JALNA

Of the origin of the now famous 'Whiteoaks' series,
the author, Mazo de la Roche, wrote in her auto-
biography, *RINGING THE CHANGES*, 1957:

'*Jalna* was inspired by that part of Southern Ontario
where we had built Trail Cottage. The descendants of
the retired military and naval officers who had settled
there, clung stoutly to British traditions. No house in
particular was pictured, no family portrayed. From
the very first the characters created themselves. They
leaped from my imagination and from memories of
my own family. The grandmother, Adeline Whiteoak,
refused to remain a minor character but arrogantly,
supported on either side by a son, marched to the
centre of the stage'.

Mazo de la Roche died in 1961, and by the time of
her death no less than twelve million volumes of the
Whiteoaks novels had been sold and enjoyed throughout the world, both in English and in many other
languages.

The 'Whiteoak' novels in chronological order

JALNA

MAZO DE LA ROCHE

UNABRIDGED

PAN BOOKS, TORONTO AND LONDON

First published in 1927 by Macmillan & Co. Ltd.
This edition published 1952 by Pan Books Ltd.,
100 Lesmill Road, Toronto, and
33 Tothill Street, London, S.W.1

ISBN 0 330 10132 3

2nd Printing 1954
New Edition 1962
4th Printing 1962
5th Printing 1965
6th Printing 1966
7th Printing 1969
8th Printing 1971
9th Printing 1971
10th Printing 1972

Printed in Canada by
Ronalds-Federated Ltd.
6300 Park Avenue
Montreal, Que.

CONTENTS

TO THE MEMORY OF
MY FATHER

WHITEOAKS OF JALNA

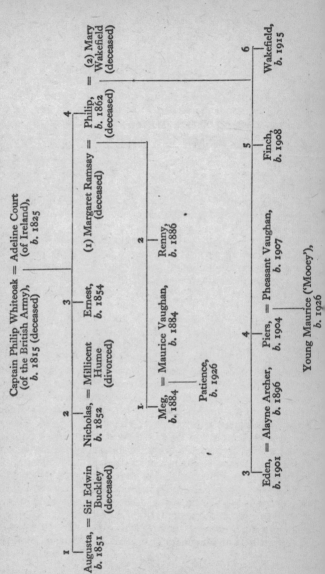

Captain Philip Whiteoak = Adeline Court
(of the British Army),   (of Ireland),
b. 1815 (deceased)   b. 1825

1
Augusta, = Sir Edwin
b. 1851   Buckley
    (deceased)

2
Nicholas, = Millicent
b. 1852   Hume
    (divorced)

3
Ernest,
b. 1854

4
Philip, = (2) Mary
b. 1862   Wakefield
(deceased)   (deceased)

(1) Margaret Ramsay =
(deceased)

1
Meg, = Maurice Vaughan,
b. 1884   b. 1884

2
Renny,
b. 1886

Patience,
b. 1926

3
Eden, = Alayne Archer,
b. 1901   b. 1896

4
Piers, = Pheasant Vaughan,
b. 1904   b. 1907

5
Finch,
b. 1908

6
Wakefield,
b. 1915

Young Maurice ('Mooey'),
b. 1926

1

THE RAKE'S PROGRESS

WAKEFIELD WHITEOAK ran on and on, faster and faster, till he could run no farther. He did not know why he had suddenly increased his speed. He did not even know why he ran. When, out of breath, he threw himself face down on the new spring sod of the meadow, he completely forgot that he had been running at all, and lay, his cheek pressed against the tender grass, his heart thudding against his ribs, without a thought in his head. He was no more happy or unhappy than the April wind that raced across his body or the young grass that quivered with life beneath it. He was simply alive, young, and pressed by the need of violent exertion.

Looking down into the crowding spears of grass, he could see an ant hurrying eagerly, carrying a small white object. He placed his finger before it, wondering what it would think when it found its way blocked by this tall, forbidding tower. Ants were notoriously persevering. It would climb up the finger, perhaps, and run across his hand. No, before it touched his finger, it turned sharply aside and hurried off in a fresh direction. Again he blocked its path, but it would not climb the finger. He persisted. The ant withstood. Harried, anxious, still gripping its little white bundle, it was not to be inveigled or bullied into walking on human flesh. Yet how often ants had scrabbled over him when he had least wanted them! One had even run into his ear once and nearly sent him crazy. In sudden anger, he sat up, nipped the ant between his thumb and forefinger, and placed it firmly on the back of his hand. The ant dropped its bundle and lay down on its back, kicking its legs in the air and twisting its body. It was apparently in extreme anguish. He threw it away, half in disgust, half in shame. He had spoiled the silly old ant's day for it. Perhaps it would die.

Briskly he began to search for it. Neither body nor bundle of ant was to be seen, but a robin, perched on a swinging branch of a wild cherry tree, burst into song. It filled the air with its rich throaty notes, tossing them on to the bright sunshine like ringing coins. Wakefield held an imaginary gun to his shoulder and took aim.

9

"Bang!" he shouted, but the robin went on singing just as though it had not been shot.

"Look here," complained Wakefield, "don't you know when you're dead? Dead birds don't sing, I tell you."

The robin flew from the cherry tree and alighted on the topmost twig of an elm, where it sang more loudly than ever to show how very much alive it was. Wakefield lay down again, his head on his arm. The moist sweet smell of the earth was in his nostrils; the sun beat warmly on his back. He was wondering now whether that big white cloud that he had seen sailing up from the south was overhead yet. He would lie still and count one hundred—no, a hundred was too much, too sustained a mental effort on a morning like this; he would count up to fifty. Then he would look up, and if the cloud were overhead he would—well, he didn't know what he would do, but it would be something terrific. Perhaps he would run at full speed to the creek and jump across, even if it were at the widest part. He pushed one hand into the pocket of his knickers and fingered his new agate marbles as he counted. A delicious drowsiness stole over him. A tender recollection of the lovely warm breakfast he had eaten filled him with peace. He wondered if it were still in his stomach, or had already changed into blood and bone and muscle. Such a breakfast should do a great deal of good. He clenched the hand belonging to the arm stretched under his head to test its muscle. Yes, it felt stronger—no doubt about that. If he kept on eating such breakfasts, the day would come when he would not stand any nonsense from Finch or from any of his brothers, even up to Renny. He supposed he would always let Meg bully him, but then Meg was a woman. A fellow couldn't hit a woman, even though she was his sister.

There came no sound of a footstep to warn him. He simply felt himself helpless in the grasp of two iron hands. He was dazed by a shake, and set roughly on his feet, facing his eldest brother, who was frowning sternly. The two clumber spaniels at Renny's heels jumped on Wakefield, licking at his face and almost knocking him down in their joy at discovering him.

Renny, still gripping his shoulder, demanded: "Why are you loafing about here, when you ought to be at Mr Fennel's? Do you know what time it is? Where are your books?"

Wakefield tried to wriggle away. He ignored the first two

questions, feeling instinctively that the third led to less dangerous channels. "Left them at Mr Fennel's yesterday," he murmured.

"Left them at Fennel's? How the devil did you expect to do your home work?"

Wakefield thought a moment. "I used an old book of Finch's for my Latin. I knew the poetry already. The history lesson was just to be the same thing over again, so's I'd have time to think up my opinion of Cromwell. The Scripture, of course, I could get out of Meg's Bible at home, and"—he warmed to his subject, his large dark eyes shining—"and I was doing the arithmetic in my head as you came along." He looked earnestly up into his brother's face.

"A likely story." But Renny was somewhat confused by the explanation, as he was meant to be. "Now look here, Wake, I don't want to be hard on you, but you've got to do better. Do you suppose I pay Mr Fennel to teach you for the fun of it? Just because you're too delicate to go to school isn't any excuse for your being an idle little beast without an idea in your head but play. What have you got in your pockets?"

"Marbles—just a few, Renny."

"Hand them over."

Renny held out his hand while the marbles were reluctantly extracted from the child's pockets and heaped on his own palm. Wakefield did not feel in the least like crying, but his sense of the dramatic prompted him to shed tears as he handed over his treasures. He could always cry when he wanted to. He had only to shut his eyes tightly a moment and repeat to himself, "Oh, how terrible! How terrible!"—and in a moment the tears would come. When he made up his mind not to cry, no amount of abuse would make him. Now, as he dropped the marbles into Renny's hand, he secretly moaned the magic formula, "Oh, how terrible! How terrible!" His chest heaved, the muscles in his throat throbbed, and soon tears trickled down his cheeks like rain.

Renny pocketed the marbles. "No snivelling now." But he did not say it unkindly. "And see that you're not late for dinner." He lounged away, calling his dogs.

Wakefield took out his handkerchief, a clean one, still folded in a little square, put in his pocket by his sister that morning, and wiped his eyes. He watched Renny's tall retreating figure till Renny looked back over his shoulder at him, then he broke into a jogtrot toward the rectory. But the freedom of the morning was no longer his. He was full of care, a slender, sallow boy of nine, whose dark brown eyes seemed too large for his pointed face, wearing a greenish tweed jacket and shorts, and green stockings that showed his bare brown knees.

He crossed the field, climbed a sagging rail fence, and began to trot along a path that led beside a muddy, winding road. Soon the blacksmith shop appeared, noisy and friendly, between two majestic elms. An oriole was darting to and fro from elm to elm, and, when the clanging on the anvil ceased for a moment, its sweet liquid song was scattered down in a shower. Wakefield stopped in the doorway to rest.

"Good morning, John," he said to John Chalk, the smith, who was paring the hoof of a huge, hairy-legged farm horse.

"Good morning," answered Chalk, glancing up with a smile, for he and Wake were old friends. "It's a fine day."

"A fine day for those that have time to enjoy it. I've got beastly old lessons to do."

"I suppose you don't call what I'm doing work, eh?" returned Chalk.

"Oh, well, it's nice work. Interesting work. Not like history and comp."

"What's 'comp'?"

"Composition. You write about things you're not interested in. Now, my last subject was 'A Spring Walk'."

"Well, that ought to be easy. You've just had one."

"Oh, but that's different. When you sit down to write about it, it all seems stupid. You begin, 'I set out one fine spring morning,' and then you can't think of a single thing to write about."

"Why not write about me?"

Wakefield gave a jeering laugh. "Who'd want to read about you! This comp. stuff has got to be *read*, don't you see?"

Conversation was impossible for a space, while the blacksmith hammered the shoe into place. Wakefield sniffed the delicious odour of burnt hoof that hung almost visibly on the air.

Chalk put down the large foot he had been nursing, and remarked:

"There was a man wrote a piece of poetry about a blacksmith

12

once. 'Under a spreading chestnut tree', it began. Ever read it? He must have wrote it to be read, eh?"

"Oh, I know that piece. It's awful bunk. And besides, he wasn't your kind of blacksmith. He didn't get drunk and give his wife a black eye and knock his kids around——"

"Look here!" interrupted Chalk with great heat. "Cut out that insultin' kind of talk or I'll shy a hammer at you."

Wakefield backed away, but said, judicially, "There you go. Just proving what I said. You're not the kind of blacksmith to write comp. or even poetry about. You're not beautiful. Mr Fennel says we should write of beautiful things."

"Well, I know I ain't beautiful," agreed Chalk, reluctantly. "But I ain't as bad as all that."

"All what?" Wakefield successfully assumed Mr Fennel's air of schoolmasterish probing.

"That I can't be writ about."

"Well, then, Chalk, suppose I was to write down everything I know about you and hand it to Mr Fennel for comp. Would you be pleased?"

"I say I'll be pleased to fire a hammer at you if you don't clear out!" shouted Chalk, backing the heavy mare toward the door.

Wakefield moved agilely aside as the great dappled flank approached, then he set off down the road—which had suddenly become a straggling street—with much dignity. The load of care that he had been carrying slid from him, leaving him light and airy. As he approached a cottage enclosed by a neat wicket fence, he saw a six-year-old girl swinging on the gate.

"Oo, Wakefield!" she squealed, delightedly. "Come an' swing me. Swing me!"

"Very well, my little friend," agreed Wakefield, cheerily. "You shall be swung, *ad infinitum. Verbum sapienti.*"

He swung the gate to and fro, the child laughing at first, then shrieking, finally uttering hiccoughing sobs as the swinging became wilder, and her foothold less secure, while she clung like a limpet to the palings.

The door of the cottage opened and the mother appeared.

"Let her be, you naughty boy!" she shouted, running to her daughter's assistance. "You see if I don't tell your brother on you!"

"Which brother?" asked Wakefield, moving away. "I have four, you know."

"Why, the oldest to be sure. Mr Whiteoak that owns this cottage."

Wakefield spoke confidentially now. "Mrs Wigle, I wouldn't if I were you. It upsets Renny terribly to have to punish me, on account of my weak heart—I can't go to school because of it—and he'd have to punish me if a lady complained of me, of course, though Muriel did ask me to swing her and I'd never have swung her if I hadn't thought she was used to being swung, seeing the way she was swinging as I swung along the street. Besides, Renny mightn't like to think that Muriel was racking the gate to pieces by swinging on it, and he might raise your rent on you. He's a most peculiar man, and he's liable to turn on you when you least expect it."

Mrs Wigle looked dazed. "Very well," she said, patting the back of Muriel, who still sobbed and hiccoughed against her apron; "but I do wish he'd mend my roof, which leaks into the best room like all possessed every time it rains."

"I'll speak to him about it. I'll see that it's mended at once. Trust me, Mrs Wigle." He sailed off, erect and dignified.

Already he could see the church, perched on an abrupt, cedar-clad knoll, its square stone tower rising, almost menacing, like a battlement against the sky. His grandfather had built it seventy-five years before. His grandfather, his father, and his mother slept in the churchyard beside it. Beyond the church and hidden by it was the rectory, where he had his lessons.

Now his footsteps lagged. He was before the shop of Mrs Brawn, who had not only sweets but soft drinks, buns, pies, and sandwiches for sale. The shop was simply the front room of her cottage, fitted with shelves and a counter, and her wares were displayed on a table in the window. He felt weak and faint. His tongue clove to the roof of his mouth with thirst. His stomach felt hollow and slightly sick. Plainly, no one on earth had ever needed refreshment more than he, and no one on earth had less means for the payment for such succour. He examined the contents of his pockets, but, though there was much in them of great value to himself, there was not one cent in hard cash, which was all that Mrs Brawn really cared about. He could see her crimson face inside the window, and he smiled ingratiatingly, for he owed her thirteen cents and he did not see where he was ever going to get the money to pay it. She came to the door.

"Well, young man, what about that money you owe me?" She was brusque indeed.

"Oh, Mrs Brawn, I aren't feeling very well this morning. I get these spells. I dare say you've heard about them. I'd like a bottle of lemon soda, please. And about paying——" He passed his hand across his brow and continued hesitatingly: "I don't believe I should have come out in the sun without my cap, do you? What was I saying? Oh, yes, about paying. Well, you see my birthday's coming very soon, and I'll be getting money presents from all the family. Eighteen cents will seem no more to me than thirteen then. Even a dollar will be nothing."

"When does your birthday come?" Mrs Brawn was weakening.

Again he passed his hand across his forehead, then laid it on his stomach, where he believed his heart to be. "I can't ezactly remember, 'cos there are so many birthdays in our family I get mixed up. Between Grandmother's great age and my few years and all those between, it's a little confusing, but I know it's very soon." As he talked, he had entered the shop and stood leaning against the counter. "Lemon soda, please, and *two* straws," he murmured.

Peace possessed him as Mrs Brawn produced the bottle, uncorked it, and set it before him with the straws.

"How is the old lady?" she inquired.

"Nicely, thank you. We're hoping she'll reach one hundred yet. She's trying awfully hard to. 'Cos she wants to see the celebration we'll have. A party, with a big bonfire and sky-rockets. She says she'd be sorry to miss it; though of course we won't have it if she's dead, and she couldn't miss what never really happened, could she, even if it was her own birthday party?"

"You've a wonderful gift of the gab." Mrs Brawn beamed at him admiringly.

"Yes, I have," he agreed, modestly. "If I hadn't, I'd have no show at all, being the youngest of such a large family. Grandmother and I do a good deal of talking, she at her end of the line and I at mine. You see, we both feel that we may not have many years more to live, so we make the most of everything that comes our way."

"Oh, my goodness, don't talk that way. You'll be all

right." She was round-eyed with sympathy. "Don't worry, my dear."

"I'm not worrying, Mrs Brawn. It's my sister does the worrying. She's had a terrible time raising me, and of course I'm not raised yet." He smiled sadly, and then bent his small dark head over the bottle, sucking ecstatically.

Mrs Brawn disappeared into the kitchen behind the shop. A fierce heat came from there, and the tantalizing smell of cakes baking, and the sound of women's voices. What a good time women had! Red-faced Mrs Brawn especially. Baking all the cakes she wanted and selling all those she couldn't eat, and getting paid for them. How he wished he had a cake. Just one little hot cake!

As he drew the lovely drink up through the straws, his eyes, large and bright, roved over the counter. Near him was a little tray of packets of chewing-gum. He was not allowed to chew it, but he yearned over it, especially that first moment of chewing, when the thick, sweet, highly-flavoured juice gushed down the throat, nearly choking him. Before he knew it—well, almost before he knew it—he had taken a packet from the tray, dropped it into his pocket, and gone on sucking, but now with his eyes tightly closed.

Mrs Brawn returned with two hot little sponge cakes on a plate and set them down before him. "I thought you'd like them just out of the oven. They're a present, mind. They'll not go on your account."

He was almost speechless with gratitude. "Oh, thank you, thank you," was all he could say, at first. Then, "But what a shame! I've gone and drunk up all my soda and now I'll have to eat my cakes dry, unless, of course, I buy another bottle of something." His eyes flew over the shelves. "I believe I'll take ginger ale this time, Mrs Brawn, thank you. And those same straws will do."

"All right." And Mrs Brawn opened another bottle and plumped it down before him.

The cakes had a delicious crisp crust and, buried in the heart of each, about six juicy currants. Oh, they were lovely!

As he sauntered from the shop and then climbed the steep steps to the church, he pondered on the subjects assigned for today's lessons. Which of his two most usual moods, he wondered, would Mr Fennel be in? Exacting, alert, or absent-minded and drowsy? Well, whatever the mood, he was now at the mercy of it, little, helpless, alone.

He trotted through the cool shadow of the church, among the gravestones, hesitating a moment beside the iron fence which enclosed his family's plot. His eyes rested on the granite plinth bearing the name 'Whiteoak'; then, wistfully, on the small stone marked 'Mary Whiteoak, wife of Philip Whiteoak'. His mother's grave. His grandfather lay there too; his father; his father's first wife—the mother of Renny and Meg; and several infant Whiteoaks. He had always liked this plot of ground. He liked the pretty iron fence and the darling little iron balls that dangled from it. He wished he could stay there this morning and play beside it. He must bring a big bunch of the kingcups that he had seen spilled like gold along the stream yesterday, and lay them on his mother's grave. Perhaps he would give a few to the mother of Renny and Meg also, but none to the men, of course; they wouldn't care about them; nor to the babies, unless to 'Gwynneth, aged five months', because he liked her name.

He had noticed that when Meg brought flowers to the graves she always gave the best to her own mother, 'Margaret', while to 'Mary'—his mother and Eden's and Piers' and Finch's —she gave a smaller, less beautiful bunch. Well, he would do the same. Margaret should have a few, but they should be inferior—not wilted or anything, but not quite so fine and large.

The rectory was a mellow-looking house with a long sloping roof and high-pointed gable. The front door stood open. He was not expected to knock, so he entered quietly, first composing his face into an expression of meek receptiveness. The library was empty. There lay his books on the little desk in the corner at which he always sat. Feebly he crossed the worn carpet and sank into his accustomed chair, burying his head in his hands. The tall clock ticked heavily, saying, 'Wake-field—Wake-field —Wake—Wake—Wake—Wake——' Then, strangely, 'Sleep —sleep—sleep—sleep . . .'

The smell of stuffy furniture and old books oppressed him. He heard the thud of a spade in the garden. Mr Fennel was planting potatoes. Wakefield dozed a little, his head sinking nearer and nearer the desk. At last he slept peacefully.

He was awakened by Mr Fennel's coming in, rather earthy, rather dazed, very contrite.

"Oh, my dear boy," he stammered, "I've kept you waiting, I'm afraid. I was just hurrying to get my potatoes in before the full of the moon. Superstitious, I know, but still—— Now, let's see; what Latin was it for today?"

The clock buzzed, struck twelve.

Mr Fennel came and bent over the little boy. "How have you got on this morning?" He was peering at the Latin textbook that Wakefield had opened.

"As well as could be expected, by myself, thank you." He spoke with gentle dignity, just touched by reproach.

Mr Fennel leaned still closer over the page. "Um-m, let's see. *Etsi in his locis—maturae sunt hiemes——*"

"Mr Fennel," interrupted Wakefield.

"Yes, Wake." He turned his shaggy beard, on which a straw was pendent, toward the boy.

"Renny wondered if you would let me out promptly at twelve today. You see, yesterday I was late for dinner, and it upset Grandmother, and at her age——"

"Certainly, certainly. I'll let you off. Ah, that was too bad, upsetting dear Mrs Whiteoak. It must not happen again. We must be prompt, Wakefield. Both you and I. Run along then, and I'll get back to my potatoes." Hurriedly he assigned the tasks for tomorrow.

"I wonder," said Wakefield, "if Tom" (Mr Fennel's son), "when he's got the pony and cart out this afternoon, would drop my books at the house for me. You see, I'll need both dictionaries and the atlas. They're pretty heavy, and as I am late already I'll need to run every bit of the way."

He emerged into the noontide brightness, light as air, the transportation of his books arranged for, his brain untired by encounters with Caesar or Oliver Cromwell, and his body refreshed by two sponge cakes and two bottles of soft drink, ready for fresh pleasurable exertion.

He returned the way he had come, only pausing once to let an importunate sow, deeply dissatisfied with the yard where she was imprisoned, into the road. She trotted beside him for a short distance, pattering along gaily, and when they parted, where an open garden gate attracted her, she did not neglect to throw a glance of roguish gratitude over her shoulder to him.

Glorious, glorious life! When he reached the field where the

18

stream was, the breeze had become a wind that ruffled up his hair and whistled through his teeth as he ran. It was as good a playfellow as he wanted, racing him, blowing the clouds about for his pleasure, shaking out the blossoms of the wild cherry tree like spray.

As he ran, he flung his arms forward alternately like a swimmer; he darted off at sudden tangents, shying like a skittish horse, his face now fierce with rolling eyes, now blank as a gambolling lamb's.

It was an erratic progress, and, as he crept through his accustomed hole in the cedar hedge on to the shaggy lawn, he began to be afraid that he might, after all, be late for dinner. He entered the house quietly and heard the click of dishes and the sound of voices in the dining-room.

Dinner was in progress, the older members of the family already assembled, when the youngest (idler, liar, thief, wastrel that he was!) presented himself at the door.

2

THE FAMILY

THERE SEEMED a crowd of people about the table, and all were talking vigorously at once. Yet, in talking, they did not neglect their meal, which was a hot, steaming dinner; for dishes were continually being passed, knives and forks clattered energetically, and occasionally a speaker was not quite coherent until he had stopped to wash down the food that impeded his utterance with a gulp of hot tea. No one paid any attention to Wakefield as he slipped into his accustomed place on the right of his half sister Meg. As soon as he had begun to come to table he had been set there, first in a high chair, then, as he grew larger, on a thick volume of *British Poets*, an anthology read by no member of the family and, from the time when it was first placed under him, known as 'Wakefield's book'. As a matter of fact, he did not need its added inches to be able to handle competently his knife and fork now, but he had got used to it, and for a Whiteoak to get used to anything meant a tenacious and stubborn clinging to it. He liked the feel of its hard boards under him, though occasionally, after painful acquaintance with Renny's shaving strop or Meg's slipper, he could have wished the *Poets* had been padded.

"I want my dinner!" He raised his voice, in a very different tone from the conciliatory one he had used to Mrs Brawn, Mrs Wigle, and the rector. "My dinner, please!"

"Hush." Meg took from him the fork with which he was stabbing the air. "Renny, will you please give this child some beef. He won't eat the fat, remember. Just nice lean."

"He ought to be made to eat the fat. It's good for him." Renny hacked off some bits of the meat, adding a rim of fat.

Grandmother spoke, in a voice guttural with food: "Make him eat the fat. Good for him. Children spoiled nowadays. Give him nothing but the fat. I eat fat and I'm nearly a hundred."

Wakefield glared across the table at her resentfully. "Shan't eat the fat. I don't want to be a hundred."

Grandmother laughed throatily, not at all ill-pleased. "Never fear, my dear, you won't do it. None of you will do it but me. Ninety-nine, and I never miss a meal. Some of the dish gravy, Renny, on this bit of bread. Dish gravy, please."

She held up her plate, shaking a good deal. Uncle Nicholas, her eldest son, who sat beside her, took it from her and passed it to Renny, who tipped the platter till the ruddy juice collected in a pool at one end. He put two spoonfuls of this over the square of bread. "More, more," ordered Grandmother, and he trickled a third spoonful. "Enough, enough," muttered Nicholas.

Wakefield watched her, enthralled, as she ate. She wore two rows of artificial teeth, probably the most perfect, most efficacious that had ever been made. Whatever was put between them they ground remorselessly into fuel for her endless vitality. To them many of her ninety-and-nine years were due. His own plate, to which appetizing little mounds of mashed potatoes and turnips had been added by Meg, lay untouched before him while he stared at Grandmother.

"Stop staring," whispered Meg, admonishingly, "and eat your dinner."

"Well, take off that bit of fat, then," he whispered back, leaning toward her.

She took it on to her own plate.

The conversation buzzed on in its former channel. What was

it all about, Wake wondered vaguely, but he was too much interested in his dinner to care greatly. Phrases flew over his head, words clashed. Probably it was just one of the old discussions provocative of endless talk: what crops should be sown that year; what to make of Finch, who went to school in town; which of Grandmother's three sons had made the worst mess of his life—Nicholas, who sat on her left, and who had squandered his patrimony on fast living in his youth; Ernest, who sat on her right, and who had ruined himself by nebulous speculations and the backing of notes for his brothers and his friends; or Philip, who lay in the churchyard, who had made a second marriage (and that beneath him!) which had produced Eden, Piers, Finch, and Wakefield, unnecessary additions to the family's already too great burdens.

The dining-room was a very large room, full of heavy furniture that would have overshadowed and depressed a weaker family. The sideboard, the cabinets towered toward the ceiling. Heavy cornices glowered ponderously from above. Inside shutters and long curtains of yellow velours, caught back by cablelike cords, with tassels at the ends shaped like the wooden human figures in a Noah's ark, seemed definitely to shut out the rest of the world from the world of the Whiteoaks, where they squabbled, ate, drank, and indulged in their peculiar occupations.

Those spaces on the wall not covered by furniture were covered by family portraits in oil, heavily framed, varied in one instance by the bright Christmas supplement of an English periodical, framed in red velvet by the mother of Renny and Meg, when she was a gay young bride.

Chief among the portraits was that of Captain Philip Whiteoak in his uniform of a British officer. He was Grandfather, who, if he were living, would have been more than a hundred, for he was older than Grandmother. The portrait showed a well-set-up gentleman of fair skin, waving brown hair, bold blue eyes, and sweet, stubborn mouth.

He had been stationed at Jalna, in India, where he had met handsome Adeline Court, who had come out from Ireland to visit a married sister. Miss Court not only had been handsome and of good family—even better than the Captain's own, as she had never allowed him to forget—but had had a pleasing little fortune of her very own, left to her by a maiden great-aunt, the daughter of an earl. The pair had fallen deeply in love, she with his sweet, stubborn mouth, and he with her long, graceful form, rendered more graceful by voluminous hooped skirts, her 'waterfall' of luxuriant dark red hair, and most of all with her passionate red-brown eyes.

They had been married in Bombay in 1848, a time of great uneasiness and strife almost throughout the world. They felt no unease and anticipated no strife, though enough of that and to spare followed, when much of the sweetness of his mouth was merged into stubbornness, and the tender passion of her eyes was burned out by temper. They were the handsomest, most brilliant couple in the station. A social gathering without them was a tame and disappointing affair. They had wit, elegance, and more money than any others of their youth and military station in Jalna. All went well till a baby girl arrived, a delicate child, unwanted by the pleasure-loving couple, who with its wailing advent brought a train of physical ills to the young mother which, in spite of all that the doctors and a long and dull sojourn in the hills could do, seemed likely to drag her down into invalidism. About the same time Captain Whiteoak had a violent quarrel with his colonel, and he felt that his whole world, both domestic and military, had somehow suddenly become bewitched.

Fate seemed to have a hand in bringing the Whiteoaks to Canada, for just at the moment when the doctor insisted that the wife, if she were to be restored to health, must live for some time in a cool and bracing climate, the husband got notice that an uncle, stationed in Quebec, had died, leaving him a considerable property.

Philip and Adeline had decided simultaneously—the only decision of moment except their marriage that they ever arrived at without storm and stress—that they were utterly sick of India, of military life, of trying to please stupid and choleric superiors, and of entertaining a narrow, gossiping, middle-class set of people. They were made for a freer, more unconventional life. Suddenly their impetuous spirits yearned toward Quebec. Philip had had letters from his uncle, eloquent on the subject of the beauties of Quebec, its desirability as a place of residence, its freedom from the narrow conventionalities of the Old World, combined with a grace of living bequeathed by the French.

Captain Whiteoak had a very poor opinion of the French—he had been born in the year of Waterloo, and his father had been killed there—but he liked the descriptions of Quebec, and when he found himself the owner of property there, with a legacy of money attached, he thought he would like nothing better than to go there to live—for a time, at any rate. He visualized a charming picture of himself and his Adeline, clinging to his arm, parading the terrace by the river after Sunday morning service, he no longer in an uncomfortable uniform but in tight, beautifully fitting trousers, double-breasted frock coat, and glittering top hat, all from London, while Adeline seemed literally to float amid fringes, ruches, and gaily-tinted veils. He had other visions of himself in company with lovely French girls when Adeline would possibly be occupied with a second accouchement, though, to do him justice, these visions never went beyond the holding of velvety little hands and the tranced gazing into dark-fringed eyes.

He sold his commission, and the two sailed for England with the delicate baby and a native ayah. The few relations they had in England did not proffer them a very warm welcome, so their stay there was short, for they were equally proud and high-spirited. They found time, however, to have their portraits painted by a really first class artist, he in the uniform he was about to discard, and she in a low-cut yellow evening gown with camellias in her hair.

Armed with the two portraits and a fine collection of inlaid mahogany furniture—for their position must be upheld in the Colony—they took passage in a large sailing vessel. Two months of battling with storms and fogs and even icebergs passed like a nightmare before they sighted the battlements of Quebec. On the way out the ayah died and was buried at sea, her dark form settling meekly into the cold Western waters. Then there was no one to care for the baby girl but the young, inexperienced parents. Adeline herself was ill almost to death. Captain Whiteoak would sooner have set out to subdue a rebellious hill tribe than the squalling infant. Cursing and sweating, while the vessel rolled like a thing in torture and his wife made sounds such as he had never dreamed she could utter, he tried to wrap the infant's squirming chafed legs in a flannel barrow-coat. Finally he pricked it with a safety pin, and when he saw blood trickling from the tiny wound he could stand it no longer; he carried the child into the common cabin, where he cast it into the lap of a poor Scotswoman who already had five of her own to look after, commanding her to care for his daughter as best she could. She cared for her very capably, neglecting her own hardy bairns, and the Captain paid her well for it. The weather cleared, and they sailed into Quebec on a beautiful crisp May morning.

But they lived for only a year in that city. The house in the Rue St Louis was flush with the street—a dim, chilly French house, sad with ghosts from the past. The sound of church bells was never out of their ears, and Philip, discovering that Adeline sometimes went secretly to those Roman churches, began to fear that she would under such influence become a papist. But, as they had lingered in London long enough to have their portraits done, so they lingered in Quebec long enough to become the parents of a son. Unlike little Augusta, he was strong and healthy. They named him Nicholas, after the uncle who had left Philip the legacy (now himself 'Uncle Nicholas', who sat at his mother's right hand when Wakefield entered the dining-room).

With two young children in a cold draughty house; with Adeline's health a source of anxiety; with far too many French about Quebec to be congenial to an English gentleman; with a winter temperature that played coyly about twenty dazzling degrees below zero, the Whiteoaks felt driven to find a more suitable habitation.

Captain Whiteoak had a friend, a retired Anglo-Indian colonel who had already settled on the fertile southern shore of Ontario. 'Here,' he wrote, 'the winters are mild. We have little snow, and in the long, fruitful summer the land yields grain and fruit in abundance. An agreeable little settlement of *respectable* families is being formed. You and your talented lady, my dear Whiteoak, would receive the welcome here that people of your consequence *merit*.'

The property in Quebec was disposed of. The mahogany furniture, the portraits, the two infants, and their nurse were somehow or other conveyed to the chosen Province. Colonel Vaughan, the friend, took them into his house for nearly a year while their own was in process of building.

Philip Whiteoak bought from the Government a thousand acres of rich land, traversed by a deep ravine through which ran a stream lively with speckled trout. Some of the land was cleared, but the greater part presented the virgin grandeur of the primeval forest. Tall, unbelievably dense pines, hemlocks, spruces, balsams, with a mingling of oak, ironwood, and elm, made a sanctuary for countless song birds, wood pigeons, partridges, and quail. Rabbits, foxes, and hedgehogs abounded. The edge of the ravine was crowned by slender silver birches, its banks by cedars and sumachs, and along the brink of the stream was a wild sweet-smelling tangle that was the home of water rats, minks, raccoons, and blue herons.

Labour was cheap. A small army of men was employed to make the semblance of an English park in the forest, and to build a house that should overshadow all others in the county. When completed, decorated, and furnished, it was the wonder of the countryside. It was a square house of dark red brick, with a wide stone porch, a deep basement where the kitchens and servants' quarters were situated, an immense drawing-room, a library (called so, but more properly a sitting-room, since few books lived there), a dining-room, and a bedroom on the ground floor; and six large bedrooms on the floor above, topped by a long, low attic divided into two bedrooms. The wainscoting and doors were of walnut. From five fireplaces the smoke ascended through picturesque chimneys that rose among the treetops.

In a burst of romantic feeling, Philip and Adeline named the place Jalna, after the military station where they had first met. Everyone agreed that it was a pretty name, and Jalna became a place for gaiety. An atmosphere of impregnable well-being grew up around it. Under their clustering chimneys, in the midst of their unpretentious park with its short, curving drive, with all their thousand acres spread like a green mantle around them, the Whiteoaks were as happy as the sons of man can be. They felt themselves cut off definitely from the mother country, though they sent their children to England to be educated.

Two boys were born to them at Jalna. One was named Ernest, because Adeline, just before his birth, had been entranced by the story of Ernest Maltravers. The other was given the name Philip, after his father. Nicholas, the eldest son, married in England, but after a short and stormy life together his wife left him for a young Irish officer, and he returned to Canada, never to see her again. Ernest remained unmarried, devoting himself with almost monastic preoccupation to the study of Shakespeare and the care of himself. He had always been the delicate one. Philip, the youngest, married twice. First, the daughter of a Scottish physician who had settled near Jalna, and who had brought his future son-in-law into the world. She had given him Meg and Renny. His second wife was the pretty young governess of his two children who were early left motherless. The second wife, treated with coldness by all his family, had four sons, and died shortly after the birth of Wakefield. Eden, the eldest of these, was now twenty-three; Piers was twenty; Finch, sixteen; and little Wake, nine.

Young Philip had always been his father's favourite, and when the Captain died it was to Philip that he left Jalna and its acres—no longer, alas, a thousand, for land had to be sold to meet the extravagances of Nicholas and the foolish credulities of Ernest with his penchant for backing other men's notes. They had had their share, "more than their share, by God," swore Captain Whiteoak.

He had never had any deep affection for his only daughter, Augusta. Perhaps he had never quite forgiven her the bad time she had given him on the passage from England to Canada. But if he had never loved her, at least he had never had any cause to worry over her. She had married young—an insignificant young Englishman, Edwin Buckley, who had surprised them all by inheriting a baronetcy, through the sudden deaths of an uncle and a cousin.

If Augusta's father had never been able to forgive her for the intricacies of her toilet on that memorable voyage, how much more difficult was it for her mother to forgive her for attaining a social position above her own! To be sure, the Courts were a far more important family than the Buckleys; they were above title-seeking; and Sir Edwin was only the fourth baronet; still, it was hard to hear Augusta called 'her ladyship'. Adeline was unfeignedly pleased when Sir Edwin died and was succeeded by a nephew, and thus Augusta, in a manner, was shelved.

All this had happened years ago. Captain Whiteoak was long dead. Young Philip and both his wives were dead. Renny was master of Jalna, and Renny himself was thirty-eight.

The clock seemed to stand still at Jalna. Renny's uncles, Nicholas and Ernest, thought of him as only a headlong boy.

And old Mrs Whiteoak thought of her two sons as mere boys, and of her dead son, Philip, as a poor dead boy.

She had sat at that same table for nearly seventy years. At that table she had held Nicholas on her knee, giving him little sips out of her cup. Now he slouched beside her, a heavy man of seventy-two. At that table Ernest had cried with fright when first he heard the explosion of a Christmas cracker. Now he sat on her other side, white-haired—which she herself was not. The central chamber of her mind was hazy. Its far recesses were lit by clear candles of memory. She saw them more clearly as little boys than as they now appeared.

Countless suns had shone yellowly through the shutters on Whiteoaks eating heartily as they ate today, talking loudly, disagreeing, drinking quantities of strong tea.

The family was arranged in orderly fashion about the table with its heavy plate and vegetable dishes, squat cruets, and large English cutlery. Wakefield had his own little knife and fork, and a battered silver mug which had been handed down from brother to brother and had many a time been hurled across the room in childish tantrums. At one end sat Renny, the head of the house, tall, thin, with a small head covered with dense, dark red hair, a narrow face, with something of foxlike sharpness about it, and quick-tempered red-brown eyes; facing him, Meg, the one sister. She was forty, but looked older because of her solid bulk, which made it appear that, once seated, nothing could budge her. She had a colourless, very round face, full blue eyes, and brown hair with a strand of grey springing from each temple. Her distinguishing feature was her mouth, inherited from Captain Whiteoak. In comparison with the mouth in the portrait, however, hers seemed to show all its sweetness with none of its stubbornness. In her it became a mouth of ineffable feminine sweetness. When she laid her cheek against her hand, her short thick arm resting on the table, she seemed to be musing on that which filled her with bliss. When she raised her head and looked at one of her brothers, her eyes were cool, commanding, but the curve of her mouth was a caress. She ate little at the table, attending always to the wants of others, keeping the younger boys in order, cutting up her grandmother's food for her, sipping endless cups of China tea. Between meals she was always indulging in little

lunches, carried to her own room on a tray—thick slices of
fresh bread and butter with gooseberry jam, hot muffins with
honey, or even French cherries and pound cake. She loved all
her brothers, but her love and jealousy for Renny sometimes
shook her solidity into a kind of ecstasy.

The half brothers were ranged in a row along one side of
the table, facing the window. Wakefield; then Finch (whose
place was always vacant at dinner time because he was a day
boy at a school in town); next Piers, he too resembling Captain
Whiteoak, but with less of the sweetness and more of the
stubbornness in his boyish mouth; last Eden, slender, fair,
with the appealing gaze of the pretty governess, his mother.

Across the table the grandmother and the two uncles; Ernest
with his cat, Sasha, on his shoulder; Nicholas with his Yorkshire
terrier, Nip, on his knees. Renny's two clumber spaniels lay on
either side of his armchair.

Thus the Whiteoaks at table.

"What is accepted?" shouted Grandmother.

"Poems," explained Uncle Ernest, gently. "Eden's poems.
They've been accepted."

"Is that what you're all chattering about?"

"Yes, Mamma."

"Who is she?"

"Who is who?"

"The girl who's accepted them."

"It's not a girl, Mamma. It's a publisher."

Eden broke in: "For God's sake, don't try to explain to
her!"

"He shall explain it to me," retorted Grandmother, rapping
the table violently with her fork. "Now then, Ernest, speak up!
What's this all about?"

Uncle Ernest swallowed a juicy mouthful of rhubarb tart,
passed up his cup for more tea, and then said: "You know that
Eden has had a number of poems published in the university
magazine and—and in other magazines, too. Now an editor—
I mean a publisher—is going to bring out a book of them. Do
you understand?"

She nodded, the ribbons on her large purple cap shaking.
"When's he going to bring it out? When's he coming? If he's
coming to tea I want my white cap with the mauve ribbons on.
Is he going to bring it out in time for tea?"

"My God!" groaned Eden, under his breath, "listen to her! Why do you try to tell her things? I knew how it would be."

His grandmother glared across at him. She had heard every word. In spite of her great age, she still bore traces of having been a handsome woman. Her fierce eyes still were bright under her shaggy reddish eyebrows. Her nose, defiant of time, looked as though it had been moulded by a sculptor who had taken great pains to make the sweep of the nostrils and arch of the bridge perfect. She was so bent that her eyes stared straight on to the victuals that she loved.

"Don't you dare to curse at me!" She thrust her face toward Eden. "Nicholas, order him to stop cursing at me."

"Stop cursing at her," growled Nicholas, in his rich, deep voice. "More tart, Meggie, please."

Grandmother nodded and grinned, subsiding into her tart, which she ate with a spoon, making little guttural noises of enjoyment.

"Just the same," said Renny, carrying on the conversation, "I don't altogether like it. None of us have ever done anything like that."

"You seemed to think it was all right for me to write poetry when I only had it published in the 'varsity magazine. Now when I've got a publisher to bring it out——"

Grandmother was aroused. "Bring it out! Will he bring it today? If he does, I shall wear my white cap with mauve——"

"Mamma, have some more tart," interrupted Nicholas. "Just a little more tart."

Old Mrs Whiteoak's attention was easily diverted by an appeal to her palate. She eagerly held out her plate, tilting the juice from it to the cloth, where it formed a pinkish puddle.

Eden, after sulkily waiting for her to be helped to some tart, went on, a frown indenting his forehead: "You simply have no idea, Renny, how difficult it is to get a book of poems published. And by a New York house, too! I wish you could hear my friends talk about it. They'd give a good deal to have accomplished what I have at my age."

"It would have been more to the point," returned Renny, testily, "to have passed your exams. When I think of the money that's been wasted on your education——"

"Wasted! Could I have done this if I hadn't had my education?"

"You've always been scribbling verses. The question is, can you make a living by it?"

"Give me time! Good Lord, my book isn't in the printer's hands yet. I can't tell what it may lead to. If you—any of you—only appreciated what I've really done——"

"I do, dear!" exclaimed his sister. "I think it's wonderfully clever of you, and, as you say, it may lead to—to anywhere."

"It may lead to my being obliged to go to New York to live, if I'm going to go in for writing," said Eden. "One should be near one's publishers."

Piers, the brother next to him, put in: "Well, it's getting late. One must go back to one's spreading of manure. One's job may be lowly—one regrets that one's job is not writing poetry."

Eden pocketed the insult of his tone, but retorted: "You certainly smell of your job."

Wakefield tilted back in his chair, leaning toward Piers. "Oh, I smell him!" he cried. "I think the smell of stable is very appetizing."

"Then I wish," said Eden, "that you'd change places with me. It takes away my appetite."

Wakefield began to scramble down, eager to change, but his sister restrained him. "Stay where you are, Wake. You know how Piers would torment you if you were next him. As for you going to New York, Eden—you know how I should feel about that." Tears filled her eyes.

The family rose from the table and moved in groups toward the three doorways. In the first group Grandmother dragged her feet heavily, supported by a son on either side, Nicholas having his terrier tucked under one arm and Ernest his cat perched on his shoulder. Like some strange menagerie on parade, they slowly traversed the faded medallions of the carpet toward the door that was opposite Grandmother's room. Renny, Piers, and Wakefield went through the door that led into a back passage, the little boy trying to swarm up the back of Piers, who was lighting a cigarette. Meg and Eden disappeared through the double doors that led into the library.

Immediately the manservant, John Wragge, known as 'Rags', began to clear the table, piling the dishes precariously on an immense black tray decorated with faded red roses, preparatory to carrying it down the long steep stairs to the basement kitchen. He and his wife inhabited the regions below, she doing the cooking, he carrying, besides innumerable trays up the steep stairs, all the coal and water, cleaning brasses and windows, and waiting on his wife in season and out. Yet she complained that he put the burden of the work on her, while he declared that he did his own and hers too. The basement was the scene of continuous quarrels. Through its subterranean ways they pursued each other with bitter recriminations, and occasionally through its brick-floored passages a boot hurtled or a cabbage flew like a bomb. Jalna was so well built that none of these altercations were audible upstairs. In complete isolation the two lived their stormy life together, usually effecting a reconciliation late at night, with a pot of strong tea on the table between them.

Rags was a drab-faced, voluble little Cockney, with a pert nose and a mouth that seemed to have been formed for a cigarette holder. He was at the head of the backstairs as Renny, Piers, and Wakefield came along the passage. Wakefield waited till his brothers had passed, and then leaped on Rags' back, scrambling up him as though he were a tree, and nearly precipitating themselves and the loaded tray down the stairs.

"Ow!" screamed Rags. " 'E's done it again! 'E's always at it! This time 'e nearly 'ad me down. There goes the sugar bison! There goes the grivy boat! Tike 'im orf me, for pity's sike, Mr W'iteoak!"

Piers, who was nearest, dragged Wakefield from Rags' back, laughing hilariously as he did so. But Renny came back frowning. "He ought to be thrashed," he said, sternly. "It's just as Rags says—he's always after him." He peered down the dim stairway at the Whiteoak butler gathering up the debris.

"I'll stand him on his head," said Piers.

"No—don't do that. It's bad for his heart."

But Piers had already done it, and the packet of gum had fallen from Wakefield's pocket.

"Put him on his feet," ordered Renny. "Here, what's this?" And he picked up the pink packet.

Wake hung a bewildered, buzzing head. "It's g-gum," he said, faintly. "Mrs Brawn gave it to me. I didn't like to offend her by saying I wasn't allowed to chew it. I thought it was better not to offend her, seeing that I owe her a little bill. But you'll notice, Renny"—he raised his large eyes pathetically to his brother's face—"you'll notice it's never been opened."

"Well, I'll let you off this time." Renny threw the packet down the stairs after Rags. "Here, Rags, throw this out!"

Rags examined it, then his voice came unctuously up the stairway: "Ow, naow, Mr W'iteoak, I'll give it to the missus. I see it's flivoured with vaniller. 'Er fivourite flivour. It'll do 'er a world of good to chew this when one of 'er spells comes on."

Renny turned to Wakefield. "How much do you owe Mrs Brawn?"

"I think it's eighteen cents, Renny. Unless you think I ought to pay for the gum. In that case it would be twenty-three."

Renny took out a handful of silver and picked out a quarter. "Now take this and pay Mrs Brawn, and don't run into debt again."

Grandmother had by this time reached the door of her room, but, hearing sounds that seemed to contain the germ of a row, which she loved only second to her meals, she ordered her sons to steer her in the direction of the backstairs. The three bore down, clasped closely together, presenting a solid, overwhelming front, awe-inspiring to Wakefield as a Juggernaut. The sun, beaming through a stained-glass window behind them, splashed bright patches of colour over their bodies. Grandmother's taste ran to gaudy hues. It was she who had installed the bright window there to light the dim passage. Now, clad in a red velvet dressing-gown, clasping her gold-headed ebony stick, she advanced toward the grandsons, long-beaked, brilliant as a parrot.

"What's this going on?" she demanded. "What's the child been doing, Piers?"

"Climbing up Rags' back, Gran. He nearly threw him downstairs. Renny promised him a licking next time he did it, and now he's letting him off."

Her face turned crimson with excitement. She looked more like a parrot than ever. "Let him off, indeed!" she cried. "There's too much letting off here. That's what's the matter. I say flog him. Do you hear, Renny? Flog him well. I want to see it done. Get a cane and flog him."

With a terrified scream, Wakefield threw his arms about Renny's waist and hid his face against him. "Don't whip me, Renny!" he implored.

"I'll do it myself," she cried. "I've flogged boys before now. I've flogged Nicholas. I've flogged Ernest. I'll flog this spoiled little rascal. Let me have him!" She shuffled toward him, eager with lust of power.

"Come, come, Mamma," interposed Ernest, "this excitement's bad for you. Come and have a nice peppermint pâté or a glass of sherry." Gently he began to wheel her around.

"No, no, no!" she screamed, struggling, and Nip and Sasha began to bark and mew.

Renny settled it by picking up the little boy under his arm and hurrying along the passage to the side entrance. He set him down on the flagged path outside and shut the door behind them with a loud bang. Wakefield stood staring up at him like a ruffled young robin that has just been tossed from its nest by a storm, very much surprised, but tremendously interested in the world in which it finds itself.

"Well," observed Renny, lighting a cigarette, "that's that."

Wakefield, watching him, was filled with a passion of admiration for Renny—his all-powerful brown hands, his red head, his long, sharp-featured face. He loved him. He wanted Renny's love and Renny's pity more than anything else in the world. He must make Renny notice him, be kind to him, before he strode off to the stable after Piers.

Closing his eyes, he repeated the potent words that never failed to bring tears to his eyes. "This is terrible! Oh, it is terrible!" Something warm swelled within him. Something gushed upward, tremulous, through his being. He felt slightly dizzy, then tears welled sweetly into his eyes. He opened them and saw Renny through their iridescent brilliance, staring at him with amused concern.

"What!" he demanded. "Did Gran frighten you?"

"N-no. A little."

"Poor old fellow!" He put his arm around Wakefield and pressed him against his side. "But look here. You mustn't cry so easily. That's twice today I've seen you. You won't have the life of a dog when you go to school if you keep on like this."

Wake twisted a button on Renny's coat.

"May I have my marbles—and—ten cents?" he breathed. "You see, it will take the quarter to pay Mrs Brawn, and I would like just one little drink of lemon sour."

Renny handed over ten cents and the marbles.

Wake threw himself on the grass, flat on his back, staring up at the friendly blue of the sky. A sense of joyous peace possessed him. The afternoon was before him. He had nothing to do but enjoy himself. Lovingly he rattled the marbles in one pocket and the thirty-five cents in the other. Life was rich, full of infinite possibilities.

Presently a hot sweet smell assailed his sensitive nostrils. It was rising from the window of the basement kitchen near him. He rolled over and sniffed again. Surely he smelled cheese cakes. Delicious, crusty, lovely cheese cakes. He crept briskly on his hands and knees to the window and peered down into the kitchen. Mrs Wragge had just taken a pan of them out of the oven. Rags was washing the dishes and already chewing the gum. Mrs Wragge's face was crimson with heat. Looking up, she saw Wakefield.

"Have a cake?" she asked, and handed one up to him.

"Oh, thanks. And—and—Mrs Wragge, please may I have one for my friend?"

"You ain't got no friend with yer," said Rags, vindictively champing the gum.

Wakefield did not deign to answer him. He only held out one thin little brown hand for the other cake. Mrs Wragge laid it on his palm. "Look out it don't burn ye," she advised.

Blissfully he lay on the shaggy grass of the lawn, munching one cake and gazing quietly at the other recumbent on the grass before him. But when he came to it he really had not room for the second cake. If Finch had been there, he could have given it to him and Finch would have asked no uncomfortable questions. But Finch was at school. Was his whole glorious afternoon to be spoiled by the responsibility of owning a cake too many?

What did dogs do when they had a bone they didn't need at the moment? They buried it.

He walked round and round the perennial border, looking for a nice place. At last, near the root of a healthy-looking bleeding-heart he dug a little hole and placed the cake therein. It looked so pretty there he felt like calling Meg out to see it. But no—better not. Quickly he covered it with the moist warm earth and patted it smooth. Perhaps one day he would come and dig it up.

3

ERNEST AND SASHA

Ernest Whiteoak was at this time seventy years old. He had reached the age when after a hearty dinner a man likes repose of body and spirit. Such scenes as the one his mother had just staged inclined to upset his digestion, and it was with as petulant a look as ever shadowed his gentle face that he steered her at last to her padded chair by her own fire and ensconced her there. He stood looking down at her with a singular mixture of disgust and adoration. She was a deplorable old vixen, but he loved her more than any one else in the world.

"Comfortable, Mamma?" he asked.

"Yes. Bring me a peppermint. A Scotch mint—not a humbug."

He selected one from a little tin box on the dresser and brought it to her in his long pale fingers that seemed almost unnaturally smooth.

"Put it in my mouth, boy." She opened it, pushing forward her lips till she looked like a hungry old bird.

He popped in the peppermint, withdrawing his fingers quickly as though he were afraid she would bite him.

She sucked the sweet noisily, staring into the dancing firelight from under shaggy red brows. On the high back of her chair her brilliantly coloured parrot, Boney, perched, vindictively pecking at the ribbons on her cap. She had brought a parrot with her from India, named Boney in derision of Bonaparte. She had had several since the first one, but the time was long past when she was able to differentiate between them. They were all 'Boney', and she frequently would tell a visitor of the time she had had fetching this one across the ocean seventy-five years ago. He had been almost as much trouble as the baby, Augusta. Grandmother and her two sons had each a pet, which gave no love to any one but its owner. The three with their pets kept to their own apartments like superior boarders, seldom emerging except for meals and to pay calls on each other, or to sit in the drawing-room at whist in the evening.

Grandmother's room was thickly carpeted and curtained.

It smelled of sandalwood, camphor, and hair oil. The windows were opened only once a week, when Mrs Wragge 'turned it out' and threw the old lady into a temper for the day.

Her bed was an old painted leather one. The head blazed with oriental fruit, clustered about the gorgeous plumage of a parrot and the grinning faces of two monkeys. On this Boney perched all night, only at daylight flapping down to torment his mistress with pecks and Hindu curses which she herself had taught him.

He began to swear now at Sasha, who, standing on her hind legs, was trying to reach his tail with a curving grey paw.

"Kutni! Kutni! Kutni!" he rapped out. "Paji! Paji! Shaitan ka katla!" He rent the air with a metallic scream.

"Pick up your horrid cat, Ernest," ordered his mother. "She's making Boney swear. Poor Boney! Pretty Boney! Peck her eyes out, Boney!"

Ernest lifted Sasha to his shoulder, where she humped furiously, spitting out in her turn curses less coherent but equally vindictive.

"Comfortable now, Mamma?" Ernest repeated, fondling the ribbon on her cap.

"M-m. When's this man coming?"

"What man, Mamma?"

"The man that's going to bring out Eden's book. When's he coming? I want to have on my écru cap with the mauve ribbons."

"I'll let you know in time, Mamma."

"M-m. . . . More wood. Put more wood on the fire. I like to be warm as well as any one."

Ernest laid a heavy piece of oak log on the fire and stood looking down at it till slender flames began to caress it; then he turned to look at his mother. She was fast asleep, her chin buried in her breast. The Scotch mint had slipped out of her mouth and Boney had snatched it up and carried it to a corner of the room, where he was striking it on the floor to crack it, imagining it was some rare sort of nut. Ernest smiled and retreated, gently closing the door after him.

He slowly mounted the stairs, Sasha swaying on his shoulder, and sought his own room. The door of his brother's room stood open, and as he passed he had a glimpse of Nicholas sprawling in an armchair, his gouty leg supported on a beaded ottoman, his untidy head enveloped in cigar smoke. In his own room he was surprised and pleased to find his nephew, Eden. The young men did not often call on him; they favoured Nicholas, who had ribald jokes to tell. Nevertheless, he liked their company, and was always ready to lay aside his work—the annotating of Shakespeare—for the sake of it.

Eden was sitting on the edge of a book-littered table, swinging his leg. He looked self-conscious and flustered.

"I hope I'm not troubling you, Uncle," he said. "Just say the word if you don't want me and I'll clear out."

Ernest sat down in the chair farthest from his desk, to show that he had no thought of study. "I'm glad to have you, Eden. You know that. I'm very pleased about this success of yours—this book, and all the more so because you've read a good many of the poems to me in this very room. I take a great interest in it."

"You're the only one that really understands," answered Eden. "Understands the difference the publishing of this book will make in my life, I mean. Of course, Uncle Nick has been very nice about praising my poems——"

"Oh," interrupted Ernest, with a hurt feeling, "you read them to Nicholas in his room, also, eh?"

"Just a few. The ones I thought would interest him. Some of the love poems. I wanted to see how they affected him. After all, he's a man of the world. He's experienced a good deal in his time."

"And how did they affect him?" asked Ernest, polishing the nails of one hand against the palm of the other.

"They amused him, I think. Like yourself, he has difficulty in appreciating the new poetry. Still, he thinks I have good stuff in me."

"I wish you could have gone to Oxford."

"I wish I could. And so I might if Renny could have been brought to see reason. Of course, he feels now that the education he has given me has been wasted, since I refuse to go on with the study of law. But I can't, and that's all there is to it. I'm awfully fond of Renny, but I wish he weren't so frightfully materialistic. The first thing he asked about my book was whether I could make much money out of it. As though one ever made much out of a first book."

"And poetry at that," amended Ernest.

"He doesn't seem to realize that I'm the first one of the family

37

who has done anything to make our name known to the world——" The armour of his egotism was pierced by a hurt glance from Ernest and he hastened to add, "Of course, Uncle, there's your work on Shakespeare. That will get a lot of attention when it comes out. But Renny won't see anything in either achievement to be proud of. I think he's rather ashamed for us. He thinks a Whiteoak should be a gentleman farmer or a soldier. His life's been rather cramped, after all."

"He was through the War," commented Ernest. "That was a great experience."

"And what impressions did he bring back from it?" demanded Eden. "Almost the first questions he asked when he returned were about the price of hay and steers, and he spent most of his first afternoon leaning over a sty, watching a litter of squirming young pigs."

"I sympathize with you very greatly, my dear boy. And so does Meggie. She thinks you're a genius."

"Good old Meg. I wish she could convince the rest of the clan of that. Piers is a young beast."

"You mustn't mind Piers. He gibes at everything connected with learning. After all, he's very young. Now tell me, Eden, what shall you do? Shall you take up literature as a profession?" Eager to be sympathetic, he peered into the boy's face. He wanted very much to hold him, to keep his confidence.

"Oh, I'll look about me. I'll go on writing. I may join an expedition into the North this summer. I've an idea for a cycle of poems about the Northland. Not wild, rugged stuff, but something delicate, austere. One thing is certain—I'm not going to mix up law and poetry. It wouldn't do for me at all. Let's see what sort of reviews I get, Uncle Ernie."

They discussed the hazards of literature as a means of livelihood. Ernest spoke as a man of experience, though in all his seventy years he had never earned a dollar by his pen. Where would he be now, Eden wondered, if it were not for the shelter of Renny's roof. He supposed Gran would have had to come across with enough to support him, though to get money from her was to draw blood from a stone.

When Eden had gone, Ernest remained motionless in his chair by the window, looking out over the green meadows, and thinking also of his mother's fortune. It was the cause of much disturbing thought to him. Not that it was what one could call a great fortune, but a comfortable sum it certainly was. And there it was lying, accumulating for no one knew whom. In moments of the closest intimacy and affection with her, she never could be ever so gently led to disclose in whose favour her will was made. She knew that much of her power lay in keeping that tantalizing secret. He felt sure, by the mirthful gleam he had discovered in her eyes when the subject of money or wills was approached, that in secret she hugged the joy of baffling them all.

Ernest loved his family. He would feel no deep bitterness should any one of them inherit the money. He greatly longed, nevertheless, to be the next heir himself, to be in his turn the holder of power at Jalna, to experience the thrill of independence. And if he had it, he would do such nice things for them all, from brother Nicholas down to little Wake! By means of that power he would guide their lives into the channels that would be best for them. Whereas, if Nicholas inherited it—it had been divulged by Mrs Whiteoak that the money was to be left solidly to one person—well, Ernest could not quite think dispassionately of Nicholas as his mother's heir. He might do something reckless. Nicholas frequently made very reckless jokes about what he would do when he got it—he seemed to take it for granted that, as the eldest, he would get it—jokes which Ernest was far too generous to repeat to his mother, but it made him positively tremble to think where the family might end if Nicholas had a fling with it. In himself he was aware of well-knit faculties, cool judgment, a capacity for power. Nicholas was headstrong, arbitrary, ill balanced.

As for Renny, he was a good fellow, but he was letting the place run down. It had deteriorated while he was away at the War, and his return had not stayed the downward progression. The younger nephews could scarcely be looked on as rivals. Still, one never could be certain where the whim of an aged woman was in question.

Ernest sighed and looked toward the bed. He thought he should take a little nap after such a substantial dinner. With a last look at the pretty green meadows, he drew down the blind and laid his slender body along the coverlet. Sasha leaped up after him, snuggling her head close to his on the pillow. They gazed into each other's eyes, his blue and

39

drowsy, hers vivid green in the shadowed room, speculative, mocking.

She stretched out a round paw and laid it on his cheek, then, lest he should rest too secure in her love, she put out her claws just a little way and let him feel their sharpness.

"Sasha, dear, you're hurting me," he breathed.

She withdrew her claws, patted him, and uttered short throaty purrs.

"Pretty puss," sighed Ernest, closing his eyes. "Gentle puss!" She was sleepy, too, so they slept.

4

NICHOLAS AND NIP

As nephew Eden had sought out Uncle Ernest that he might discuss his future with him, so that same afternoon nephew Renny sought out Uncle Nicholas that they too might discuss Eden's prospects.

Both rooms, the scenes of these conversations, would appear to an outside observer overfurnished. The two elderly men had collected there all the things which they particularly fancied or to which they thought they had a claim, but while Ernest's taste ran to pale water-colours, china figures, and chintz-covered chairs, Nicholas had the walls of his room almost concealed by hunting prints and pictures of pretty women. His furniture was leather-covered. An old square piano, the top of which was littered with pipes, several decanters and a mixer, medicine bottles—he was always dosing himself for gout—and music, stood by the window.

Nip, the Yorkshire terrier, had a bone on the hearth-rug when Renny entered. Hearing the step, he darted forward, nipped Renny on the ankle, and darted back to his bone, snarling as he gnawed. Nicholas, his bad leg stretched on the ottoman, looked up from his book with a lazy smile.

"Hullo, Renny! Come for a chat? Can you find a chair? Throw those slippers on to the floor. Place always in a mess —yet if I let Rags in here to tidy up he hides everything I use, and what with my knee—well, it puts me in the devil of a temper for a week."

"I know," agreed Renny. He dropped the slippers to the floor and himself into the comfort of the chair. "Have you got a good book, Uncle Nick? I never seem to have any time for reading."

"I wish I hadn't so much, but when a man's tied to his chair, as I am a great deal of the time, he must do something. This is one Meggie got the last time she was in town. An English authoress. The new books puzzle me, Renny. My God! if everything in this one is true, it's amazing what nice women will do and think these days. The thoughts of this heroine—my goodness, they're appalling. Have a cigar?"

Renny helped himself from a box on the piano. Nip, thinking Renny had designs on his bone, darted forth once more, bit the intruder's ankle, and darted back growling, fancying himself a terrifying beast.

"Little brute!" said Renny. "I really felt his teeth that time. Does he think I'm after his bone?"

Nicholas said: "Catch a spider! Catch a spider, Nip!" Nip flew to his master, tossing his long-haired body round and round him, and yapping loudly.

A loud thumping sounded through the thick walls. Nicholas smiled maliciously. "It always upsets Ernie to hear Nip raise his voice. Yet I'm expected to endure the yowls of that cat of his at any hour of the night." He clapped his palms together at the little dog. "Catch a spider, Nip! Catch a spider!" Hysterically yelping, Nip sped around the room, looking in corners and under chairs for an insect. The thumping on the wall became frantic.

Renny picked up the terrier and smothered his barks under his arm. "Poor Uncle Ernest! You'll have him unnerved for the rest of the day. Shut up, Nip, you little scoundrel."

Nicholas' long face, the deep downward lines of which gave an air of sagacity to his most trivial remarks, was lit by a sardonic smile. "Does him good to be stirred up," he remarked. "He spends too much time at his desk. Came to me the other day jubilant. He had got what he believed to be two hundred and fifty mistakes in the text of Shakespeare's plays. Fancy trying to improve Shakespeare's text at this time. I tell him he has not an adequate knowledge of the handwriting of the day, but he thinks he has. Poor Ernie, he always was a little nutty."

Renny puffed soberly at his cigar. "I hope to God Eden is not going to take after him. Wasting his time over poetry. I feel a bit upset about this book of his. It's gone to his head. I believe the young fool thinks he can make a living from poetry. You don't think so, do you, Uncle Nick?" He regarded Nicholas almost pathetically.

"I don't believe it's ever been done. I like his poetry, though. It's very nice poetry."

"Well, he must understand he's got to work. I'm not going to waste any more money on him. He's quite made up his mind he won't go on with his profession. After all I've spent on him! I only wish I had it back."

Nicholas tugged at his drooping moustache. "Oh, he had to have a university education."

"No, he didn't. Piers hasn't. He didn't want it. Wouldn't have it. Eden could have stopped at home. We could find plenty of work for him on one of the farms."

"Eden farming? My dear Renny! Don't worry. Let him go on with his poetry and wait and see what happens."

"It's such a damned silly life for a man. All very well for the classic poets——"

"They were young fellows once. Disapproved of by their families, too."

"*Is* his poetry good enough?"

"Well, it's good enough to take the fancy of this publisher. For my part, I think it's very adroit. A sort of delicate perfection—a very wistful beauty that's quite remarkable."

Renny stared at his uncle, suspiciously. Was he making fun of Eden? Or was he just pulling the wool over his own eyes to protect Eden? 'Adroit, delicate, wistful'—the adjectives made him sick. "One thing's damned certain," he growled; "he'll not get any more money out of me."

Nicholas heaved himself about in his chair, achieving a more comfortable position. "How are things going? Pretty close to the wind?"

"Couldn't be closer," Renny assented.

Nicholas chuckled. "And yet you would like to keep all the boys at Jalna instead of sending them out into the world to shift for themselves. Renny, you have the instincts of the patriarch. To be the head of a swarming tribe. To mete out justice and rewards, and grow a long red beard."

Renny, somewhat nettled, felt like saying that both Nicholas and his brother Ernest had taken advantage of this instinct in him, but he satisfied himself by pulling the little dog's ears. Nip growled.

"Catch a spider, Nip," commanded his master, clapping his hands at him.

Once again Nip hurled himself into a frenzy of pursuit after an imagined insect. The thumping on the wall broke out anew. Renny got up to go. He felt that his troubles were not being taken seriously. Nicholas, looking up from under his shaggy brows, saw the shadow on Renny's face. He said, with sudden warmth: "You're an uncommonly good brother, Renny, *and* nephew. Have a drink?"

Renny said he would, and Nicholas insisted on getting up to mix it for him. "Shouldn't take one myself with this damn knee——" but he did, hobbling about his liquor cabinet in sudden activity.

"Well, Eden can do as he likes this summer," said Renny, cheered by his glass, "but by fall he's got to settle down, either in business or here at Jalna."

"But what would the boy do at Jalna, Renny?"

"Help Piers. Why not? If he would turn in and help, we could take over the land that is rented to old Hare and make twice as much out of it. It's a good life. He could write poetry in his spare time if he wanted to. I'd not say a word against it, so long as I wasn't asked to read it."

"The ploughman poet. It sounds artless enough. But I'm afraid he has very different ideas for his future. Poor young whelp. Heavens! How like his mother he is!"

"Well," mumbled Renny. "He'll not get around me. I've wasted enough on him. To think of him refusing to try his finals! I've never heard of such a thing. Now he talks of going down to New York to see his publisher."

"I expect this particular germ has been working in him secretly for a long time. Perhaps the boy's a genius, Renny."

"Lord! I hope not."

Nicholas made the subterranean noises that were his laughter. "You're a perfect Court, Renny. No wonder Mamma is partial to you."

"Is she? I'd never noticed it. I thought Eden was her pet. He has a way with women of all ages. Well, I'm off. Hobbs,

43

up Mistwell way, is having a sale of Holsteins. I may buy a cow or two."

"I should go with you if it were horses, in spite of my knee, but I can't get worked up over cows. Never liked milk."

Renny had got to the door when Nicholas asked suddenly: "How about Piers? Have you spoken to him of the girl yet?"

"Yes. I've told him he must cut out these meetings with her. He never dreamed they'd been seen. He was staggered."

"He seemed all right at dinnertime."

"Oh, we had our little talk two days ago. He's not a bad youngster. He took it very well. There aren't many girls about here—attractive ones—and there's no denying Pheasant is pretty."

Nicholas' brows darkened. "But think what she is. We don't want that breed in the family. Meg would never stand it."

"The girl is all right," said Renny, in his contradictory way. "She didn't choose the manner of her coming into the world. The boys have always played about with her."

"Piers will play about with her once too often."

"That's all right," returned Renny, testily. "He knows I'll stand no nonsense." He went out, shutting the door noisily, as he always did.

Nip was still busy with his bone. Regarding him, Nicholas feared that he would be in for an attack of indigestion if he got any more of the gristle off it. He dragged the treasure from here, and with difficulty straightened himself. Once bent over, it was no joke to rise. What a responsibility a little pet dog was! "No, no, no more gristle. You'll get a tummy-ache."

Nip protested, dancing on his hind legs. Nicholas laid the bone on the piano and wiped his fingers on the tail of his coat. Then the bottle of Scotch and the siphon caught his eye. He took up his glass. "Good Lord, I shouldn't be doing this," he groaned, but he mixed himself another drink. "Positively the last today," he murmured, as he hobbled toward his chair, glass in hand.

A deep note was struck on the piano. Nip had leaped to the stool and from there to the keys. Now he had stretched his head to recapture the bone. Nicholas sank with a grunt of mingled pain and amusement into his chair. "I suppose we may as well kill ourselves," he commented, ruefully,

> "You in your small corner,
> And I in mine."

Nip growled, gnawing his bone on the top of the piano.

Nicholas sipped his whisky and soda dreamily. The house was beautifully quiet now. He would doze a little, just in his chair, when he had finished his glass and Nip his bone. The rhythmic crunching of Nip's teeth as he excavated for marrow was soothing. A smile flitted over Nicholas' face as he remembered how the little fellow's barking had upset Ernest. Ernest did get upset easily, poor old boy! Well, he was probably resting quietly now beside his beloved Sasha. Cats. Selfish things. Only loved you for what they could get out of you. Now Nip—there *was* devotion.

He stretched out his hand and looked at it critically. Yes, that heavy ring with the square green stone in its antique setting became it. He was glad he had inherited his mother's hands—Court hands. Renny had them, too, but badly cared for. No doubt about it, character, as well as breeding, showed in hands. A vision of the hands of his wife, Millicent, came before him—clawlike hands with incredibly thin, very white fingers, and large curving nails. . . . She was still living; he knew that. Good God, she would be seventy! He tried to picture her at seventy, then shook his head impatiently—no, he did not want to picture her at either seventy or seventeen. He wanted to forget her. When Mamma should die, as she must soon, poor old dear, and he should inherit the money, he would go to England for a visit. He'd like to see old England once again before he—well, even he would die some day, though he expected to live to be at least ninety-nine like Mamma. He was a Court, and they were famous for their longevity and—what was the other? Oh, yes, their tempers. Well, thank goodness, he hadn't inherited the Court temper. It would die with Mamma, though Renny when he was roused was a fierce fellow.

Nip was whining to be lifted from the piano top. He was tired of his bone, and wanted his afternoon nap. Little devil, to make him get out of his chair again just when he was so comfortable!

With a great grunt he heaved himself on to his feet and limped to the piano. He took up the little dog, now entirely gentle and confiding, and carried him back under his arm. His knee gave him a sharp twinge as he lowered his weight into the chair once more, but his grimace of pain changed to a smile at the shaggy little face that was turned up to his. He had a sudden impulse to say, "Catch a spider, Nip!" and start a fresh skirmish. He even framed the words with his lips, and a sudden tenseness in Nip's body, a gleam in his eye, showed that he was ready; but he must not upset old Ernie again, and he was very drowsy—that second drink had been soothing. "No, no, Nip," he murmured, "go to sleep. No more racketing, old boy." He stroked the little dog's back with a large, indolent hand.

Nip lay along his body, as he half reclined, gazing into his eyes. Nicholas blew into Nip's face. Nip thumped his tail on Nicholas' stomach.

They slept.

5

PIERS AND HIS LOVE

IT WAS almost dark when Piers crossed the lawn, passed through a low wicket gate in the hedge, and pressed eagerly along a winding path that led across a paddock where three horses were still cropping the new grass. The path wandered then down into the ravine; became, for three strides, a little rustic bridge; became a path again, still narrower, that wound up the opposite steep, curved through a noble wood; and at last, by a stile, was wedded to another path that had been shaped for no other purpose but to meet it on the boundary between Jalna and the land belonging to the Vaughans.

Down in the ravine it was almost night, so darkly the stream glimmered amid the thick undergrowth and so close above him hung the sky, not yet pricked by a star. Climbing up the steep beyond, it was darker still, except for the luminous shine of the silver birches that seemed to be lighted by some secret beam within. A whippoorwill darted among the trees, catching insects, uttering, each time it struck, a little throaty cluck, and showing a gleam of white on its wings. Then suddenly, right over his head, another whippoorwill burst into its loud lilting song.

When he reached the open wood above, Piers could see that there was still a deep red glow in the west, and the young leaves of the oaks had taken a burnished look. The trees were lively with the twittering of birds seeking their nests, their love-making over for the day—his just to begin.

His head was hot and he took off his cap to let the cool air fan it. He wished that his love for Pheasant were a calmer love. He would have liked to stroll out with her in the evenings, just pleasantly elated, taking it as a natural thing, as natural as the life of these birds, to love a girl and be loved by her. But it had come upon him suddenly, after knowing her all his life, like a storm that shook and possessed him. As he hurried on through the soft night air, each step drawing him nearer to the stile where Pheasant was to meet him, he tormented himself by picturing his disappointment if she were not there. He saw, in his fancy, the stile, bare as a waiting gallows, mocking the sweet urge that pressed him. He saw himself waiting till dark night and then stumbling back to Jalna filled with despair because he had not held her in his arms. What was it that had overtaken them both that day, when, meeting down in the ravine, she had been startled by a water-snake and had caught his sleeve and had pointed down into the stream where it had disappeared? Bending over the water, they had suddenly seen their two faces reflected in a still pool, looking up at them not at all like the faces of Piers and Pheasant who had known each other all their days. The faces reflected had had strange, timid eyes and parted lips. They had turned to look at each other. Their own lips had met.

Remembering that kiss, he began to run across the open field toward the stile.

She was sitting on it, waiting for him, her drooping figure silhouetted against the blur of red in the west. He slackened his pace as soon as he saw her, and greeted her laconically as he came up.

"Hullo, Pheasant!"

"Hullo, Piers! I've been waiting quite a while."

"I couldn't get away. I had to stop and admire a beastly cow Renny bought at the Hobbs' sale today."

He climbed to the stile and sat down beside her. "It's the first warm evening, isn't it?" he observed, not looking at her. "I got as hot as blazes coming over. I wasn't letting the grass grow under my feet, I can tell you." He took her hand and drew it against his side. "Feel that."

"Your heart is beating rather hard," she said, in a low voice. "Is it because you hurried or because——" She leaned against his shoulder and looked into his face.

It was what Piers had been waiting for, this moment when she would lean toward him. Not without a sign from her would he let the fountain of his love leap forth. Now he put his arms about her and pressed her to him. He found her lips and held them with his own. The warm fragrance of her body made him dizzy. He was no longer strong and practical. He wished in that moment that they two might die thus happily clasped in each other's arms in the tranquil spring night.

"I can't go on like this," he murmured. "We simply must get married."

"Remember what Renny has said. Are you going to defy him? He'd be in a rage if he knew we were together here now."

"Renny be damned! He's got to be taught a lesson. It's time he was taught that he can't lord it over every one. He's spoiled, that's the trouble with him. I call him the Rajah of Jalna."

"After all, you have the right to say who you will marry, even if the girl is beneath you, haven't you?"

He felt a sob beneath her breast; her sudden tears wet his cheek.

"Oh, Pheasant, you little fool," he exclaimed. "You beneath me? What rot!"

"Well, Renny thinks so. All your family think so. Your family despise me."

"My family may go to the devil. Why, after all, you're a Vaughan. Everybody knows that. You're called by the name."

"Even Maurice looks down on me. He's never let me call him Father."

"He deserves to be shot. If I had ever done what he did, I'd stand by the child. I'd brave the whole thing out, by God!"

"Well, he has—in a way. He's kept me. Given me his name."

"His parents did that. He's never liked you or been really kind to you."

"He thinks I've spoiled his life."

"With Meggie, you mean. Picture Meg and Maurice married!" He laughed and kissed her temple, and, feeling her silky brow touch his cheek, he kissed that, too.

She said: "I can picture that more easily than I can our own marriage. I feel as though we should go on and on, meeting and parting like this for ever. In a way I think I'd like it better, too."

"Better than being married to me? Look here, Pheasant, you're just trying to hurt me."

"No, really. It's so beautiful, meeting like this. All day I'm in a kind of dream, waiting for it; then after it comes the night, and you're in the very heart of me all night——"

"What if I were beside you?"

"It couldn't be so lovely. It couldn't. Then in the morning, the moment I waken, I am counting the hours till we meet again. Maurice might not exist. I scarcely see or hear him."

"Dreams don't satisfy me, Pheasant. This way of living is torture to me. Every day as the spring goes on it's a greater torture. I want you—not dreams of you."

"Don't you love our meeting like this?"

"Don't be silly! You know what I mean." He moved away from her on the stile and lighted a cigarette. "Now," he went on, in a hard, businesslike tone, "let us take it for granted that we're going to be married. We are, aren't we? Are we going to be married, eh?"

"Yes. . . . You might offer me a cigarette."

He gave her one and lighted it for her.

"Very well. Can you tell me any reason for hanging back? I'm twenty, you're seventeen. Marriageable ages, eh?"

"Too young, they say."

"Rot. They would like us to wait till we're too decrepit to creep to this stile. I'm valuable to Renny. He's paying me decent wages. I know Renny. He's good-natured at bottom, for all his temper. He'd never dream of putting me

49

out. There's lots of room at Jalna. One more would never be noticed."

"Meg doesn't like me. I'm rather afraid of her."

"Afraid of Meggie! Oh, you little coward! She's gentle as a lamb. And Gran always liked you. I'll tell you what, Pheasant, we'll stand in with Gran. She has a lot of influence with the family. If we make ourselves pleasant to her, there's no knowing what she may do for us. She's often said that I am more like my grandfather than any of the others, and she thinks he was the finest man that ever lived."

"What about Renny? She's always talking about his being a perfect Court. Anyhow, I expect her will was made before we were born."

"Yes, but she's always changing it or pretending that she does. Only last week she had her lawyer out for hours, and the whole family was upset. Wake peeked in at the keyhole and he said all she did was feed the old fellow with peppermints. Still, you can never tell." He shook his head sagaciously and then heaved a gusty sigh. "One thing is absolutely certain: I can't go on like this. I've either got to get married or go away. It's affecting my nerves. I scarcely knew what I was eating at dinner today, and such a hullabaloo there was over this book of Eden's. Good Lord! Poetry! Think of it! And at teatime Finch had come home with a bad report from one of his masters and there was another row. It raged for an hour."

But Pheasant had heard nothing but the calculated cruelty of the words 'go away'. She turned toward him a frightened, wide-eyed face.

"Go away! How can you say such a thing? You know I'd die in this place without you."

"How pale you've got," he observed, peering into her face. "Why are you turning pale? Surely it wouldn't matter to you if I went away. You could go right on dreaming about me, you know."

Pheasant burst into tears and began to scramble down from the stile. "If you think I'll stop here to be tortured!" she cried, and began to run from him.

"Yet you expect me to stay and be tortured!" he shouted.

She ran into the dusk across the wet meadow, and he sat obstinately staring after her, wondering if her will would

50

hold out till she reached the other side. Already her steps seemed to be slackening. Still her figure became less clear. What if she should run on and on till she reached home, leaving him alone on the stile with all his love turbulent within him? The mere thought of that was enough to make him jump down and begin to run after her, but even as he did so he saw her coming slowly back, and he clambered again to his seat just in time to save his dignity. He was thankful for that.

She stopped within ten paces of him.

"Very well," she said, in a husky voice, "I'll do it."

He was acutely aware of her nearness in every sensitive nerve, but he puffed stolidly at his cigarette a moment before he asked gruffly: "When?".

"Whenever you say." Her head drooped and she gave a childish sob.

"Come here, you little baggage," he ordered peremptorily. But when he had her on the stile again a most delicious tenderness took possession of him and withal a thrilling sense of power. He uttered endearments and commands with his face against her hair.

All the way home he was full of lightness and strength, though he had worked hard that day. Half way down the steep into the ravine a branch of an oak projected across the path above him. He leaped up and caught it with his hands and so hung aloof from the earth that seemed too prosaic for his light feet. He swung himself gently a moment, looking up at the stars that winked at him through the young leaves. A rabbit ran along the path beneath, quite unaware of him. His mind was no longer disturbed by anxiety, but free and exultant. He felt himself one with the wild things of the wood. It was spring, and he had chosen his mate.

When he crossed the lawn he saw that the drawing-room was lighted. Playing cards as usual, he supposed. He went to one of the french windows and looked in. By the fire he could see a table drawn up, at which sat his grandmother and his uncle Ernest, playing at draughts. She was wrapped in a bright green-and-red plaid shawl, and wearing a much beribboned cap. Evidently she was beating him, for her teeth were showing in a broad grin and a burst of loud laughter made the bridge players at the other table turn in their chairs with looks of annoyance. The long aquiline face of Uncle Ernest drooped wistfully above the board. On the blackened walnut mantelpiece Sasha lay curled beside a china shepherdess, her gaze fixed on her master with a kind of ecstatic contempt.

At the bridge table sat Renny, Meg, Nicholas, and Mr Fennel, the rector. The faces of all were illumined by fire-light, their expressions intensified: Nicholas, sardonic, watch-ful; Renny, frowning, puzzled; Meg, sweet, complacent; Mr Fennel, pulling his beard and glowering. Poor creatures all, thought Piers, as he let himself in at the side door and softly ascended the stair, playing their little games, their paltry pastimes, whilst he played the great game of life.

A light showed underneath Eden's door. More poetry, more paltry pastime! Had Even ever loved? If he had, he'd kept it well to himself. Probably he only loved his Muse. His Muse—ha, ha! He heard Eden groan. So it hurt, did it, loving the pretty Muse? Poetry had its pain, then. He gave a passing thump to the door.

"Want any help in there?"

"You go to hell," rejoined the young poet, "unless you happen to have a rag about you. I've upset the ink."

Piers poked his head in at the door. "My shirt isn't much better than a rag," he said. "I can let you have that."

Eden was mopping the stained baize top of the desk with blotting paper. On a sheet of a writing pad was neatly written what looked like the beginning of a poem.

"I suppose you get fun out of it," remarked Piers.

"More than you get from chasing a girl about the wood at night."

"Look here, you'd better be careful!" Piers raised his voice threateningly, but Eden smiled and sat down at his desk once more.

It was uncanny, Piers thought, as he went on to his room. How ever had Eden guessed? Was it because he was a poet? He had always felt, though he had given the matter but little thought, that a poet would be an uncommonly unpleasant person to have in the house, and now, by God, they had a full-fledged one at Jalna. He didn't like it at all. The first bloom of his happy mood was gone as he opened the door into his bedroom.

He shared it with sixteen-year-old Finch. Finch was now humped over his Euclid, an expression of extreme melancholy lengthening his already long sallow face. He had been the centre of a whirlpool of discussion and criticism all tea-time, and the effect was to make his brain, never quite under his control, completely unmanageable. He had gone over the same problem six or seven times and now it meant nothing to him, no more than a senseless nursery rhyme. He had stolen one of Piers' cigarettes to see if it would help him out. He had made the most of it, inhaling slowly, savouring each puff, retaining the stub between his bony fingers till they and even his lips were burned, but it had done no good. When he heard Piers at the door he had dropped the stub, a mere crumb, to the floor and set his foot on it.

Now he glanced sullenly at Piers out of the corners of his long light eyes.

Piers sniffed. "H-m. Smoking, eh? One of my fags, too, I bet. I'll just thank you to leave them alone, young man. Do you think I can supply you with smokes? Besides, you're not allowed."

Finch returned to his Euclid with increased melancholy. If he could not master it when he was alone, certainly he should never learn it with Piers in the room. That robust, domineering presence would crush the last spark of intelligence from his brain. He had always been afraid of Piers. All his life he had been kept in a state of subjection by him. He resented it, but he saw no way out of it. Piers was strong, handsome, a favourite. He was none of these things. And yet he loved all his family, in a secret, sullen way, even Piers who was so rough with him. Now, if Piers had been like some brothers one might ask him to give one a helping hand with the Euclid; Piers had been good at the rotten stuff. But it would never do to ask Piers for help. He was too impatient, too intolerant of a fellow who got mixed up for nothing.

"I'd thank you," continued Piers, "to let my fags, likewise my handkerchiefs, socks, and ties, alone. If you want to pinch other people's property, pinch Eden's. He's a poet and probably doesn't know what he has." He grinned at his reflection in the glass as he took off his collar and tie.

Finch made no answer. Desperately he sought to clamp

his attention to the problem before him. Angles and triangles tangled themselves into strange patterns. He drew a grotesque face on the margin of the book. Then horribly the face he had created began to leer at him. With a shaking hand he tried to rub it out, but he could not. It was not his to erase. It possessed the page. It possessed the book. It was Euclid personified, sneering at him!

Piers had divested himself of all his clothes and had thrown open the window. A chill night wind rushed in. Finch shivered as it embraced him. He wondered how Piers stood it on his bare skin. It fluttered the pages of a French exercise all about the room. There was no use in trying; he could not do the problem.

Piers, in his pyjamas now, jumped into bed. He lay staring at Finch with bright blue eyes, whistling softly. Finch began to gather up his books.

"All finished?" asked Piers, politely. "You got through in a hurry, didn't you?"

"I'm not through," bawled Finch. "Do you imagine I can work with a cold blast like that on my back and you staring at me in front? It just means I'll have to get up early and finish before breakfast."

Piers became sarcastic. "You're very temperamental, aren't you? You'll be writing poetry next. I dare say you've tried it already. Do you know, I think it would be a good thing for you to go down to New York in the Easter holidays and see if you can find a publisher."

"Shut up," growled Finch, "and let me alone."

Piers was very happy. He was too happy for sleep. It would ease his high spirts to bait young Finch. He lay watching him speculatively while he undressed his long, lanky body. Finch might develop into a distinguished-looking man. There was something arresting even now in his face; but he had a hungry, haunted look, and he was uncomfortably aware of his long wrists and legs. He always sat in some ungainly posture and, when spoken to suddenly, would glare up, half defensively, half timidly, as though expecting a blow. Truth to tell, he had had a good many, some quite undeserved.

Piers regarded his thin frame with contemptuous amusement. He offered pungent criticisms of Finch's prominent shoulder blades, ribs, and various other portions of his anatomy. At last the boy, trembling with anger and humiliation, got into his nightshirt, turned out the light, and scrambled over Piers to his place next the wall. He curled himself up with a sigh of relief. It had been a nervous business scrambling over Piers. He had half expected to be grabbed by the ankle and put to some new torture. But he had gained his corner in safety. The day with its miseries was over. He stretched out his long limbs.

They lay still, side by side, in the peaceful dark. At length Piers spoke in a low, accusing tone.

"You didn't say your prayers. What do you mean by getting into bed without saying your prayers?"

Finch was staggered. This was something new. Piers, of all people, after him about prayers! There was something ominous about it.

"I forgot," he returned, heavily.

"Well, you've no right to forget. It's an important thing at your time of life to pray long and earnestly. If you prayed more and sulked less, you'd be healthier and happier."

"Rot. What are you givin' us?"

"I'm in dead earnest. Out you get and say your prayers."

"You don't pray yourself," complained Finch, bitterly. "You haven't said prayers for years."

"That's nothing to you. I've a special compact with the Devil, and he looks after his own. But you, my little lamb, must be separated from the goats."

"Oh, let me alone," growled Finch. "I'm sleepy. Let me alone."

"Get up and say your prayers."

"Oh, Piers, don't be a——"

"Be careful what you call me. Get out."

"Shan't." He clutched the blankets desperately, for he feared what was coming.

"You won't get up, eh? You won't say your prayers, eh? I've got to force you, eh?"

With each question Piers' strong fingers sought a tenderer spot in Finch's anatomy.

"Oh—oh—oh! Piers! Please let me up! Ow-eee-ee!" With a last terrible squeak Finch was out on the floor. He stood rubbing his side cautiously. Then he almost blubbered: "What the hell do you want me to do, anyway?"

"I want you to say your prayers properly. I'm not going to have you start being lax at your age. Down on your knees."

Finch dropped to his knees on the cold floor. Kneeling by the bedside in the pale moonlight, he was a pathetic young figure. But the sight held no pathos for Piers.

"Now, then," he said. "Fire away." Finch pressed his face against his clenched hands.

"Why don't you begin?" asked Piers, rising on his elbow and speaking testily.

"I—I have begun," came in a muffled voice.

"I can't hear you. How do you expect the Almighty to hear you if I can't? Speak up."

"I c-can't. I won't!"

"You *shall*. Or you'll be sorry."

In the stress of the moment, all Finch's prayers left him, as earlier all his Euclid had done. In the dim chaos of his soul only two words of supplication remained. "O God," he muttered, hoarsely, and because he could think of nothing else, and must pray or be abused by that devil Piers, he repeated the words again and again in a hollow, shaking voice.

Piers lay listening blandly. He thought Finch the most ridiculous duffer he had ever known. He was a mystery Piers would never fathom. Suddenly he thought: 'I'm fed up with this,' and said: "Enough, enough. It's not much of a prayer you've made, but still you've a nice intimate way with the Almighty. You'd make a good Methodist of the Holy Roller variety." He added, not unkindly, "Hop into bed now."

But Finch would not hop. He clutched the counterpane and went on sobbing, "O God!" The room was full of the presence of the Deity to him, now wearing the face of the terrible, austere Old Testament God, now, miraculously, the handsome, sneering face of Piers. Only a rap on the head brought him to his senses. He somehow got his long body back into bed, shivering all over.

Eden threw the door open. "One might as well," he complained in a high voice, "live next door to a circus. You're the most disgusting young——" and he delivered himself of some atrocious language. He interrupted himself to ask, cocking his head, "Is he crying? What's he crying for?"

"Just low-spirited, I expect," replied Piers, in a sleepy voice. "What are you crying for, Finch?"

"Let me alone, can't you?" screamed Finch, in a sudden fury. "You let me alone!"

"I think he's snivelling over his report. Renny was up in the air about it," said Piers.

"Oh, is that it? Well, study will do more than snivelling to help that." And Eden disappeared as he had come.

The two brothers lay in the moonlight. Finch was quiet save for an occasional gulp. Piers' feelings toward him were magnanimous now. He was such a helpless young fool. Piers thought it rather hard that he had been born between Eden and Finch. Wedged in between a poet and a fool. What a sandwich! Of a certainty, he was the meaty part.

His thoughts turned to Pheasant. She was of never-failing interest to him: her pretty gestures, her reckless way of throwing her heart open to him, her sudden withdrawals, the remoteness of her profile. He could see her face in the moonlight as though she were in the room with him. Soon she would be, instead of snuffling young Finch! He loved her with every inch of his body. He alone of all the people in Jalna knew what real love was. Strange that, being absorbed by love as he was, he should have time to play with young Finch and make him miserable. No denying that there lurked a mischievous devil in him. Then, too, he had suffered so much anxiety lately that to have everything settled, to be certain of having his own way, made him feel like a young horse suddenly turned out into the spring pastures, ready to run and kick and bite his best friend from sheer high spirits.

Poor old Finch! Piers gave the bedclothes a jerk over Finch's protruding shoulder and put an arm around him.

6

PHEASANT AND MAURICE

TWO WEEKS later Pheasant awakened one morning at sunrise. She could not sleep, because it was her wedding day. She jumped out of bed and ran to the window to see whether the heavens were to smile on her.

The sky was radiant as a golden sea, and just above the sun a cloud shaped like a great red whale floated as in a dream. Below her window, shutting in the lawn, the cherry orchard had burst into a sudden perfection of bloom. The young trees stood in snowy rows like expectant young girls awaiting their first communion. A cowbell was jangling down in the ravine.

Pheasant leaned across the sill, her cropped brown hair all on end, her nightdress falling from one slim shoulder. She was happy because of the gay serenity of the morning, because the cherry trees had come into bloom for her wedding day; yet she was depressed, because it was her wedding day and she had nothing new to wear. Besides, she would have to go to live at Jalna, where nobody wanted her except Piers.

She was to meet him at two o'clock. He had borrowed a car, and they were to drive to Stead to be married. This was outside Mr Fennel's parish. Then they were to go to the city for the night, but they must be back at Jalna the next day because Piers was anxious about the spring sowing. What sort of reception would the family at Jalna give them? They had been kind always, but would they be kind to her as Piers' wife? Still, Piers would take care of her. She would face the world with him at her side.

She drummed her white fingers on the sill, watching the sun twinkle on her engagement ring which thus far she had only dared to wear at night. She thought of that blissful moment when each had stared into the other's face, watching love flower there like the cherry tree bursting into bloom. She would love him always, let him cuddle his head against her shoulder at night, and go into the fields with him in the morning. She was glad he had chosen the land as his job, instead of one of the professions. She was too ignorant to be the wife of a learned young man. To Piers she could unfold her childish speculations about life without embarrassment.

For the hundredth time she examined the few clothes she had laid in an immense shabby portmanteau for her wedding journey—her patent-leather shoes and her one pair of silk stockings, a pink organdie dress, really too small for her, four handkerchiefs—well, she had plenty of them, at least, and one never knew when one might shed tears—a nightdress, and an India shawl that had been her grandmother's. She did not suppose she would need the shawl; she had never worn it except when playing at being grown up, but it helped to make a more impressive trousseau, and it might be necessary to have a wrap at dinner in the hotel, or if they went to the opera. She felt somewhat cheered as she replaced them and fastened the spongy leather straps. After all, they might have been fewer and worse.

She got out her darning things and mended—or rather puckered together—a large hole in the heel of a brown stocking she was to wear on the journey. She mended the torn buttonholes of her brown coat, sprinkled a prodigious amount of cheap perfume over the little brown dress that lay in a drawer ready to put on, and found herself chilled, for she had not yet dressed.

She hastily put on her clothes, washed her face, and combed her hair, staring at herself in the glass. She thought dismally: 'Certainly I am no beauty. Nannie has trimmed my hair badly. I'm far too thin, and I haven't at all that sleek look becoming in a bride. No one could imagine a wreath of orange blossoms on my head. A punchinello's cap would be more appropriate. Ah, well, there have been worse-looking girls led to the altar, I dare say.'

Maurice Vaughan was already at the table, eating sausages and fried potatoes. He did not say good morning, but he put some of the food on a plate and pushed it toward her. Presently he said:

"Jim Martin is coming with a man from Brancepeth today. Have Nannie put the dinner off till one. We'll be busy."

Pheasant was aghast. She was to meet Piers at two. How could she get away in time? And if she did not turn up for dinner Maurice might make inquiries, get suspicious. Her hands shook as she poured her tea. She could not properly see the breakfast things.

Maurice stared at her coldly. "Did you hear what I said?" he asked. "What's the matter with you this morning?"

"I was busy thinking. Yes, you want dinner at two; I heard."

"I said one o'clock. I'd better give the order myself, if you haven't the wit."

Pheasant was regaining her self-possession.

"How easily you get out of temper," she said, coolly. "Of course I'll remember. I hope Mr Martin will be soberer than he was the last time he was here. He put a pickle in his tea instead of sugar, and slept all evening, I remember, in his chair."

"I don't."

"I dare say you don't. You were pretty far gone yourself."

Vaughan burst out laughing. The audacities of this only half-acknowledged young daughter of his amused him. Yet, perversely, when she was meek and eager to please, he was often unkind to her, seeming to take pleasure in observing how she had inherited a capacity for suffering equal to his own.

Maurice Vaughan was the grandson and only male descendant of the Colonel Vaughan whose letters had persuaded Philip Whiteoak to remove westward from Quebec. He was an only child, who had come to his parents late in life. He had been too gently reared, and had grown into a heavily built, indolent, arrogant youth, feeling himself intellectually above all his associates, even Renny Whiteoak, whom he loved. At twenty he nourished the illusion that he would become a great man in the affairs of his country with no effort on his part. At twenty-one he became engaged to Meg Whiteoak, charmed by that ineffably sweet smile of hers and her drowsy quiescence toward himself. The parents of the two were almost beside themselves with pleasure. They scarcely dared to breathe lest a breath too hot or too cold should damp the ardour of the young pair and the so desirable match be not consummated.

Meggie would not be hurried. A year's engagement was proper, and a year's engagement she would have. Maurice, idle and elegant, attracted the attention of a pretty, sharp-featured village girl, Elvira Gray. She took to picking bramble-berries in the woods where Maurice slouched about with his gun—the same woods where Piers and Pheasant now met. Maurice, while he waited impatiently for Meg, was comforted by the love of Elvira.

A month before the marriage was to take place, a tiny bundle containing a baby was laid one summer night on the Vaughans' doorstep. Old Mr Vaughan, awakened by its faint cry, went downstairs in his slippers, opened the front door, and found the bundle, on which a note was pinned, which read: 'Maurice Vaughan is the father of this baby. Please be kind to it. It hasn't harmed no one.'

Mr Vaughan fell in a faint on the steps and was found, lying beside the baby, by a farm labourer who read the note and quickly spread the news. The child was carried into the house and the news of its arrival to Jalna.

As proper in the heroine of such a tragedy, Meg locked herself in her room, and refused to see any one. She refused to eat. Maurice, after a heartrending morning with his parents, during which he acknowledged everything, went and hid himself in the woods. It was found that Elvira, an orphan, had disappeared.

Meg's father, accompanied by his brothers, Nicholas and Ernest, went to thrash out the matter with Mr Vaughan. They were quite twenty years younger than he, and they all raged around the poor distracted man at once, in true Whiteoak fashion. Still, in spite of their outraged feelings, they agreed that the engagement was not to be broken, that the marriage must take place at the appointed time. A home could be found for the baby. They drove back to Jalna, after having had some stiff drinks, feeling that, thank God, everything had been patched up, and it would be a lesson to the young fool, though rather rough on Meggie.

Meggie could not be persuaded to leave her room. Trays of food placed outside her door were left untouched. One night, after four days of misery, young Maurice rode over to Jalna on his beautiful chestnut mare. He threw a handful of gravel against Meggie's window and called her name. She made no answer. He repeated it with tragic insistence. Finally Meg appeared in the bright moonlight, framed as a picture by the vine-clad window. She sat with her elbow on the sill and her chin on her palm, listening, while he, standing with the mare's bridle over his arm, poured out his contrition. She listened impassively, with her face raised moonward, till he had done, and then said: "It is all over. I cannot marry you, Maurice. I shall never marry anyone."

Maurice could not and would not believe her. He was unprepared for such relentless stubbornness beneath such a sweet exterior. He explained and implored for two hours. He threw himself on the ground and wept, while the mare cropped the grass beside him.

Renny, whose room was next to Meg's, could bear it no longer. He flew downstairs to Maurice's side and joined his supplications to his friend's in rougher language. Nothing could move Meggie. She listened to the impassioned appeals of the two youths with tears raining down her pale cheeks; then, with a final gesture of farewell, she closed the window.

Meggie was interviewed by each of her elders in turn. Her father, her uncles, her young stepmother—who had hoped so soon to be rid of her—all exercised their powers of reasoning with her. Grandmother also tried her hand, but the sight of Meggie, suave yet immovable as Gibraltar, was too much for the old lady. She hit her on the head, which caused Philip Whiteoak to intervene, and say that he would not have his little girl forced into any distasteful marriage, and that it was small wonder if Meggie couldn't stomach a bridegroom who had just made a mother of a chapped country wench.

Meggie emerged from her retirement, pale but tranquil. Her life suffered little outward derangement from this betrayal of her affections. However, she cared less for going out with other young people, and spent many hours in her bedroom. It was at this time that she acquired the habit of eating almost nothing at the table, getting ample nourishment from agreeable little lunches carried to her room. She became more and more devoted to her brothers, pouring out on them a devotion with which she sought to drown the image of her lover.

Maurice never again came nearer to Jalna than its stables. The friendship between him and Renny still endured. Together they went through the hardships of the War years later. When Pheasant was three years old, Mr and Mrs Vaughan died within the year, and she was left to the care of an unloving young father whom she could already call 'Maurice'. Misfortune followed close upon bereavement. Mining stocks in which nearly all the Vaughans' money was invested became worthless and Maurice's income declined from ten thousand a year to less than two. He made something from breeding horses, but as Pheasant grew up she never knew what it was to have two coins to rub together or attractive garments with which to clothe her young body.

The thousand acres bought from the Government by the first Vaughan had dwindled to three hundred. Of these only fifty lay under cultivation; the rest were in pasture and massive oak woods. The ravine that traversed Jalna narrowly spread into a valley through Vaughanlands, ending in a shallow basin, in the middle of which stood the house, with hanging shutters, sagging porch, and moss-grown roof.

The one servant now kept was an old Scotswoman, Nannie, who spoke but rarely and then in a voice scarcely above a whisper. Beside Jalna, teeming with loud-voiced, intimate, inquisitive people, Vaughanlands seemed but an echoing shell, the three who dwelt there holding aloof in annihilating self-absorption.

Dinner at one, instead of half past twelve as usual, threw Pheasant's plans into confusion. She felt suddenly weak, defenceless, insecure. She felt afraid of herself. Afraid that she would suddenly cry out to Maurice: 'I'm going to run away to be married at half past one! Dinner *must* be at the regular time.'

What a start that would give him! She pictured his heavy, untidy face startlingly concentrated into dismay.

'What's that?' he would exclaim. 'What's that, you little devil?'

Then she would hiss: 'It's true. I'm going to be married this very day. And I'm going to marry into the Jalna family who wouldn't have you, my fine fellow.'

Instead of this she said meekly: "Oh, Maurice, I'm afraid I'll have to take my dinner at half past twelve. I've an appointment with the dentist in Stead at two o'clock."

She wondered why she had said that, for she had never been to a dentist in her life. She did not know the name of one.

"What are you making appointments with the dentist for?" he growled. "What's the matter with your teeth?"

"I've been troubled by toothache lately," she said, truthfully, and he remembered an irritating smell of liniment about her at odd times.

They went on with their breakfast in silence, she, a wave of relief sweeping over her at the absence of active opposition, drinking cup after cup of strong tea; he thinking that after all it were better the child should not be at the table with the two men who were coming. Martin had a rough tongue. Not the sort of man a decent fellow would want to introduce to his young daughter, he supposed. But then, what was the use of trying to protect Pheasant? She was her mother's daughter and he had had no respect for her mother; he had very little for himself, her father. Not all the beastly allegations about the countryside against him since his first mishap were true, but they had damaged his opinion of himself, his dignity. He knew he was considered a rip, and always would be even when the patch of white that was coming above one temple spread over his whole head.

As for Pheasant, she was filled by sudden unaccountable compassion for him. Poor Maurice! Tomorrow morning, and all the mornings to come, he would be eating breakfast alone. To be sure, they seldom spoke, but still she was there beside him; she carried his messages to Nannie; she poured his tea; and she had always gone with him to admire the new colts. Well, perhaps when she was not there he would be sorry that he had not been nicer to her.

She was so inexperienced that she thought of going to live at Jalna as of removal to a remote habitation where she would be cut off permanently from all her past life.

When Maurice had swallowed the last mouthful of tea, he rose slowly and went to the bow window, which, being shadowed by a veranda, gave only a greenish half light into the room. He stood with his back toward her and said, "Come here."

Pheasant started up from her chair, all nerves. What was he going to do to her? She had a mind to run from the room. She gasped: "What do you want?"

"I want you to come here."

She went to his side with an assumed nonchalance.

"You seem to be playing the heavy father this morning," she said.

"I want to see that tooth you're talking about."

"I wasn't talking about it. It's you who are talking about it. I only said I was going to have it filled."

"Please open your mouth," he said, testily, putting his hand under her chin.

She prayed, 'O God, let there be a large hole in it,' and opened her mouth so wide that she looked like a young robin beseeching food.

"H-m," growled Maurice. "It should have been attended to some time ago." He added, giving her chin a grudging stroke: "You've pretty little teeth. Get the fellow to fix them up properly."

Pheasant stared. He was being almost loving. At this late hour! He had stroked her chin—given it a little dab with his fingers, anyway. She felt suddenly angry with him. The idea of getting demonstratively affectionate with her at this late hour! Making it harder for her to leave him.

"Thanks," she said. "I'll be a beauty if I keep on, shan't I?"

He answered seriously: "You're too skinny for beauty. But you'll fill out. You're nothing but a filly."

"This is the way fillies show their pleasure," she said, and rubbed her head against his shoulder. "I wish I could whinny! But I *can* bite."

"I know you can," he said, gravely. "You bit me when you were five. And I held your head under the tap for it."

She was glad he had reminded her of that episode. It would be easier to leave him after that.

He went into the hall and took his hat from a peg.

"Goodbye," she called after him.

She watched him go along the path toward the stables, filling his pipe, walking with his peculiar, slouching, hangdog gait. She threw open the window and called after him:

"Oh, hullo, Maurice!"

"Yes?" he answered, half wheeling.

"Oh—goodbye!"

"Well, I'll be——" she heard him mutter, as he went on.

He must think her a regular little fool. But, after all, it was a very serious goodbye. The next time they met, if ever they met again, she would be a different person. She would have an honourable name—a name with which she could face the world. She would be Mrs Piers Whiteoak.

7

PIERS AND PHEASANT MARRIED

HE HAD arrived on the very tick of two. She had been there twenty minutes earlier, very hot, but pale from excitement and fatigue; she had jogged—sometimes breaking into a run—for nearly half a mile, lugging the heavy portmanteau. She had been in a state of panic at the approach of every vehicle, thinking she was pursued. Three times she had fled to the shelter of a group of wayside cedars, to hide while a wagon lumbered or a car sped by.

Piers stowed the portmanteau in the back of the car, and she flung herself into the seat beside him. He started the car—a poor old rattletrap, but washed for the occasion—with a jerk. He looked absurdly Sundayish in his rigid best serge suit, and with an expression rather more wooden than exultant.

"They needed this car at home today," he said. "I'd a hard time getting away."

"So had I. Maurice was having two guests to dinner, and it had to be later, and he wanted me there to receive them."

"H-m. Who were they?"

"A Mr Martin and another man. Both horse breeders."

" 'Receive them!' Good Lord! You do say ridiculous things!"

She subsided into her corner, crushed. Was this what it was like to elope? A taciturn, soap-shining lover in a bowler hat, who called one ridiculous just at the moment when he should have been in an ecstasy of daring and protective love!

"I think you're very arrogant," she said.

"Perhaps I am," he agreed, letting the speed out. "I can't help it if I am," he added, not without complaisance. "It's in the blood, I expect."

She took off her hat and let the wind ruffle her hair. Road signs rushed past, black-and-white cattle in fields, cherry orchards in full bloom, and apple orchards just coming into bud.

"Gran said at dinner that I need disciplining. You'll have to do it, Pheasant." He looked around at her, smiling, and seeing her with her hair ruffled, her eyes shining, he added: "You precious darling!"

He snatched a kiss, and Pheasant put her hand on the wheel beside his. They both stared at the hand, thinking how soon the wedding ring must outshine the engagement ring in importance. They experienced a strange mixture of sensations, feeling at the same moment like runaway children (for they had both been kept down by their elders) and tremendous adventurers, not afraid of anything in this shining spring world.

They were married by the rector of Stead, a new man who had barely heard the names of their families, with perhaps a picturesque anecdote attached. Piers was so sunburned and solid that he looked like nothing but an ordinary young countryman, and Pheasant's badly cut dress and cheap shoes transformed her young grace into coltish awkwardness. He hoped they would come regularly to his church, he said, and he gave them some very good advice in the cool vestry. When they had gone and he examined the fee which Piers had given him in an envelope, he was surprised at its size, for Piers was determined to carry everything through as a Whiteoak should.

As they flew along the road, which ran like a trimming of white braid on the brown shore that skirted the lake, Piers began to shout and sing in an ecstasy of achievement.

"We're man and wife!" he chanted. "Man and wife! Pheasant and Piers! Man and wife!"

His exuberance and the speed at which they drove the car made people stare. The greenish-blue lake, still stirred by a gale which had blown all night, but had now fallen to a gentle breeze, beat on the shore a rhythmic accompaniment, an extravagant wedding march. Cherry orchards flung out the confetti of their petals on the road before them, and the air was unimaginably heavy with the heady incense of spring. Piers stopped the wagon of a fruit vendor and bought oranges, of which Pheasant thrust sections into his mouth as he drove, and ate eagerly herself, for excitement made them thirsty. As they neared the suburbs of the city she threw the rinds into the ditch and scrubbed her lips and hands on her handkerchief. She put on her hat and sat upright then, her hands in her lap, feeling that everyone who met them must realize that they were newly married.

Piers had spoken for rooms in the Queen's Hotel which the Whiteoaks had frequented for three generations. He had not been there very much himself—a few times to dinner in company with Renny, twice for birthday treats as a small boy with Uncle Nicholas.

Now on his wedding day he had taken one of the best bedrooms with bath adjoining. His blood was all in his head as the clerk gave a surreptitious smile and handed the key to a boy. The boy went lopsidedly before them to the bedroom, carrying the antiquated portmanteau. All the white closed doors along the corridor made Pheasant feel timid. She fancied there were ears against all the panels, eyes to the keyholes. What if Maurice should suddenly pounce out on them? Or Renny? Or terrible Grandmother Whiteoak?

When they were alone in the spacious, heavily furnished hotel bedroom, utterly alone, with only the deep rumble of the traffic below to remind them of the existence of the world, a sudden feeling of frozen dignity, of aloofness from each other, took possession of them.

"Not a bad room, eh? Think you'll be comfortable here?" And he added, almost challengingly: "It's one of the best rooms in the hotel, but if there's anything you'd like different——"

"Oh, no. It's nice. It'll do nicely, thank you."

Could they be the young runaway couple who had raced along the lake-shore road, singing and eating oranges?

"There's your bag," he said, indicating the ponderous portmanteau.

"Yes," she agreed. "I've got the bag all right."

"I wonder what we'd better do first," he added, staring at her. She looked so strange to him in this new setting that he felt as though he were really seeing her for the first time.

"What time is it?"

"Half past five."

She noticed then that the sun had disappeared behind a building across the street, and that the room lay in a yellowish shadow. Evening was coming.

"Hadn't you better send the telegrams?"

"I expect I had. I'll go down and do that, and see that we've a table reserved; and, look here, shouldn't you like to go to the theatre tonight?"

Pheasant was thrilled at that. "Oh, I'd love the theatre! Is there something good on?"

"I'll find out, and get tickets, and you can be changing. Now about those telegrams. How would it do if I just send one to Renny, something like this: 'Pheasant and I married. Home tomorrow. Tell Maurice.' Would that be all right?"

"No," she said, firmly. "Maurice must have a telegram all to himself, from me. Say: 'Dear Maurice——' "

"Good Lord! You can't begin a telegram, 'Dear Maurice'. It isn't done. Tell me what you want to say and I'll put it in the proper form."

Pheasant spoke in an incensed tone. "See here; is this your telegram or mine? I've never written a letter or sent a telegram to Maurice in my life and I probably never shall again. So it's going to begin: 'Dear Maurice'."

"All right, my girl. Fire away."

"Say, 'Dear Maurice: Piers and I are married. Tell Nannie. Yours sincerely, Pheasant.' That will do."

Piers could not conceal his mirth at such a telegram, but he promised to send it, and after giving her body a convulsive squeeze and receiving a kiss on the sunburned bridge of his nose he left her.

She was alone. She was married. All the old life was over and the new just beginning. She went to the dressing-table and stood before the three-sectioned mirror. It was wonderful to see her own face there, from all sides at once. She felt that she had never really seen herself before—no wonder her reflection looked surprised. She turned this way and that, tilting her head like a pretty bird. She took off her brown dress and stood enthralled by the reflection of her charms in knickers and a little white camisole. She turned on the electric light, and made a tableau with her slender milky arms upraised and her eyes half closed. She wished she could spend a long time playing with these magical reflections, but Piers might come back and find her not dressed.

A bell in some tower struck six.

She saw that her hands needed washing and hoped there would be soap in the bathroom. She gasped when she had pressed the electric button and flooded the room with a hard white light. The fierce splendour of it dazzled her. At home there was a bathroom with a bare uncovered floor on which stood an ancient green tin bath, battered and disreputable. The towels were old and fuzzy, leaving bits of lint all over one's body, and the cake of soap was always like jelly, because Maurice would leave it in the water. Here were glistening tile and marble, nickel polished like new silver, an enormous tub of virgin whiteness, and a row of towels fit only for a bride. "And, by my halidom," she exclaimed—for she was devoted to Sir Walter Scott—"I am the bride!"

She locked herself in and took a bath, almost reverently handling the luxurious accessories. Such quantities of steaming water! Such delicate soap! Such satiny towels! As she stepped dripping on to the thick bath mat she felt that never till that moment had she been truly clean.

Her hair was sleekly brushed, and she was doing up her pink-and-white dress when Piers arrived. He had sent off the telegrams—and not neglected the 'Dear' for Maurice. He had got orchestra chairs for a Russian vaudeville. He took her to the ladies' drawing-room and set her in a white-and-gold chair where she waited while he scrubbed and beautified himself.

They were at their own table in a corner where they could see the entire dining-room: rows and rows of white-clothed tables, glimmering with silver, beneath shaded lights; a red-faced waiter with little dabs of whisker before his ears, who took a fatherly interest in their dinner.

Piers whispered: "What will you have, Mrs Piers Whiteoak?" —and put everything out of her head but those magic words.

Piers ordered the dinner. Delicious soup. A tiny piece of fish with a strange sauce. Roast chicken. Asparagus. Beautiful but rather frightening French pastries—one hardly knew how to eat them. Strawberries like dissolving jewels. ("But where do they come from, Piers, at this time of year?") Such dark coffee. Little gold-tipped cigarettes, specially bought for her. The scented smoke circled about their heads, accentuating their isolation.

Four men at the table next them did not seem able to keep their eyes off her. They talked earnestly to each other, but their eyes, every now and again, would slide toward her, and sometimes, she was sure, they were talking about her. The odd thing was that the consciousness of their attention did not confuse her. It exhilarated her, gave her a certainty of poise and freedom of gesture which otherwise she would not have had.

She had carried the gold-embroidered India shawl that had been her grandmother's down to dinner, and when she became aware that these four dark men were watching her, speculating about her, some instinct, newly awakened, told her to put the shawl about her shoulders, told her that there was something about the shawl that suited her better than the little pink-and-white dress. She held it closely about her, sitting erect, looking straight into Piers' flushed face, but she was conscious of every glance, every whisper from the four at the next table.

When she and Piers passed the men on their way out, one of them was brushed by the fringe of her shawl. His dark eyes were raised to her face, and he inclined his head toward the shawl as though he sought the light caress from it. He was a man of about forty. Pheasant felt that the shawl was a magic shawl, that she floated in it, that it bewitched all it touched. Her small brown head rose out of its gorgeousness like a sleek flower.

The Russian company was a new and strange experience. It opened the gates of an undreamed-of and exotic world. She heard the 'Volga Boat Song' sung in a purple twilight by only dimly discerned foreign seamen. She heard the ragings and pleadings in a barbarous tongue when a savage crew threw their captain's mistress overboard because she had brought them ill luck. The most humorous acts had no smile from her. They were enthralling, but never for a moment funny. The moon-faced showman, with his jargon of languages, had a dreadful fascination for her, but she saw nothing amusing in his patter. To her he was the terrifying magician who had created all this riot of noise and colour. He was a sinister man, at whom one gazed breathlessly, gripping Piers' hand beneath the shawl. She had never been in a theatre before. And Piers sat, brown-faced, solid, smiling steadily at the stage, and giving her fingers a steady pressure.

Passing through the foyer, there was a dense crowd that surged without haste toward the outer doors. Pheasant pressed close to Piers, looking with shy curiosity at the faces about her. Then someone just behind took her wrist in his hand, and slid his other hand lightly along her bare arm to beneath the shoulder, where it rested a moment in casual caress, then was withdrawn.

Pheasant trembled all over, but she did not turn her head. She knew without looking that the hand had been the hand of the man whose head she had brushed with her shawl. When she and Piers reached the street she saw the four men together, lighting cigarettes, just ahead.

She felt old in experience.

It was only a short distance to the hotel. They walked among other laughing, talking people, with a great full moon rising at the end of the street, and with the brightness of the electric light giving an air of garish gaiety to the scene. Pheasant felt that it must last for ever. She could not believe that tomorrow it would be all over, and they would be going back to Jalna, facing the difficulties there.

From their room there was quite an expanse of sky visible. Piers threw the window open and the moon seemed then to stare in at them.

They stood together at the window, looking up at it.

"The same old moon that used to shine down on us in the woods," Piers said.

"It seems ages ago."

"Yes. How do you feel? Tired? Sleepy?"

"Not sleepy. But a little tired."

"Poor little girl!"

He put his arms about her and held her close to him. His whole being seemed melting into tenderness toward her. At the same time his blood was singing in his ears the song of possessive love.

8

WELCOME TO JALNA

THE CAR moved slowly along the winding driveway toward the house. The driveway was so darkened by closely ranked balsams that it was like a long greenish tunnel, always cool and damp. Black squirrels flung themselves from bough to bough, their curving tails like glossy notes of interrogation. Every now and again a startled rabbit showed its downy brown hump in the long grass. So slowly the car moved, the birds scarcely ceased their jargon of song at its approach.

Piers felt horribly like a schoolboy returning after playing truant. He remembered how he had sneaked along this drive, heavy-footed, knowing he would 'catch it', and how he had caught it, at Renny's efficient hands. He slumped in his seat as he thought of it. Pheasant sat stiffly erect, her hands clasped tightly between her knees. As the car stopped before the broad wooden steps that led to the porch, a small figure appeared from the shrubbery. It was Wakefield, carrying in one hand a fishing-rod, and in the other a string from which dangled a solitary perch.

"Oh, hullo," he said, coming over the lawn to them. "We got your telegram. Welcome to Jalna!"

He got on to the runningboard and extended a small fishy hand to Pheasant.

"Don't touch him," said Piers. "He smells beastly."

Wakefield accepted the rebuff cheerfully.

"I like the smell of fish myself," he said pointedly to Pheasant. "And I forgot that some people don't. Now Piers likes the smell of manure better because working with manure is his job. He's used to it. Granny says that one can get used——"

"Shut up," ordered Piers, "and tell me where the family is."

"I really don't know," answered Wakefield, flapping the dead fish against the door of the car, "because it's Saturday, you see, and a free day for me. I got Mrs Wragge to put me up a little lunch—just a cold chop and a hard-boiled egg, and a lemon tart and a bit of cheese, and——"

"For heaven's sake," said Piers, "stop talking and stop flapping that fish against the car! Run in and see what they're doing. I'd like to see Renny alone."

"Oh, you can't do that, I'm afraid. Renny's over with Maurice this afternoon. I expect they're talking over what they will do to you two. It takes a lot of thought and talk, you see, to arrange suitable punishments. Now the other day Mr Fennel wanted to punish me and he simply couldn't think

73

of anything to do to me that would make a suitable impression. Already he'd tried——"

Piers interrupted, fixing Wakefield with his eye: "Go and look in the drawing-room windows. I see firelight there. Tell me who is in the room."

"All right. But you'd better hold my fish for me, because someone might look out of the window and see me, and, now I come to think of it, Meggie told me I wasn't to go fishing today, and it slipped right out of my head, the way things do with me. I expect it's my weak heart."

"If I don't thrash you," said his brother, "before you're an hour older, my name isn't Piers Whiteoak. Give me the fish." He jerked the string from the little boy's hand.

"Hold it carefully, please," admonished Wakefield over his shoulder, as he lightly mounted the steps. He put his face against the pane, and stood motionless a space.

Pheasant saw that the shadows were lengthening. A cool damp breeze began to stir the shaggy grass of the lawn, and the birds ceased to sing.

Piers said: "I'm going to throw this thing away."

"Oh, no," said Pheasant, "don't throw the little fellow's fish away." A nervous tremor ran through her, more chill than the breeze. She almost sobbed: "Ugh, I'm so nervous!"

"Poor little kid," said Piers, laying his hand over hers. His own jaws were rigid, and his throat felt as though a hand were gripping it. The family had never seemed so formidable to him. He saw them in a fierce phalanx bearing down on him, headed by Grandmother ready to browbeat—abuse him. He threw back his shoulders and drew a deep breath. Well—let them! If they were unkind to Pheasant, he would take her away. But he did not want to go away. He loved every inch of Jalna. He and Renny loved the place as none of the others did. That was the great bond between them. Piers was very proud of this fellowship of love for Jalna between him and Renny.

"Confound the kid!" he said. "What is he doing?"

"He's coming."

Wakefield descended the steps importantly.

"They're having tea in the parlour just as though it were Sunday," he announced. "A fire lighted. It looks like a plate

74

of Sally Lunn on the table. Perhaps it's a kind of wedding feast. I think we'd better go in. I'd better put my fish away first, though."

Piers relinquished the perch, and said: "I wish Renny were there."

"So do I," agreed Wakefield. "A row's ever so much better when he's in it. Gran always says he's a perfect Court for a row."

Piers and Pheasant went slowly up the steps and into the house. He drew aside the heavy curtains that hung before the double doors of the drawing-room and led her into the room that seemed very full of people.

There were Grandmother, Uncle Nicholas, Uncle Ernest, Meg, Eden, and young Finch, who was slumped on a beaded ottoman devouring seed-cake. He grinned sheepishly as the two entered, then turned to stare at his grandmother, as though expecting her to lead the attack. But it was Uncle Nicholas who spoke first. He lifted his moustache from his teacup, and raised his massive head, looking rather like a sardonic walrus. He rumbled:

"By George, this is nothing more than I expected! But you pulled the wool over Renny's eyes, you young rascal."

Meg broke in, her soft voice choked with tears:

"Oh, you deceitful, unfeeling boy! I don't see how you can stand there and face us. And that family—Pheasant—I never spoke to you about it, Piers—I thought you'd *know* how I'd feel about such a marriage."

"Hold your tongues!" shouted Grandmother, who so far had only been able to make inarticulate sounds of rage. "Hold your silly tongues, and let me speak." The muscles in her face were twitching, her terrible brown eyes were burning beneath her shaggy brows. She was sitting directly in front of the fire, and her figure in its brilliant tea-gown was illumined with a hellish radiance. Boney, sitting on the back of her chair, glowed like an exotic flower. His beak was sunken on his puffed breast, and he spread his feathers to the warmth in apparent oblivion to the emotion of his mistress.

"Come here!" she shouted. "Come over here in front of me. Don't stand like a pair of ninnies in the doorway."

"Mamma," said Ernest, "don't excite yourself so. It's bad for you. It'll upset your insides, you know."

"My insides are better than yours," retorted his mother. "I know how to look after them."

"Come closer, so she won't have to shout at you," ordered Uncle Nicholas.

"Up to the sacrificial altar," adjured Eden, who lounged near the door. His eyes laughed up at them as they passed toward Mrs Whiteoak's chair. Pheasant gripped Piers' coat in icy fingers. She cast an imploring look at Nicholas, who had once given her a doll and remained a kind of god in her eyes ever since, but he only stared down his nose, and crumbled the bit of cake on his saucer. If it had not been for the support of Piers' arms, she felt that she must have sunk to her knees, she trembled so.

"Now," snarled Grandmother, when she had got them before her, "aren't you ashamed of yourselves?"

"No," answered Piers, stoutly. "We've only done what lots of people do. Got married on the quiet. We knew the whole family would get on their hind feet if we told them, so we kept it to ourselves, that's all."

"And do you expect"—she struck her stick savagely on the floor—"do you expect that I shall allow you to bring that little brat here? Do you understand what it means to Meg? Maurice was her fiancé and he got this brat——"

"Mamma!" cried Ernest.

"Easy, old lady," soothed Nicholas.

Finch exploded in sudden, hysterial laughter.

Meg raised her voice. "Don't stop her. It's true."

"Yes, what was I saying? Don't dare to stop me! This brat —this brat—he got her by a slut——"

Piers bent over her, glaring into her fierce old face.

"Stop it!" he shouted. "Stop it, I say!"

Boney was roused into a sudden passion by the hurricane about him. He thrust his beak over Grandmother's shoulder, and, riveting his cruel little eyes on Piers' face, he poured forth a stream of Hindu abuse:

"Shaitan! Shaitan ka bata! Shaitan ka butcha! Piakur! Piakur! Jab kutr!"

This was followed by a cascade of mocking, metallic laughter, while he rocked from side to side on the back of Grandmother's chair.

It was too much for Pheasant. She burst into tears, hiding

76

her face in her hands. But her sobs could not be heard for the cursing of Boney; and Finch, shaking from head to foot, added his hysterical laughter.

Goaded beyond endurance, his sunburned face crimson with rage, Piers caught the screaming bird by the throat and threw him savagely to the floor, where he lay, as gaily coloured as painted fruit, uttering strange coughing sounds.

Grandmother was inarticulate. She looked as though she would choke. She tore at her cap and it fell over one ear. Then she grasped her heavy stick. Before anyone could stop her—if indeed they had wished to stop her—she had brought it with a resounding crack on to Piers' head.

"Take that," she shouted, "miserable boy!"

At the instant that the stick struck Piers' head, the door from the hall was opened and Renny came into the room, followed by Wakefield, who, behind the shelter of his brother, peered timidly yet inquisitively at the family. All faces turned toward Renny, as though his red head were a sun and they sun-gazing flowers.

"This is a pretty kettle of fish," he said.

"He's abusing Boney," wailed Grandmother. "Poor dear Boney! Oh, the young brute! Flog him, Renny! Give him a sound flogging!"

"No! No! No! No!" screamed Pheasant.

Nicholas heaved himself about in his chair, and said:

"He deserved it. He threw the bird on the floor."

"Pick poor Boney up, Wakefield dear," said Ernest. "Pick him up and stroke him."

Except his mistress, Boney would allow no one but Wakefield to touch him. The child picked him up, stroked him, and set him on his grandmother's shoulder. Grandmother, in one of her gusts of affection, caught him to her and pressed a kiss on his mouth. "Little darling," she exclaimed. "Gran's darling! Give him a piece of cake, Meg."

Meg was crying softly behind the teapot. Wakefield went to her, and, receiving no notice, took the largest piece of cake and began to devour it.

Renny had crossed to Piers' side and was staring at his head.

"His ear is bleeding," he remarked. "You shouldn't have done that, Granny."

"He was impudent to her," said Ernest.

Eden cut in: "Oh, rot! She was abusing him and the girl horribly."

Grandmother thumped the floor with her stick.

"I wasn't abusing him. I told him I wouldn't have that girl in the house. I told him she was a bastard brat, and so she is. I told him—bring me more tea—more tea—where's Philip? Philip, I want tea!" When greatly excited she often addressed her eldest son by his father's name.

"For God's sake, give her some tea," growled Nicholas. "Make it hot."

Ernest carried a cup of tea to her, and straightened her cap.

"More cake," she demanded. "Stop your snivelling, Meggie."

"Grandmother," said Meg, with melancholy dignity, "I am not snivelling. And it isn't much wonder if I do shed tears, considering the way Piers has acted."

"I've settled him," snorted Grandmother. "Settled him with my stick. Ha!"

Piers said, in a hard voice: "Now, look here, I'm going to get out. Pheasant and I don't have to stop here. We only came to see what sort of reception we'd get. Now we know, and we're going."

"Just listen to him, Renny," said Meg. "He's lost all his affection for us, and it seems only yesterday that he was a little boy like Wake."

"Heaven knows whom Wakefield will take up with," said Nicholas. "The family's running to seed."

"Will you have some tea, Renny?" asked Meg.

"No, thanks. Give the girl some. She's awfully upset."

"I don't want tea!" cried Pheasant, looking wildly at the hostile faces about her. "I want to go away! Piers, please, please, take me away!" She sank into a wide, stuffed chintz chair, drew up her knees, covered her face with her hands, and sobbed loudly.

Meg spoke with cold yet furious chagrin.

"If only he *could* send you home and have done with you! But here you are, bound fast to him. You'd never rest till you'd got him bound fast. I know your kind."

Nicholas put in: "They don't wait till they're out of pina-fores—that kind."

78

Eden cried: "Oh, for God's sake!"

But Piers' furious voice drowned him out.

"Not another word about her. I won't stand another word!"

Grandmother screamed: "You'll stand another crack on the head, you young whelp!" Crumbs of cake clung to the hairs on her chin. Wake regarded them, fascinated. Then he blew on them, trying to blow them off. Finch uttered hysterical croaking sounds.

"Wakefield, don't do that," ordered Uncle Ernest, "or you'll get your head slapped. Mamma, wipe your chin."

Meg said: "To think of the years that I've kept aloof from the Vaughans! I've never spoken to Maurice since that terrible time. None of them have set foot in this house. And now his daughter—that child—the cause of all my unhappiness—brought here to live as Piers' wife."

Piers retorted: "Don't worry, Meg. We're not going to stay."

"The disgrace is here for ever," she returned bitterly, "if you go to the other end of the earth." Her head rested on her hand, supported by her short plump arm. Her sweetly curved lips were drawn in at the corners, in an expression of stubborn finality. "You've finished things. I was terribly hurt at the very beginning of my life. I've tried to forget. Your bringing this girl here has renewed all the hurt. Shamed me, crushed me—I thought you loved me, Piers——"

"Oh Lord, can't a man love his sister and another too?" exclaimed Piers, regarding her intently, with scarlet face, cut to the heart, for he loved her.

"No one who loved his sister could love the daughter of the man who had been so faithless to her."

"And besides," put in Nicholas, "you promised Renny you'd give the girl up."

"Oh, oh," cried Pheasant, sitting up in her chair. "Did you promise that, Piers?"

"No, I didn't."

Nicholas roared: "Yes, you did! Renny told me you did."

"I never promised. Be just, now, Renny! I never promised, did I?"

"No," said Renny. "He didn't promise. I told him to cut it out. I said there'd be trouble."

"Trouble—trouble—trouble," moaned Grandmother, "I've

had too much trouble. If I didn't keep my appetite, I'd be dead. Give me more cake, someone. No, not that kind—devil's cake. I want devil's cake!" She took the cake that Ernest brought her, bit off a large piece, and snorted through it: "I hit the young whelp a good crack on the head!"

"Yes, Mamma," said Ernest. Then he inquired, patiently, "*Must* you take such large bites?"

"I drew the blood!" she cried, ignoring his question, and taking a still larger bite. "I made the lad smart for his folly."

"You ought to be ashamed, Gran," said Eden, and the family began to argue noisily as to whether she had done well or ill.

Renny stood looking from one excited face to another, feeling irritated by their noise, their ineffectuality, yet, in spite of all, bathed in an immense satisfaction. This was his family. His tribe. He was head of his family. Chieftain of his tribe. He took a very primitive, direct, and simple pleasure in lording it over them, caring for them, being badgered, harried, and importuned by them. They were all of them dependent on him except Gran, and she was dependent, too, for she would have died away from Jalna. And beside the fact that he provided for them, he had the inherent quality of the chieftain. They expected him to lay down the law; they harried him till he did. He turned his lean red face from one to the other of them now, and prepared to lay down the law.

The heat of the room was stifling; the fire was scarcely needed; yet now, with sudden fervour, it leaped and crackled on the hearth. Boney, having recovered from Piers' rough handling, was crying in a head-splitting voice, "Cake! Cake! Devil cake!"

"For God's sake, somebody give him cake," said Renny.

Little Wake snatched up a piece of cake and held it toward Boney, but just as the parrot was at the point of taking it he jerked it away. With flaming temper Boney tried three times, and failed to snatch the morsel. He flapped his wings and uttered a screech that set the blood pounding in the ears of those in the room.

It was too much for Finch. He doubled up on his footstool, laughing hysterically; the footstool slipped—or did Eden's foot push it?—and he was sent sprawling on the floor.

Grandmother seized her cane and struggled to get to her feet. "Let me at them!" she screamed.

"Boys! Boys!" cried Meggie, melting into sudden laughter. This was the sort of thing she loved—'rough-house' among the boys, and she sitting solidly, comfortably in her chair, looking on. She laughed; but in an instant she was lachrymose again, and averted her eyes from the figure of Finch stretched on the floor.

Renny was bending over him. He administered three hard thumps on the boy's bony, untidy person, and said:

"Now, get up and behave yourself."

Finch got up, red in the face, and skulked to a corner. Nicholas turned heavily in his chair, and regarded Piers.

"As for you," he said, "you ought to be flayed alive for what you've done to Meggie."

"Never mind," Piers returned. "I'm getting out."

Meg looked at him scornfully. "You'd have to go a long way to get away from scandal—I mean, to make your absence really a help to me, to all of us."

Piers retorted: "Oh, we'll go far enough to please you. We'll go to the States—perhaps." The 'perhaps' was mumbled on a hesitating note. The sound of his own voice announcing that he would go to a foreign country, far from Jalna and the land he had helped to grow things on, the horses, his brothers, had an appalling sound.

"What does he say?" asked Grandmother, roused from one of her sudden dozes. Boney had perched on her shoulder and cuddled his head against her long flat cheek. "What's the boy say?"

Ernest answered: "He says he'll go to the States."

"The States? A Whiteoak go to the States? A Whiteoak a Yankee? No, no, no! It would kill me. He mustn't go. Shame, shame on you, Meggie, to drive the poor boy to the States! You ought to be ashamed of yourself. Oh, those Yankees! First they take Eden's book and now they want Piers himself. Oh, don't let him go!" She burst into loud sobs.

Renny's voice was raised, but without excitement.

"Piers is not going away—anywhere. He's going to stay right here. So is Pheasant. The girl and he are married. I presume they've lived together. There's no reason on earth why she shouldn't make him a good wife——"

Meg interrupted:

"Maurice has never forgiven me for refusing to marry him. He has made this match between his daughter and Piers to punish me. He's done it. I know he's done it."

Piers turned to her. "Maurice has known nothing about it."

"How can you know what schemes were in his head?" replied Meg. "He's simply been waiting his chance to thrust his brat into Jalna."

Piers exclaimed: "Good God, Meggie! I didn't know you had such a wicked tongue."

"No back chat, please," rejoined his sister.

Renny's voice, with a vibration from the chest which the family knew foreboded an outburst if he were opposed, broke in.

"I have been talking the affair over with Maurice this afternoon. He is as upset about it as we are. As for his planning the marriage to avenge himself on you, Meg, that is ridiculous. Give the man credit for a little decency—a little sense. Why, your affair with him was twenty years ago. Do you think he's been brooding over it ever since? And he was through the War too. He's had a few things to think of besides your cruelty, Meggie!"

He smiled at her. He knew how to take her. And she liked to have her 'cruelty' referred to. Her beautifully shaped lips curved a little, and she said, with almost girlish petulance:

"What's the matter with him, then? Everyone agrees that there's something wrong with him."

"Oh, well, I don't think there is very much wrong with Maurice, but if there is, and you are responsible, you shouldn't be too hard on him, or on this child, either. I told Piers that if he went on meeting her there'd be trouble, and there has been, hasn't there? Lots of it. But I'm not going to drive him away from Jalna. I want him here—and I want my tea, terribly. Will you pour it out, Meggie?"

Silence followed his words, broken only by the snapping of the fire and Grandmother's peaceful, bubbling snores. Nicholas took out his pipe and began to fill it from his pouch. Sasha leaped from the mantelpiece to Ernest's shoulder and began to purr loudly, as though in opposition to Grandmother's snores. Wakefield opened the door of a cabinet filled with curios from India, with which he was not allowed to play, and stuck his head inside.

"Darling, don't," said Meg, gently.

Renny, the chieftain, had spoken. He had said that Piers was not to be cast out from the tribe, and the tribe had listened and accepted his words as wisdom. All the more readily because not one of them wanted to see Piers cast out, even though they must accept with him an unwelcome addition to the family. Not even Meg. In truth, Renny was more often the organ of the family than its head. They knew beforehand what he would say in a crisis, and they excited, harried, and goaded him till he said it with great passion. Then, with apparent good grace, they succumbed to his will.

Renny dropped into a chair with his cup of tea and a piece of bread and butter. His face was redder than usual, but he looked with deep satisfaction at the group about him. He had quelled the family riot. They depended on him, from savage old Gran down to delicate little Wake. They depended on him to lead them. He felt each one of them bound to him by a strong, invisible cord. He could feel the pull of the cords, drawn taut from himself to each individual in the room. To savage old Gran. To beastly young Finch. To that young fool Piers with his handkerchief against his bleeding ear. To Meggie, who pictured Maurice as brooding in black melancholy all these years. Well, there was no doubt about it, Maurice was a queer devil. He had let two women make a very different man of him from what Nature had intended him to be. Renny felt the cords from himself stretching dark and strong to each member of the family. Suddenly he felt a new drawing, a fresh cord. It was between Pheasant and him. She was one of them now. His own. He looked at her, sitting upright in the big chair, her eyes swollen from crying, but eating her tea like a good child. Their eyes met, and she gave a little watery pleading smile. Renny grinned at her encouragingly.

Rags had come in and Meg was ordering a fresh pot of tea.

This was the Whiteoak family as it was when Alayne Archer came into their midst from New York.

9

EDEN AND ALAYNE

E DEN FOUND that his steps made no noise on the thick rug
that covered the floor of the reception room of the New
York publishing firm of Cory and Parsons, so he could pace
up and down as restlessly as he liked without fear of attracting
attention. He was horribly nervous. He had a sensation in his
stomach that was akin to hunger, yet his throat felt so oddly
constricted that to swallow would have been impossible.

A mirror in a carved frame gave him, when he hesitated
before it, a greenish reflection of himself that was not re-
assuring. He wished he had not got such a brazen coat of
tan in the North that summer. These New Yorkers would
surely look on him as a Canadian backwoodsman. His hands,
as he grasped the package containing his new manuscript,
were almost black, it seemed to him, and no wonder, for he
had been paddling and camping among the Northern lakes
for months. He decided to lay the manuscript on a table,
picking it up at the last minute before he entered Mr Cory's
private office. It had been Mr Cory with whom he had
corresponded about his poems, who had expressed himself as
eager to read the long narrative poem composed that summer.
For the book published in midsummer was being well re-
viewed, American critics finding an agreeable freshness and
music in Eden's lyrics. As books of poems went, it had had a
fair sale. The young poet would get enough out of it perhaps
to buy himself a new winter overcoat. He stood now, tall and
slender in his loosely fitting tweeds, very British-looking,
feeling that this solemn, luxurious room was the threshold over
which he would step into the world of achievement and fame.

The door opened and a young woman entered so quietly
that she was almost at Eden's side before he was aware of her
presence.

"Oh," he said, starting, "I beg your pardon. I'm waiting to
see Mr Cory."

"You are Mr Whiteoak, aren't you?" she asked in a tranquil
voice.

He flushed red, very boyishly, under his tan.

"Yes. I'm Eden Whiteoak. I'm the——"

Just in time he choked back what he had been about to say: that he was the author of *Under the North Star*. It would have been a horrible way to introduce himself—just as though he had expected the whole world to know about his book of poems.

However, she said, with a little excited catch of the breath:

"Oh, Mr Whiteoak, I could not resist coming to speak to you when I heard you were here. I want to tell you how very, very much I have enjoyed your poems. I am a reader for Mr Cory, and he generally gives me the poetry manuscripts, because—well, I am very much interested in poetry."

"Yes, yes, I see," said Eden, casting about to collect his thoughts.

She went on in her low even voice:

"I cannot tell you how proud I was when I was able to recommend your poems to him. I have to send in adverse reports on so many. Your name was new to us. I felt that I had discovered you. Oh, dear, this is very unbusinesslike, telling you all this, but your poetry has given me so much pleasure that—I wanted you to know."

Her face flashed suddenly from gravity into smiling. Her head was tilted as she looked into his eyes, for she was below medium height. Eden, looking down at her, thought she was like some delicately tinted yet sturdy spring flower, gazing upward with a sort of gentle defiance.

He held the hand she offered in his own warm, deeply tanned one.

"My name is Alayne Archer," she said. "Mr Cory will be ready to see you in a few minutes. As a matter of fact he told me to have a little talk with you about your new poem. It is a narrative poem, is it not? But I did so want to tell you that I was the 'discoverer' of your first."

"Well then, I suppose I may as well hand the manuscript over to you at once."

"No. I should give it to Mr Cory."

They both looked down at the packet in his hand, then their eyes met and they smiled.

"Do you like it very much yourself?" she asked. "Is it at all like the others?"

"Yes, I like it—naturally," he answered, "and yes, I think it has the same feeling as the others. It was good fun writing it, up there in the North, a thousand miles from anywhere."

"It must have been inspiring," she said. "Mr Cory is going to visit the North this fall. He suffers from insomnia. He will want to hear a great deal about it from you." She led the way toward two upholstered chairs. "Will you please sit down and tell me more about the new poem? What is it called?"

"'The Golden Sturgeon.' Really, I can't tell you about it. You'll just have to read it. I'm not used to talking about my poetry. In my family it's rather a disgrace to write poetry."

They had sat down, but she raised herself in her chair and stared at him incredulously. She exclaimed in a rather hushed voice: "Poetry? A disgrace?"

"Well, not so bad as that, perhaps," said Eden, hurriedly. "But a handicap to a fellow—something to be lived down."

"But are they not proud of you?"

"Y-yes. My sister is. But she doesn't know anything about poetry. And one of my uncles. But he's quite old. Reads nothing this side of Shakespeare."

"And your parents? Your mother?" It seemed to her that he must have a mother to adore him.

"Both dead," he replied, and he added: "My brothers really despise me for it. There is a military tradition in our family."

She asked: "Were you through the War?"

"No. I was only seventeen when peace came."

"Oh, how stupid I am! Of course you were too young."

She began then to talk about his poetry. Eden forgot that he was in a reception room of a publisher's office. He forgot everything except his pleasure in her gracious, self-possessed, yet somehow shy presence. He heard himself talking, reciting bits of his poems—he had caught something of the Oxford intonation from his uncles—saying beautiful and mournful things that would have made Renny wince with shame for him, could he have overheard.

A stenographer came to announce that Mr Cory would see Mr Whiteoak. They arose, and looking down on her, he thought he had never seen such smooth, shining hair. It was coiled about her head like bands of shimmering satin.

He followed the stenographer to Mr Cory's private room,

and was given a tense handshake and a tenser scrutiny by the publisher.

"Sit down, Mr Whiteoak," he said, in a dry, precise voice. "I am very glad that you were able to come to New York. I and my assistant, Miss Archer, have been looking forward to meeting you. We think your work is exceedingly interesting."

Yet his pleasure seemed very perfunctory. After a short discussion of the new poem which Mr Cory took into his charge, he changed the subject abruptly, and began to fire at Eden question after question about the North. How far north had he been? What supplies were needed? Particularly, what underwear and shoes. Was the food very bad? He suffered at times from indigestion. He supposed it was very rough. His physicians had told him that a hunting trip up there would set him up, make a new man of him. He was strong enough but—well, insomnia was a disagreeable disorder. He couldn't afford to lower his efficiency.

Eden was a mine of information. He knew something about everything. As Mr Cory listened to these details he grew more animated. A faint ashes-of-roses pink crept into his greyish cheeks. He tapped excitedly on his desk with the tips of his polished fingernails.

Eden in his mind was trying to picture Mr Cory in that environment, but he could not, and his fancy instead followed Miss Archer, with her bands of shimmering hair and her grey-blue eyes, set wide apart beneath a lovely white brow. He followed her shadow, grasping at it as it disappeared, imploring it to save him from Mr Cory, for he had begun to hate Mr Cory, since he believed he had found out that he was interesting to the publisher only as a Canadian who knew all about the country to which a physician had ordered him.

Yet at that moment Mr Cory was asking him almost genially to dinner at his house that night.

"Miss Archer will be there," added Mr Cory. "She will talk to you about your poetry with much more understanding than I can, but I like it. I like it very well indeed."

And, naturally, Eden suddenly liked Mr Cory. He suddenly seemed to discover that he was very human, almost boyish, like a very orderly greyish boy who had never been really young. But he liked him, and shook his hand warmly as he thanked him, and said he would be glad to go to dinner.

Eden had no friends in New York, but he spent the afternoon happily wandering about. It was a brilliant day in mid-September. The tower-like skyscrapers and the breezy canyons of the streets fluttering bright flags—he did not know what the occasion was—exhilarated him. Life seemed very full, brimming with movement, adventure, poetry, singing in the blood, crying out to be written.

Sitting in a tea-room, the first lines of a new poem began to take form in his mind. Pushing his plate of cinnamon toast to one side, he jotted them down on the back of an envelope. A quiver of nervous excitement ran through him. He believed they were good. He believed the idea was good. He found that he wanted to discuss the poem with Alayne Archer, to read those singing first lines to her. He wanted to see her face raised to his with that look of mingled penetration and sweet enthusiasm for his genius—well, she herself had used the word once; in fact, one of the reviewers of *Under the North Star* had used the word, so surely he might let us slide through his own mind now and again, like a stimulating draught. Genius. He believed he had a spark of the sacred fire, and it seemed to him that she, by her presence, the support of her admiration, had the power to fan it to a leaping flame.

He tried to sketch her face on the envelope. He did not do so badly with the forehead, the eyes, but he could not remember her nose—rather a soft feature, he guessed—and when the mouth was added, instead of the look of a spring flower, gentle but defiant, that he had tried to achieve, he had produced a face of almost Dutch stolidity. Irritably he tore up the sketch and his poem with it. She might not be strictly beautiful, but she was not like that.

That evening, in his hotel, he took a good deal of care with his dressing. His evening clothes were well fitting, and the waistcoat, of the newest English cut, very becoming. If it had not been for that Indian coat of tan, his reflection would have been very satisfying. Still, it made him look manlier. And he had a well-cut mouth. Girls had told him it was fascinating. He smiled and showed a row of gleaming teeth, then snapped his lips together. Good Lord! He was acting like a movie star! Or a dentifrice advertisement. Ogling, just that. If Renny could have seen him ogling himself in the glass, he would have knocked his block off. Perhaps it were better than genius (that word again!) should be encased in a wild-eyed, unkempt person. He scowled, put on his hat and coat, and turned out the light.

Mr Cory lived on Sixty-first Street, in an unpretentious house, set between two very pretentious ones. Eden found the rest of the guests assembled except one, an English novelist who arrived a few minutes later than himself. There were Mr Cory; his wife; his daughter, a large-faced young woman with straight black shingled hair; a Mr Gutweld, a musician; and a Mr Groves, a banker, who it was soon evident was to accompany Mr Cory on his trip to Canada; Alayne Archer; and two very earnest middle-aged ladies.

Eden found himself at dinner between Miss Archer and one of the earnest ladies. Opposite were the English novelist, whose name was Hyde, and Miss Cory. Eden had never seen a table so glittering with exquisite glass and slender, shapely cutlery. His mind flew for an instant to the dinner table at Jalna with its huge platters and cumbersome old English plate. For an instant the faces of those about him were blotted out by the faces of the family at home, affectionate, arrogant, high-tempered—faces that, once seen, were not easily forgotten. And when one had lived with them all one's life——But he put them away from him and turned to the earnest lady. Alayne Archer's shoulder was toward him as she listened to Mr Groves on her other side.

"Mr Whiteoak," said the lady, in a richly cultivated voice, "I want to tell you how deeply I appreciate your poetry. You show a delicate sensitiveness that is crystal-like in its implications." She fixed him with her clear grey eyes, and added: "And such an acute realization of the poignant transiency of beauty." Having spoken, she conveyed an exquisite silver spoon filled with exquisite clear soup unflinchingly to her lips.

"Thanks," mumbled Eden. "Thank you very much." He felt overcome with shyness. Oh, God, that Gran were here! He would like to hide his head in her lap while she warded off this terrible woman with her stick. He looked at her, a troubled expression shadowing his blue eyes, but she was apparently satisfied, for she went on talking. Presently Mr Cory claimed her attention and he turned to Alayne Archer.

"Speak to me. Save me," he whispered. "I've never felt so

stupid in my life. I've just been asked what my new poem was about and all I could say was—'a fish'!"

She was looking into his eyes now and he felt an electrical thrill in every nerve at her nearness, and an intangible something he saw in her eyes.

She said: "Mr Groves has something he wants to ask you about supplies for a hunting trip to Canada."

Mr Groves leaned nearer. "How about canned goods?" he said. "Could we take all our supplies over from here, or must we buy them in Canada?"

They talked of tinned meats and vegetables, till Mr Groves turned to examine cautiously, through his glasses, a new dish offered by the servant. Then Miss Archer said softly:

"So you are feeling shy? I do not wonder. Still, it must be very pleasant to hear such delightful things about your poetry."

Looking down over her face he thought her eyelids were like a Madonna's. "I tried to make a sketch of you today, but I tore it up—and some verses with it. You'll scarcely believe it, but I made you look quite Dutch."

"That is not so surprising," she answered. "On my mother's side I am of Dutch extraction. I think I show it quite plainly. My face is broad and rather flat, and I have high cheek bones."

"You draw an engaging picture of yourself, certainly."

"But it is quite true, is it not?" She was smiling with a rather malicious amusement. "Come, now, I do look a stolid Dutch Fräulein; acknowledge it."

He denied it stoutly, but it was true that the Dutch blood explained something about her. A simplicity, a directness, a tranquil tenacity. But with her lovely rounded shoulders, her delicately flushed cheeks, those Madonna eyelids, and that wreath of little pink and white flowers in her hair, he thought she was a thousand times more charming than any girl he had ever met.

Hyde, the novelist, was saying, in his vibrant tones: "When I come to America, I always feel that I have been starved at home. I eat the most enormous meals here, and such meals! Such fruit! Such cream! I know there are cows in England. I've seen them with my own eyes. I ran against one once with my car. But they don't give cream. Their milk is skimmed—pale blue when it comes. Can anyone explain why? Mr Whiteoak, tell me, do you have cream in Canada?"

"We only use reindeer's milk there," replied Eden.

After dinner Hyde sauntered up to him.

"You are the lucky dog! The only interesting woman here. Who is she?"

"Miss Alayne Archer. She is an orphan. Her father was an old friend of Mr Cory's."

"Does she write?"

"No. She reads. She is a reader for the publishing house. It was she who——" But he bit that sentence off just in time. He wasn't going to tell this bulgy-eyed fellow anything more.

Hyde said: "Mr Whiteoak, had you a relative in the Buffs? A red-haired chap?"

"Yes. A brother—Renny. Did you know him?"

Hyde's eyes bulged a little more.

"Did I know him? Rather. One of the best. Oh, he and I had a hell of a time together. Where is he now? In Canada?"

"Yes. He farms."

Hyde looked Eden over critically. "You're not a bit like him. I can't imagine Whiteoak writing poetry. He told me he had a lot of young brothers. 'The whelps', he used to call you. I should like to see him. Please remember me to him."

"If you can manage it, you must come to see us."

Hyde began to talk about his adventures with Renny in France. He was wound up. He seemed to forget his surroundings entirely and poured out reminiscences ribald and bloody which Eden scarcely heard. His own eyes followed Alayne Archer wherever she moved. He could scarcely forbear leaving Hyde rudely and following her. He saw the eyes of Mr Cory and Mr Groves on him, and he saw gleaming in them endless questions about hunting in the North. It seemed as though walls were closing in on him. He felt horribly young and helpless among these middle-aged and elderly men. In desperation he interrupted the Englishman.

"You said you would like to meet Miss Archer."

Hyde looked blank, then agreed cheerfully: "Yes, yes, I did."

Eden took him over to Alayne, turning his own back firmly on the too eager huntsmen.

"Miss Archer," he said, and saw a swift colour tinge her cheeks and pass away, leaving them paler than before. "May I introduce Mr Hyde?"

The two shook hands.

"I have read your new book in the proof sheets," she said to Hyde, "and I think it is splendid. Only I object very strongly to the way you make your American character talk. I often wish that Englishmen would not put Americans into their books. The dialect they put into their mouths is like nothing spoken on land or sea." She spoke lightly, but there was a shadow of real annoyance in her eyes. She had plenty of character, Eden thought; she was not afraid to speak her mind. He pretended to have noticed the same thing. The Englishman laughed imperturbably.

"Well, it's the way it sounds to us," he said. "Then my man, you remember, is a Southerner. He doesn't speak as you do here."

"Yes, but he is an educated Southerner, who would not prefix every sentence with 'Gee' and call other men 'guys', and continually say 'It sure is'—I hope I'm not being rude?"

But Hyde was not annoyed. He was merely amused. No protests could change his conception of American speech. He said to Eden: "Why don't you Canadians write about Americans and see if you have better luck?"

"I shall write a poem about Americans," laughed Eden, and the glance that flashed from his eyes into Alayne's was like a sunbeam that flashes into clear water and is held there.

Would they never be alone together? Yes, the pianist was sitting down before the piano. They melted into a quiet corner. There was no pretending. Each knew the other's desire to escape from the rest. They sat without speaking while the music submerged them like a sea. They were at the bottom of a throbbing sea. They were hidden. They were alone. They could hear the pulsing of the great heart of life. They could feel it in their own heartbeats.

He moved a little nearer to her, staring into the room straight ahead of him, and he could almost feel her head on his shoulder, her body relaxing into his arms. The waves of Chopin thundered on and on. Eden scarcely dared to turn his face toward her. But he did, and a faint perfume came to him from the wreath of little French flowers she wore. What beautiful hands lying in her lap! Surely hands for a poet's love. God, if he could only take them in his and kiss the palms! How tender and delicately scented they would be——

The pianist was playing Debussy. Miss Cory had switched off the lights, all but a pale one by the piano. The sea was all delicate singing wavelets then. He took Alayne's hands and held them to his lips.

As he held them, his being was shaken by a throng of poems rushing up within him, crying out to be born, touched into life by the contact of her hands.

10

ALAYNE AND LIFE

ALAYNE ARCHER was twenty-eight years old when she met Eden Whiteoak. Her father and mother had died within a few weeks of each other, during an epidemic of influenza three years before. They had left their daughter a few hundreds in the bank, a few thousands in life insurance, and an artistic stucco bungalow in Brooklyn, overlooking golf links and a glimpse of the ocean. But they had left her an empty heart, from which the love that had been stored increasingly for them during the twenty-five years flowed in an anguished stream after them into the unknown. It had seemed to her at first that she could not live without those two precious beings whose lives had been so closely entwined with hers.

Her father had been professor of English in a New York State college, a pedantic but gentle man, who loved to impart information to his wife and to instruct his daughter, but who, in matters other than scholastic, was led by them as a little child.

Her mother was the daughter of the principal of a small theological college in the state of Massachusetts, who had got into trouble more than once because of his advanced religious views—had, in fact, escaped serious trouble only because of his personal magnetism and charm. These qualities his daughter had inherited from him, and had in her turn transmitted them to her own daughter Alayne.

Though an earnest little family who faced the problems of the day and their trips to Europe anxiously, they were often filled by the spirit of gentle fun. The grey bungalow resounded to professorial gaiety and the youthful response from Alayne. Professor and Mrs Archer had married young, and they often remarked that Alayne was more like an adored young sister to them than a daughter. She had no intimate friends of her own age. Her parents sufficed. For several years before his death Professor Archer had been engaged in writing a history of the American Revolutionary War, and Alayne had thrown herself with enthusiasm into helping him with the work of research. Her admiration had been aroused for those dogged Loyalists who had left their homes and journeyed northward into Canada to suffer cold and privation for the sake of an idea. It was glorious, she thought, and told her father so. They had argued, and after that he had called her, laughingly, his little Britisher; and she had laughed, too, but she did not altogether like it, for she was proud of being an American. Still, one could see the other person's side of a question.

Mr Cory had been a lifelong friend of her father's. When Professor Archer died, he came forward at once with his assistance. He helped Alayne to dispose of the bungalow by the golf links—those golf links where Alayne and her father had had many a happy game together, with her mother able to keep her eye on them from the upstairs sitting-room window; he had looked into the state of her father's financial affairs for her, and had given her work in reading for the publishing house of Cory and Parsons.

The first blank grief, followed by the agony of realization, had passed, and Alayne's life settled into a sad tranquillity. She had taken a small apartment near her work, and night after night she pored over her father's manuscript, correcting, revising, worrying her young brain into fever over some debatable point. Oh, if he had only been there to settle it for her! To explain, to elucidate his own point of view in his precise and impressive accents! In her solitude she could almost see his long thin scholar's hands turning the pages, and tears swept down her cheeks in a storm, leaving them flushed and hot, so that she would have to go to the window, and press her face to the cool pane, or throw it open and lean out, gazing into the unfriendly street below.

The book was published. It created a good impression, and reviewers were perhaps a little kinder to it because of the recent death of the author. It was praised for its modern liberality. But a few critics pointed out errors and contradictions, and Alayne, holding herself responsible for these, suffered great humiliation. She accused herself of laxness and stupidity. Her dear father's book! She became so white that Mr Cory was worried about her. At last Mrs Cory and he persuaded her to share an apartment with a friend of theirs, Rosamond Trent, a commercial artist, a woman of fifty.

Miss Trent was efficient, talkative, and nearly always good humoured. It was when Alayne joined Miss Trent that she settled down into tranquillity. She read countless manuscripts, some of them very badly typed, and the literary editor of Cory and Parsons learned to rely on her judgment, especially in books other than fiction. In fiction her taste, formed by her parents, was perhaps too conventional, too fastidious. Many of the things she read in manuscript seemed horrid to her. And they had a disconcerting way of cropping up in her mind afterward, like strange weeds that, even after they are uprooted and thrown away, appear again in unexpected places.

She would sit listening to Rosamond Trent's good humoured chatter, her chin in her curled palm, her eyes fixed on Miss Trent's face, yet not all of her was present in the room. Another Alayne, crying like a deserted child, was wandering through the little bungalow; wandering about the garden among the rhododendrons and the roses, where the grass was like moist green velvet, and not a dead leaf was allowed by the professor to lie undisturbed; wandering, weeping over the links with the thin grey shadow of her father, turning to wave a hand to the watching mother in the window.

Sometimes the other Alayne was different, not sad and lonely but wild and questioning. Had life nothing richer for her than this? Reading, reading manuscripts, day in, day out, sitting at night with gaze bent on Miss Trent's chattering face, or going to the Corys' or some other house, meeting people who made no impression on her. Was she never going to have a real friend to whom she could confide everything—well, almost everything? Was she never—for the first time in her life she asked herself this question in grim earnest—was she never going to have a lover?

Oh, she had had admirers—not many, for she had not encouraged them. If she went out with them she was sure

95

to miss something delightful that was happening at home. If they came to the house they seldom fitted in with the scheme of things. Sexually she was one of those women who develop slowly; who might, under certain conditions, marry, rear a family, and never have the well-spring of her passions unbound.

There had been one man who might almost have been called a lover, a colleague of her father's, but several years younger. He had come to the house, first as her father's friend, then more and more as hers. He had fitted into their serious discussions, even into their gaieties. Once he had gone to Europe with them. In Sorrento, on a morning when the spring was breaking and they had been walking up a narrow pathway across a hill, filled with the wonder of that ecstatic awakening, he had asked her to marry him. She had begged him to wait for his answer till they returned to America, for she was afraid that her delight was not in him but in Italy.

They had been back in America only a month when her mother was taken ill. The next two months were passed in heart-piercing suspense and agony. Then, at the end, she found herself alone. Again her father's friend, in old-fashioned phrasing, which she loved in books but which did not move her in real life, asked her to marry him. He loved her and he wanted to care for her. She knew that her father had approved of him, but her heart was drained empty, and its aching spaces desired no new occupant.

When the manuscript of young Whiteoak's book was given her to read, Alayne was in a mood of eager receptivity to beauty. The beauty, the simplicity, the splendid abandon of Eden's lyrics filled her with a new joy. When the book appeared, she had an odd feeling of possession toward it. She rather hated seeing Miss Trent's large plump hands caressing it—"Such a ducky little book, my dear!"—and she hated to hear her read from it, stressing the most striking phrases, sustaining the last word of each line with an upward lilt of her throaty voice—"Sheer beauty, that bit, isn't it, Alayne dear?" She felt ashamed of herself for grudging Miss Trent her pleasure in the book, but she undoubtedly did grudge it.

She rather dreaded meeting Eden for fear he should be disappointing. Suppose he were short and thickset, with beady black eyes and a long upper lip. Suppose he had a hatchet face and wore horn-rimmed spectacles.

Well, however he looked, his mind was beautiful. But she· had quaked as she entered the reception-room.

When she saw him standing tall and fair, with his crest of golden hair, his sensitive features, his steady but rather wistful smile, she was trembling, almost overcome with relief. He seemed to carry some of the radiance of his poetry about his own person. Those brilliant blue eyes in that tanned face! Oh, she could not have borne it had he not been beautiful!

It seemed as natural to her that they two should seek a quiet corner together, that he should, when the opportunity offered, take her hands in his and press ecstatic kisses upon them, as that two drops of dew should melt into one, or two sweet chords blend.

It seemed equally natural to her to say yes when, two weeks later, he asked her to marry him.

He had not intended to ask her that. He realized in his heart that it was madness to ask her, unless they agreed to a long engagement, but the autumn night was studded with stars and heavy with the teasing scents of burning leaves and salt air. They were gliding slowly along an ocean driveway in Rosamond Trent's car. Rosamond was slouching over the wheel, silent for once, and they two in the back seat alone, in a world apart. He could no more stop himself from asking her to marry him than he could help writing a poem that burned to be expressed.

His love for her was a poem. Their life together would be an exquisite, enchanted poem, a continual inspiration for him. He could not do without her. The thought of holding her intimately in his arms gave him the tender sadness of a love poem to be written. Yet he must not ask her to marry him. He must not and—he did.

"Alayne, my beautiful darling—will you marry me?"

"Eden—Eden——" She could scarcely speak, for the love now filling her heart that had been drained empty of love almost drowned her senses. "Yes—I will marry you if you want me. I want you with all my soul."

11

BELOVED, IT IS MORN

"I LIKE YOUR young poet immensely," said Rosamond Trent.

"He must be a delightful lover. But, Alayne dear—now you must not mind my saying this; I am so much older— don't you think it is rather reckless to plunge into matrimony without waiting to see how he gets on in the world? You are both such dears, but you are so inexperienced. Here are you, giving up a good position, and going to a country you know nothing about, arranging to spend some months with a family you have never seen——"

"His sister," said Alayne patiently, "has written me a delightful letter. They have a big old house. She seems to want me. Even the dear grandmother sent me a message of welcome. Then I have a little money of my own; I shall not be quite dependent. And if it were ever necessary, I——"

"Oh, my dear, I am sure it will be all right. But you are so precipitate. If you would only wait a little."

"I have been waiting for Eden all these years!" exclaimed Alayne, flushing. "I realize that now. Neither he nor I feel like wasting any of the precious time we might be together. After we are married I shall visit his people, and Eden will look about. If he cannot get into anything satisfactory that will leave him plenty of time in which to develop his talent, or if I do not like Canada, we shall come back to New York. I know he could have something with Mr Cory in the publishing business, but—oh, I do not want him to do anything that will hamper him. I want him to live for his art."

Miss Trent made a little gesture of impatience. Then she made a large gesture of great affection, and gathered Alayne to her heart.

"You two darlings!" she said. "I know it will be all right. And why waste time when you are young and beautiful!"

She realized that such were the glamour and wonder of Alayne's feeling toward Eden that it was useless to reason with her. Alayne herself was conscious of such subtleties in her love for him that she felt at times bewildered. He was a young god of the sun, a strong deliverer from her prison of heartbreak; he was a fledgling genius; he was a stammering, sunburned, egotistical young Canadian with not too good an education; he was a blue-eyed, clinging-fingered child; he was a suddenly wooden and undemonstrative young Britisher. An evening with him excited her so that she could not sleep after it. And as she spent every evening with him, she grew drowsy-eyed from lying awake thinking of him. The curves of her mouth became more tender, more yielding from those same thoughts.

Eden had begun the letter to Meg telling her of his engagement in much trepidation. But as he wrote he gained confidence, and told of Alayne's beauty, her endearing qualites, her influential friends who would be able to do so much for him in the publishing world. And she was independent—not an heiress, not the rich American girl of fiction; still, she would be a help, not a handicap to him. Meg was to believe that she was absolutely desirable.

The family at Jalna, always credulous, with imaginations easily stirred, snatched with avidity at the bare suggestion of means. They settled it among themselves that Alayne was a rich girl, and that Eden for some reason wished to depreciate her wealth.

"He's afraid some of us will want to borrow a few bucks," sneered Piers.

"He'd have never been such a fool as to marry if the girl had not had lots of brass," growled Nicholas.

"He was bound to attract some cultivated rich woman with his talents, his looks, and his lovely manners," said Meg, her smile of ineffable calm sweetness curving her lips. "I shall be very nice to her. Who knows, she may do something for the younger boys. American women are noted for their generosity. Wakefield is delicate and he's very attractive. Finch is——"

"Neither delicate nor attractive," put in Renny, grinning, and Finch, who was wrestling in a corner with his Latin, blushed a deep pink and gave a snort of mingled amusement and embarrassment.

Grandmother shouted: "When is she coming? I must wear my cream-coloured cap with the purple ribbons."

Piers said: "Eden always was an impulsive fool. I'll bet he's making a fool marriage." He rather hoped that Eden was, for he found it hard to endure the thought of Eden making a marriage which would be welcomed by the whole family while he himself was continually forced to feel that he had made a mess of his life.

Meg wrote her letter to Alayne, inviting her to come to Jalna for as long as she liked. She was to consider Jalna her home. All the family were so happy in dear Eden's happiness. Dear Grandmother sent her love. ("Have you got that down, Meggie? That I send my love? Underline it. No mistake.") Alayne was deeply touched by this letter.

What delight she took in showing New York to her lover! Theatres, museums, cathedrals, shops, and queer little tea-rooms. Down dingy steps they went, she feeling thrilled because he was thrilled, into dim rooms, lighted by candles, where waitresses wore smocks or other distinctive regalia, and the places bore such names as The Pepper Pot, The Samovar, The Mad Hatter, or The Pig and Whistle. Together they stood, as the evening fell, looking down from the twentieth story of a pale, column-like building into the street below, where the electric signs became a chain of burning jewels, out across the Hudson and the harbour with its glittering ferryboats, or, raising their happy eyes, saw all the dim towers flower into fairy brightness.

She took him up the Hudson to visit her two aunts, the sisters of her father, who lived in a house with a pinkish roof overlooking the river. They were delighted with Alayne's young Canadian. He had such an easy, pleasant voice, he was so charmingly deferential to them. Even while they regretted that Alayne was going away, for a time at least, they were exhilarated, elated by her bliss. They took Eden to their hearts, and, seated in their austerely perfect little living-room, they asked him innumerable questions about his family. He, lounging much less than when in Alayne's apartment, looked with curiosity into the clear eyes of those two elderly women, wondering whether they had always been so earnest, so elegantly poised, so essentially well behaved. Yes, he thought so. He pictured them sitting in high chairs, investigating rubber dolls and rattles with the selfsame expression. They were inclined to stoutness. Their faces were just pleasantly lined. Their greying hair was rolled back from their foreheads with well-groomed precision. Their dresses of soft neutral tints blended perfectly with the delicate self-tones of the wallpaper and hangings. Groups of little black framed prints and etchings of the doorways of European cathedrals, old bridges, or quiet landscapes gave distinction to the walls. Yet, in spite of the studied austerity, Eden felt that these two elderly ladies were incurably romantic. He was nervous lest he should say something to shatter the brittle atmosphere in which they had their being. He tried, when questioned, to present the family at Jalna in as neutral tints as possible. But it was difficult. He realized for the first time that they were high-coloured and flamboyant.

Miss Harriet was asking:

"Let me see, there are six of you, aren't there? How very interesting. Just imagine Alayne having brothers and sisters, Helen. She used always to be praying for them when she was little, didn't you, Alayne?"

"There is only one sister," said Eden.

"She wrote Alayne such a kind letter," murmured Miss Helen.

Miss Harriet proceeded: "And your older brother went through all the terrors of the War, did he not?"

"Yes, he was through the War," replied Eden, and he thought of Renny's rich vocabulary.

"And the brother next to you is married, Alayne tells us. I do hope his wife and Alayne will be friends. Is she about Alayne's age? Have you known her long?"

"She is seventeen. I've known her all my life. She's the daughter of a neighbour." His mind flew for an instant to the reception given to Piers and Pheasant when they returned to Jalna after their marriage. He remembered the way poor young Pheasant had howled, and Piers had stood holding his bleeding ear.

"I trust Alayne and she will be congenial. Then there are the two younger brothers. Tell us about them."

"Well, Finch is rather a—oh, he's just at the hobbledehoy period, Miss Archer. We can hardly tell what he'll be. At present he's immersed in his studies. Wake is a pretty little chap. You'd quite like him. He is too delicate to go to school, and has all his lessons with our rector. I'm afraid he's very indolent, but he's an engaging young scamp."

"I am sure Alayne will love him. And she will have uncles,"

too. I am glad there are no aunts. Yes, Alayne, we were saying only this morning we are glad there are no aunts. We really want no auntly opposition in loving you."

"Then," put in Miss Helen, "there is Eden's remarkable grandmother. Ninety-nine, did you say, Eden? And all her faculties almost unimpaired. It is truly wonderful."

"Yes, a regular old—yes, an amazing old lady, Grandmother is." And he suddenly saw her grinning at him, the graceless ancient, with her cap askew, Boney perched on her shoulder, rapping out obscene Hindu oaths in his raucous voice. He groaned inwardly and wondered what Alayne would think of his family.

He had written asking Renny to be best man for him. Renny had replied: 'I have neither the *time*, the *togs*, nor the *tin* for such a bust-up. But I enclose a cheque for my wedding present to you, which will help to make up for my absence. I am glad Miss Archer has money. Otherwise I should think you insane to tie yourself up at this point in your career, when you seem to be going in several directions at once and arriving nowhere. However, good luck to you and my very best regards to the lady. Your aff. bro. Renny.'

The cheque was sufficient to pay for the honeymoon trip and to take them home to Jalna. Eden, with his head among the stars, thanked God for that.

They were married in the austerely perfect living-room of Alayne's aunts' house on the Hudson. Late roses of so misty a pink that they were almost mauve, and asters of so uncertain a mauve that they were almost pink, blended with the pastel shades worn by the tremulously happy aunts. A Presbyterian minister united them, for the Misses Archer were of that denomination. They had felt it keenly when their brother had embraced Unitarian doctrines, though they had never reproached him for his change of faith. Intellectually Alayne was satisfied with Unitarianism, but she had sometimes wished that the faith in which she had been reared were more picturesque even though less intellectual. In truth, religious speculation had played a very small part in her life, and when bereavement came to her she found little consolation in it. With a certain sad whimsicality, she liked at times to picture the spirit of her father meticulously going over the golf course, stopping now and again to wave a ghostly hand to the spirit of her mother peering from an upper window of the stucco bungalow.

She thought of them a good deal on this her wedding day. They would have been so happy in her happiness. They would have loved Eden. He looked so radiant, sun-burned, and confident as he smiled down at her that she became radiant and confident too.

The Corys, Rosamond Trent, and the other friends at the wedding repast thought and said that they had never seen a lovelier couple.

As they motored to New York to take their train Eden said: "Darling, I have never met so many well-behaved people in my life. Darling, let us be wild and half mad and delirious with joy! I'm tired of being good."

She hugged him to her. She loved him intensely, and she longed with great fervour to experience life.

12

WELCOME AGAIN TO JALNA

WAKEFIELD SLEPT late that morning, just when he had intended to be about early. When he opened his eyes he found that Renny's head was not on the pillow next his as usual. He was not even dressing. He was gone, and Wake had the bed and the room to himself. He slept with Renny because he sometimes had a 'bad turn' in the night and it was to his eldest brother he clung at such times.

He spreadeagled himself on the bed, taking up all the room he could, and lay luxuriously a few minutes, rejoicing in the fact that he did not have to go to Mr Fennel's for lessons on this day, because it had been proclaimed a holiday by Grandmother. It was the day on which Eden and his bride were expected to arrive at Jalna. Their train was to reach the city at nine that morning and Piers had already motored to fetch them the twenty-five miles to Jalna, where a great dinner was already in preparation.

The loud wheezing that preceded the striking of the grandfather's clock in the upstairs hall now began. Wake listened. After what seemed a longer wheeze than usual the clock struck nine. The train carrying the bride and groom must at this moment be arriving at the station. Wakefield had seen pictures of wedding parties, and he had a vision of Eden travelling in a top hat and long-tailed coat with a white flower in his buttonhole, seated beside his bride, whose face showed but faintly through a voluminous veil and who carried an immense bouquet of orange blossoms. He did wish that Meg had allowed him to go in the car to meet them. It seemed too bad that such a lovely show should be wasted on Piers, who had not seemed at all keen about meeting them.

Wake thought that he had better give his rabbit hutches a thorough cleaning, for probably one of the first things the bride would wish to inspect would be his rabbits. It would be some time before they arrived, for they were to have breakfast in town. He began to kick the bedclothes from him. He kicked them with all his might till he had nothing over him, then he lay quite still a moment, his small dark face turned impassively toward the ceiling, before he leaped out of bed and ran to the window.

It was a day of thick yellow autumn sunshine. A circular bed of nasturtiums around two old cedar trees burned like a slow fire. The lawn still had a film of heavy dew drawn across it, and a procession of bronze turkeys, led by the red-faced old cock, left a dark trail where their feet had brushed it.

"Gobble, gobble, gobble," came from the cock, and his wattles turned from red to purple. He turned and faced his hens and wheeled before them, dropping his wings with a metallic sound.

Wake shouted from the window: "Gobble, gobble, gobble! Get off the lawn! I say, get off the lawn!"

"Clang, clang, clang," responded the gobbler's note of anger, and the hens made plaintive piping sounds.

"I suppose you think," retorted Wakefield, "that you're fifteen brides and a groom. Well, you're not. You're turkeys; and you'll be eaten first thing, you know. The real bride and groom will eat you, so there!"

"Gobble, gobble, gobble."

The burnished procession passed into the grape arbour. Between purple bunches of grapes, Wake could see the shine of plumage, the flame of tossing wattles.

It was a lovely morning! He tore off his pyjamas and, stark

naked, ran round and round the room. He stopped breathless before the washstand, where the brimming basin foaming with shaving lather showed how complete had been Renny's preparations for the bride and groom.

Wakefield took up the shaving soap and the shaving brush, and immersed the brush in the basin. He made a quantity of fine, fluffy, and altogether delightful lather. First he decorated his face, then produced a nice epaulette for each shoulder. Then he made a collar for his round brown neck. Up and down, he decorated his small person. By twisting about before the mirror he managed to do even his back. It took most of the shaving stick, but the effect when his toilet was completed was worth all the trouble. He stood in rapt admiration before the glass, astonished at what a little ingenuity and a lot of lather could do. He pictured himself receiving the bride and groom in this simple yet effective attire. He was sure that Alayne would think it worth while travelling all the way from New York to see a sight like this.

He was lost in reverie when a smothered scream disturbed him. It was uttered by Mrs Wragge, who stood in the doorway, one hand clapped to her mouth, the other carrying a slop-pail.

"My Gawd!" she cried. "Wot a norrible sight! Ow, wot a turn it give me! My 'eart's doawn in my boots and my stummick's in the top of my 'ead."

She was too funny standing there, red-faced and open-mouthed. Wakefield could not refrain from doing something to her. He danced toward her and, before she realized the import of the brandished shaving brush, she had a snowy meringue of lather fairly between the eyes and down the bridge of the nose. With a scream, this time unsmothered, Mrs Wragge dropped the pail of slops and pawed blindly at her ornate face. Meg, giving a last satisfied examination to Eden's room, which had been prepared for the bridal pair, hurried toward the sounds of distress from her handmaiden, and, catching the little boy by the ankle just as he was disappearing under the big four-poster, dragged him forth and administered three sharp slaps.

"There," she said, "and there, and *there*! As though I hadn't enough to do!"

When Wakefield descended the stairs half an hour later, his expression was somewhat subdued but he carried himself with dignity, and he was conscious of looking extremely well in his best Norfolk suit and a snowy Eton collar. He had begged for just a little haircream to make his hair lie flat, but Meg liked it fluffy, and he had not wished to insist on anything on a morning when she was already somewhat harassed.

As he passed the door of his grandmother's room, he could hear her saying in a cajoling tone to Boney: "Say 'Alayne' now, Boney. 'Pretty Alayne'. Say 'Alayne'. Say 'Hail, Columbia'." Then her voice was drowned by the raucous tones of Boney uttering a few choice Hindu curses.

Wakefield smiled and entered the dining-room. The table was cleared, but a tray was laid on a small table in a corner. Bread and butter, marmalade, milk. He knew that if he rang the bell Rags would bring him a dish of porridge from the kitchen. It was an old silver bell in the shape of a little fat lady. He loved it, and handled it caressingly a moment before ringing it long and clearly.

He went to the head of the basement stairs and listened. He could hear Rags rattling things on the stove. He heard a saucepan being scraped. Nasty, sticky, dried-up old porridge! He heard Rags' step on the brick floor approaching the stairway. Lightly he glided to the clothes cupboard and hid himself inside the door, just peeping through a narrow crack while Rags mounted the stairs and disappeared into the dining-room, a cigarette stuck between his pale lips and the plate of porridge tilted at a precarious angle. Wakefield reflected without bitterness that Rags would not have dared to wait on any other member of the family with such a lack of decorum. But he smiled slyly as he glided down the stairs into the basement, leaving Rags and the porridge in the dining-room alone.

The kitchen was an immense room with a great unused fireplace and a coal range that was always in use. The table and dressers were so heavy that they were never moved, and one wall was covered by an oak rack filled with platters from successive Whiteoak dinner-sets. Many of these would have given delight to a collector, but the glazing on all was disfigured by innumerable little cracks from being placed in ovens far too hot.

Wakefield gave one longing look into the pantry. How he would have liked to forage for his breakfast among those richly laden shelves! He saw two fat fowls trussed up in a roasting-pan ready to put into the oven, and a huge boiled ham, and a brace of plum tarts. But he dared not. Rags would be returning at any moment. On the kitchen table he found a plate of cold toast and a saucer of anchovy paste. Taking a slice of toast and the anchovy paste, he trotted out of the kitchen and along the brick passage into the coal cellar. He heard Rags clattering down the kitchen stairs, muttering as he came. A window in the coal cellar stood open, and mounted on an empty box he found he could easily put his breakfast out on the ground and climb out after it.

He was sorry to see how black his hands and bare knees had become in the operation. He scrubbed them with his clean handkerchief, but the only result was that the handkerchief became black. He did not like to return such a black rag to the pocket of his best suit, so he pushed it carefully out of sight in a crack just under the sill of the cellar window. Some little mouse, he thought, would be glad to find it and make a nice little nest of it.

He carried his toast and anchovy paste to the old carriage house, and sought a favourite retreat of his. This was a ponderous closed carriage that Grandfather Whiteoak had sent to England for when he and Grandmother had first built Jalna. It had a great shell-like body, massive lamps, and a high seat for the coachman. It must have been a splendid sight to see them driving out. It had not been used for many years. Wakefield slumped on the sagging seat, eating his toast and anchovy paste with unhurried enjoyment. The fowls clucking and scratching in the straw made a soothing accompaniment to his thoughts.

'Now, if I had my way I'd meet the brideangroom with this beautiful carriage, drawn by four white horses. I'd have the wheels all done up in wreaths of roses like the pictures of carnivals in California. And a big bunch of roses for her to carry, and a trumpeter sitting on the seat beside the coachman tooting a trumpet. And a pretty little dwarf hanging on behind, with a little silver whistle to blow when the trumpeter stopped tooting. What a happy brideangroom they'd be!'

'Brideangroom. . . . Brideangroom.' He liked the pleasant

way those words ran together. Still, he must not linger here too long or he would not be on hand to welcome them. He decided that there was no time left for cleaning the rabbit hutches. He would go across the meadow to the road, and wait by the church corner. Then he would have a chance to meet them before the rest of the family. He clambered out of the carriage, a cobweb clinging to his hair and a black smudge across his cheek. He set the saucer containing the remainder of the anchovy on the floor and watched five hens leap simultaneously upon it, a tangle of wings and squawks, while a rooster side-stepped about the scrimmage, watching his wives with a distracted yellow eye.

He trotted across the meadow, climbed the fence, and gained the road. He stopped long enough to pass the time of day with Chalk, the blacksmith, and was almost by the Wigles' cottage when Muriel accosted him from the gate:

"I've got ten thents."

He hesitated, looking at the little girl over his shoulder. "Have you? Where did you get it?" he asked with polite interest.

"It'th a birthday prethent. I'm thaving up to buy a dolly."

Wake went to her and said kindly: "Look here, Muriel, you're awfully silly if you do that. A doll costs a dollar or more, and if you save ten cents every single birthday it'd be years and years before you'd have enough to buy one. By that time you'd be too old to play with it. Better come to Mrs Brawn's now and buy yourself a chocolate bar. I'll buy you a bottle of cream soda to drink with it.

"I don't like cream thoda," replied Muriel, petulantly. She opened her small hot palm and examined the coin lying on it.

Wakefield bent over it. "Why, it's a Yankee dime," he exclaimed. "Goodness, Muriel, you'd better hurry up and spend it, because likely as not it'll be no good by next week."

Mrs Wigle put her head out of the window of the cottage. "When's your brother goin' to mend my roof?" she demanded. "It's leakin' like all possessed."

"Oh, he was just speaking about that this morning, Mrs Wigle. He says that just as soon as he gets this wedding reception off his hands, he's going to attend to your roof."

"Well, I hope he will," she grumbled, and withdrew her head.

"Come along now, Muriel," said Wake. "I haven't much time to spare, but I'll go with you to Mrs Brawn's so's you won't feel shy."

He took her hand and the little girl trotted beside him with a rather dazed expression. They presented themselves before Mrs Brawn's counter.

"Well, Master Whiteoak," she said, "I hope you've come to pay your account."

"I'm afraid not this morning," replied Wake. "We're so very busy getting ready for the brideangroom that I forgot. But Muriel here wants a bottle of cream soda and a chocolate bar. It's her birthday, you see."

They sat on the step outside the shop with the refreshments, Wakefield sucking the sickly drink placidly through a straw, Muriel nibbling the chocolate.

"Have a pull, Muriel," he offered.

"Don't like it," she said. "You have a bite of chocolate." She held the bar to his lips, and so they contentedly ate it, bite about.

How happy he was! 'Brideangroom. . . . Brideangroom.' The pleasant words went singing through his head. A spiral of wood smoke curled upward from a mound of burning leaves in a yard across the street. A hen and her half grown brood scratched blithely in the middle of the road. Muriel was gazing into his face with slavish admiration.

A car was coming. Their own car. He recognized its peculiar hiccoughing squeaks. Hastily he drained the last drops and pushed the bottle into Muriel's hands.

"You may return the bottle, Muriel," he said. "I must go to meet the brideangroom."

The car was in sight. He espied a clump of Michaelmas daisies growing by the side of the road, and he swiftly ran and plucked a long feathery spray. It was rather dusty, but still very pretty, and he stood clasping it, with an expectant smile on his face, as the car approached. Piers, who was driving, would have gone by and left him standing there, but Eden sharply told him to stop, and Alayne leaned forward full of eager curiosity.

Wakefield mounted the runningboard and held the Michaelmas daisies out to her.

"Welcome to Jalna," he said.

13

INSIDE THE GATES OF JALNA

E DEN HAD not been sorry to see his little brother waiting at the roadside with daisies for Alayne. The meeting with Piers, the breakfast in his company at the Queen's, and the subsequent drive home had not been altogether satisfactory. Alayne had been tired and unusually quiet, Piers actually taciturn. Eden resented this taciturnity because he remembered having been very decent to Piers and Pheasant on the occasion of their humiliating return to Jalna. He had been the first, and the only one except Renny, to stand up for them. He regarded his brother's solid back and strong sunburned neck with growing irritation as the car sped along the lakeshore road.

Alayne gazed out over the misty blue expanse of the lake with a feeling approaching sadness. This sea that was not a sea, this land that was not her land, this new brother with the unfriendly blue eyes and the sulky mouth, she must get used to them all. They were to be hers. Ruth—'amid the alien corn'.

But she should not feel that they were alien. It was a lovely land. The language was her own. Even this new brother was probably only rather shy. She wished that Eden had told her more about his family. There were so many of them. She went over their names in her mind to prepare herself for the meeting. A tiny shudder of apprehension ran through her nerves. She put her hand on Eden's and gripped his fingers.

"Cheer up, old dear," he said. "We'll soon be there."

They had left the lake shore and were running smoothly over a curving road. A quaint old church, perched on a wooded knoll, rose before them. Then a diminutive shop, two children staring, Eden's voice saying, "There's young Wake, Piers!" And a little boy on the runningboard, pushing flowers into her hand.

"Welcome to Jalna," he said, in a sweet treble, "and I thought maybe you'd like these Michaelmas daisies. I've been waiting ever so long."

"Hop in," commanded Eden, opening the door.

He hopped in, and squeezed his slender body between theirs on the seat. Piers had not looked round. Now he started the car with a jerk.

Wakefield raised his eyes to Alayne's face and scrutinized her closely. 'What eyelashes!' she thought. 'What a darling!' His little body pressed against her seemed the most delightful and pathetic thing. Oh, she could love this little brother. And he was delicate, too. Not strong enough to go to school. She would play with him, help to teach him. They smiled at each other. She looked across his head at Eden and formed the words 'A darling' with smiling lips.

"How is everyone at home?" asked Eden.

"Nicely, thank you," said Wakefield, cheerfully. "Granny has had a little cough, and Boney imitates her. Uncle Ernest's nose is rather pink from hay fever. Uncle Nick's gout is better. Meggie eats very little, but she is getting fatter. Piers took the first prize with his bull at the Durham show. It wore the blue ribbon all the way home. Finch came out fifty-second in his Greek exam. I can't think of any news about Pheasant and Rags and Mrs Wragge except that they're there. I hope you like your flowers, Alayne. I should have got more, but I saw your car coming just as I was beginning to gather them."

"They are beautiful," said Alayne, holding them to her face, and Wakefield close to her side. "I am so very glad you came to meet me."

In truth she was very glad. It seemed easier to meet the family with the little boy by her side. Her cheeks flushed a pretty pink, and she craned her neck eagerly to catch a first glimpse of the house as they passed between the stalwart spruces along the drive.

Jalna looked very mellow in the golden sunlight, draped in its mantle of reddening Virginia creeper and surrounded by freshly clipped lawns. One of Wake's rabbits was hopping about, and Renny's two clumber spaniels were stretched on the steps. A pear tree near the house had dropped its fruit in the grass, where it lay richly yellow, giving to the eyes of a town dweller an air of negligent well-being to the scene. Alayne thought that Jalna had something of the appearance of an old manorial farmhouse, set among its lawns and orchards. The spaniels lazily beat their plumed tails on the step, too indolent to rise.

"Renny's dogs," commented Eden, pushing one of them out of the way with his foot that Alayne might pass. "You'll have to get used to animals. You'll find them all over the place."

"That will not be hard. I have always wanted pets." She bent to stroke one of the silken heads.

Eden looked down at her curiously. How would she and his family get on, he wondered. Now that he had brought her home he realized suddenly that she was alien to his family. He had a disconcerting sensation of surprise at finding himself married. After all, he was not so elated as he had expected to be when Rags opened the door and smiled a self-conscious welcome.

Rags was always self-conscious when he wore his livery. It consisted of a shiny black suit with trousers very tight for him and a coat a size too large, and a stiff white collar, and a greenish-black bow tie. His ash-blond hair was clipped with convict-like closeness, his pallid face showed a cut he had given himself when shaving. His air had something of the secretive smirk of an undertaker.

"Welcome 'ome, Mr Eden," he said, sadly. "Welcome 'ome, sir."

"Thanks, Rags. Alayne, this is Wragge, our——" Eden hesitated, trying to decide how Mr Wragge should be described, and continued, "our factotum."

"Welcome 'ome, Mrs Whiteoak," said Rags, with his curiously deprecating yet impudent glance. It said to Eden silently but unmistakably: 'Ow, you may fool the family, young man, but you can't fool me. You 'aven't married a heiress. And 'ow we're to put up with another young woman 'ere, Gawd only knows."

Alayne thanked him, and at the same moment the door of the living-room was opened and Meg Whiteoak appeared on the threshold. She threw her arms about Eden's neck and kissed him with passionate tenderness. Then she turned to Alayne, her lips, with their prettily curved corners, parted in a gentle smile.

"So this is Alayne. I hope you will like us all, my dear. We're so happy to have you."

Alayne found herself enfolded in a warm plump embrace. She thought it was no wonder the brothers adored their sister —Eden had told her they did—and she felt prepared to make a sister, a confidante, of her. How delightful! A real sister. She held tightly to Meg's hand as they went into the living-room where more of the family had assembled.

It was so warm that even the low flameless fire seemed too much; none of the windows were open. Slanting bars of sunlight penetrating between the slats of the inside shutters converged at one point, the chair where old Mrs Whiteoak sat. Like fiery fingers they seemed to point her out as the most significant presence in the room. Yet she was indulging in one of her unpremeditated naps. Her head, topped by a large purple cap with pink rosettes, had sunk forward so that the only part of her face visible was her heavy jaw and row of too perfect under-teeth. She wore a voluminous tea-gown of purple velvet, and her shapely hands clasping the gold top of her ebony stick were heavy with rings worn for the occasion. A steady bubbling snore escaped her. The two elderly men came forward, Nicholas frowning because of the painful effort of rising, but enfolding Alayne's hand in a warm grasp. They greeted her in mellow whispers, Ernest excusing their mamma's momentary oblivion.

"She must have these little naps. They refresh her. Keep her going."

Wakefield, who stood gazing into his grandmother's face, remarked: "Yes. She winds herself up, rather like a clock, you know. You can hear her doing it, can't you? B-z-z-z-z——"

Meg smiled at Alayne. "He thinks of everything," she said. "His mind is never still."

"He ought to be more respectful in speaking of his grand-mamma," rebuked Ernest. "Don't you think so, Alayne?"

Nicholas put his arm about the child. "She'd probably be highly amused by the comparison, and talk of nothing else for an hour." He turned with his sardonic smile to Alayne. "She's very bright, you know. She can drown us all out when she——"

"Begins to strike," put in Wake, carrying on the clock simile. Nicholas rumpled the boy's hair.

"We had better sit down," said Meg, "till she wakens and has a little talk with Alayne. Then I'll take you up to your room, my dear. You must be tired after the journey. And hungry, too. Well, we're going to have an early dinner."

"Chicken and plum tart! Chicken and plum tart!" exploded Wakefield, and old Mrs Whiteoak stirred in her sleep.

Uncle Nicholas covered the child's face with his hand, and the family's gaze was fixed expectantly on the old lady. After a moment's contortion, however, her face resumed the calm of peaceful slumber; everyone sat down, and conversation was carried on in hushed tones.

Alayne felt as though she were in a dream. The room, the furniture, the people were so different from those to which she was accustomed that their strangeness made even Eden seem suddenly remote. She wondered wistfully whether it would take her long to get used to them. Yet in looking at the faces about her she found that each had a distinctive attraction for her. Or perhaps it was fascination. Certainly there was nothing attractive about the grandmother unless it were the bizarre strength of her personality.

"I lived in London a good many years," mumbled Uncle Nicholas, "but I don't know much about New York. I visited it once in the nineties, but I suppose it has changed a lot since then."

"Yes, I think you would find it very changed. It is changing constantly."

Uncle Ernest whispered: "I sailed from there once for England. I just missed seeing a murder."

"Oh, Uncle Ernest, I wish you'd seen it!" exclaimed Wakefield, bouncing up and down on the padded arm of his sister's chair.

"Hush, Wake," said Meg, giving his thigh a little slap. "I'm very glad he didn't see it. It would have upset him terribly. Isn't it a pity you have so many murders there? And lynchings, and all?"

"They don't have lynchings in New York, Meggie," corrected Uncle Ernest.

"Oh, I forgot. It's Chicago, isn't it?"

Eden spoke for almost the first time. "Never met so many orderly people in my life as I met in New York."

"How nice," said Meg. "I do like order, but I find it so hard to keep, with servants' wages high, and so many boys about, and Granny requiring a good deal of waiting on."

The sound of her own name must have penetrated Mrs Whiteoak's consciousness. She wobbled a moment as though she were about to fall, then righted herself and raised her still handsome, chiselled nose from its horizontal position and looked about. Her eyes, blurred by sleep, did not at once perceive Alayne.

"Dinner," she observed. "I want my dinner."

"Here are Eden and Alayne," said Ernest, bending over her.

"Better come over to her," suggested Nicholas.

"She will be so glad," said Meg.

Eden took Alayne's hand and led her to his grandmother. The old lady peered at them unseeingly for a moment; then her gaze brightened. She clutched Eden to her and gave him a loud, hearty kiss.

"Eden," she said. "Well, well, so you're back. Where's your bride?"

Eden put Alayne forward, and she was enfolded in an embrace of surprising strength. Sharp bristles scratched her cheek, and a kiss was planted on her mouth.

"Pretty thing," said Grandmother, holding her off to look at her. "You're a very pretty thing. I'm glad you've come. Where's Boney, now?" She released Alayne and looked around sharply for the parrot. At the sound of his name he flapped heavily from his ring perch to her shoulder. She stroked his bright plumage with her jewelled hand.

"Say 'Alayne'," she adjured him. "Say 'Pretty Alayne'. Come, now, there's a darling boy!"

Boney, casting a malevolent look on Alayne with one topaz eye, for the other was tight shut, burst into a string of curses.

"Kutni! Kutni! Kutni!" he screamed. "Shaitan ke khatla! Kambakht!"

Grandmother thumped her stick loudly on the floor. "Silence!" she thundered. "I won't have it. Stop him, Nick. Stop him!"

"He'll bite me," objected Nicholas.

"I don't care if he does. Stop him!"

"Stop him yourself, Mamma."

"Boney, Boney, don't be so naughty. Say 'Pretty Alayne'. Come, now."

Boney rocked himself on her shoulder in a paroxysm of rage.

"Paji! Paji! Kuzabusth! Iflatoon! Iflatoon!" He glared into his mistress's face, their two hooked beaks almost touching, his scarlet and green plumage, her purple and pink finery, blazing in the slanting sun rays.

"Please don't trouble," said Alayne, soothingly. "I think he is very beautiful, and he probably does not dislike me as much as he pretends."

"What's she say?" demanded the old lady, looking up at her sons. It was always difficult for her to understand a stranger, though her hearing was excellent, and Alayne's slow and somewhat precise enunciation was less clear to her than Nicholas' rumbling tones or Ernest's soft mumble.

"She says Boney is beautiful," said Nicholas, too indolent to repeat the entire sentence.

Grandmother grinned, very well pleased. "Aye, he's beautiful. A handsome bird, but a bit of a devil. I brought him all the way from India seventy-three years ago. A game old bird, eh? Sailing-vessels then, my dear. I nearly died. And the ayah did die. They put her overboard. But I was too sick to care. My baby Augusta nearly died, poor brat, and my dear husband, Captain Philip Whiteoak, had his hands full. You'll see his portrait in the dining-room. The handsomest officer in India. I could hold my own for looks, too. Would you think I'd ever been a beauty, eh?"

"I think you are very handsome now," replied Alayne, speaking with great distinctness. "Your nose is really——"

"What's she say?" cried Grandmother.

Ernest murmured: "She says your nose——"

"Ha, ha, my nose is still a beauty, eh? Yes, my dear, it's a good nose. A Court nose. None of your retroussé, surprised-looking noses. Nothing on God's earth could surprise my nose. None of your pinched, sniffing, cold-in-the-head noses, either. A good reliable nose. A Court nose." She rubbed it triumphantly.

"You've a nice-looking nose, yourself," she continued. "You and Eden make a pretty pair. But he's no Court. Nor a Whiteoak. He looks like his poor pretty flibbertigibbet mother."

Alayne, shocked, looked indignantly toward Eden, but he wore only an expression of tolerant boredom, and was putting a cigarette between his faintly smiling lips.

Meg saw Alayne's look and expostulated: "Grandmamma!"

"Renny's the only Court among 'em," pursued Mrs White-oak. "Wait till you see Renny. Where is he? I want Renny." She thumped the floor impatiently with her stick.

"He'll be here very soon, Granny," said Meg. "He rode over to Mr Probyn's to get a litter of pigs."

"Well, I call that very boorish of him. Boorish. Boorish. Did I say boorish? I mean Boarish. There's a pun, Ernest. You enjoy a pun. Boarish. Ha, ha!"

Ernest stroked his chin and smiled deprecatingly. Nicholas laughed jovially.

The old lady proceeded with a rakish air of enjoyment. "Renny prefers the grunting of a sow to sweet converse with a young bride——"

"Mamma," said Ernest, "shouldn't you like a peppermint?"

Her attention was instantly distracted. "Yes. I want a peppermint. Fetch me my bag."

Ernest brought a little old bead-embroidered bag. His mother began to fumble in it, and Boney, leaning from her shoulder, pecked at it and uttered cries of greed.

"A sweet!" he babbled. "A sweet—Boney wants a sweet—Pretty Alayne—Pretty Alayne—Boney wants a sweet!"

Grandmother cried in triumph: "He's said it! He's said it! I told you he could. Good Boney." She fumbled distractedly in the bag.

"May I help you?" Alayne asked, not without timidity.

The old lady pushed the bag into her hand. "Yes, quickly. I want a peppermint. A Scotch mint. Not a humbug."

"Boney wants a humbug!" screamed the parrot, rocking from side to side. "A humbug—Pretty Alayne—Kutni! Kutni! Shaitan ke khatla!"

Grandmother and the parrot leaned forward simultaneously for the sweet when it was found, she with protruding wrinkled lips, he with gaping beak. Alayne hesitated, fearing to offend either by favouring the other. While she hesitated Boney snatched it, and with a whir of wings flew to a far corner of the room. Grandmother, rigid as a statue, remained with protruding mouth till Alayne unearthed another sweet and popped it between her lips, then she sank back with a sigh of satisfaction, closed her eyes, and began to suck noisily.

Alayne longed to wipe her fingers, but she refrained. She

looked at the faces about her. They were regarding the scene with the utmost imperturbability, except Eden, who still wore his look of faintly smiling boredom. A cloud of smoke about his head seemed to emphasize his aloofness.

Meg moved closer to him and whispered: "I think I shall take Alayne upstairs. I've had new chintzes put in your room, and fresh curtains, and I've taken the small rug from Renny's room and covered the bare spot on the carpet with it. I think you'll be pleased when you see it, Eden. She's a perfect dear."

Brother and sister looked at Alayne, who was standing with the two uncles at a window. They had opened the shutters and were showing her the view of the oak woods that sloped gradually down to the ravine. A flock of sheep were quietly grazing, tended by an old sheepdog. Two late lambs were vying with each other in plaintive cries.

Meg came to Alayne and put an arm through hers. "I know you would like to go to your room," she said.

The two women ascended the stairway together. When they reached Eden's door, Meg impetuously seized Alayne's head between her plump hands and kissed her on the forehead. "I'm sure we can love each other," she explained, with childish enthusiasm, and Alayne returned the embrace, feeling that it would be easy to love this warm-blooded woman with a mouth like a Cupid's bow.

When Eden came up, he found Alayne arranging her toilet articles on the dressing-table and humming a happy little song. He closed the door after him and came to her.

"I'm glad you can sing," he said. "I had told you that my family were an unusual set of people, but when I saw you among them I began to fear they'd be too much for you—that you'd get panicky, perhaps, and want to run back to New York."

"Is that why you were so quiet downstairs? You had an odd expression. I could not quite make it out. I thought you looked bored."

"I was. I wanted to have you to myself." He took her in his arms.

Eden was at this moment inexplicably two men. He was the lover, strongly possessive and protective. As opposed to this, he was the captive, restless, nervous, hating the thought of the responsibility of introducing his wife to his family, of translating one to the other in terms of restraint and affection.

She said, stroking his hair, which was like a shining metallic casque over his head: "Your sister—Meg—was delightful to me. She seems quite near already. And she tells me she had this room done over for me—new chintz and curtains. I am so glad it looks out over the park and the sheep. I can scarcely believe I shall have sheep to watch from my window."

"Let me show you my things," cried Eden, gaily, and he led her about the room, pointing out his various belongings from schooldays on, with boyish naïveté. He showed her the ink-stained desk at which he had written many of his poems.

"And to think," she exclaimed, "that I was far away in New York, and you were here, at that desk, writing the poems that were to bring us together!" She stroked the desk as though it were a living thing, and said, "I shall always want to keep it. When we have our own house, may we take it there, Eden?"

"Of course." But he wished she would not talk about having their own house yet. To change the subject he asked, "Did you find Gran rather overpowering? I'm afraid I scarcely prepared you for her. But she can't be explained. She's got to be seen to be credible. The uncles are nice old boys."

"Do you think"—she spoke hesitatingly, yet with determination—"that it is good for her to spoil her so? She absolutely dominated the room."

He smiled down at her quizzically. "My dear, she will be a hundred on her next birthday. She was spoiled before we ever saw her. My grandfather attended to that. Quite possibly she was spoiled before ever he saw her. She probably came into the world spoiled by generations of tyrannical hot-tempered Courts. You will just have to make the best of her."

"But the way she spoke about your mother. I cannot remember the word—flibberty-something. It hurts me, dearest."

Eden ran his hand through his hair in sudden exasperation. "You must not be so sensitive, Alayne. Words like that are a mere caress compared to what Gran can bring out on occasion."

"But about your dear mother," she persisted.

"Aren't women always like that about their daughters-in-law? Wait till you have one of your own and see. Wait till you are ninety-nine. You may be no more sweet-tempered than Gran by then."

Eden laughed gaily, but with an air of dismissing the subject, and drew her to the chintz-covered window-seat. "Let's sit down here a bit and enjoy Meggie's new decoration. I think she's done us thundering well, don't you?"

Alayne leaned against him, breathing deeply of the tranquil air of Indian summer that came like a palpable essence through the open window. The earth, after all its passion of bearing, was relaxed in passive and slumbrous contentment. Its desires were fulfilled, its gushing fertility over. In profound languor it seemed to brood neither on the future nor on the past, but on its own infinite relation to the sun and to the stars. The sun had become personal. Red and rayless, he hung above the land as though listening to the slow beating of a great heart.

She became aware that Eden was observing someone in the grounds outside. She heard the sound of a horse's hoofs and, turning, saw a man leaning from his horse to fasten the gate behind him. Her beauty-loving eye was caught first by the satin shimmer of the beast's chestnut coat. Then she perceived that the rider was tall and thin, that he stooped in the saddle with an air of slouching accustomedness, and, as he passed beneath the window, that he had a red, sharp-featured face that looked rather foxlike beneath his peaked tweed cap.

The two clumber spaniels had rushed out to greet him and were bounding about the horse, their long silken ears flapping. Their barking irritated the horse, and, after a nip or two at them, he broke into a canter and disappeared with his rider behind a row of Scotch firs that hid the stables from the house.

"Renny," murmured Eden, "back from his porcine expedition."

"Yes, I thought it must be Renny, though he is not like what I expected him to be. Why did you not call to him?"

"He's rather a shy fellow. I thought it might embarrass both of you to exchange your first greetings from such different altitudes."

Alayne, listening to the muffled sound of hoofs, remarked: "He gives the impression of a strong personality."

"He has. And he's as wiry and strong as the devil. I've never known him to be ill for a day. He'll probably live to be as old as Gran."

'Gran—Gran,' thought Alayne. Every conversation in this family seemed to be punctuated by remarks about that dreadful old woman.

"And he owns all this," she commented. "It does not seem quite fair to all you others."

"It was left that way. He has to educate and provide for the younger family. The uncles had their share years ago. And of course Gran simply hoards hers. No one knows who will get it."

'Gran', again.

A gentle breeze played with a tendril of hair on her forehead. Eden brushed his lips against it. "Darling," he murmured, "do you think you can be happy here for a while?"

"Eden! I am gloriously happy."

"We shall write such wonderful things—together."

They heard steps on the gravelled path that led to the back of the house. Alayne, opening her eyes, heavy with a momentary sweet languor, saw Renny enter the kitchen, his dogs at his heels. A moment later a tap sounded on the door.

"Please," said Wake's voice, "will you come down to dinner?"

He could not restrain his curiosity about the bride and groom. It seemed very strange to find this young lady in Eden's room, but it was disappointing that there were no confetti and orange blossoms about.

Alayne put her arm around his shoulders as they descended the stairs, feeling more support from his little body in the ordeal of meeting the rest of the family than the presence of Eden afforded her. There were still Renny and the wife of young Piers.

Their feet made no sound on the thick carpet of the stairs. The noontide light falling through the coloured glass window gave the hall an almost churchlike solemnity, and the appearance at the far end of old Mrs Whiteoak emerging from her room, supported on either side by her sons, added a final processional touch. Through the open door of the dining-room

Alayne could see the figures of Renny, Piers, and a young girl advancing toward the table. Meg already stood at one end of it, surveying its great damask expanse as some high priestess might survey the sacrificial altar. On a huge platter already lay two rotund roasted fowls. Rags stood behind a drawn-back chair, awaiting Mrs Whiteoak. As the old lady saw Alayne and her escorts approaching the door of the dining-room, she made an obviously heroic effort to reach it first, shuffling her feet excitedly, and snuffing the good smell of the roast with the excitement of an old warhorse smelling blood.

"Steady, Mamma, steady," begged Ernest, steering her past a heavily carved hall chair.

"I want my dinner," she retorted, breathing heavily. "Chicken. I smell chicken. And cauliflower. I must have the pope's nose, and plenty of bread sauce."

Not until she was seated was Alayne introduced to Renny and Pheasant. He bowed gravely, and murmured some only half intelligible greeting. She might have heard it more clearly had her mind been less occupied with the scrutiny of him at sudden close quarters. She was observing his narrow, weatherbeaten face, the skin like red-brown leather merging in colour into the rust-red of his hair, his short thick eyelashes, his abstracted, yet fiery eyes. She observed too his handsome, hard-looking nose, which was far too much like his grandmother's.

Pheasant she saw as a flowerlike young girl, a fragile *Narcissus poeticus* in this robust, highly coloured garden of Jalna.

Alayne was seated at Renny Whiteoak's left, and at her left Eden, and next him Pheasant and Piers. Wakefield had been moved to the other side of the table, between his sister and Uncle Ernest. Alayne had only glimpses of him around the centrepiece of crimson and bronze dahlias, flowers that in their rigid and uncompromising beauty were well fitted to withstand the overpowering presence of the Whiteoaks. Whenever Alayne's eyes met the little boy's, he smiled. Whenever her eyes met Meg's, Meg's lips curved in their own peculiar smile. But when her eyes met those of Mrs Whiteoak, the old lady showed every tooth in a kind of ferocious friendliness, immediately returning to her dinner with renewed zeal, as though to make up for lost time.

The master of Jalna set about the business of carving with

the speed and precision of one handing out rations to an army. But there was nothing haphazard about his method of apportioning the fowl. With carving-knife poised, he shot a quick look at the particular member of the family he was about to serve, then, seeming to know either what they preferred or what was best for them, he slashed it off and handed the plate to Rags, who glided with it to Meg, who served the vegetables.

To one accustomed to a light luncheon, the sight of so much food at this hour was rather disconcerting. Alayne, looking at those enormous dinner plates mounded with chicken, bread sauce, mashed potatoes, cauliflower, and green peas, thought of little salad lunches in New York with mild regret. They seemed very far away. Even the table silver was enormous. The great knife and fork felt like implements in her hands. The salt cellars and pepper pots seemed weighted by memories of all the bygone meals they had savoured. The long-necked vinegar bottle reared its head like a tawny giraffe in the massive jungle of the table.

Renny was saying, in his vibrant voice that was without the music of Eden's, "I'm sorry I could not go to your wedding. I could not get away at that time."

"Yes," chimed in Meg, "Renny and I wanted so very much to go, but we could not arrange it. Finch had a touch of tonsillitis just then, and Wakefield's heart was not behaving very well, and of course there is Grandmamma."

Mrs Whiteoak broke in: "I wanted to go, but I'm too old to travel. I did all my travelling in my youth. I've been all over the world. But I sent my love. Did you get my love? I sent my love in Meggie's letter. Did you get it, eh?"

"Yes, indeed," said Alayne. "We were so very glad to get your message."

"You'd better be. I don't send my love to everyone, helter-skelter." She nodded her cap so vigorously that three green peas bounced from her fork and rolled across the table. Wakefield was convulsed with laughter. He said, "Bang!" as each pea fell, and shot one of his own after them. Renny looked down the table sharply at him, and he subsided.

Grandmother peered at her fork, shrewdly missing the peas.

"My peas are gone," she said. "I want more peas; more cauliflower and potatoes, too."

She was helped to more vegetables, and at once began to mould them with her fork into a solid mass.

"Mamma," objected Ernest, mildly, "must you do that?"

Sasha, who was perched on his shoulder, observing that his attention was directed away from his poised fork, stretched out one furry paw and drew it toward her own whiskered lips. Ernest rescued the morsel of chicken just in time. "Naughty, naughty," he said.

As though there had been no interruption, Meg continued: "It must have been such a pretty wedding. Eden wrote us all about it."

By this time Renny had attacked the second fowl with his carvers. Alayne had made no appreciable inroads on her dinner, but all the Whiteoaks were ready for more.

"Renny, did you get the pigs?" asked Piers, breaking in on conversation about the wedding with, Alayne thought, ostentatious brusqueness.

"Yes. You never saw a grander litter. Got the nine and the old sow for a hundred dollars. I offered ninety; Probyn wanted a hundred and ten. I met him half way." The master of Jalna began to talk of the price of pigs; and with gusto. Everyone talked of the price of pigs; and everyone agreed that Renny had paid too much.

Only the dishevelled carcase of the second fowl remained on the platter. Then it was removed, and a steaming blackberry pudding and a large plum tart made their appearance.

"You are eating almost nothing, dear Alayne," said Meg. "I do hope you will like the pudding."

Renny was looking at Alayne steadily from under his thick lashes, the immense pudding spoon expectantly poised.

"Thank you," she answered. "But I really could not. I will take a little of the pie."

"Please don't urge her, Meggie," said Eden. "She is used to luncheon at noon."

"Oh, but the pudding," sighed Meg. "It's such a favourite of ours."

"I like it," said the grandmother with a savage grin; "please give me some."

She got her pudding and Alayne her tart, but when Meg's turn arrived, she breathed: "No, thank you, Renny. Nothing for me." And Renny, knowing of the trays carried to her room, made no remark, but Eden explained in an undertone: "Meggie eats nothing—at least almost nothing at the table. You'll soon get used to that."

Meggie was pouring tea from a heavily chased silver pot. Even little Wake had some; but how Alayne longed for a cup of coffee, for the plum tart, though good, was very rich. It seemed to cry out for coffee.

Would she ever get used to them, Alayne wondered. Would they ever seem near to her—like relatives? As they rose from the table and moved in different directions, she felt a little oppressed, she did not quite know whether by the weight of the dinner or by the family, which was so unexpectedly foreign to her.

Old Mrs Whiteoak pushed her son Ernest from her, and, extending a heavily ringed hand to Alayne, commanded:

"You give me your arm, my dear, on this side. You may as well get into the ways of the family at once."

Alayne complied with a feeling of misgiving. She doubted whether she could efficiently take the place of Ernest. The old woman clutched her arm vigorously, dragging with what seemed unnecessary and almost intolerable weight. The two, with Nicholas towering above them, shuffled their way to Mrs Whiteoak's bedroom and established her there before the fire by painful degrees. Alayne, flushed with the exertion, straightened her back and stared with surprise at the unique magnificence of the painted leather bedstead, the inlaid dresser and tables, the Indian rugs and flamboyant hangings.

Mrs Whiteoak pulled at her skirt. "Sit down, my girl, sit down on this footstool. Ha—I'm out o' breath. Winded——" She panted alarmingly.

"Too much dinner, Mamma," said Nicholas, striking a match on the mantelpiece and lighting a cigarette. "If you will overeat, you will wheeze."

"You're a fine one to talk," retorted his mother, suddenly getting her breath. "Look at your own leg, and the way you eat and swill down spirits."

Boney, hearing the voice of his mistress raised in anger, roused himself from his after-dinner doze on the foot of the bed, and screamed: "Shaitan! Shaitan ka bata! Shaitan ka butcha! Kunjus!"

Mrs Whiteoak leaned over Alayne, where she now sat on

the footstool, and stroked her neck and shoulders with a hand not so much caressing as appraising. She raised her heavy red eyebrows to the lace edging of her cap and commented with an arch grin:

"A bonny body. Well covered, but not too plump. Slender, but not skinny. Meg's too plump. Pheasant's skinny. You're just right for a bride. Eh, my dear, but if I was a young man I'd like to sleep with you."

Alayne, painfully scarlet, turned her face away from Mrs Whiteoak toward the blaze of the fire. Nicholas was comfortingly expressionless.

"Another thing," chuckled Mrs Whiteoak, "I'm glad you've lots of brass. I am indeed."

"Easy now," cried Boney. "Easy does it!"

At that moment Grandmother fell into one of her sudden naps. Nicholas smiled down tolerantly at his sleeping parent.

"You mustn't mind what she says. Remember, she's ninety-nine, and she's never had her spirit broken by life—or by the approach of death. You're not offended, are you?"

"N-no. But she says I am—brazen. Why, it almost makes me laugh. I've always been considered rather retiring—even diffident."

Nicholas made subterranean sounds of mirth that had in them a measure of relief, but he offered no explanation. Instead, he took her hand and drew her to her feet.

"Come," he said, "and I'll show you my room. I expect you to visit me often there, and tell me all about New York, and I'll tell you about London in the old days. I'm a regular fossil now, but if you'll believe me, I was a gay fellow once."

He led the way to his room, heaving himself up the stairs by the hand railing. He installed her by the window, where she could enjoy the splendour of the autumn woods and where the light fell over her, bringing out the chestnut tints in her hair and the pearl-like pallor of her skin. It was so long since he had met a young woman of beauty and intelligence that the contact exhilarated him, made the blood quicken in his veins. Before he realized it, he was telling her incidents of his life of which he had not spoken for years. He even unearthed a photograph of his wife in a long-trained evening gown, and showed it to her. His face, massive and heavily lined, looked, as he recalled those bygone days, like a rock from which the

126

sea has long receded, but which bears on its seamed and battered surface irrevocable evidence of the fury of past storms.

He presented her, as a wedding present, with a silver bowl in which he had been accustomed to keep his pipes, first brightening it up with a silk handkerchief.

"You are to keep roses in it now, my dear," he said, and quite casually he put his fingers under her chin, raised her face, and kissed her. Alayne was touched by the gift, a little puzzled by a certain smiling masterfulness in the caress.

A moment later Ernest Whiteoak appeared at the door. Alayne must now inspect his retreat. No, Nicholas was not wanted, just Alayne.

"He intends to bore you with his melancholy annotating of Shakespeare. I warn you," exclaimed Nicholas.

"Nonsense," said Ernest. "I just don't want to feel utterly shelved. Don't be a beast, Nick. Alayne is as much interested in me as she is in you; aren't you, Alayne?"

"She's not interested in you at all," retorted Nicholas, "but she's enthralled by my sweet discourse; aren't you, Alayne?"

They seemed to take pleasure in the mere pronouncing of her name; using it on every occasion.

To Ernest's room she was led then, and because of his brother's gibe he at first would not speak of his hobby, contenting himself with showing her his water-colours, the climbing rose whose yellow flowers still spilled their fragrance across his window-sill, and the complaisant feline tricks of Sasha. But when Alayne showed an unmistakable interest in the annotation of Shakespeare and an unexpected knowledge of the text, his enthusiasm overflowed like Niagara in spring-time. Two hours flew by, in which they established the intimacy of congenial tastes. Ernest's thin cheeks were flushed; his blue eyes had become quite large and bright. He drummed the fingers of one hand incessantly on the table.

So Meg found them when she came to carry Alayne away for an inspection of the house and garden. Eden was off somewhere with Renny, Meg explained, and Alayne had a sudden feeling of anger toward this brother who so arrogantly swept Eden from her side, and who was so casually polite to her himself.

It was warm enough to have tea on the lawn, Meg announced, and when she and Alayne returned from their tour of the mass of overgrown lilacs, syringas, and guelder-rose trees that was called 'the shrubbery', and the sleepy kitchen garden where the rows of cabbages and celery and rank bed of parsley were flanked by scarlet sage and heavy-headed dahlias, they found that Rags had arranged the tea things on the wicker table. Some of the family were already disposed about it in deck chairs or on the grass, according to their years.

Alayne's eyes missed no detail of the scene before her: the emerald-green lawn lying in rich shadow, while the upper portions of the surrounding trees were bathed in lambent sunshine which so intensified their varying autumn hues that they had the unreal splendour of colours seen under water. Near the tea-table Grandmother dozed in her purple velvet tea-gown. Nicholas was stretched, half recumbent, playing idly with the ears of Nip, whose pointed muzzle was twitching expectantly toward the plates of cakes; Ernest stood courteously by his chair; on the grass sprawled bare-kneed Wake with a pair of rabbits, and bony long-limbed Finch, whom she now saw for the first time. Eden, Piers, and Renny did not appear, but before the second pot of tea was emptied young Pheasant slipped into the scene, carrying a branch of scarlet maple leaves, which she laid across the knees of Nicholas.

A mood of gentle hilarity possessed them all. As she ate cucumber sandwiches and cheese cakes, Alayne felt more in harmony with the life that was to be hers among this family. She was relieved by the absence of the three who did not join the party. With Eden away, she could more readily submerge herself in the family, explore the backwater of their relations with each other. In the case of Piers, she felt only relief from a presence that was at least covertly hostile. As for Renny, she could not make him out. She would need time for that. Just now his dominating personality, combined with his air of abstraction, puzzled and rather irritated her.

Eden had told her that Renny did not like his poetry, that he did not like any poetry. She thought of him as counting endless processions of foals, calves, lambs, and young pigs, always with an eye on the market. She would have been surprised, could she have followed him to his bedroom that night, to find how gentle he was toward little Wake, who was tossing about, unable to sleep after the excitement of the day. Renny rubbed his legs and patted his back as a mother might have done. In fact, in his love for his little brother he combined the devotion of both father and mother. Meg was all grown-up sister.

Wake, drowsy at last, curled up against Renny's chest and murmured: "I believe I could go to sleep more quickly if we'd pretend we were somebody else, Renny, please."

"Do you? All right. Who shall we be? Living people or people out of the books? You say."

Wake thought a minute, getting sleepier with each tick of Renny's watch beneath the pillow; then he breathed: "I think we'll be Eden and Alayne."

Renny stifled a laugh. "All right. Which am I?"

Wake considered again, deliciously drowsy, sniffing at the nice odour of tobacco, Windsor soap, and warm flesh that emanated from Renny.

"I think you'd better be Alayne," he whispered.

Renny, too, considered this transfiguration. It seemed difficult, but he said resignedly: "Very well. Fire away."

There was silence for a space; then Wakefield whispered, twisting a button of Renny's pyjamas: "You go first, Renny. Say something."

Renny spoke sweetly: "Do you love me, Eden?"

Wake chuckled, then answered, seriously: "Oh, heaps. I'll buy you anything you want. What would you like?"

"I'd like a limousine, and an electric toaster, and—a feather boa."

"I'll get them all first thing in the morning. Is there anything else you'd like, my girl?"

"M—yes. I'd like to go to sleep."

"Now, see here, you can't," objected the pseudo-groom. "Ladies don't pop straight off to sleep like that."

But apparently this lady did. The only response that Wakefield could elicit was a gentle but persistent snore.

For a moment Wake was deeply hurt, but the steady rise and fall of Renny's chest was soothing. He snuggled closer to him, and soon he too was fast asleep.

14

FINCH

THE COMING of Alayne had made a deep and rather overwhelming impression on young Finch. She was unlike any
one he had ever met; she filled his mind with curiosity and
tremulous admiration; he could not put the thought of her
aside on that first night. Her face was between him and the
dry pages over which he pored. He was driven to rise once in
the middle of wrestling with a problem in algebra and creep
half way down the stairs, just to watch her for a few minutes
through the open door of the drawing-room, where the family
sat at bridge and backgammon. Her presence in the house
seemed to him a most lovely and disturbing thing, like a
sudden strain of music.

He longed to touch her dress, which was of a material he
could not remember having seen before, and of a colour he
could not name. He longed to touch her hands, the flesh of
which looked so delicate and yet so firm. As he crouched over
his uncongenial tasks in the untidy bedroom, strange thoughts
and visions blurred the dog's-eared page before him. A chill
breeze coming in at the window carried the sounds and scents
of the late autumn countryside: the rustle of leaves that were
losing their fresh resilience and becoming sapless and crisp;
the scrape of two dead branches, one on the other, as though
the oak tree to which they belonged strove to play a dirge for the
dead summer; the fantastic tapping of a vine against the pane,
dancing a skeleton dance to the eerie music of the oak; the
smell of countless acres of land lying heavy and dank, stupefied
by the approach of barrenness.

What did it all mean? Why had he been put into this
strange confusion of faces, voices, bewildering sounds of night
and day? Who was there in the world to love him and care
for him as Alayne loved and cared for Eden? No one, he was
sure. He belonged to the lonely, fretful sounds which came in
at the window rather than to warm human arms and clinging
human lips.

His mind dwelt on the thought of kissing the mouth of

Eden's wife. He was submerged in an abyss of dreaming, his head sunk on his clenched hands. A second self, white and wraithlike, glided from his breast and floated before him in a pale greenish ether. He watched it with detached exultation in its freedom. It often freed itself from his body at times like these, sometimes disappearing almost instantly, at others floating near him as though beckoning him to follow. Now it moved face downward like one swimming, and another dim shape floated beside it. He pressed his knuckles into his eyes, drawing fiery colours from the lids, trying to see, yet afraid to see, the face of the other figure. But neither of the floating figures had a discernible face. One, he knew, belonged to him because it had emerged from his own body, but the other, fantastically floating, whence came it? Had it risen from the body of the girl in the drawing-room below, torn from her by the distraught questing of his own soul? What was she? What was he? Why were they here, all the warm-blooded hungry people, in this house called Jalna?

What was Jalna? The house, he knew very well, had a soul. He had heard it sighing, moving about in the night. He believed that from the churchyard sometimes the spirits of his father and his father's wives, his grandfather, and even the dead infant Whiteoaks, congregated under this roof to refresh themselves, to drink of the spirit of Jalna, that spirit which was one with the thin and fine rain that now began to fall. They pressed close to him, mocking him—the grandfather in hussar's uniform, the infants in long pale swaddling clothes.

His temples throbbed, his cheeks burned, his hands were clammy and very cold. He rose, letting his books fall to the floor, and went to the window. He knelt there and leaned across the sill, holding his hands out into the rain, in an attitude of prayer, his thin wrists projecting from the frayed edges of his sleeves.

By degrees peace descended on him, but he did not want to look back into the room. He thought of the nights when he had shared the bed with Piers. He had always been longing for the time when he might sleep in peace, free from his brother's tormenting. Now he felt that he would be glad of Piers' wholesome presence to protect him from his own thoughts.

Why did God not protect him? Finch believed desperately

and yet gloriously in God. During the Scripture study at school, while other boys were languishing in their seats, his eyes were riveted on the pages that seemed to burn with the grandeur and terror of God. The words of Jesus, the thought of that lonely figure of an inspired young man, were beautiful to him, but it was the Old Testament that shook his soul. When the time came for questions and examinations in Scripture, Finch was so incoherent, so afraid of disclosing his real feelings, that he usually stood at the foot of the class.

"A queer devil, Finch Whiteoak," was the verdict of his schoolfellows, "not in it with his brothers." For Renny's athletic prowess was still remembered; Eden's tennis, his running, his prizewinning in English literature and languages; Piers as captain of the Rugby team. Finch did nothing well. As he travelled back and forth to school in the train, slouching in a corner of the seat, his cap with the school badge pulled over his eyes, he wondered, with a bitterness unusual at his age, what he would do with his life. He seemed fitted for nothing in particular. No business or profession of which he had ever heard awakened any response of inclination in him. He would have liked to stay at home and work with Piers, but he quailed before the thought of a life subject to his brother's tyranny.

Sometimes he dreamed of standing in the pulpit of a vast, dim cathedral, such as he had seen only in pictures, and swaying a multitude by his burning eloquence. He, Finch Whiteoak, in a long white surplice and richly embroidered stole—a bishop—an archbishop, the very head of the Church, next to God Himself. But the dream always ended by the congregation's fleeing from the cathedral, a panic-stricken mob; for he had unwittingly let them have a glimpse of his own frightened, craven soul, howling like a poor hound before the terror of God.

'Wilt thou break a leaf driven to and fro? and wilt thou pursue the dry stubble?'

He was growing quieter now as he hung across the sill, letting the fine mist of rain moisten his hands and head. Below, on the lawn, a bright square of light fell from a window of the drawing-room. Someone came and stood at the window, throwing the shadow of a woman into the bright rectangle. Which of them? Meg, Pheasant, Alayne? Alayne, he felt sure.

There was something in the poise.... Again he thought of her lips, of kissing them. He drew in his hands, wet with rain, and pressed them against his eyeballs. 'For thou writest bitter things against me, and makest me to possess the iniquities of my youth.' Why could he remember these torturing texts when nothing else would stay in his head? 'Make me to hear joy and gladness; that the bones which thou hast broken may rejoice.' He pressed his fingers closer, and there began going through his brain things that a Scottish labourer on the farm had told. The man had formerly been a factory hand in Glasgow. Finch remembered an endless jigging song he had sung in a kind of whisper, that had ribald words. He remembered a scene of which he had been an undiscovered witness.

It had been in the pine grove, the last remnant of the primeval forest thereabout. This grove was as dark as a church at twilight, and was hidden in the heart of a great sunny wood of silver birches, maples, and oak, full of bird song and carpeted with glossy wintergreen leaves, which in springtime were starred with windflowers and star-of-Bethlehem and tiny purple orchids. There was little bird song in the pine grove, and no flowers, but the air in there was always charged with the whisperings and the pungent scent of pine needles. The deeply shaded aisles between the trees were slippery with them, and there what little sunshine filtered in was richly yellow.

It was a place of deep seclusion. Finch liked nothing so well as to spend a Saturday morning there by himself, and give himself up to the imaginings that were nearly always free and beautiful among the pines.

He had gone there early on that morning to escape Meg, who had wanted him to do some disagreeable task about the house. He had heard her calling and calling as he had run across the lawn and dived into the shrubbery. He had heard her call to Wake, asking if he had seen him. He had stretched his long legs across the meadow and the pasture, leaped the stream, and disappeared from the sight of all into the birch wood. His pulses had been throbbing and his heart leaping with joy in his freedom. Among the gay, light-foliaged trees he had passed, eager for the depth and solitude of the pines, which with an air of gentle secrecy they seemed to guard. But he had found that he was not alone. In the dimmest recess, where the grove dipped into a little hollow, he had discovered Renny standing with a woman in his arms. He was kissing her with a certain fierce punctiliousness on the mouth, on the neck, while she caressed him with slavish tenderness. While Finch stood staring, they had parted, she smoothing the strands of her long hair as she hurried away, Renny looking after her for a space, waving his hand to her when she looked back over her shoulder and then sauntering with bent head toward home.

Finch had never been able to find out who that woman was, though he had looked eagerly in the faces of all the women he had met for a long time. He had even gone to the pine grove and lain there motionless for hours, hoping, yet fearing, that she and Renny would return, his heart beating expectantly at every sound; but they had never come. He often gazed with envious curiosity into Renny's lean red face, wondering what thoughts were in his head. Piers had observed once to him that women always 'fell' for Renny. He could understand why, and he reflected forlornly that they would never fall for him.

He heard Wakefield calling to him plaintively from his bed: "Finch, Finch! Come here, please!"

He went down the hallway, passing Meg's door, which was covered by a heavy chenille curtain that gave an air of cosy seclusion to her sanctum.

"Well?" he asked, putting his head into Renny's room, where Wake sat up in bed, flushed and bright-eyed in the yellow lamplight.

"Oh, Finch, I can't sleep. My legs feel like cotton wool. When do you think Renny'll come?"

"How can I tell?" Finch answered gruffly. "You go to sleep. That's all nonsense about your legs. They're no more cotton wool than mine are."

"Oh, Finch, please come in. Don't leave me alone! Just come and talk for a little while. Just a minute, *please*."

Finch came in and sat down on the foot of the bed. He took a lone, somewhat dishevelled cigarette wrapped in silver paper from his pocket, unwrapped and lighted it.

Wake watched him, the strained look of loneliness passing from his little face.

"Give me a puff or two," he begged, "just a few puffs, please, Finch."

"No," growled Finch, "you'll make yourself sick. You're not allowed."

"Neither are you."

"Yes, I am."

"Well, not many."

"You don't call this many, do you?"

"I've seen you twice, no—three times before today."

Finch raised his voice. "You see a darned sight too much."

"Why, I'd never tell on you, Finch." Wake's tone was aggrieved. "I only want one little puff."

With a growl, Finch took the cigarette from his own lips and stuck it between his small brother's. "Now, then," he said, "make the best of your time."

Wake inhaled deeply, luxuriously, his eyes beaming at Finch through the smoke. He exhaled. Again, again. Then he returned the cigarette to its owner, still more battered and very moist. Finch looked at it doubtfully a moment, and then put it back philosophically into his own mouth. He felt happier. He was glad after all that Wake had called him. Poor little devil, he had his own troubles.

The darkness pouring into the room from the strange, dreamlike world outside had a liberating effect on the minds of the two boys. The tiny light of the candle, reflected in the mirror on the dresser, only faintly illuminated their faces, seeming to draw them upward from an immense void.

"Finch," asked Wake, "do you believe in God?"

A tremor ran through Finch's body at the question. He peered at the child, trying to make out whether he had divined any of his imaginings.

"I suppose I do," he answered. Then he asked, almost timidly, "Do you?"

"Yes. But what I'm wondering is—what kind of face has He? Has He a real face, Finch, or—just something flat and white where His face ought to be? That's what I think sometimes." Wake's voice had fallen to a whisper, and he pulled nervously at the coverlet.

Finch clutched his knees, staring at the candle that was now spluttering, almost out.

"His face is always changing," he said. "That's why you can't see it. Don't you ever try to see it, Wake; you're too young. You're not strong enough. You'd go nutty."

"Have you seen it, Finch?" This conversation was like a ghost story to Wake, frightening, yet exhilarating. "Do tell me what you've seen."

"Shut up," shouted Finch, springing up from the bed. "Go to sleep. I'm going." He lunged toward the door, but the candle had gone out and he had to grope his way.

"Finch, Finch, don't leave me," Wake was wailing.

But Finch did not stop till he reached his own bed, and threw himself face downward upon it. There he lay until he heard the others coming up the stairs.

15

MORE ABOUT FINCH

THE NEXT morning a mild, steady wind was blowing, which had appropriated to itself every pungent autumn scent in its journeying across wood and orchard. It blew in at the window and gently stirred the hair on Finch's forehead, and brought to his cheeks a childish pink. He did not hurry to get up, but stretched at ease a while, for it was a Saturday morning. His morbid fancies of the night before were gone, and his mind was now occupied in making a momentous decision. Should he put on some old clothes and steal out of the house with only something snatched from the kitchen for breakfast, thus avoiding a meeting with Eden's wife, for this morning he was shy of her; or should he dress with extra care and make a really good impression on her by appearing both well-turned-out and at ease?

Those who were early risers would have had their breakfast by now and be about the business of the day, but Eden never showed up till nine, and Finch supposed that a New York girl would naturally keep late hours. He wanted very much to make a good impression on Alayne.

He got up at last, and after carefully washing his face and hands and scrubbing his neck at the washstand, he took from its hanger his new dark-blue flannel suit. When it was on and his best blue-and-white striped shirt, he was faced by the problem of a tie. He had a really handsome one of blue and grey which Meggie had given him on his last birthday, but he was nervous about wearing it. Meg would be sure to get on her hind feet if she caught him sporting it on a mere Saturday. Even wearing the suit was risky. He thought he had better slip upstairs after breakfast and change into an old one. Perhaps he had better change now. He was a fool to try to please Alayne's fastidious New York eye. He hesitated, admiring his reflection in the looking-glass. He longingly fingered the tie. The thought of going to Piers' room and borrowing one of his ties entered his mind, but he put it aside. Now that Piers was married, young Pheasant was always about.

Damn it all! The tie was his, and he would wear it if he wanted to.

He tied it carefully. He cleaned and polished his nails on a wornout buffer Meggie had thrown away. Meticulously he parted and brushed his rather lank fair hair, plastered it down with a little pomade which he dug out of an empty jar Eden had thrown aside.

A final survey of himself in the glass brought a grin, half pleased, half sheepish, to his face. He sneaked past the closed door of his sister's room and slowly descended the stairs.

It was as he had hoped. Eden and Alayne were the only occupants of the dining-room. They sat close together at one side of the table. His place was on Alayne's left. With a muttered "Good morning" he dragged forth his chair and subsided into it, crimson with shyness.

After one annoyed glance at the intruder, Eden vouch-safed him no attention whatever, speaking to Alayne in so low a tone that Finch, with ears strained to catch these gentle morning murmurings of young husband to young wife, could make out no word. He devoted himself to his porridge, humbly taking what pleasure he could draw from the proximity of Alayne. A fresh sweetness seemed to emanate from her. Out of the corner of his eye he watched the movements of her hands. He tried very hard not to make a noise over his porridge and milk, but every mouthful descended his throat with a gurgling sound. His very ears burned with embarrassment.

Alayne thought she had never before seen anyone eat such an immense plate of cereal. She hated cereals. She had said to Eden almost pettishly: "I do not want any cereal, thank you, Eden." And he had almost forced her to take it.

"Porridge is good for you," he had said, heavily sugaring his own.

He did not seem to notice that this breakfast was not at all the sort to which she was used. There was no fruit. Her soul cried out for coffee, and there was the same great pot of tea, this time set before her to pour. Frizzled fat bacon, so much buttered toast, and bitter orange marmalade did not tempt her. Eden partook of everything with hilarity, crunching the toast crusts in his strong white teeth, trying brazenly to put his arm about her waist before the inquisitive eyes of the boy. Something fastidious in her was not pleased with him this morning. Suddenly she found herself wondering whether if she had met him first in his own home she would so quickly have fallen in love. But one look into his mocking yet tender eyes, one glance at his sensitive, full-lipped mouth, reassured her. She would, oh yes, she would!

She addressed a sentence now and again to Finch, but it seemed hopeless to draw him into the conversation. He so plainly suffered when she attempted it that she gave up trying.

As they got up from the table Eden, who was already cherishing a cigarette between his lips, turned to his brother as if struck with an idea.

"Look here, Finch. I wish you'd show Alayne the pine grove. It's wonderful on a morning like this. It's deep and dark as a well in there, Alayne, and all around it grow brambles with the biggest, juiciest berries. Finch will get you some, and he'll likely be able to show you a partridge and her young. I've got something in my head that I want to get out, and I must have solitude. You'll take care of her, won't you, Finch?"

In spite of the lightness of his tone, Alayne discovered the fire of creative desire in it. Her gaze eagerly explored his face. Their eyes met in happy understanding.

"Do go off by yourself and write," she agreed. "I shall be quite content to wander about by myself if Finch has other plans."

She almost hoped he had. The thought of a tête-à-tête with this embarrassed hobbledehoy was not alluring. He drooped over his chair, his bony hands resting on the back, and stared at the disarranged table.

"Well," said Eden, sharply, "what are your plans, brother Finch?"

Finch grinned sheepishly. "I'd like to take her. Yes, thank

you," he replied, gripping the back of the chair till his knuckles turned white.

"Good boy," said Eden. He ran upstairs to get a sweater coat for Alayne, and she and Finch waited his return in absolute silence. Her mind was absorbed by the thought that Eden was going to write. He had said one day that he had an idea for a novel. Little tremors of excitement ran through her as she pictured him beginning it that very morning. She stood in the bow-window looking out at the dark hemlocks, from which issued a continuous chirping as a flock of swallows gathered for their flight south.

Rags was beginning to clear the table. His cynical light eyes took in every detail of Finch's attire. They said to the boy, as plainly as words: 'Ho, ho, my young feller! You've decked yerself all up for the occasion, 'aven't yer? You think you've made an impression on the lidy, don't yer? But if you could only see yerself! *And* just you wait till the family catches you in your Sunday clothes. There won't be nothink doing, ow naow!'

Finch regarded him uncomfortably. Was it possible that these thoughts were in Rags' head, or did he just imagine it? Rags had such a secret sneering way with him.

Eden followed them to the porch. They met Meg in the hall, and the two women kissed, but it was dim there and Finch, clearing his throat, laid one hand on the birthday necktie and concealed it.

It was a day of days. As golden, as mature, as voluptuous as a Roman matron fresh from the bath, the October morning swept with indolent dignity across the land. Alayne said something like this to the boy as they followed a path over the meadows, and, though he made no reply, he smiled in a way that lighted up his plain face with such sudden sweetness that Alayne's heart warmed to him. She talked without waiting for him to reply, till by degrees his shyness melted, and she found herself listening to him. He was telling her how this path that led through the birch wood was an old Indian trail, and how it led to the river six miles away where the traders and Indians had long ago been wont to meet to barter skins of fox and mink for ammunition and blankets. He was telling her of the old fiddler, 'Fiddler Jock', who had had his hut in this wood before the Whiteoaks had bought Jalna.

"My Grandad let him stay on. He used to play his fiddle at

weddings and parties of all sorts. But one night some people gave him such a lot of drink before he started for his hut that he got dazed, and it was a bitterly cold night, and he could not find his way home through the snow. When he got as far as Grandad's barnyard he gave up and he crawled into a straw stack and was frozen to death. Gran found him two days after when she was out for a walk. He was absolutely rigid, his frozen eyes staring out of his frozen face. Gran was a young woman then, but she's never forgotten it. I've often heard her tell of finding him. She had Uncle Nick with her. He was only a little chap, but he's never forgotten the way the old fellow had his fiddle gripped, just as though he'd been playing when he died."

Alayne looked curiously at the boy. His eyes had a hallucinated expression. He was evidently seeing in all its strangeness the scene he had just described.

They had now entered the pine grove. A shadow had fallen over the brightness of the morning like the wing of a great bird. In here there was a cathedral hush, broken only by the distant calling of crows. They sat down on a fallen tree, on the trunk of which grew patches of moss of a peculiarly vivid green, a miniature forest in itself.

"I don't believe I'd mind," said Finch, "going about with a fiddle and playing tunes at the weddings of country people. It seems to me I'd like it." Then he added, with a shade of bitterness in his tone, "I guess I've just the right amount of brains for that."

"I do not see why you should speak of yourself in that way," exclaimed Alayne. "You have a very interesting face." She made the statement with conviction, though she had just discovered the fact.

Finch made a sardonic grimace that was oddly reminiscent of Uncle Nicholas. "I dare say it's interesting, and I shouldn't be surprised if old fiddler Jock's was interesting, especially when it was frozen stiff."

She felt almost repelled by the boy's expression, but her interest in him was steadily growing.

"Perhaps you are musical? Have you ever had lessons?"

"No. They'd think it a waste of money. And I haven't the time for practising. It takes all my time to keep from the foot of the form."

He seemed determined to present himself in an unprepossessing light to her. And this after all the anxious care over his toilet. Perhaps the truth was that, having seen a gleam of sympathy in her eyes, he was hungry for more of it. But it was difficult to account for the reactions of Finch Whiteoak.

Alayne saw in him a boy treated with clumsy stupidity by his family. She saw herself fiercely taking up cudgels for him. She was determined that he should have music lessons if her influence could bring them about. She drew him on to talk, and he lay on the ground, sifting the pine needles through his fingers and giving his confidence more freely than he had ever given it before. But even while he talked with boyish eagerness, his mind more than once escaped its leash and ran panting after strange visions. Himself, alone with her in this dark mysterious place, embracing her with ecstasy, not with the careless passion of Renny's caressing of the strange woman. After one of these excursions of the mind he would draw himself up sharply and try to look into her eyes with the same expression of friendly candour which she gave him.

As they were returning to the house and Alayne's thoughts were flying back to Eden, they came upon a group in the orchard consisting of Piers and several farm labourers, who, under his supervision, were preparing a number of barrels of apples for shipment. Piers, with a piece of chalk in his sunburned hand, was going about marking the barrels with the number of their grade. He pretended not to notice the approach of his brother and Alayne, but when he could no longer ignore them he muttered a sulky "Good morning", and turned to one of the labourers with some directions about carting the apples to the station.

Finch led Alayne from barrel to barrel with a self-consciously possessive air, knowing that the farm hands were regarding them with furtive curiosity. He explained the system of grading to her, bringing for comparison apples from the different barrels. He asked her to test the flavour of the most perfect specimen he could find, glossy, red, and flawless as a drop of dew.

"Mind that you replace that apple, Finch," said Piers curtly in passing. "You should know better than to disturb apples after they are packed. They'll be absolutely rattling about by the time they reach Montreal." He took a hammer from one of the men and began with deafening blows to 'head in' a barrel.

Finch noticed Alayne's discomposure, and his own colour rose angrily as he did as he was bid. When they had left the orchard Alayne asked: "Do you think Piers dislikes me?"

"No. It's just his way. He's got a beastly way with him. I don't suppose he dislikes me, but sometimes——" He could not finish what he had been going to say. One couldn't tell Alayne the things Piers did.

Alayne continued reflectively:

"And his wife—I just noticed her a moment ago disappearing into the shrubbery when she saw us approach. I am afraid she does not approve of me either."

"Look here," cried Finch, "Pheasant's shy. She doesn't know what to say to you." But in his heart he believed that both Piers and Pheasant were jealous of Alayne.

He parted with her at the front door and went himself to the side entrance, for he was afraid of meeting his sister. He entered a little washroom next the kitchen—which served as a sort of downstairs lavatory for the brothers—to wash his hands. The instant he opened the door he discovered Piers already there, but it was not possible to retreat, for Piers had seen him. He was washing before going to the station with the fruit. His healthy face, still red from the towel, took on an unpleasant sneer.

"Well," he observed, "of all the asses I've ever known! The suit—the tie—the hair—good Lord! Has she taken you on as her dancing partner? Or what is your particular capacity? Pheasant and I want to know."

"Let me alone," growled Finch, moving toward the basin and twitching up his cuffs. "Somebody has to be decent to the girl, I guess."

Piers, drying his hands, moved close to him, surveying him jocularly.

"The tie, the hair, 'the skin you love to touch'," he chuckled. "You are all the toilet advertisements rolled into one, aren't you?"

Finch, breathing heavily, went on lathering his hands.

Piers assumed the peculiarly irritating smile characteristic of Mr Wragge.

"I do 'ope," he said, unctuously, "that the young lidy appreciates all your hefforts to be doggish, sir."

Goaded beyond bearing, Finch wheeled, and slapped a handful of soapy water full in his brother's face. A moment later Renny, entering the washroom, found young Finch sprawling on the floor, the birthday tie ruined by a trickle of blood from his nose.

"What's this?" demanded the eldest Whiteoak, sternly looking first at the recumbent figure, then at the erect, threatening one.

"He's too damned fresh," returned Piers. "I was chaffing him about dressing up as though he were going to a party when he was escorting Eden's wife to the bush, and he threw some dirty water in my face, so I knocked him down."

Renny took in the boy's costume with a grin, then he gently prodded him with his boot.

"Get up," he ordered, "and change out of that suit before it's mussed up."

When Finch had gone, he turned to Piers and asked: "Where is Eden this morning?"

"Oh, he's writing in the summerhouse, with a few sprays of lilies of the valley on the table beside him. Pheasant peeked in and saw him. I expect it's another masterpiece."

Renny snorted, and the two went out together.

16

'IN THE PLACE WHERE THE TREE FALLETH'

ALAYNE FOUND Eden in the summerhouse, a vine-smothered, spiderish retreat, with a very literary-looking pipe in his mouth, his arms folded across his chest, and a thoughtful frown indenting his brow.

"May I come in?" she breathed, fearing to disturb him, yet unable to endure the separation any longer.

He smiled an assent, gripping the pipe between his teeth.

"Have you begun the—you know what?"

"I do *not* know what."

"The n-o-v-e-l," she spelled.

He shook his head. "No; but I've written a corking thing. Come in and hear."

"A poem! I am so glad you are really beginning to write

again. It is the first, you know, since we have been married, and I was beginning to be afraid that instead of being an inspiration——"

"Well, listen to this and tell me whether I'm the better or worse for being married."

"Before you begin, Eden, I should just like to remark the way the sunlight coming in through those vines dapples your hair and cheek with gold."

"Yes, darling, and if you had been here all morning you might have remarked how the insect life took to me. They let themselves down from every corner and held a sort of county fair on me, judging spider stallions, fat ladybugs' race, and earwig baby show. In each case the first, second, third, and consolation prize was a bite of me."

"You poor lamb," said Alayne, settling herself on the bench beside him, her head on his shoulder. "How you suffer for your art!" She searched his face for the mark of a bite, and, really finding one on his temple, she kissed it tenderly.

"Now for the poem," he exclaimed. He read it, and it gained not a little from his mellow voice and expressive, mobile face. Alayne was somewhat disconcerted to find that she had no longer the power to regard his writing judicially. She now saw it coloured by the atmosphere of Jalna, tempered by the contacts of their life together. She asked him to read it again, and this time she closed her eyes that she might not see him, but every line of his face and form was before her still, as though her gaze were fixed on him.

"It is splendid," she said, and she took it from him and read it to herself. She was convinced that it was splendid, but her conviction did not have the same austere clarity that it had carried when she was in New York and he an unknown young poet in Canada.

After that Eden spent each morning in the summerhouse, not seeming to mind the increasing dampness and chill as the autumn drew on. The Whiteoaks seemed to be able to endure an unconscionable amount of either heat or cold. Alayne began to be accustomed to these extremes of temperature, to an evening spent before the blistering heat of the drawing-room fire, and a retiring to a bedroom so chill that her fingers grew numb before she was undressed.

From the summerhouse issued a stream of graceful, carelessly buoyant lyrics like young birds. Indeed, Piers with brutal jocularity remarked to Renny that Eden was like a sparrow, hatching out an egg a day in his lousy nest under the vines.

It became the custom for Eden, Alayne, Ernest, and Nicholas to gather in the latter's room every afternoon to hear what Eden had composed that morning. The four became delightfully intimate in this way, and they frequently—Nicholas making his leg an excuse for this—had Rags bring their tea there. As Grandmother could not climb the stairs, Alayne felt joyously certain of no intrusions from her. The girl found almost past endurance the old lady's way of breaking her cake into her tea and eating it from a spoon with the most aggravating snortlings and gurglings. It was pleasant to pour the tea in Nicholas' room for the three men from an old blue Coalport teapot that wore a heathenish woolly 'cosy'; and after tea Nicholas would limp to the piano and play from Mendelssohn, Mozart, or Liszt.

Alayne never forgot those afternoons, the late sunshine touching with a mellow glow the massive head and bent shoulders of Nicholas at the piano, Ernest shadowy in a dim corner with Sasha, Eden beside her, strong in his shapely youth. She grew to know the two elderly men as she knew no other member of Eden's family except poor young Finch. They seemed close to her; she grew to love them.

Piers, when Meg told him of these meetings, was disgusted. They made him sick with their poetry and music. He pictured his two old uncles gloating imaginatively over Alayne's sleek young womanhood. Eden, he thought, was a good-for-nothing idler—a sponger. Meggie herself did not want to join the quartette in Uncle Nick's room. It was not the sort of thing she cared about. But she did rather resent the air of intimacy which was apparent between the uncles and Alayne, an intimacy which she had not achieved with the girl. Not that she had made any great effort to do so. Persistent effort, either mental or physical, was distasteful to Meg, yet she could, when occasion demanded, get her own way by merely exerting her power of passive stubbornness. But passive stubbornness will not win a friend, and as a matter of fact Meg did not greatly desire the love of Alayne. She rather liked her, though she found her hard to talk to—'terribly different'—and she told her grandmother that Alayne was a 'typical American girl.' "I won't have it," Grandmother had growled, getting very red, and Meg had hastened to add, "But she's very agreeable, Gran, and what a blessing it is that she has money!"

To be sure, there was no sign of excess of wealth. Alayne dressed charmingly, but with extreme simplicity. She had shown no disposition to shower gifts upon the family, yet the family, with the exception of Renny and Piers, were convinced that she was a young woman of fortune. Piers did not believe it, simply because he did not want to believe it; Renny had cornered Eden soon after his return and had wrested from him the unromantic fact that he had married a girl of the slenderest means, and had come home for a visit while he 'looked about him'. And so strong was the patriarchal instinct in the eldest Whiteoak that Eden and Alayne might have lived on at Jalna for the rest of their lives without his doing more than order Eden to help Piers on the estate.

On one occasion Eden did spend a morning in the orchard grading apples, but Piers, examining the last of the consignment and finding the grading erratic, to say the least of it, had leaped in a fury into his Ford and rushed to the station, where he had spent the rest of the day in a railway car, wrenching the tops from barrels and regrading them. There had been a family row after this, with Renny and Pheasant on the side of Piers, and the rest of the family banded to protect Eden. They had the grace to wait till Alayne went to bed before beginning it. She had gone to her room early that night, feeling something electric in the air, and no sooner had her door closed than the storm burst forth below.

She had been brought up in an atmosphere of a home peaceful as a nest of doves, and this sudden transplanting into the noisy raillery and hawklike dissensions of the Whiteoaks bewildered her. Up in her room she quaked at the thought of her oddness among these people. When Eden came up an hour later he seemed exhilarated rather than depressed by the squall. He sat on the side of the bed, smoking endless cigarettes, and told her what this one had said and how he had squelched that one, and how Gran had thrown her velvet bag in Renny's face; and Alayne listened, languid in the reassurance of his love. He even sat down at his desk before he came to bed and wrote a wild and joyous poem about a gypsy girl, and came

146

back to the bed and read it loudly and splendidly, and Nip, in Uncle Nick's room across the hall, started up a terrific yapping.

One of Eden's cigarette stubs had burned a hole in the quilt.

Lying awake long afterward, while Eden slept peacefully beside her, Alayne wondered if she could be the same girl who had laboured over her father's book and paid decorous little visits to her aunts up the Hudson. She wondered, with a feeling of apprehension, when Eden was going to bestir himself to get a position. After the affair of the apples he spent more and more time in the summerhouse, for he had begun another long narrative poem. Proof sheets of his new book had arrived from New York, and they demanded their share of his time.

Alayne, who was supposed to be the inspiration of this fresh wellspring of poetry, found that during the fierce hours of composition the most helpful thing she could do for the young poet was to keep as far away from him as possible. She explored every field and grove of Jalna, followed the stream in all its turnings, and pressed her way through thicket and bramble to the deepest part of the ravine. She came to love the great unwieldy place, of which the only part kept in order was the farm run by Piers. Sometimes Finch or Wakefield accompanied her, but more often she was alone.

On one of the last days of autumn she came upon Pheasant, sitting with a book in the orchard. It was one of those days so still that the very moving of the sphere seemed audible. The sun was a faint blur of red in the hazy heaven, and in the north the smoke of a distant forest fire made a sullen gesture. This conflagration far away seemed to be consuming the very corpse of summer, which, being dead indeed, felt no pain in the final effacement.

Pheasant was sitting with her back against the bole of a gnarled old apple tree, the apples of which had not been gathered but were lying scattered on the grass about her. The ciderish smell of their decay was more noticeable here than the acrid smell of smoke. The young girl had thrown down her book and, with head tilted back and eyes closed, was more than half asleep. Alayne stood beside her, looking down at her, but Pheasant did not stir, exposing her face to the gaze of the almost stranger with the wistful unconcern of those who slumber. It seemed to Alayne that she had never before really seen this child—for she was little more than a child. With her cropped brown head, softly parted lips, and childish hands with their limply upturned palms, she was a different being from the secretive, pale girl always on her guard whom Alayne met at table and in the drawing-room at cards. Then she seemed quite able to take care of herself, even faintly hostile in her attitude. Now, in this relaxed and passive pose, she seemed to ask for compassion and tenderness.

As Alayne was about to turn away, Pheasant opened her eyes, and, finding Alayne's eyes looking down into them with an expression of friendliness, she smiled as though she could not help herself.

"Hullo," she said, with boyish brevity. "You caught me asleep."

"I hope I did not waken you."

"Oh, I was only cat-napping. This air makes you drowsy."

"May I sit down beside you?" Alayne asked, with a sudden desire to get better acquainted with the young girl.

"Of course." Her tone was indifferent, but not unfriendly. She picked up her hat, which was half full of mushrooms, and displayed them. "I was gathering these," she said, "for Piers' breakfast. He can eat this many all himself."

"But aren't you afraid you will pick poison ones? I should be."

Pheasant smiled scornfully. "I've been gathering mushrooms all my life. These are all alike. The orchard kind. Except this dear little pink one. I shall give it to Wake. It's got a funny smoky taste and he likes it." She twirled the pink mushroom in her slim brown fingers. "In the pine woods I get lots of morels. Piers likes them too, only not so well. Piers thinks it's wonderful the way I can always find them. He has them for breakfast almost every morning."

Everything was in terms of Piers. Alayne asked:

"What is your book? Not so interesting as the mushrooms?"

"It's very good. It belongs to Piers. One of Jules Verne's."

Alayne had hoped that they might talk about the book, but she had read nothing of Jules Verne. She asked instead:

"Have you known Piers many years? I suppose you have, for you were neighbours, weren't you?"

Pheasant stiffened. She did not answer for a moment, but

148

bent forward plucking at the coarse orchard grass. Then she said in a low voice, "I suppose Eden has told you about me."

"Nothing except that you were a neighbour's daughter."

"Come, now. Don't hedge. The others did, then. Meg—Gran—Uncle Nick?"

"No one," answered Alayne firmly, "has told me anything about you."

"Humph. They're a funny lot. I made sure they'd tell you first thing." She mused a moment, biting a blade of grass, and then added: "I suppose they didn't want to tell you anything so shocking. You're so frightfully proper, and all that."

"Am I?" returned Alayne, rather nettled.

"Well, aren't you?"

"I had not thought about it."

"It was one of the first things I noticed about you."

"I hope it hasn't turned you against me," said Alayne lightly. Pheasant reflected, and said she did not think so.

"Then what is it?" persisted Alayne, her tone still light, but her face becoming very serious.

Pheasant picked up one of the misshapen apples of the old tree and balanced it on her palm.

"Oh, you're different; that's the principal thing. You don't seem to know anything about real life."

Alayne could have laughed aloud at the answer, that this ignorant little country girl should doubt her experience of life. Yet it was true enough that she did not know life as they in this backwater knew it, where no outside contacts modified the pungent vitality of their relations with each other.

She sat a moment in thought and then she said, gently:

"You are mistaken if you think that I should be easily upset by anything you would care to tell me. Not that I want to urge your confidence."

"Oh, it's not a matter of confidence," exclaimed Pheasant. "Everybody in the world knows it but you, and, of course, you'll hear it sooner or later, so I may as well tell you."

She laid the apple on the grass, and, clasping her ankles in her brown hands, sat upright, with the air of a precocious child, and announced: "I'm illegitimate—what Gran in her old-fashioned way calls a bastard. There you are." A bright colour dyed her cheeks, but she flung out the words with pathetic bravado.

"I am sorry," murmured Alayne, "but you do not suppose that that will affect my feelings for you, do you?"

"It does most people's." The answer came in a low husky voice, and she went on hurriedly: "My father was the only child of an English colonel. His parents doted on him. He was the delight of their old age. My mother was a common country girl and she left me on their doorstep with a note, exactly the way they do in books. They took me in and kept me, but it broke the old people's hearts. They died not long after. My father——"

"Did you live with him?" Alayne tried to make it easier for her by a tone of unconcern, but her eyes were filled with tears of pity for the child who in such quaint phraseology—'the delight of their old age,' indeed—told of the tragedy of her birth.

"Yes, till I was married. He just endured me. But I expect the sight of me was a constant reminder—of what he'd lost, I mean."

"Lost?"

"Yes, Meg Whiteoak. He'd been engaged to her, and she broke it off when I appeared on the scene. That's why she has that glassy stare for me. All the Whiteoaks were against the marriage, of course. It was adding insult to injury, you see."

"Oh, my dear."

The significance of looks and chance phrases that had puzzled her became apparent. She was pierced by a vivid pain at the thought of all the unmerited suffering of Pheasant.

"You have had rather a hard time, but surely that is all over. Meg cannot go on blaming you for what is not your fault, and I think the others are fond of you."

"Oh, I don't know."

"I should be if you would let me." Her hand moved across the grass to Pheasant's. Their fingers intertwined.

"All right. But I warn you, I'm not a bit proper."

"Perhaps I am not so proper as you think." Their fingers were still warmly clutched. "By the way, why doesn't Piers like me? I feel that it will not be altogether simple to be your friend when he is so—well, distant."

"He is jealous of you—for my sake, I think. I just think that, mind you; he's never said so. But I think he finds it pretty beastly that you should be thought so much of and me so little, and that you should be made so welcome and me so unwelcome, when after all we're just two girls, except that you're rich and I'm poor, and you're legitimate and I'm up against the bar sinister, and Piers has always taken such an interest in the place and worked on it, and Eden only cares for poetry and having his own way."

Alayne was scarlet. Out of the tangle of words one phrase menaced her. She said, with a little gasp: "Whatever made you think I was rich? My dear child, I am poor—poor. My father was a college professor. You know they are poor enough, in all conscience."

"You may be what you call poor, but you're rich to us," answered Pheasant, sulkily.

"Now listen," continued Alayne, sternly. "My father left me five thousand dollars insurance, and a bungalow which I sold for fourteen thousand, which makes nineteen thousand dollars. That is absolutely all. So you see how rich I am."

"It sounds a lot," said Pheasant, stolidly, and their hands parted and they both industriously plucked at the grass.

The significance of other allusions was now made plain to Alayne. She frowned as she asked: "What put such an idea into your head, Pheasant? Surely the rest of the family are not suffering from that hallucination."

"We all thought you were frightfully well off. I don't know exactly how it came about—someone said—Gran said—no, Meg said it was——" She stopped short, suddenly pulled up by a tardy caution.

"Who said what?" insisted Alayne.

"I think it was Uncle Nick who said——"

"Said what?"

"That it was a good thing that Eden—oh, bother, I can't remember what he said. What does it matter, anyhow?"

Alayne had to subdue a feeling of helpless anger before she answered, quietly: "It does not matter. But I want you not to have the notion that I am rich. It is ridiculous. It puts me in a false position. You knew that I worked for my living before I married Eden. Why did you think I did that?"

"We knew it was publishing books. It didn't seem like work."

"My child, I was not publishing. I only read manuscripts for the publisher. Do you see the difference?"

Pheasant stared at her uncomprehendingly, and Alayne, moved by a sudden impulse, put her arm about her and kissed her. "How silly of me to mind! May we be friends, then?"

Pheasant's body relaxed against her with the abandon of a child's. "It's lovely of you," she breathed, "not to mind about my——"

Alayne stopped her words with a kiss. "As though that were possible! And I hope Piers will feel less unfriendly to me when he knows everything."

Pheasant was watching over Alayne's shoulder two figures that were approaching along the orchard path.

"It's Renny," she said, "and Maurice. I wonder what they're up to. Renny's got an axe."

The men were talking and laughing rather loudly over some joke, and did not see the girls at once. Alayne sat up and stroked her hair.

"I'll bet it is some war joke," whispered Pheasant. "They're always at it when they're together." Pheasant took up an apple and rolled it in their direction. "Hullo, Maurice, why such hilarity?"

The two came up, Maurice removing his tweed cap. Renny, already bareheaded, nodded, the reminiscent grin fading from his face.

"Alayne," he said, "this is Maurice Vaughan, our nearest neighbour."

They shook hands, and Alayne, remembering having heard a reference to the fact that Vaughan drank a good deal, thought he showed it in his heavy eyes and relaxed mouth. He gave Pheasant a grudging smile, and then turned to Renny.

"Is this the tree?" he asked.

"Yes," returned Renny, surveying it critically.

"What are you going to do?" asked Alayne.

"Cut it down. It's very old, and it's rotting. It must make room for a new one."

Alayne was filled with dismay. To her the old apple tree was beautiful, standing strong, and yet twisted with age in the golden October sunshine. From it seemed to emanate the spirit of all the seasons the tree had known, with their scents of fragile apple blossoms and April rains, of moist orchard earth and mellowing fruit. A lifetime of experience was recorded on its rugged trunk, the bark of which enfolded it in mossy layers, where a myriad tiny insects had their being.

She asked, trying not to look too upset, for she was never certain when the Whiteoaks would be amused at what they thought soft-heartedness or affection, "Must it come down? I was just thinking what a grand old tree it is. And it seems to have borne a good many apples."

"It's diseased," returned Renny. "Look at the shape of the apples. This orchard needs going over rather badly."

"But this is only one tree and it is such a beautiful shape."

"You must go over to the old orchard. You will find dozens like this there." He pulled off his coat and began to roll up the sleeves from his lean, muscular arms. Alayne fancied that an added energy was given to his movements by her opposition.

She said nothing more, but with a growing feeling of antagonism watched him pick up the axe and place the first blow against the stalwart trunk. She imagined the consternation among the insect life on the tree at that first shuddering shock, comparable to an earthquake on our own sphere. The tree itself stood with a detached air, only the slightest quiver stirring its glossy leaves. Another and another blow fell, and a wedge-shaped chip, fresh with sap, sprang out on to the grass. Renny swung the axe with ease, it and his arms moving in rhythmic accord. Another chip fell, and another, and the tree sent up a groaning sound, as the blows at last penetrated its vitals.

"Oh, oh! Let me get my things," cried Pheasant, and would have darted forward to rescue her hat and mushrooms had not Vaughan caught her by the wrist and jerked her out of the way.

It seemed that the dignity of the gnarled old tree would never be shaken. At each blow a shiver ran through its far-spreading branches and, one by one, the remaining apples fell, but for a long time the great trunk and massive primal limbs received the onslaughts of the axe with a sort of rugged disdain. At last, with a straining of its farthest roots, it crashed to the ground, creating a gust of air that was like the last fierce outgoing of breath from a dying man.

Renny stood, lean, red-faced, triumphant, his head moist with sweat. He glanced shrewdly at Alayne and then turned to Vaughan.

"A good job well done, eh, Maurice?" he asked. "Can you give me a cigarette?"

Vaughan produced a box, and Pheasant, without waiting to be asked, snatched one for herself and, with it between her lips, held up her face to Vaughan's for a light.

"There's a bold little baggage for you," remarked Renny to Alayne, with an odd look of embarrassment.

Pheasant blinked at Alayne through smoke. "Alayne knows I've been badly brought up."

"I think the result is delightful," said Alayne, but she disapproved of Pheasant at that moment.

Pheasant chuckled. "Do you hear that, Maurice? Aren't you proud?"

"Perhaps Alayne doesn't realize that he is your happy parent," said Renny, taking the bull by the horns.

Vaughan gave Alayne a smile, half sheepish, half defiant, and wholly, she thought, unprepossessing. "I expect Mrs Whiteoak has heard of all my evil doings," he said.

"I did not connect you two in my mind at all. I only heard today—a few minutes ago—that Pheasant had a father living. I had stupidly got the idea that she was an orphan."

"I expect Maurice wishes I were, sometimes," said Pheasant. "I don't mean that he wishes himself dead——"

"Why not?" asked Vaughan.

"Oh, because it's such fun being a man, even an ill-tempered one. I mean that he wishes he had no encumbrance in the shape of me."

"You encumber him no longer," said Renny. "You encumber me; isn't that so?"

"Will somebody please get my hat and book and mushrooms?" pleaded the young girl. "They're under the tree."

Renny began to draw aside the heavy branches, the upper ones of which were raised like arms in prayer. An acrid scent of crushed overripe apples rose from among them. His hands, when he had rescued the treasures, were covered by particles of bark and tiny terrified insects.

Vaughan turned toward home, and Pheasant ran after him, showing, now that they were separated, a demonstrative affection toward him that baffled Renny, who was not much given to speculation concerning the feelings of his fellows.

As for Alayne, her mind was puzzled more and more by

these new connections who were everything that her parents and her small circle of intimates were not. Even while their conduct placed her past life on a plane of dignity and reticence, their warmth and vigour made that life seem tame and even colourless. The response of her nature to the shock of this change in her environment was a variety of moods to which she had never before been accustomed. She had sudden sensations of depression, tinged with foreboding, followed by unaccountable flights of gaiety, when she felt that something passionately beautiful was about to happen to her.

Renny, lighting a cigarette, looked at her gravely. "Do you know," he said, "I had no idea that you were so keen about that tree, or I should have left it as it was. Why didn't you make me understand?"

"I did not want to make too much fuss. I thought you would think I was silly. Anyone who knew me at all well would have known how I felt about it. But then—you do not know me very well. I cannot blame you for that."

His gaze on her face became more intense. "I wish I did understand you. I'm better at understanding horses and dogs than women. I never understand them. Now, in this case, it wasn't till the tree was down and I saw your face that I knew what it meant to you. Upon my word, I wouldn't have taken anything—why, you looked positively tragic. You've no idea what a brute I feel." He gave a rueful cut at the fallen tree to emphasize his words.

"Oh, don't!" she exclaimed. "Don't hurt it again!"

He stood motionless among the broken branches, and she moved to his side. He attracted her. She wondered why she had never noticed before how striking he was. But then, she had never before seen him active among outdoor things. She had seen him rather indifferently riding his roan horse. In the house she had thought of him as rather morose and vigilant, though courteous when he was not irritated or excited by his family; and she had thought he held rather an inflated opinion of his own importance as head of the house. Now, axe in hand, with his narrow red head, his red foxlike face and piercing red-brown eyes, he seemed the very spirit of the woods and streams. Even his ears, she noticed, were pointed, and his hair grew in a point on his forehead.

He, having thrown down the axe at her words of entreaty,

stood among the broken branches, motionless as a statue, with apparently a statue's serene detachment under inspection. He scarcely seemed to breathe.

One of those unaccountable soarings of the spirit to which she had of late been subject possessed her at this moment. Her whole being was moved by a strange exhilaration. The orchard, the surrounding fields, the autumn day, seemed but a painted background for the gesture of her own personality. She had moved to Renny's side. Now, from a desire scarcely understood by herself, to prove by the sense of touch that she was really she and he was no one more faunlike than Renny Whiteoak, she laid her hand on his arm. He did not move, but his eyes slid toward her face with an odd, speculative look in them. He was faintly hostile, she believed, because of her supersensitiveness about the tree. She smiled up at him, trying to show that she was not feeling childishly aggrieved, and trying at the same time to hide that haunting and wilful expectancy fluttering her nerves.

The next moment she found herself in his arms with his lips against hers, and all her sensations crushed for the moment into helpless surrender. She felt the steady thud of his heart, and against it the wild tapping of her own. At last he released her and said, with a rather whimsical grimace: "Did you mind so much? I'm awfully sorry. I suppose you think me more of a brute than ever now."

"Oh," she exclaimed quiveringly, "how could you do that? How could you think I would be willing——"

"I didn't think at all," he said. "I did it on the spur of the moment. You looked so—so—oh, I can't think of a word to describe how you looked."

"Please tell me. I wish to know," she said icily.

"Well—inviting, then."

"Do you mean consciously inviting?" There was a dangerous note in her voice.

"Don't be absurd! Unconsciously, of course. You simply made me forget myself. I'm sorry."

She was trembling all over.

"Perhaps," she said, courageously, "you were not much more to blame than I."

"My dear child—as though you could help the way you looked."

156

"Yes, but I went over to you, deliberately, when—oh, I cannot say it!" Yet, perversely, she wanted to say it.

"When you knew you were looking especially lovely—is that what you mean?"

"Not at all. It's no use—I cannot say it."

"Why make the effort? I'm willing to take all the blame. After all, a kiss isn't such a terrible thing, and I'm a relation. Men occasionally kiss their sisters-in-law. It will probably never happen again unless, as you say, you brazenly approach me when—what *were* you trying to say, Alayne? Now I come to think of it, I believe I have the right to know. It might save me more stabs of conscience."

"Oh, you make it all seem ridiculous. You make me feel very childish—very stupid."

He had seated himself on the fallen tree. Now he raised his eyes contritely to hers.

"Look here. That's the last thing on earth I want to do. I'm only trying to get you not to take it too seriously, and I want all the blame."

Her earnest eyes now looked full into his, taking a great deal of courage, for his were sparkling, so full of interest in her, and at the same time so mocking.

"I see that I must tell you. It is this: I have had odd feelings lately of unrest, and a kind of anticipation, as though just around the corner some moving, thrilling experience were waiting for me. This sensation makes me reckless. I felt it just before I moved toward you, and, I think—I think——"

"You think I was playing up to you?"

"Not quite that. But I think you felt something unusual about me."

"I did, and I do. You're not like any woman I've ever known. Tell me, have you thought of me as—caring for you, thinking a good deal about you?"

"I thought you rather disliked me. But please let us forget about all this. I never want to think of it again."

"Of course not," he assented gravely.

With a stab of almost physical pain, she remembered that she had half unconsciously kissed him back again. Her face and neck were dyed crimson. With a little gasp she said: "Of the two I am the more to blame."

"Is this the New England conscience that I've heard so much about?" he asked, filled with amazement.

"I suppose so."

He regarded her with the same half mocking, half quizzical look in his eyes, but his voice deepened.

"Oh, my dear, you are a sweet thing! And to think that you are Eden's wife, and that I must never kiss you again!"

She could not meet his eyes now. She was afraid of him, and still more afraid of herself. She felt that the strange expectancy of mood that had swayed her during these weeks at Jalna was nothing but the premonition of this moment. She said, trying to take herself in hand:

"I am going back to the house. I think I heard the stable clock strike. It must be dinnertime." She turned away and began to walk quickly over the rough orchard grass.

It was significant of the eldest Whiteoak that he made no attempt to follow her, but sat with his eyes on her retreating form, confident that she would look back at him. As he expected, she turned after a dozen paces and regarded him with dignity but with a certain childlike pleading in her voice.

"Will you promise never to think of me as I have been this morning?" he asked.

"Then I must promise never to think of you at all," he returned with composure.

"Then never think of me. I should prefer that."

"Come, Alayne, you know that's impossible."

"Well, promise to forget this morning."

"It is forgotten already."

But, hurrying away through the orchard, she felt that if he could forget as easily as that it would be more terrible to her than if he had brooded on it in his most secret thoughts.

17

PILGRIM'S PROGRESS

ALAYNE HAD been accustomed to church, but the systematic upheaval of Sunday mornings at Jalna was a revelation to her. She had been used to the intellectual, somewhat detached worship of the Unitarian church, where, seated between her father and mother, she had followed reverently the minister's meticulous analysation of the teachings of the man Jesus. She had listened, in a church that rather resembled a splendid auditorium, to the unaccompanied singing of a superb quartette. She had seen collection plates all aflutter with crisp American banknotes, and been scarcely conscious of the large congregation of well-groomed, thoughtful men and women.

When she had lived alone after the death of her parents, she had gone less regularly to church, attending the evening service rather than the morning, and when Rosamond Trent had come to live with her she had gone with still less regularity, for Rosamond was one of those who believe that churchgoing is for those who have nothing better to do.

At Jalna there was an iron rule that every member of the family should attend morning service unless suffering from extreme physical disability. Being only half sick would not do at all. One must be prostrated. Alayne had seen Meg almost stumble into the motor, dazed from headache, a bottle of smelling-salts held to her nose, and sit through the entire services with closed eyes. She had seen young Finch dragged off, regardless of a toothache.

She was inclined to rebel at first, but when she found Eden slavishly acquiescent, she too succumbed. After all, she thought, there was something rather fine in such devotion, even though religion seemed to play so small a part in it. For the Whiteoaks were not, according to Alayne's standards, a religious family. In fact, she never heard the subject mentioned among them. She remembered the intelligent discussions on religious subjects in her father's house: Would Science destroy Religion? The quoting of Dean Inge, Professor Bury, Pasteur, and Huxley.

The only mention of the Deity's name at Jalna was when Grandmother mumbled an indistinguishable grace, or when one of the young men called on the Almighty to witness that he would do such and such a thing, or that something else was damned. Yet with what heroism they herded themselves into those hard adjacent pews each Sunday!

Wakefield summed it all up for Alayne in these words:

"You see, Grandfather built the church, and he never missed a Sunday till he died. Gran never misses a Sunday, and she's almost a hundred. She gets awfully sick if any of the rest of us stop home. And the rector and the farmers and other folk about count us every Sunday, and if one is missing, why it doesn't seem like Sunday to them at all." The little boy's eyes were shining. He was very much in earnest.

Grandmother had never ridden in a motor car, and never expected to ride in one consciously. But she had given orders for the motor hearse from Stead to bear her body to her grave. "For," she said, "I like to think I'll have one swift ride before I'm laid away."

The old phaeton was brought to the front steps every Sunday morning at half past ten. The two old bay horses, Ned and Minnie, were freshly groomed, and the stout stableman, Hodge, wore a black broadcloth coat with a velvet collar. With his long whip he flicked the flies off the horses, and every moment cast an anxious look at the door and set his hat at a more Sundayish angle.

At a quarter to eleven old Mrs Whiteoak emerged, supported by Renny and Piers, for it needed plenty of muscle to negotiate the passage from her room to the phaeton. For church she always wore a black moiré silk dress, a black velvet fur-trimmed cloak, and voluminous widow's weeds of the heaviest crêpe. Alayne thought that the old lady never looked so dignified, so courageous, as she did on these occasions, when, like some unseaworthy but gallant old ship, her widow's veil billowing like a sail, she once again set forth from her harbour. When she was installed in a corner of the seat, with a cushion at her back, the old horses invariably made a forward plunge, for they were instantly aware of her arrival, and Rags as invariably, with a loud adjuration to Hodge to "'old 'ard", leaped to the horses' heads with a great show of preventing a runaway.

Her two sons next appeared: Nicholas, with a trace of his elegance of the old days; Ernest, mildly exhilarated, now that he had passed through the stage of preparation. The old phaeton creaked as their weight was simultaneously added to its burden. Then came Meg, usually flustered over some misdeed of Wake's or Finch's. The little boy made the last of the phaeton party, climbing to the seat beside Hodge, and looking, in comparison with that burly figure, very small and dignified in his snowy Eton collar and kid gloves.

The rest of the family followed in the motor car, excepting

Finch, who walked through fields and lanes. He preferred to do this because there was not room for him in either vehicle without squeezing, and it was hard enough for him to know what to do with his long legs and arms on ordinary occasions. He liked this Sunday walk by himself, alone with his own thoughts.

Renny drove the car, and it was his chief concern to overtake and pass the phaeton as soon as possible, for if he did not accomplish this before the narrow sloping Evandale road was reached, it was probable that the rest of the drive would take place behind the slow-trotting horses, for Grandmother would not allow Hodge to move aside so that a motor might pass her on the road. She did not want to end her days in a ditch, she said. And she would sit with the utmost composure while Renny's car, with perhaps half a dozen others behind it, moved at a funeral pace, urging her onward with desparing honkings of their horns.

This morning was one such occasion. The drowsy Indian-summer heat still continued, but the air had become heavier. The various odours from the earth and fields did not mingle or move about, but hung like palpable essences above the spot from which they rose. All objects were veiled in a thick yellowish haze, and the road dust stirred by the horses' hoofs descended in an opaque cloud on the motor behind.

It was the morning after the scene in the orchard. Alayne had slept little. All night, as she lay tossing, changing sharply from one position to another as the recollection of Renny's kisses made her cheeks burn and her nerves quiver, she had tried to see her position clearly to ascertain whether she had been truly culpable or merely the passive object of Renny's calculated passion. But here in Jalna she found that she could not think with the same freedom of initiative as formerly. Fantastic visions floated between her and the situation she was trying to puzzle out. At last, in the pale abnormal earth light before the dawn, a friendly languor enfolded her and she sank into a quiet sleep.

Now, sitting behind Renny, she saw only the side of his face when he turned it momentarily toward Piers. She saw his thin cheekbone, the patch of reddish hair at his temple, and the compressed line of his lip and chin. Had he slept soundly, giving scarcely a second thought to what had so disturbed her? He had not appeared at dinner, tea, or supper, sending a message to the house that he and Maurice Vaughan had gone together to a sale of horses. This morning the determination to pass his grandmother's chariot before it reached the Evandale road seemed to absorb him. Pheasant had kept them waiting, and on her he threw a black look as she scrambled into the car.

The engine balked, then started jarringly. Eden, sitting between the girls, took a hand of each and exclaimed: "Oh, my dears, let us cling together! We will come through this safely if we only cling together. Pheasant, give me your little paw."

But, speed though the eldest Whiteoak did, he could not overtake his grandmother before she reached the Evandale road. There was the phaeton creaking along in leisurely fashion in a cloud of yellow dust, resembling an old bark in a heavy fog, Grandmother's veil streaming like a black pirate flag.

Renny, with half closed eyes, squinted down the road where it dropped steeply into a dusty ditch, grey with thistles. "I believe I could get by," he muttered to Piers. "I've a mind to try."

The occupants of the phaeton recognized the peculiar squeakings of the family motor. They turned their heads, peering out of the dust fog like mariners sighting a hostile craft. Renny emphatically sounded his horn.

They could hear Grandmother shout to Hodge. At once the two old horses were restrained to a walk.

"By Judas!" exclaimed Renny. "I'd like to give the old lady a bump!"

Again he cast his eyes along the narrow strip of road between the phaeton wheels and the ditch. "I believe I'll risk it," he said. "Just go by like the devil and give them a scare."

Piers protested: "You'll put us head-first into those thistles if you do. And you might frighten the nags."

"True," said Renny, gloomily, and sounded his horn with passionate repetition. Grandmother's face glared out of the fog.

"No back chat!" she shouted; but it was evident that she was enjoying herself immensely.

Farmer Tompkins and Farmer Gregg drew up their respective cars behind, and sounded their horns simultaneously. The eldest Whiteoak frowned. It was all very well for him to torment his ancient relative, but those yokels should not. He slumped in his seat, resigning himself to the progress of a snail. He took off his hat.

The sight of his narrow head suddenly bared, the pointed ears lying close against the closely cropped red hair, had a remarkable and devastating effect on Alayne. She wanted to reach forward, put a hand on either side of it, and hold it tightly. She desired to stroke it, to caress it. She gave a frightened look toward Eden, as though to implore him to cast out these devils that were destroying her. He smiled back encouragingly. "We shall arrive," he said, "in God's good time. Behind us is Tompkins, who is a churchwarden, and he's suffering torture at the thought of being late. I've known him since I was three and he has only been twice late in all that time, and on each occasion it was Gran's fault. Tompkins is much worse off than we are."

Alayne scarcely heard what he said, but she slipped her hand in his and clung to it. She was lost in speculation about what thoughts might be in that head toward which her hands were yearning. Were they of her, or had the scene in the orchard been only one of many careless encounters with women? She believed that last was not so, for he had avoided the house for the rest of the day, and this morning had palpably avoided her. There was a sombre melancholy in his face as she caught a glimpse of his reflection in the little mirror before him. But perhaps that was only because he was baffled by old Mrs Whiteoak.

What had he done to her that had filled her with such unrest? She had got up in the night and crept to the window and, in the mystery of the moonlight, seen the orchard, and even been able to discern the curving bulk of the tree he had felled. She had felt again the hot passion of his kisses.

One thing of which she was keenly sensible this morning was her new intimacy with Pheasant. Every time their eyes met, the young girl gave her a little smile, ingenuous as a child's. Alayne even fancied that Piers was less surly with her than formerly. She had told Eden of the talk with Pheasant, and he had seemed rather amused at Alayne's desire to make friends with her. "She's a dear quaint kid," he had remarked. "But she'll soon bore you. However, perhaps you're so bored already that even the company of Pheasant——"

"Nonsense," she had interrupted, more shortly than she had ever before spoken to him. "I am not bored at all, but Pheasant attracts me. I think I could become very fond of her. She has unusual possibilities."

Now Eden sat between them, holding a hand of each and smiling tolerantly. He did not care if they never got to church.

The bell was ringing as the car chugged up the steep little hill and passed through the gate behind the church. Heads of people mounting the precipitous steps at the front could be seen bobbing upward, as though ascending from a well. Golden sunshine lay like a caress on the irregular green mounds and mossgrown headstones of the churchyard. There was one new grave, on the fresh sandy top of which a wreath of drooping flowers lay.

Wakefield came and put his hand into Alayne's.

"That's Mrs Miller's grave," he said. "She had a baby, and they're both in there. Isn't it terrible? It was a nice little girl and they'd named it Ruby Pearl. However, Miller has five girls left, so it might be worse."

"Hush, dear," said Alayne, squeezing his hand. "Are you going to sit with me?"

Wakefield had taken pride in sitting by Alayne and finidng, with a great fluttering of leaves, the places in the prayerbook for her. Now he looked doubtful.

"I'd like to," he said, "but I think Meggie feels lonely at my leaving her. You see, I've sat beside her ever since I was very little and used to go to sleep with my head on her lap. Look, they're getting Granny out of the phaeton. I think I'd better rush over and see that the sexton's holding the door wide open."

He flew across the grass.

Old Mrs Whiteoak shuffled, with scarcely perceptible progress, along the slat walk that led to the church door. Renny and Piers supported her, and Nicholas, Ernest, and Meg followed close behind, carrying her various bags, books, and cushions. Under her beetling rust-coloured brows her piercing gaze swept the face of those she passed. From side to side her massive old head moved with royal condescension. Sometimes her face was lighted by a smile, as she recognized an old friend, but this was seldom, for most of her friends were long dead. The smile flashed—the mordant and mischievous grin for which the Courts had been famous—at the Misses Lacey, daughters of a retired British admiral. "How's your father, girls?" she panted.

The 'girls', who were sixty-four and sixty-five, exclaimed simultaneously: "Still bedridden, dear Mrs Whiteoak, but *so* bright!"

"No right to be bedridden. He's only ninety. How's your mother?"

"Ah, dear Mrs Whiteoak, Mamma has been dead nine years!" cried the sisters in unison.

"God bless me, I forgot! I'm sorry." She shuffled on.

Now the grin was bestowed on a bent labourer nearly as old as herself, who stood, hat in hand, to greet her, the fringe of silvery hair that encircled his pink head mingling with his patriarchal beard. He had driven Nicholas and Ernest about in their pony cart when they were little boys.

"Good morning, Hickson. Ha! These slats are hard to get over. Grip my arm tighter, Renny! Stop staring about like a fool, Piers, and hang on to me."

The old man pressed forward, showing his smooth gums in a smile of infantile complacence.

"Mrs Whiteoak, ma'am, I just am wantin' to tell ye that I've got my first great-great-grandchild."

"Good for you, Hickson! You're smarter than I am—I haven't got even one great yet. Don't drag at me, Piers. One would think I was a load of hay—ha! and you a carthorse. Tell Todd to stop clanging that bell. It's deafening me. Ha! Now for the steps."

Eden and Alayne had fallen in behind Pheasant and Meg, who had Wakefield by the hand. Alayne wondered what the Corys and Rosamond Trent would have thought if they could have seen her at that moment, moving in that slow procession, rather like courtiers behind an ancient queen. Already Alayne felt a family pride in the old lady. There was a certain fierce grandeur about her. Her nose was magnificent. She looked as though she should have a long record of intrigues, lovers, and duels behind her, yet she had been buried most of her life in this backwater. Ah, perhaps that was the secret of her strong individualism. The individualism of all the Whiteoaks. They thought, felt, and acted with Victorian intensity. They threw themselves into living, with unstudied sincerity. They did not philosophize about life, but no emotion was too timeworn, too stuffy, to be dragged forth by them and displayed with vigour and abandon.

Now they were in the cool, dim church.

The bell had ceased. They were ranged in two pews, one behind the other. Their heads, blond, brown, and grey, were bent. Grandmother's great veil fell across Wake's thin shoulders. She wheezed pathetically.

Little Miss Pink at the organ broke into the processional hymn. Wakefield could see, between the forms of those grown-ups before him, the white-clad figure of Mr Fennel. How different he looked on Sunday, with his beard all tidy and his hair parted with moist precision! And there was Renny, surpliced too. How had he got into the vestry and changed so quickly? A Whiteoak always read the Lessons. Grandfather had done it for years. Then Father had had his turn. And Uncle Ernest still read them sometimes when Renny was away—all the time Renny had been at the War. Would Wakefield ever read them himself, he wondered? He pictured himself rolling out the words grandly, not in Renny's curt, inexpressive way.

A burst of melody rose from the Whiteoak pews. Strong voices, full of vitality, that bore down upon little Miss Pink and her organ like boisterous waves and swept them along, gasping and wheezing, while the choir tried vainly to hold back. And even Renny in the chancel was against the choir and with the family. The choir, with the organ so weak and Miss Pink so vacillating, had no chance at all against the Whiteoaks.

"Rend your heart, and not your garments, and turn unto the Lord your God; for he is gracious and merciful, slow to anger, and of great kindness, and repenteth him of the evil."

Mr Fennel's voice was slow and sonorous. Heavy autumn sunshine lay in translucent planes across the kneeling people. Alayne had come to love this little church, its atmosphere of simplicity, of placid acceptance of all she questioned. She kept her eyes on the prayerbook which Eden and she shared. Grandmother, in a husky whisper, directly behind them, was asking Meggie for a peppermint. When it was given to her she dropped it, and it rolled under the seat and was lost. She was given another, and sucked it triumphantly. The odours of the peppermint and of the stuff of her crêpe veil were exuded from her. Wakefield dropped his collection money, and Uncle Nick tweaked his ear. Piers and Pheasant whispered, and Grandmother poked at Piers with her stick. Renny mounted the step behind the brass eagle of the lectern and began to read the First Lesson.

"If the clouds be full of rain, they empty themselves upon the earth: and if the tree fall toward the south, or toward the north, in the place where the tree falleth, there it shall be.

"He that observeth the wind shall not sow; and he that regardeth the clouds shall not reap.

"As thou knowest not what is the way of the spirit, nor how the bones do grow in the womb of her that is with child: even so thou knowest not the works of God who maketh all."

The family stared at their chief as he read.

Old Mrs Whiteoak thought: 'A perfect Court! Look at that head, will you? My nose—my eyes. I wish Philip could see him. Ha, where's my peppermint? Must have swallowed it. How far away the lad looks. He's in his nightshirt—going to bed—time for bed——'

She slept.

Nicholas thought: 'Renny's wasted here. Ought to be having a gay time in London. Let's see; he's thirty-eight. When I was that age—God, I was just beginning to hate Millicent! What a life!'

He heaved himself in his seat and eased his gouty knee.

Ernest thought: 'Dear boy, how badly he reads! Still his voice is arresting. I always enjoy old Ecclesiastes. I do hope there will not be plum tart for dinner—I shall be sure to eat it and sure to suffer. Mamma is dropping her peppermint——'

He whispered to her: "Mamma, you are losing your peppermint."

Meg thought: 'I wish Renny would not get such a close haircut. How splendid he looks. Really, what strange things the Bible says. But very true, of course. How sweet Wake looks! So interested. He has the loveliest eyelashes. He's getting ready to kick Finch on the ankle——'

She bent over Wakefield, and laid a restraining hand on his leg.

Renny's voice read on:

"Truly the light is sweet, and a pleasant thing it is for the eyes to behold the sun."

Eden thought: 'He was a poet, the old chap who wrote that. "Truly the light is sweet—and a pleasant thing it is for the eyes to behold——" Strange I never noticed before how lovely Pheasant is. Her profile——'

He shifted his position a little, so that he might the better see it.

Piers thought: 'I wonder if that piece of land needs potash. I believe I'll try it. Don't see what the dickens can be wrong with the sick ewe. Walking in a circle, like a fool animal in a roundabout. Perhaps she's got gid or sturdy. Must have the vet. to her. Let's see—fourteen and twenty-one is thirty-five, and seven is forty-two—owe Baxter forty-two. Pheasant daren't look at me—little rogue—darling little kid——'

He pressed his knee against hers, and looked at her under his lashes.

Pheasant thought: 'How big and brown Piers' hands always look on Sunday! Regular fists. I like them that way, too. I wish Eden wouldn't stare. I know perfectly well he's thinking how dowdy I am beside Alayne. Oh dear, how hard this seat gets! I shall never get used to churchgoing—I wasn't caught young enough. My whole character was completely formed when I married. Neither Maurice nor I have any religion. How nice it was to see him yesterday in the orchard—quite friendly he was, too. Now religion—take Renny: there he stands in his surplice, reading out of the Bible, and yesterday I heard him swearing like a trooper just because a pig ran under his horse. To be sure, it nearly threw him, but then, what good is religion if it doesn't teach forbearance? I don't think he is a bit better than Piers. I wish Piers wouldn't try to make me smile.'

She bit her lip and turned her head away.

Wakefield thought: 'I do hope there'll be plum tart for dinner—if there isn't plum tart, I hope there'll be lemon tart. ... But Mrs Wragge was in a terrible temper this morning. How glad I am I was in the coal cellar when she and Rags had their row! Why, he called her a—hold on, no, I'd better not think of bad things in church. I might be struck dead—dead as a doornail, the very deadest thing. How pretty the

168

lectern is—how beautifully Renny reads. Some day I shall read the Lessons just like that—only louder—that is, of course, if I live to grow up. By stretching my legs very far under the seat in front, I can kick Finch's ankle. Now—oh, bother Meggie, bother Meggie, always interfering—bother her, I say!'

He looked up innocently into his sister's face.

Finch thought: 'Tomorrow is the algebra exam, and I shall fail—I shall fail. . . . If only my head did not get confused! If only I were more like Renny! Nothing in the world will ever tempt me to stand up behind the lectern and read the Lessons. What a beastly mess I'd make of it——'

He became conscious of the words his brother was reading:

"Rejoice, O young man, in thy youth; and let thy heart cheer thee in the days of thy youth, and walk in the ways of thine heart, and in the sight of thine eyes: but know thou, that for all these things God will bring thee into judgment."

Finch twisted unhappily in his seat. Why these eternal threats? Life seemed compact of commands and threats—and the magic of the words in which these old, old threats were clothed. The dark, heavy foreboding. Magic—that was it: their magic held and terrified him. . . . If he could but escape from the cruel magic of words. If he could only have sat by Alayne, that he might have touched her dress as they knelt!

He closed his eyes, and clenched his bony hands tightly on his thighs.

Alayne thought: 'How strange his brogues look under his surplice! I noticed this morning how worn and how polished they are—good-looking brogues. . . . How can I think of brogues when my mind is in torment? Am I growing to love him? What shall I do in that case? Eden and I would have to leave Jalna. No, I do not love him. I will not let myself. He fascinates me—that is all. I do not even like him. Rather, I dislike him. Standing there before that brass thing, in his brogues—his red hair—the Court nose—that foxlike look—he is repellant to me.'

She too closed her eyes, and pressed her fingers against them.

"Here endeth the First Lesson."

Then, with Miss Pink and the organ tremulously leading the

way, and the choir fatuously fancying themselves masters of the situation, the *Te Deum* burst forth from every Whiteoak chest save Grandmother's, and she was gustily blowing in a doze. From the deep baritone of Nicholas to the silver pipe of Wake, they informed the heavens and the earth that they praised the Lord and called Him Holy.

That night, after the nine-o'clock supper of cold beef and bread and tea, with oatmeal scones and milk for Grandmother and Ernest (who, alas, had partaken of plum tart at dinner as he feared), Meg said to Alayne:

"Is it true, Alayne, that Unitarians do not believe in the divinity of Christ?"

"What's that?" interrupted Grandmother. "What's that?"

"The divinity of Christ, Gran. Mrs Fennel was telling me yesterday that Unitarians do not believe in the divinity of Christ."

"Nonsense," said Mrs Whiteoak. "Rubbish. I won't have it. More milk, Meggie."

"I suppose you do not believe in the Virgin Birth, either," continued Meg, pouring out the milk. "In that case, you will not find the Church of England congenial."

"I like the service of your church very much," said Alayne, guardedly. There had been something that savoured of an attack in this sudden question.

"Of course she does," said Mrs Whiteoak, heartily. "She's a good girl. Believes what she ought to believe. And no nonsense. She's not a heathen. She's not a Jew. Not believe in the Virgin Birth? Never heard of such a thing in decent society. It's not respectable."

"Why talk of religion?" said Nicholas. "Tell us a story, Mamma. One of your stories, you know."

His mother cocked an eyebrow at him. Then, looking down her nose, she tried to remember a risqué story. She had had quite a store of these, but one by one they were slipping her memory.

"The one about the curate on his holiday," suggested Nicholas, like a dutiful son.

"Nick!" remonstrated Ernest.

"Yes, yes," said the old lady. "This curate had worked for years and years without a holiday. And—and—oh dear, what comes next?"

"Another curate," prompted Nicholas, "who was also over-worked."

"I think the boys should go to bed," said Meg, nervously.

"She'll never remember it," replied Renny, with calm.

"Oh, Wakefield is playing with the Indian curios!" cried Meg. "Do stop him, Renny!"

Renny took the child forcibly from the cabinet, gave him a gentle cuff, and turned him toward the door. "Now, to bed," he ordered.

"Let him say good-night, first!" shouted Grandmother. "Poor little darling, he wants to kiss his Gran goodnight."

Boney, disturbed from slumber, rocked on his perch and screamed in far-away nasal tones:

"Ka butcha! Ka butcha! Haramzada!"

Wakefield made the rounds, distributing kisses and hugs with a nice gauging of the character of the recipient. They ranged in all varieties, from a bearlike hug and smack to Gran, to a courteous caress to Alayne, a perfunctory offering of his olive cheek to his brothers, except Finch, to whom he administered a punch in the stomach which was returned by a sly but wicked dig in the short rib.

The Whiteoaks had a vocation for kissing. Alayne thought of that as she watched the youngest Whiteoak saluting the family. They kissed upon the slightest provocation. Indeed, the grandmother would frequently, on awakening from a doze, cry out pathetically:

"Kiss me, somebody, quick!"

Ah, perhaps Renny had regarded the kissing of her in the orchard as a light thing!

A sudden impulse drew her to him where he stood before the cabinet of curios, a little ivory ape in his hand.

"I want to speak to you about Finch," she said, steadily.

The light was dim in that corner. Renny scanned her face furtively.

"Yes?"

"I like him very much. He is an unusual boy. And he is at a difficult age. There is something I should like you to do for him."

He regarded her suspiciously. What was the girl up to?

"Yes?" His tone was mildly questioning.

"I want you to give him music lessons. Music would be

splendid for him. He is a very interesting boy, and he needs some outlet besides geometry and things like that. I am sure you will not be sorry if you do it. Finch is worth taking a great deal of trouble for."

He looked genuinely surprised.

"Really? I always thought him rather a dull young whelp. And no good at athletics, either. That would be some excuse for being at the bottom of his form most of the time. None of us think of him as 'interesting'."

"That is just the trouble. Every one of you thinks the same about Finch, and in consequence he feels himself inferior—the ugly duckling. You are like a flock of sheep, all jumping the one way."

Her enthusiasm for Finch made her forget her usual dignified reticence, and with it her embarrassment. She looked at him square and accusingly.

"And you look on me as the bell-wether, eh? If you turn my woolly wooden head in another direction, the others will follow. I am to believe that Finch will turn out to be the swan, then?"

"I should not be surprised."

"And you think his soul needs scales and finger exercises?"

"Please do not make fun of me."

"I shall have the family in my wool, you know. They'll hate the strumming."

"They will get used to it. Finch *is* important, though none of you may think so."

"What makes you sure he has musical talent?"

"I am not sure. But I know he appreciates music, and I think he is worth the experiment. Did you ever watch his face when your Uncle Nicholas is playing?"

"No."

"Well, he is playing now. From here you can see Finch quite clearly. Isn't his expression beautiful, revealing?"

Renny stared across the room at his young brother.

"He looks rather idiotic to me," he said, "with his jaw dropped and his head stuck forward."

"Oh, you are hopeless!" she said, angrily.

"No, I'm not. He's going to have his music and I am going to endure the curses of the family. But for my life and soul I can't see anything of promise in him at this moment. Now

172

Uncle Nick, with the lamplight falling on that grey lion's head of his, looks rather splendid."

"But Finch—don't you see the look in his eyes? If only you could understand him—be a friend to him——" Her eyes were pleading.

"What a troubled little thing you are! I believe you do a lot of worrying. Perhaps you are even worrying about me?" He turned his intense gaze into her eyes.

Deep chords from the piano, Grandmother and Boney making love to each other in Hindu. The yellow lamplight, which left the corners of the room in mysterious shadow, isolated them, giving the low tones of their voices a significance that their words did not express.

A passionate unrest seized upon her. The walls of the room seemed to be pressing in on her; the group of people yonder, stolid, inflexible, full-blooded, arrogant, seemed to be crushing her individuality. She wanted to snatch the ivory ape from Renny's hands and hurl it into their midst, frightening them, making the parrot scream and squawk.

Yet she had just been granted a favour that lay near her heart: music for poor young Finch.

The contradictions of her temperament puzzled and amused the eldest Whiteoak. He discovered that he liked to startle her. Her unworldliness, as he knew the world, her reticence, her honesty, her academic ardours, her priggishness, the palpable passion that lay beneath all these, made her an object of calculated sexual interest to him. At the same time he felt an almost tender solicitude for her. He did not want to see her hurt, and he wondered how long it would be before Eden would most certainly hurt her.

"I have forgotten yesterday, as I promised. Have you forgiven?"

"Yes," she returned, and her heart began to beat heavily.

"But giving Finch those music lessons will never make up for cutting down the tree, I'm afraid. You've made me very tenderhearted."

"Are you sorry for that?"

"Yes. I have especial need of hardness just now."

The parrot screamed: "Chore! Chore! Haramzada! Chore!"

"What are you two talking about?" shouted Grandmother.

"Eastern lore," replied her grandson.

"Did you say the War? I like to hear about the War as well as anyone. Do you know the Buffs, Alayne? That was Renny's regiment. Did your country go to war, Alayne?"

"Yes, Mrs Whiteoak."

"Yes, *Gran*, please!"

"Yes, Gran."

"Ah, I hadn't heard of it. Renny was in the Buffs. One of the most famous regiments in England. Ever hear of the Buffs, Alayne?"

"Not till I came to Jalna, Gran."

"What's that? What's that? Not heard of the Buffs? The girl must be mad! I won't have it!" Her face grew purple with rage. "Tell her about the Buffs, somebody. I forget the beginning of it. Tell her instantly!"

"I'll tell her," said Renny.

Nicholas put the loud pedal down. Grandmother fell into one of her sudden dozes, by which she always recaptured the strength lost in a rage.

They were boring, Alayne thought. They were maddening. They oppressed her, and yet a strange burden of beauty lay on the high-walled room, emanating from the figures disposed about it: Gran and Boney; Nicholas at the piano; Meg, all feminine curves and heavy sweetness; Piers and Eden playing cribbage; Sasha, curled on the mantelpiece.

"I must not get to care for you," Renny said, in a muffled voice. "Nor you for me. It would make an impossible situation."

"Yes," murmured Alayne, "it would be impossible."

18

IN THE WIND AND RAIN

"HERE'S A LETTER from New York to say they've got the proofs all right," observed Eden. "They think the book will be ready by the first of March. Do you think that is a good time?"

"Excellent," said Alayne. "Is the letter from Mr Cory?"

"Yes. He sends his regards to you. Says he misses you awfully. They all do. And he's sending you a package of new books to read."

Alayne was delighted. "Oh, I am so glad. I am hungry for new books. When I think how I used literally to wallow in them! Now the thought of a package of new ones seems wonderful."

"What a brute I am!" exclaimed Eden. "I never think of anything but my damned poetry. Why didn't you tell me you had nothing to read? I've seen you with books, and I didn't realize that they were probably forty years old. What have you been reading?"

"I've been working with Uncle Ernest a good deal. I like that; and I've been indulging in Ouida for the first time, fancy! And reading *Rob Roy* to Wake. I have not done badly."

"You darling! Why don't you simply jump on me when I'm stupid? Here you are, cooped up at Jalna, with no amusements, while it streams November rain, and I lose myself in my idiotic imaginings."

"I am perfectly happy, only I don't see a great deal of you. You were in town three days last week, for instance, and you went to that football match with Renny and Piers one day."

"I know, I know. It was that filthy job I was looking after in town."

"That did not come to anything, did it?"

"No. The hours were too beastly long. I'd have had no time for my real work at all. What I want is a job that will only take a part of my time. Leave me some leisure. And the pay not too bad. A chap named Evans, a friend of Renny's, who has something to do with the Department of Forestry, is going to do something for me, I'm pretty sure. He was overseas with Renny, and he married a relative of the Prime Minister."

"What is the job?"

Eden was very vague about the job. Alayne had discovered that he was very vague about work of any kind except his writing, upon which he could concentrate with hot intensity.

"I'm just a child," he would exclaim, "about worldly things. There's no use, Alayne, you'll never be able to make me grow up. You'll go on to the end of your days, making over your New York frocks, and getting shabbier and shabbier as to hats and shoes, and more and more resigned to——"

"Don't be so sure of that," she had answered with a little asperity. "I am not resigned by nature. As to being poor—

according to Pheasant I am rich. At least, she says your family think I am."

He had been staggered. He could not imagine why the family should think so, except for the reason that they thought of all American girls as rich. As for Pheasant, she was a poisonous little mischief-maker, and he would speak to Piers about her.

Alayne had found that, when Eden was irritating, he annoyed her out of all proportion to his words—made her positively want to hurt him. Now, to save her dignity, she changed the subject.

"Eden, I sometimes wish you had gone on with your profession. You would at least have been sure of it. You would have been your own master——"

"Dear," he interrupted, "wish me an ill that I deserve, trample on me, crush me, be savage, but don't wish I were a member of that stuffy, stultifying, atrophying profession. It was Meggie who put me into it, when I was too young and weak to resist. But when I found out the effect it was having on me, thank God I had the grit to chuck it. My darling, just imagine your little white rabbit spending his young life nosing into all sorts of mouldy lawsuits, and filthy divorce cases, and actions for damages to the great toe of a grocer by a motor driven by the President of the Society for the Suppression of Vice! Think of it!" He rumpled his fair hair and glared at her. "Honestly, I shouldn't survive the strain a week."

Alayne took his head to her breast and stroked it in her soft, rather sedate fashion.

"Don't, darling. You make me feel a positive ogre. And there's no hurry. I've drawn almost nothing from my account yet."

"I should hope not!" he exclaimed, savagely.

She asked after a moment: "Will the books from Mr Cory come straight here or shall we have to go to town for them?"

"It depends upon whether they are held up in the customs. If they are, we'll go in together for them. It will be a little change for you. God knows, you don't get much change."

They were in their own room. He was at his desk, and she standing beside him. He began searching through a box of stamps for a stamp that was not stuck to another one. He was mixing them up thoroughly, partially separating one from

176

another, then in despair throwing them back into the box in such disorder that she longed to snatch them from him and set them to rights, if possible, but she had learned that he did not like his things put in order. He had been helping Renny to exercise two new saddle horses, and he smelled of the stables. The smell of horses was always in the house; dogs were always running in and out, barking to get in, scratching at doors to get out; their muddy footprints were always in evidence in November. Alayne was getting accustomed to this, but at first it had been a source of irritation, even disgust. She would never forget the shock she had experienced when, coming into her bedroom one afternoon, she had discovered a shaggy, bobtailed sheepdog curled up on the middle of her bed.

She rather liked dogs, but she did not understand them. At home they had never had a dog. Her mother had kept goldfish and a canary, but Alayne had thought these rather a nuisance. She felt that she would like horses better than either dogs or canaries. She wished she could ride, but nothing had been said about her learning, and she was too reserved, too much afraid of being a trouble, to suggest it. Meg had never ridden since her engagement to Maurice had been broken off, but Pheasant rode like a boy.

Eden had at last detached a stamp. He held it against his tongue and then stuck it upside down on his letter.

Watching him, Alayne had a sudden and dispassionate vision of him as an old man, firmly established at Jalna, immovable, contented, without hope or ambition, just like Nicholas and Ernest. She saw him grey-headed, at a desk, searching for a stamp, licking it, fixing it, fancying himself busy. She felt desperately afraid.

"Eden," she said, still stroking his bright head, "have you been thinking of your novel lately? Have you perhaps made a tiny beginning?"

He turned on her, upsetting the box of stamps and giving the inkpot such a jar that she was barely able to save it.

"You're not going to start bothering me about that, are you?" Rich colour flooded his face. "Just when I'm fairly swamped with other things. I hope you're not going to begin nagging at me, darling, because I can't wangle the right sort of job on the instant. I couldn't bear that."

"Don't be silly," returned Alayne. "I have no intention of nagging. I am only wondering if you are still interested in the novel."

"Of course I am. But, my dear lady, a man can't begin a tremendous piece of work like that without a lot of thought. When I begin it I'll let you know." He took up his fountain-pen and vigorously shook it. He tried to write, but it was empty.

"Isn't it appalling," he remarked, "how the entire universe seems after one sometimes? Just before you came in, that shelf over there deliberately hit me on the head as I was getting a book from the bookcase. I dropped the book, and, when I picked it up, the sharp corner of the dresser bashed me on the other side of the head. Now my pen's empty, and there is scarcely any ink!"

"Let me fill it for you," said Alayne. "I think there is enough ink."

She filled it, kissed the bumped head, and left him.

As she descended the stairs, she had a glimpse of Piers and Pheasant in a deep window-seat on the landing. They had drawn the shabby mohair curtains before them, but she saw that they were eating a huge red apple, bite about, like children. Outside, the wind was howling and the rain was slashing down the window-pane behind them. They looked very jolly and carefree, as though life were a pleasant game. And yet, she reflected, they had their own troubles.

The front door was standing open, and Renny was in the porch, talking to a man whom Alayne knew to be a horse-dealer. He was a heavy-jowled man with a deep, husky voice and little shrewd eyes. A raw blast, smelling of the drenched countryside, rushed in at the open door. The feet of the two men had left muddy tracks in the hall, and one of the clumber spaniels was critically sniffing over them. The other spaniel was humped up in the doorway, biting himself ferociously just above the tail. In the sudden twilight of the late afternoon she could not distinguish Renny's features, but she could see his weatherbeaten face close to the dealer's as they talked together.

After all, she thought, he was little better than a horse-dealer himself. He spent more time with his horses than he did with his family. Half the time he did not turn up at meals, and when he did appear, riding through the gate on his bony grey mare, his shoulders drooping and his long back slightly bent, as likely as not some strange and horsy being rode beside him.

And the devastating fascination he had for her! Beside him, Eden upstairs at his desk seemed nothing but a petulant child. Yet Eden had bright and beautiful gifts which Renny had neither the imagination nor the intellect to appreciate.

Rags' face, screwed up with misery, appeared around a doorway at the back of the hall.

"My word, wot a draught!" she heard him mutter. "It's enough to blow the tea things off the tr'y."

"I will shut the door, Wragge," she said, kindly, but, regarding her own offer with cold criticism as she stepped over the long plumed tail of a spaniel, she came to the conclusion that she had made it for the sole reason that she might stand in the doorway an instant with the gale blowing her, and be seen by Renny. After all, she did not quite escape the plumy tail. The high heel of her shoe pinched it sharply, and the spaniel gave an outraged yelp of pain. Renny peered into the hall with a snarl: some one had hurt one of his dogs. His rough red eyebrows came down over his beak of a nose.

"I was going to close the door," explained Alayne, "and I stepped on Flossie's tail."

"Oh," said Renny, "I thought perhaps Rags had hurt her." The horse-dealer's little grey eyes twinkled at her through the gloom.

She tried to close the door, but the other spaniel humped himself against it. He would not budge. Renny took him by the scruff and dragged him into the porch.

"Stubborn things, ain't they?" remarked the horse-dealer.

"Thanks, Renny," said Alayne, and she closed the door, and found herself not alone in the hall, but out in the porch with the men.

Renny turned a questioning look on her. Now why had she done that? The wind was whipping her skirt against her legs, plastering her hair back from her forehead, spattering her face with raindrops. Why had she done such a thing?

Merlin, the spaniel, to show that there was no hard feeling, stood on his hind legs and put his paws against her skirt, licking up toward her face.

"Down, Merlin, down," said his master, and he added, perfunctorily, "Alayne, this is Mr Crowdy, the man who bought Firelight's foal. Crowdy, Mrs Eden Whiteoak."

"Pleased to meet you," said Mr Crowdy, removing his hat. "It's terrible weather, ain't it? But only what we must expect at this time of year. Rain and sleet and snow from now on, eh? You'll be wishing you was back in the States, Mrs Whiteoak."

"We have cold weather in New York, too," said Alayne, wondering what the man must think of her. She felt sure that Renny saw through her, saw that he had a pernicious fascination that had drawn her, against her will, to the porch.

"Well," observed the horse-dealer, "I must be off. Mrs Crowdy she'll have it in for me if I'm late to supper." He and Renny made some arrangement to meet at Mistwell the next day, and he drove off in a noisy Ford car.

They were alone. A gust of wind shook the heavy creeper above the porch and sent a shower of drops that drenched their hair. He fumbled for a cigarette and with difficulty lighted it.

"I felt that I had to have the air," she said. "I have been in all day."

"I suppose it does get on your nerves."

"You must have hated my coming out in the middle of your conversation with that man. I do not think I ever did anything quite so stupid before."

"It didn't matter. Crowdy was just going. But are you sure you won't take cold? Shall I get you a sweater out of the cupboard?"

"No. I am going in." But she stood motionless, looking at the sombre shapes of the hemlocks that were being fast engulfed by the approaching darkness. Thought was suspended, only her senses were alive, and they were the senses of elemental things—the rain, the wind, the engulfing darkness, the quiescent, imploring earth——

Was she in his arms—the rough tweed of his sleeve against her cheek—his lips pressing hers—his kisses torturing her, weakening her? No, he had not moved from where he stood. She was standing alone at the edge of the steps, the rain spattering her face as though with tears. Yet, so far as she was concerned, the embrace had been given, received. She felt the ecstasy, the relaxation of it.

He stood there immobile, silhouetted against the window of the library which had been, at that moment, lighted behind him. Then his voice came as though from a long way off.

"What is it? You are disturbed about something."

"No, no. I am all right."

"Are you? I thought you had come out here to tell me something."

"No, I had nothing to tell you. I came because—I cannot explain—but you and that man made a strange sort of picture out here, and I moved out into it unconsciously." She realized with an aching relief that he had not guessed the trick her senses had played her. He had only seen her standing rigid at the top of the windswept steps.

A long-legged figure came bounding along the driveway, leaped on to the steps, and almost ran against her. It was Finch back from school. He was drenched. He threw a startled look at them and moved toward the door.

"Oh, Finch, you *are* wet," said Alayne, touching his sleeve.

"That's nothing," he returned, gruffly.

"You're late," remarked Renny.

"I couldn't get the earlier train. A bunch of us were kept in."

The boy hesitated, peering at them as though they were strangers whose features he wished to distinguish and remember.

"H-m," muttered Renny. "Well, you had better change into dry things and do some practising before tea."

His tone, abstracted and curt, was unlike his usual air of indolent authority. Finch knew that he was expected to move instantly, but he could not force his legs to carry him into the house. There was something in the porch, some presence, something between those two, that mesmerized him. His soul seemed to melt within him, to go out through his chest gropingly toward theirs. His body a helpless shell, propped there on two legs, while his soul crept out toward them, fawning about them like one of the spaniels, one of the spaniels on the scent of something strange and beautiful.

"You're so wet, Finch," came distantly in Alayne's voice.

And then in Renny's: "Will you do what I tell you? Get upstairs and change."

Finch peered at them, dazed. Then, slowly, his soul skulked

back into his body like a dog into its kennel. Once more his legs had life in them.

"Sorry," he muttered, and half stumbled into the house.

Meg was coming down the stairway, and Rags had just turned on the light in the hall.

"How late you are!" she exclaimed. "Oh, what a muddy floor! Finch, is it possible you brought all that mud in? One would think you were an elephant. Will you please take it up, Wragge, at once, before it gets tramped in? How many times have I told you to wipe your boots on the mat outside, Finch?"

"I dunno."

"Well, really, this rug is getting to be a disgrace. You're late, dear. Are you starving?"

She was at the foot of the stairs now. She kissed him, and he rubbed his cheek, moist with rain, against hers, warm and velvety.

"M-m," they breathed, rocking together. Flossie, the spaniel, was scratching at the already much bescratched front door.

"What does Flossie want?" asked Meg.

"I dunno."

"Why, she wants to get out. Merlin must be out there. Was he there when you came in?"

"I didn't see him."

"Let Flossie out, Rags. She wants Merlin."

"No, don't let her out," bawled Finch. "She'll only bring more mud in. Put her in the kitchen."

"Yes, I believe that would be better. Put her in the kitchen, Rags."

Finch said: "I've got to do some practising."

"No, dear," replied his sister, firmly. "It's teatime. You can't practise now. It's time for tea."

"But, look here," cried Finch. "I shan't get any practising tonight, then. I've a lot of lessons to do."

"You shouldn't be so late coming home. That's one reason I didn't want you to have such an expensive teacher. It's so worrying when there's no opportunity for practising. But, of course, Alayne would have it."

"Darn it all!" bawled Finch. "Why can't I practise in peace?"

"Finch, go upstairs this instant and change into dry things."

The door of Gran's room opened and Uncle Nick put his head out.

"What's this row about?" he asked. "Mamma is sleeping."

"It's Finch. He is being very unruly." Meg turned her round sweet face toward Nicholas.

"You ought to be ashamed of yourself. And all the money which is being spent on your music! Get upstairs with you. You deserve to have your ears cuffed."

Finch, with his ears as red as though they had already had the cuffing, slunk up the stairs. Piers and Pheasant, still on the window-seat, had drawn the curtains tightly across, so that they were effectually concealed, except for the outline of their knees, and their feet, which projected under the edge. Finch, after a glance at the feet, was reasonably sure of their owners. What a lot of fun everyone had, but himself! Snug and dry before warm fires, or petting in corners.

He found Wakefield in his room, sprawled on the bed, reading *Huckleberry Finn*.

"Hullo," said the little boy, politely. "I hope you don't mind me being here. I wanted to lie down a bit as I aren't very well, and yours is the only bed I can tumble up without Meggie minding."

"Why don't you tell her you're not well?" asked Finch, pulling off his soaked jacket.

"Oh, she'd fuss over me, keep me on the sofa where she could watch me. I like a little privacy as well as anyone."

He was eating marshmallows and he offered Finch one.

"Thanks," said Finch, who was ravenous. "You seem always to have marshmallows lately." He looked at him with sudden severity. "Does Meggie know you've always got them?"

Wake calmly bit into another. "Oh, I don't suppose so. Any more than she knows you've always got cigarettes about you." His eyes were on his book; one cheek was distended. He looked innocent, and yet, the little devil, it had sounded like a threat.

"You mind your own affairs," broke out Finch, "or I'll chuck you into the hall."

Wakefield's bright eyes were on him. "Don't be cross, Finch. I was only thinking how yellow your second finger looked when you took that marshmallow. You'd better scrub it with pumice-stone before tea or someone may notice. You see, your hands are so large and bony that people notice them, and anyone knows that it takes more than one ciagrette to give that orangy colour."

"You see too damned much," growled Finch. "When you get to school you'll have some of the smugness knocked out of you."

"I dare say," agreed Wake, sadly. "I hope you won't let the other boys bully me, Finch."

"Why, look here, there are five hundred fellows in the school. Do you suppose I can keep an eye on you? I'll never even see you. You'll have to just shift for yourself."

"Oh, I'll manage somehow," said Wake.

Finch thought that Wake would probably be happier at school than he was. He hoped so, for he was very fond of this dark-skinned debonair little brother, so different from himself. In silence he took off his sodden socks, gave his feet a perfunctory rub with a frayed bath towel and threw it into a corner. His brain was going round like a squirrel in a cage. Finding Renny and Alayne alone in the dark, rain-drenched porch had brought something to his mind, reminding him curiously of something. He could not think at first what it was, then he remembered. It was the time he had come upon Renny and the unknown woman in the pine wood.

It was not only finding Renny alone with a woman in a dim and sheltered spot, it was something in his attitude—an air of detached attentiveness, as though he were listening, waiting for something that the woman was to do. Some sort of signal.

Finch could not understand why it had affected him so deeply to discover Renny and Alayne in the porch together, unless it was that it had reminded him of that other time. He had been determined that Meg should not know that they were there. But why? There was nothing wrong in their being there together. It was simply that he himself had the kind of mind that—oh Lord, he seemed to find possibilities of mystery, of evil, where no one else would see anything of import. He had a disturbed and beastly mind, there was no doubt about it. He deserved all the knocks that came his way. He had a horrible mind, he thought.

He did wish Meggie would let him practise his music lesson.

Meggie was antagonistic toward the music lessons. No doubt about that. But if he had been taking from Miss Pink it would have been all right. God, women were strange beings!

He went to the drawer where his underclothes were kept, and fumbled hopelessly for a pair of socks that matched.

19

A VARIETY OF SCENES

THE BOOKS from New York were held up at the custom-house in the city. The day when the official card arrived informing Alayne of this, the country was so submerged in cold November rain that a trip into town to get them seemed impossible. Alayne, with the despair of a disappointed child, wandered about the house, looking out of first one window and then another, gazing in helpless nostalgia at dripping hemlocks like funeral plumes, then at the meadows where the sheep huddled, next at the blurred wood that dipped to the wet ravine, and last, from a window in the back hall, on to the old brick oven and the clothes-drier and a flock of draggled, rowdy ducks. She thought of New York and her life there, of her little apartment, of the publishing house of Cory and Parsons, the reception room, the offices, the packing rooms. It all seemed like a dream. The streets with their cosmopolitan throngs, faces seen and instantly lost, faces seen more closely and remembered for a few hours, the splendid and terrible onward sweep of it. The image of every face here was bitten into her memory, even the faces of the farm labourers, of Rags, of the grocer's boy, and the fishmonger.

How quiet Jalna could be! It lay under a spell of silence, sometimes for hours. Now, in the hall, the only sound was the steady licking of a sore paw by the old sheep dog, and the far-away rattle of coals in the basement below. What did the Wragges do down there in the dim half light? Quarrel, re-criminate, make it up? Alayne had seen Rags, a moment ago, glide through the hall and up the stairs with a tray to Meg's room. Oh, that endless procession of little lunches! Why could not the woman eat a decent meal at the table? Why this air of stale mystery? Why this turgid storing up behind all these closed doors? Grandmother: Boney—India—crinolines—scandal—Captain Whiteoak. Nicholas: Nip—London—whisky—Millicent—gout. Ernest: Sasha—Shakespeare—old days at Oxford—debts. Meggie: broken hearts—bastards—little lunches—cosy plumpness.

And all the rest of them, getting their rooms ready for their old age—stuffy nests where they would sit and sit under the leaky roof of Jalna till at last it would crash in on them and obliterate them.

She must get Eden away from here before the sinister spell of the house caught them and held them for ever. She would buy a house with her own money, and still have enough left to keep them for a year or two, until he could make a living from his pen. She would not have him tortured by uncongenial work. Above all, she must not be in the house with Renny Whiteoak. She no longer concealed from herself the fact that she loved him. She loved him as she had never loved Eden—as she had not known that she was capable of loving anyone. A glimpse of him on his bony grey mare would make her forget whatever she was doing. His presence in the dining-room or drawing-room was so disturbing to her that she began to think of her feelings as dangerously unmanageable.

The clock struck two. The day was only half gone, and already it seemed as long as any day should be. The rain was now descending tumultuously. How such a rain would bounce again from the pavement in New York! Here it drove in unbroken shining strands like the quivering strings of an instrument. A stableman with a rubber cape thrown over his head came running across the yard, frightening the ducks, and clattered down the steps into the basement. A moment later Mrs Wragge laboriously climbed the stairs from her domain and appeared in the hall.

"Please, Mrs Whiteoak," she said. "Mr Renny 'as sent word from the stables as 'e's goin' into town by motor this afternoon and if you'll send the card from the customs back by Wright, he says, he'll get them books from the States. Or was it boots? Bless me, I've gone and forgot. And there's nothink throws 'im into a stew like a horror in a message."

"It was books," said Alayne. "I will run up to my room and find the notice. Just come to the foot of the stairs and I'll throw it down to you."

The thought of having the books that evening exhilarated her. She flew up the stairs.

Eden was not writing as she expected but emptying the books out of the secretary and piling them on the bed.

"Hullo!" he exclaimed. "See what a mess I'm in. I'm turning out all these old books. There are dozens and dozens I never look at. Taking up room. Old novels. Old *Arabian Nights*. Even old schoolbooks. And *Boys' Own*. Wake may have those."

What a state the bed was in!

"Eden, are you sure they are not dusty?"

"Dusty! I'll bet they haven't been dusted for five years. Look at my hands."

"Oh dear! Well, never mind. Renny's motoring into town and he will get the books from the customs. Oh, wherever *is* that card? I know I left it on the desk, and you have heaped books all over it. Really, Eden, you are the most untidy being I have ever known."

They argued, searching for the card, which was at last unearthed in the wastepaper basket. In the meantime the car had arrived at the door, and Mrs Wragge was panting up the stairs with another message.

"'E says 'e's late already, 'm, and will you please send the card. He says it's not half bad out, if you'd like a ride to town. But indeed, 'm, I shouldn't go if I was you, for Mr Renny, he drives like all possessed, and the 'ighway will be like treacle."

"Great idea," cried Eden. "We'll both go. Eh, Alayne? It'll do us good. I've been working like the devil. I can stir up Evans about the job, and you can do a little shopping. We'll have tea at The George and be home in time for supper. Will you do it, Alayne?"

Alayne would. Anything to be free for a few hours from the cramped and stubborn air of Jalna. Mrs Wragge panted downstairs with the message.

Alayne had never in her life before gone away leaving her room in such disorder. Impossible to keep even a semblance of order in the place where Eden worked. When they were in their own house, oh, the little cool mauve-and-yellow room she would have for her own!

If Renny were disappointed at the appearance of Eden he did not show it. Husband and wife clambered, rain-coated, into the back seats under the dripping curtains. The wet boughs of the hemlocks swept the windows as they slid along the drive.

It was true that the master of Jalna drove "like all possessed". The highway was almost deserted. Like a taut wet ribbon it stretched before them: to their left, alternate sodden woods, fields, and blurred outlines of villages; to their right, the grey expanse of the inland sea, and already, on a sandy point, a lighthouse sending its solitary beam into the mist.

Alayne was set down before a shop. "Are you sure you've plenty of money, dear?" and a half suppressed grin from Renny. Eden was taken to the customhouse, and then the elder Whiteoak went about his own strange business among legginged, swearing hostlers, and moist smelling straw, and beautiful, satin-coated creatures who bit their mangers and stamped in excess of boredom.

Alayne bought a bright French scarf to send to Rosamond Trent, "just to show her that we have some pretty things up here", two new shirts for Eden—a surprise—a box of sweets for Gran, another, richer, larger one for the family, a brilliant smock that she could not resist for Pheasant, and some stout woollen stockings for herself.

She found Eden and Renny waiting for her in the lobby of an upstairs tea-room. They chose a table near the crackling fire. In a corner on the floor Eden heaped Alayne's purchases on top of the package of books. There were quite eight books in the packet, he informed her, and he had had the devil's own time getting them out of the customs. They had been mislaid and it had taken six clerks to find them. Alayne's eyes gloated over them as they lay there. While they waited for their order, she told what she had bought and for whom—except the shirts, which were to be a surprise.

"And nothing for me?" pleaded Eden, trying to take her foot between his thick-soled boots.

"Wait and see." She sent a warm bright look toward him, trying to avoid Renny's dark gaze.

"Nor me?" he asked.

"Ha," said Eden, "there's nothing for you." And he pressed Alayne's foot.

"My God," he continued, as the waitress appeared with the tray, "the man has ordered poached eggs! Why didn't I?"

He looked enviously for a moment on the two harvest moons that lay on buttered toast before his brother, and then attacked his Sally Lunn and raspberry jam.

"What is that you have?" asked Renny, looking down his nose at Alayne's cake and ice-cream.

"You seem to forget," she replied, "that I am an American, and that I haven't tasted our national sweet for months."

"I wish you would let me order an egg for you," he returned, seriously. "It would be much more staying."

Eden interrupted: "Do you know, brother Renny, you smell most horribly horsy?"

"No wonder. I've been embracing the sweetest filly you ever saw. She's going to be mine, too. What a neck! What flanks! And a hide like brown satin." He stopped dipping a strip of toast into the yolk of an egg to gaze ecstatically into space.

Alayne gave way. She stared at him, drank in the sight of the firelight on his carved, weatherbeaten face, lost herself in the depths of his unseeing eyes.

"Always horses, never girls," Eden was saying rather thickly, through jam. "I believe you dream o' nights of a wild mane whipping your face, and a pair of dainty hoofs pawing your chest. What a bedfellow, eh, brother Renny?" His tone was affectionate and yet touched by the patronage of the intellectual toward the man who is interested only in active pursuits.

"I can think of worse," said Renny, grinning.

Safe from the wind and rain the three talked, laughed, and poured amber cups of tea from fat green pots. Golden beads of butter oozed through the pores of toasted Sally Lunns and dimpled on little green plates. Plump currants tumbled from slices of fruit cake; and Alayne gave her share of icing to Eden. A pleasant hum of careless chatter buzzed around them.

"By the way," said Eden, "Evans wants me to stop in town all night. There is a man named Brown he wants me to meet."

"Anything doing yet?" asked Renny.

Eden shook his head. "Everything here is dead in a business way. The offices positively smell mouldy. But Evans says there's bound to be a tremendous improvement in the spring."

"Why?" asked Alayne.

"I really don't know. Evans didn't say. But these fellows have ways of telling."

"Oh, yes," agreed Renny, solemnly. "They know."

'Little boys,' thought Alayne, 'that's what they are, nothing but little boys where business—city business—is concerned. Believing just what they're told. No initiative. I know five times as much about business as they.'

"So," went on Eden, "if you don't mind trusting yourself to Renny, old lady, I'll stop the night here and see this man. You'll just have to chuck those books back into the bookcase, and I'll look after them tomorrow. Too bad I left them all over the place."

"Oh, I'll manage." But she thought: "He doesn't care. He knows I shall have to handle a hundred dusty books, that the bed is all upset, they are even on the chairs and dresser, and he'll never give it a second thought. He's selfish. He's as self-centred as a cat. Like a lithe, golden, tortoiseshell cat; and Renny's like a fox; and their grandmother is an old parrot; and Meggie is another cat, the soft purry kind that is especially wicked and playful with a bird; and Ernest and Nicholas are two old owls; and Finch a clumsy half grown lamb—what a menagerie at Jalna!"

As Eden was putting her into the car he whispered: "Our first night apart. I wonder if we'll be able to sleep."

"It will seem strange," she returned.

He pushed his head and shoulders into the dimness inside and kissed her. The rain was slashing against the car. Her parcels were heaped on the seat beside her.

"Keep the rug about you. Are you warm? Now your little paw." He cuddled it against his cheek. "Perhaps you would sooner have sat in the front seat with Renny." She shook her head and he slammed the door, just as the car moved away.

They were off, through the blurred streaming streets, nosing their way through the heavily fumbling traffic; cars that were like wet black beetles lurching homeward. Every moment Renny's hand, holding a cloth, slid across the glass. No modern improvements on the Jalna car. Then out of the town. Along the shore, where a black cavern indicated the lake and one felt suddenly small and lonely. Why did he not speak to her? Say something ordinary and comforting?

They were running into a lane, so narrow that there was barely room for the motor to push through. Renny turned toward her.

"I have to see a man in here. I shan't be more than five minutes. Do you mind?"

"Of course not." But she thought: "He asks me if I mind, after we are here. If that isn't like the Whiteoaks! Of course I mind. I shall perfectly hate sitting here in the chill dark, alone in this lashing rain. But he does not care. He cares nothing about me. Possibly forgets—everything—just as he promised he would—and I cannot forget—and I suffer."

He had plunged into the darkness and was swallowed as completely as a stone dropped into a pool. There was no sound of retreating footsteps. The stamp of a horse could scarcely have been heard above the wind and rain. At one moment she saw him bent in the doorway of the car; at the next he was apparently extinguished. But after a little she heard a dog bark and then the slam of a door.

She snuggled her chin into the fur about her neck and drew the rug closer. Then she discovered that he had left the door of the motor open. He did not care whether she was wet and chilled to the bone. She could have whimpered—indeed, she did make a little whimpering sound, as she leaned over the seat and clutched at the door. She could not get it shut. She sank back and again pulled the rug closer. It was as though she were in a tiny house in the woods alone, shut in by the echoing walls of rain. Supposing that she lived in a tiny house in the woods alone—with Renny, waiting for him now to come home to her—oh God, why could she not keep him out of her thoughts? Her mind was becoming like a hound, always running, panting, on the scent of Renny—Renny, Reynard the Fox!

She and Eden must leave Jalna, have a place of their own, before she became a different being from the one he had married. Even now she scarcely recognized herself. A desperate, gypsy, rowdy something was growing in her—the sedate daughter of Professor Knowlton C. Archer.

She clutched the cord with which the books were tied as though to save herself by it. She would try to guess the titles of the books, knowing what she did of the latest Cory publications. It would be interesting to see how many she could guess correctly. What should she say to him when he came back? Just be cool and distant, or say something that would stir him to realization of her mood, her cruelly tormented mood? Rather be silent and let him speak first.

He was getting into the car. From the black earthy-smelling void into which he had dropped, he as suddenly reappeared, dropping heavily on to the seat and banging the door after him.

"Was I long?" he asked in a muffled tone. "I'm afraid I was more than five minutes."

"It seemed long." Her voice sounded faint and far away.

"I think I'll have a cigarette before we start." He fumbled for his case, then offered it to her.

She took one and he struck a light. As her face was illumined, he looked into it thoughtfully.

"I was thinking, as I came down the lane, that if you weren't the wife of Eden, I should ask you if you would like to be my mistress."

The match was out, and again they were in darkness.

"A man might cut in on another man that way," he went on, "but not one's brother—one's half brother."

"Don't you recognize sin?" she asked, out of the faint smoke cloud that veiled her head.

"No, I don't think I do. At least, I've never been sorry for anything I've done. But there are certain decencies of living. You don't really love him, do you?"

"No. I just thought I did."

"And you do love me?"

"Yes."

"It's rotten hard luck. I've been fighting against it, but I've gone under." He continued on a note of ingenuous wonder. "And to think that you are Eden's wife! What hopelessly rotten luck!"

She was thinking: "If he really lets himself go and asks me that, I shall say yes. That nothing matters but our love. Better throw decency to the winds than have this tumult inside one. I cannot bear it. I shall say yes."

Life in a dark full tide was flowing all about them. Up the lane it swept, as between the banks of a river. They were afloat on it, two leaves that had come together and were caught. They were submerged in it, as the quivering reflections of two stars. They talked in low, broken voices. When had he first begun to love her? When had she first realized that all those exultant, expectant moods of hers were flaring signals from the fresh fire that was now consuming her? But he did not again put into words his desire for her. He, who had all his life ridden desire as a galloping horse, now took for granted that in this deepest love he had known he must keep the whip-hand of desire. She, who had lived a life of self-control, was now ready to be swept away in amorous quiescence, caring for nothing but his love.

At last, mechanically, he moved under the wheel and let in the clutch. The car moved slowly backward down the sodden lane, lumbered with elephantine obstinacy through the long grass of the ditch, and slid then, hummingly, along the highway.

They scarcely spoke until they reached Jalna, except when he said over his shoulder: "Should you care to ride? This new mare is just the thing for you. She's very young, but beautifully broken, and as kind as a June day. You'd soon learn."

"But didn't you buy her as a speculation?"

"Well—I'm going to breed from her."

"If you think I can learn——"

"I should say that you would ride very well. You have the look of it—a good body."

The family were at supper. Meg ordered a fresh pot of tea for the latecomers.

"Could we have coffee instead?" asked Renny, "Alayne is tired of your everlasting tea, Meggie."

Nicholas asked: "What books did they send? I shouldn't mind reading a new novel. I'll have a cup of that coffee when it comes. Where did you get rid of Eden? Aren't you cold, child?"

His deep eyes were on them with a veiled expression, as though behind them he were engaged in some complicated thinking.

"Evans wanted him to stay in town," answered Renny, covering his cold beef with mustard.

"Do you think he will get Eden something?" asked his sister.

"Oh, I don't know. There's no hurry."

Ernest said peevishly: "As I was remarking just before you two came in, something must be done about the young cockerels. They crow, and they crow. I did not get a wink of sleep after grey daylight for them. I was told a month ago that they would soon be killed, and here they are still crowing."

"Ah, say," interrupted Finch, "don't kill all the pretty little Leghorn cockerels. They're so——"

"It doesn't matter to you, Finch," said Ernest, getting angry. "You sleep like a log. But this morning they were dreadful. The big Wyandottes experimented with every variety of crow, from a defiant clarion shout to a hoarse and broken 'cock-a-doodle-do', and then the little Leghorns with their plaintive reiterations in a minor key, 'Cock-a-doo-doo!' It's maddening."

"You do it very badly," said his brother. "It's more like this." And in stentorian tones he essayed the crow, flapping his arms as wings. Piers and Finch also crowed.

"Then a hen," pursued Ernest, "thought she would lay an egg. Fully twenty times she announced that she thought she had better lay an egg. Then she laid the egg, squawking repeatedly, that the world might know what an agonizing and important task it was. Then her screams of triumph when it was accomplished! Worst of all, every cock and cockerel in the barnyard immediately crowed in unison."

"Each imagining, poor fool," said Nicholas, "that he was the father of the egg."

"I didn't hear them at all," said Meggie.

Ernest raised a long white hand. "If I had the whole gallinaceous tribe," he said, "between the forefinger and thumb of this hand, tomorrow's sun should rise upon a cockless and henless world."

A heavy thumping sounded on the floor of Grandmother's room.

"Piers, go and see what she wants," said Meg. "I tucked her up quite an hour ago, and she dropped off instantly."

Piers went, and returned, announcing: "She wants to know who brought the rooster into the house. Says she won't have it. She wants Renny and Alayne to go and kiss her."

"Oh, I think she just wants Renny. I don't think she would trouble Alayne."

"She said she wanted them both to come and kiss her."

"Come along, Alayne," said Renny, throwing down his table napkin. They left the room together.

Just as they reached the bedroom door, a long sigh was drawn within. They hesitated, looking at each other. That quivering intake of breath went to their hearts. She was lying alone in there, the old, old woman with her own thoughts. Her fears perhaps. Of what was she thinking, stretched under her quilt, the old lungs dilating, contracting? They went in and bent over her, one on each side of the bed. She drew them down to her in turn and kissed them with sleepy, bewildered, yet passionate affection, her mouth all soft and sunken with the two sets of teeth removed.

As they tucked the bedclothes about her neck, she lay peering up at them, her eyes queerly bright under the night light, infinitely pathetic.

"Anything more, Gran?" asked Renny.

"No, darling."

"Quite comfy, Gran?" asked Alayne.

She did not answer, for she was again asleep.

Outside, they exchanged tender, whimsical smiles. They wished they did not have to return to the dining-room. They loved each other all the more because of their pity for the old woman.

As Nicholas and Ernest separated for the night, Nicholas said in his growling undertone: "Did you notice anything about those two?"

Ernest had been blinking, but now he was alert at once.

"No, I didn't. And yet, now I come to think of it— What d'ye mean, Nick?"

"They're gone on each other. No doubt about that. I'll just go in with you a minute and tell you what I noticed."

The two stepped softly into Ernest's room, closing the door after them.

Renny, in his room, was sitting in a shabby leather armchair, with a freshly filled pipe in his hand. This particular pipe and this chair were sacred to his last smoke before going to bed. He did not light up now, however, but sat with the comfort of the smooth bowl in the curve of his hand, brooding with the bitterness of hopeless love on the soft desirability of the loved one. This girl. This wife of Eden's. The infernal cruelty of it! It was not as though he loved her only carnally, as he had other women. He loved her protectingly, tenderly. He wanted to keep her from hurt. His passion, which in other affairs had burst forth like a flamboyant red flower without foliage, now reared its head almost timidly through tender leaves of protectiveness and pure affection.

There she lay in the next room, alone. And not only alone, but loving him. He wondered if she had already surrendered herself to him in imagination. No subtle vein of femininity ran through the stout fabric of his nature that might have made it possible for him to imagine her feelings. To him she was a closed book in a foreign language. He believed that there were men who understood women because of a certain curious prying in their contacts with them. To him it was scarcely decent. He took what women gave him, and asked no questions.

There she lay in the next room, alone. He had heard her moving about in her preparation for bed. She had seemed to be moving things about, and he had remembered Eden's saying something about emptying out the bookcase. The blasted fool! Leaving her to handle a lot of heavy books. He had thought of going in to do it for her, but he had decided against that. God knows what might have come of it—alone together in there—the rain on the roof, the old mossgrown roof of Jalna pressing above them, all the passions that had blazed and died beneath it dripping down on them, pressing them together.

There she lay in the next room, alone. He pictured her in a fine embroidered shift, curled softly beneath the silk eiderdown like a kitten, her hair in two long honey-coloured braids on the pillow. He got up and moved restlessly to the door, opened it, and looked out into the hall. A gulf of darkness there. And a silence broken only by the low rumble of Uncle Nick's snore and the rasping tick of the old clock. God! Why had Eden chosen to stay away tonight?

Wakefield stirred on the bed, and Renny closed the door and came over to him. He opened his eyes and smiled sleepily up at him.

"Renny—a drink."

He filled a glass from a carafe on the washstand, and held it to the child's mouth. Wake raised himself on his elbow and drank contentedly, his upper lip magnified to thickness in the water. He emptied the glass and threw himself back on the pillow, wet-mouthed and soft-eyed.

"Coming to bed, Renny?"

"Yes."

"Had your smoke?"

"Yes."

"M-m. I don't smell it."

"I believe I've forgotten it."

"Funny. I say, Renny, when you get into bed, will you play we're somebody else? I'm nervous."

"Rot. You go to sleep."

"Honestly. I'm as nervous as anything. Feel my heart."

Renny felt it. "It feels perfectly good to me." He pulled the clothes about the boy's shoulders and patted his back. "One would think you were a hundred. You're more trouble than Gran."

"May I go to the Horse Show with you?"

"I guess so."

"Hurrah. Did you buy the filly?"

"Yes."

"When will she be here?"

"Tomorrow."

"If I aren't well, may I stay home from lessons?"

"Yes." Renny had no backbone tonight, Wake saw that. He could do what he liked with him.

"May I tell Meggie you said so?"

"I suppose."

"Who shall we be when you come to bed?"

"Well—no pirates or harpooners or birds of that sort. You be thinking up a nice quiet sociable pair while I have my smoke."

A muffled tread sounded in the hall, and a low knock on the door. Renny opened it on Rags, sleep-rumpled but important.

"Sorry to disturb you, sir, but Wright is downstairs. 'E's just come in from the stible and 'e says Cora's colt 'as took a turn for the worse, sir, and would you please 'ave a look at it."

Rags spoke with the bright eagerness of hired help who have bad news to tell.

This was bad indeed, for Cora was a new and expensive purchase.

"Oh, curse the luck," growled Renny, as he and Wright, with coat collars turned up, hurried through the rain, now only a chill drizzle, toward the stable.

"Yes indeed, sir," said Wright. "It's pretty hard luck. I was just going to put the light out and go to bed"—he and two other men slept above the garage—"when I saw she was took bad. She'd just been nursed too, and we'd give her a raw egg, but she sort of collapsed and waved her head about, and I thought I'd better fetch you. She'd seemed a bit stronger today, too."

Down in the stable it was warm and dry. The electric light burned clearly—lamps in the house, electricity in the stables at Jalna—and there was a pleasant smell of new hay. The foal lay on a bed of clean straw in a loose-box. Its dam, in the adjoining stall, threw yearning and troubled glances at it over the partition. Why was not its tender nose pressing and snuffling against her? Why, when it suckled, did it pull so feebly, with none of those delicious buntings and furious pullings which, instinct told her, were normal and seemly?

Renny pulled off his coat, threw it across the partition, and knelt beside the foal. It seemed to know him, for its great liquid eyes sought his face with a pleading question in them. Why was it thus? Why had it been dropped from warm indolent darkness into this soul-piercing light? What was it? And along what dark echoing alley would it soon have to make its timid way alone?

Its head, large and carved, was raised above its soft furry body; its stiff foal's legs looked all pitiful angles.

"Poor little baby," murmured Renny, passing his hands over it, "poor little sick baby."

Wright and Dobson stood by, reiterating the things they had done for it. Cora plaintively whinnied and gnawed the edge of her manger.

"Give me the liniment the vet left," said Renny. "Its legs are cold."

He filled his palm with the liquid and began to rub the foal's legs. If only warmth and strength could pass from him into it! "By Judas," he thought, "perhaps there's some fiery virtue in my red head!"

He sent the two men to their beds, for he wanted to look after the foal himself, and they must have their sleep.

He rubbed it till his arms refused to move, murmuring encouragements to it, foolish baby talk: "Little colty—poor little young 'un—does she feel 'ittle bit better then?" and "Cora's baby girl!"

Comforting noises came from other stalls, soft blowings through wide velvety nostrils, deep contented sighs, now and again a happy munching as a wisp of left-over supper was consumed, the deep sucking-in of a drink. He took a turn through the passages between the stalls, sleepy whinnies of recognition welcoming him. In the hay-scented dusk he caught the shine of great liquid eyes, a white blaze on a forehead, a white star on a breast, or the flash of a suddenly tossed mane. God, how he loved them, these swift and ardent creatures! "Shall I ever see the foal standing tall and proud in her box like one of these?"

He went back to her.

Cora had lain down, a dark hump in the shadow of her stall. In her anxiety she had kicked her bedding into the passage, and lay on the bare floor.

The foal's eyes were half closed, but when Renny put his hand on its tawny flank, they flew wide open, and a shiver slid beneath his palm. He felt its legs. Warmer. He was going to save it. He was going to save it! It wanted to rise. He put his arms about it. "There—up she comes now!" It was on its feet, its eyes blazing with courage, its neck ridiculously arched, its legs stiffly braced. Clattering her hoofs, Cora rose, whinnying, and looked over the partition at her offspring. It answered her with a little grunt, took two wavering steps, then, as if borne down by the weight of its heavy head, collapsed again on the straw. "Hungry. Hungry. Poor old baby's hungry. She's coming, Cora. Hold on, pet." He carried the colt to its dam and supported it beneath her.

Oh, her ecstasy! She quivered from head to foot. She nuzzled it, slobbering, almost knocking it over. She nuzzled Renny, wetting his hair. She bit him gently on the shoulder. "Steady on. Steady on, old thing. Ah, the baby's got it. Now for a meal!"

Eagerly it began to suck, but had scarcely well begun when its heart failed it. The foal turned its head petulantly away. Cora looked at Renny in piteous questioning. It hung heavy in his arms. He carried it back, and began the rubbing again. It dozed. He dozed, his face glistening with sweat under the electric light.

But another light was penetrating the stable. Daylight, pale and stealthy as a cat, creeping through the straw, gliding along the cobweb-hung beams, penetrating delicately into the blackest corners. Impatient whinnies were flung from stall to stall. Low, luscious moos answered from the byre. The orchestra of cocks delivered its brazen salute to the dawn. The stallion's blue-black eyes burned in fiery morning rage, but the little foal's eyes were dim.

Renny bent over it, felt its legs, looked into its eyes. 'Oh, that long, long lonely gallop ahead of me,' its eyes said. 'To what strange pasture am I going?'

Wright came clattering down the stairs, his broad face anxious.

"How's the wee foal, sir?"

"It's dying, Wright."

"Ah, I was afraid we couldn't save her. Lord, Mr Whiteoak, you shouldn't have stopped up all night! When I saw the light burning I was sure you had, and I came straight over."

Cora uttered a loud terrified whinny.

The two men bent over the foal.

"It's gone, Wright."

"Yes, sir. Cora knows."

"Go in and quiet her. Have it taken away. God! It came suddenly at the last."

The rain was over. A mild breeze had blown a clear space in the sky. It was of palest blue, and the blown-back clouds, pearl and amethyst, were piled up, one on another, like tumbled towers. Behind the wet boles of the pines a red spark of sunrise burned like a torch.

Renny pictured the soul of the foal, strong-legged, set free, galloping with glad squeals toward some celestial meadow, its eyes like stars, its tail a flaming meteor, its flying hoofs striking bright sparks from rocky planets. 'What a blithering ass I am—worse than Eden. Writing poetry next. . . . All her foals—and theirs—generations of them—lost.'

He went in at the kitchen door, and found young Pheasant, a sweater over her nightdress. She was sitting on the table eating a thick slice of bread and butter.

"Oh, Renny, how is the little colt? I wakened before daylight, and I couldn't go to sleep again for thinking of it, and I got so hungry, and I came down as soon as it was light enough, to get something to eat, and I saw the light under your door and I was sure it was worse. Wake called to me and he said Wright had come for you."

"Yes, Wright came."

He went to the range and held his hands over it. He was

chilled through. She studied him out of the sides of her eyes. He looked aloof, unapproachable, but after a moment he said, gently:

"Make me a cup of tea, like a good kid. I'm starved with the cold in that damned stable. The kettle's singing."

She slid from the table and got the kitchen teapot, fat, brown, shiny, with a nicked spout. She dared not ask him about the colt. She cut some fresh bread and spread it, thinking how strange it was to be in the kitchen at this hour with Renny, just like Rags and Mrs Wragge. The immense, low-ceiled room, with its beamed ceiling and now unused stone fireplace, was heavy with memories of the past, long-gone Christmas dinners, christening feasts, endless roasts and boilings. The weariness, the bickerings, the laughter, the love-making of generations of servant maids and men. All the gossip that had been carried down with the trays, concerning the carryings on of those who occupied the regions above, had settled in this basement, soaked into every recess. Here lay the very soul of Jalna.

Renny sat down by the table. His thin, highly coloured face looked worn. Straws clung to his coat. His hands, which he had washed at a basin in the scullery, looked red and chapped. To Pheasant, suddenly, he was not imposing, but pathetic. She bent over him, putting her arm around his shoulders.

"Is it dead?" she whispered.

He nodded, scowling. Then she saw that there were tears in his eyes. She clasped him to her, and they cried together.

20

MERRY GENTLEMEN

EARLY IN December, Augusta, Lady Buckley, came from England to visit her family. It would probably, unless her mother proposed to live for ever, be the last Christmas the ancient lady would be on earth. At any rate, Augusta said in her letter, it would be the last visit to them in her own lifetime, for she felt herself too old to face the vagaries of ocean travel.

"She has said that on each of her last three visits," observed

Nicholas. "She makes as many farewells as Patti. I'll wager she lives to be as old as Mamma."

"Never," interrupted his mother, angrily, "never. I won't have it. She'll never live to see ninety."

"Augusta is a handsome woman," said Ernest. "She has a dignity that is never seen now. I remember her as a dignified little thing when we were in shoulder knots."

"She always has an offended air," returned Nicholas. "She looks as though something had offended her very deeply in early infancy and she had never got over it."

Mrs Whiteoak cackled. "That's true, Nick. It was on the voyage from India, when I was so sick. Your papa had to change her underthings, and he stuck her with a safety-pin, poor brat!"

The brothers laughed callously, and each squeezed an arm of the old lady. She was such an entertaining old dear. They wondered what they should ever do without her. Life would never be the same when she was gone. They would realize then that they were old, but they would never quite realize it while she lived.

They were taking her for her last walk of the season. This always occurred on a mild day in December. After that she kept to the house till the first warm spring day. Peering out between the crimson curtains of her window, she would see something in the air that marked the day as the one for her last walk. "Now," she would exclaim, "here goes for my last walk till spring!" A thrill always ran through the house at this announcement. "Gran's going for her last walk. Hullo, there, what do you suppose? Gran's off for her last toddle, poor old dear."

She invariably went as far as the wicket gate in the hedge beside the drive, a distance of perhaps fifty yards. They had arrived at the gate now, and she had put out her hands and laid them on the warm and friendly surface of it. They shook a good deal from the exertion, so that a tremor ran through her into the gate and was returned like a flash of secret recognition. Those three had stood together at that gate nearly seventy years before, when she was a lovely-shouldered young woman with auburn ringlets, and they two tiny boys in green velvet suits with embroidered cambric vests, and cockscombs of hair atop their heads.

They stood leaning against the gate without speaking, filled for the moment with quaint recollections, enjoying the mild warmth of the sun on their backs. Then Ernest said:

"Shall we turn back, Mamma?"

Her head was cocked. "No. I hear horses' hoofs."

"She does, by gad," said Nicholas. "You've better ears than your sons, Mamma."

Renny and Alayne were returning from a ride. Like soft thunder the sound of their galloping swept along the drive. Then horses and riders appeared, the tall bony grey mare and the bright chestnut; the long, drooping, grey-coated figure of the man, and the lightly poised, black-habited girl.

"Splendid!" cried Nicholas. "Isn't she doing well, Ernie?"

"One would think she had ridden all her life."

"She's got a good mount," observed Renny, drawing in his horse, and throwing a look of pride over the chestnut and his rider.

Alayne's eyes were bright with exhilaration. In riding she had found something which all her life she had lacked, the perfect outdoor exercise. She had never been good at games, had never indeed cared for them, but she had taken to riding as a waterfowl to the pond. She had gained strength physically and mentally. She had learned to love a gallop over frozen roads, against a bitter wind, as well as a canter in the temperate sun.

Renny was a severe master. Nothing but a good seat and a seemly use of the good hands nature had given her satisfied him. But when at last she rode well, dashing along before him, bright wisps of hair blown from under her hat, her body light as a bird's against the wind, he was filled with a voluptuous hilarity of merely living. He could have galloped on and on behind her, swift and arrogant, to the end of the world.

They rarely talked when they rode together. It was enough to be flying in unison along the lonely roads, with the lake gulls screaming and sweeping overhead. When they did speak it was usually about the horses. He kept a sharp eye on her mount, and when he tightened a girth for her, or adjusted a stirrup, a look into her eyes said more than any words.

Sometimes Eden and Pheasant and Piers rode with them, and once they were joined by Maurice Vaughan, to Pheasant's childlike delight. It was on this occasion that Eden's horse slipped on the edge of a cliff above the lake, and would have taken him to the bottom had not Renny caught the bridle and dragged horse and rider to safety. He had pushed Piers and Maurice aside to do this, as though with a fierce determination to save Eden himself. Did he covet the satisfaction, Alayne wondered afterward, of risking his life to save Eden's, to make up to him for winning the love of his wife, or was it only the arrogant, protective gesture of the head of the family?

Now at any time the bitterness of winter would descend on them. The rides would be few.

"Watch me," cried Grandmother. "I'm going back to the house now. This is my last walk till spring. Ha—my old legs feel wobbly. Hold me up, Nick. You're no more support than a feather bolster."

The three figures shuffled along the walk, scarcely seeming to move. The horses dropped their heads and began to crop the dank grass of December.

"You've no idea," said Renny, "how much the old lady and the two old boys mean to me."

His grandmother had reached the steps. He waved his riding-crop and shouted: "Well done! Bravo, Gran! Now you're safe till spring, eh?"

"Tell them," wheezed Gran to Nicholas, "that when they've put their nags away they're to come and kiss me."

"What does she say?" shouted Renny.

Nicholas rumbled: "She wants to be kissed."

When they had installed their mother in her favourite chair, he said in a heavy undertone to Ernest:

"Those two are getting in deeper every day. Where's it going to end? Where are Eden's eyes?"

"Oh, my dear Nick, you imagine it. You always were on the lookout for that sort of thing. I've seen nothing. Still, it's true that there is a feeling. Something in the air. But what can we do? I'd hate to interfere with an affair of Renny's. Besides, Alayne is not that sort of girl——"

"They're all that sort. Show me the woman who wouldn't enjoy a love affair with a man like Renny, especially if she were snatched up from a big city and hidden away in a sequestered hole like Jalna. I'd be tempted to have one myself if I could find a damsel decrepit enough to fancy me."

Ernest regarded his brother with a tolerant smile.

"Well, Nick, you have had affairs enough in your day. You and Millicent might be——"

"For God's sake, don't say that," interrupted Nicholas. "I'd rather be dead than have that woman about me."

"Ah, well——" Ernest subsided, but he murmured something about 'a dashed sight too many affairs'.

"Well, they're all over, aren't they?" Nicholas asked testily. "Ashes without a spark. I can't even remember their names. Did I ever kiss any one in passion? I can't recall the sensation. What I am interested in is this case of Renny and Alayne; it's serious."

"He scarcely seems to notice her in the house."

"Notice her! Oh, my dear man——" Nicholas bit off the top of a cigar, and scornfully spat it out.

"Well, for an instance, when the young Fennels were in the other night, and the gramophone was playing, Alayne danced oftener with them and Eden, and even young Finch, than with Renny. I only saw her dance with him once."

Nicholas said, pityingly: "My poor blind old brother! They only danced together once because once was all they could stand of it. I saw them dancing in the hall. It was dim there. Her face had gone white, and her eyes—well, I don't believe they saw anything. He moved like a man in a dream. He'd a stiff smile on his face, as though he'd put it on for convenience: a mask. It's serious with him this time, and I don't like it."

"There will be a pretty row if Eden gets on to it."

"Eden won't notice. He's too damned well wrapped up in himself. But I wonder Meggie hasn't."

Ernest took up a newspaper and glanced at the date. "The seventeenth. Just fancy. Augusta will arrive in Montreal tomorrow. I expect the poor thing has had a terrible passage. She always chooses such bad months for crossing." He wanted to change the subject. It upset his digestion to talk about the affairs of Renny and Alayne. Besides, he thought that Nicholas exaggerated the seriousness of it. They might be rather too interested in each other, but they were both too sensible to let the interest go to dangerous lengths. He looked forward to seeing Augusta; he and she had always been congenial.

She arrived two days later. She had made the passage without undue discomfort, never indeed missing a meal, though most of the passengers had been very ill. She had become such a hardened traveller in her infancy that it lay almost beyond the power of the elements now to disarrange her.

Lady Buckley was like a table set for an elaborate banquet at which the guests would never arrive. Her costume was intricate, elegant, with the elegance of a bygone day, unapproachable. No one would ever dare to rumple her with a healthy hug. Even old Mrs Whiteoak held her in some awe, though behind her back she made ribald and derisive remarks about her. She resented Augusta's title, pretended that she could not recall it, and had always spoken to her acquaintances of 'my daughter, Lady Buntley—or Bunting—or Bantling'.

Augusta wore her hair in the dignified curled fringe of Queen Alexandra. It was scarcely grey, though whether through the kindness of nature or art was not known. She wore high collars fastened by handsome brooches. She had a long tapering waist and shapely hands and feet, the latter just showing beneath the hem of her rather full skirt. That air of having never recovered from some deep offence, of which Nicholas had spoken, was perhaps suggested by the poise of her head, which always seemed to be drawn back as though in recoil. She had strongly arched eyebrows, dark eyes, become somewhat glassy from age, the Court nose in a modified form, and a mouth that nothing could startle from its lines of complacent composure. She was an extremely well-preserved woman, who, though she was older than Nicholas or Ernest, looked many years younger. Since it was her fate to have been born in a colony, she was glad it had been India and not Canada. She thought of herself as absolutely English, refuting as an unhappy accident her mother's Irish birth.

She was most favourably impressed by Alayne. She was pleased by a certain delicate sobriety of speech and bearing that Alayne had acquired from much association with her parents.

"She is neither hoydenish nor pert, as so many modern girls are," she observed to her mother, in her deep, well-modulated voice.

"Got a good leg on her, too," returned the old lady, grinning.

Lady Buckley and Alayne had long conversations together. The girl found beneath the remote exterior a kind and sympathetic nature. Lady Buckley was fond of all her nephews, but especially of the young boys. She would tell old-fashioned stories, some of them unexpectedly blood-curdling, to Wakefield by the hour. She would sit very upright beside Finch while he practised his music lesson, composedly praising and criticizing, and the boy seemed to like her presence in the room. She endeared herself to Alayne by being kind to Pheasant. "Let us ignore her mother's birth," she said, blandly. "Her father is of a fine old English military family, and, if her parents were not married—well, many of the nobility sprang from illegitimate stock. I quite like the child."

It was soon evident that Meg resented her aunt's attitude toward Piers' marriage, her admiration for Alayne, and her influence over Finch and Wakefield. She first showed her resentment by eating even less than formerly at the table. It would have been a marvel how she kept so sleek and plump had one not known of those tempting secret trays carried to her by Rags who, if he were loyal and devoted to anyone on earth, was loyal and devoted to Miss Whiteoak.

She then took to sitting a great deal with her grandmother with the door shut against the rest of the family, and a blazing fire on the hearth. The old lady thrived on the scorching air and gossip. There was nothing she enjoyed more than 'hauling Augusta over the coals' behind her back. To her face she gave her a grudging respect. Since Augusta approved of Finch's music lessons, it was inevitable that his practising should prove a torture to the old lady.

"Gran simply cannot stand those terrible scales and chromatics," Meg said to Renny. "Just at the hour in the day when she usually feels her brightest, her nerves are set on edge. At her age it's positively dangerous."

"If the boy were taking lessons from Miss Pink," retorted Renny, bitterly, "the practising wouldn't disturb Gran in the least."

"Why, Renny, Gran never objected to his taking from Mr Rogers! It doesn't matter to her whom he takes from, though certainly Miss Pink would never have taught him to hammer as he insists on doing."

"No, she would have taught him to tinkle out little tunes with no more pep than a toy music-box. If the youngster is musical, he's going to be properly taught. Alayne says he's very talented."

The words were scarcely out before he knew he had made a fatal mistake in quoting Alayne's opinion. He saw Meg's face harden; he saw her lips curl in a cruel little smile. He floundered.

"Oh, well, anyone can see that he's got talent. I saw it long ago; that is why I chose Mr Rogers."

She made no reply for a moment, but still smiled, her soft blue eyes searching his. Then she said:

"I don't think you realize, Renny, how strange your attitude toward Alayne is becoming. You have almost a possessive air. Sometimes I think it would be better if Eden had never brought her here. I've tried to like her, but——"

"Oh, my God!" said Renny, wheeling, and beginning to stride away. "You women make me sick. There's no peace with you. Imagine the entire family by the ears because of a kid's music lessons!" He gave a savage laugh.

Meg, watching him flounder, was aware of depths she had only half suspected. She said:

"It's not that. It's not that. It's the feeling that there's something wrong—some sinister influence at work. From the day Eden brought the girl here I was afraid."

"Afraid of what?"

"Afraid of something in her. Something fatal and dangerous. First she wormed her way——"

"'Wormed her way!' Oh, Meggie, for heaven's sake!"

"Yes, she did! She literally wormed her way into the confidence of the uncles. Then she captivated poor Finch. Just because she told him he was musical, he is willing to practise till he's worn out and Granny is ill. Then she turned Wake against me. He won't mind a thing I say. And now you, Renny! But this is dangerous. Different. Oh, I've seen it coming."

He had recovered himself.

"Meggie," he said, stifling her in a rough tweed hug, "if you would ever eat a decent meal—you know you literally starve yourself—and ever go out anywhere for a change, you wouldn't get such ideas into your head. They're not like you. You are so sane, so well balanced. None of us has as sound a head as you. I depend on you in every way. You know that."

She collapsed, weeping on his shoulder, overwhelmed by this primitive masculine appeal. But she was not convinced. Her sluggish nature was roused to activity against the machinations of Alayne and Lady Buckley.

That evening when Finch went to the drawing-room to practise he found the door locked. He sought Renny in the harness-room of the stable.

"Look here," Finch burst out, almost crying, "what do you suppose? They've gone and locked me out. I can't practise my lesson. They've been after me for a week about it, and now I'm locked out."

Renny, pipe in mouth, continued to gaze in whole-souled admiration at a new russet saddle.

"Renny," bawled Finch, "don't you hear? They've locked me out of the drawing-room, and I met Rags in the hall and he gave one of his beastly grins and said, 'Ow, Miss W'iteoak 'as locked up that pianer. She's not goin' to 'ave any pianer playin' in the 'ouse till the old lidy's recovered. She's in a pretty bad w'y, she is, with all your rattlety-bangin'.' I'd like to know what I'm to do. I may as well throw the whole thing up if I'm not allowed to practise."

Renny made sympathetic noises against the stem of his pipe and continued to gaze at the saddle.

Finch drove his hands into his pockets and slumped against the door jamb. He felt calmer now. Renny would do something, he was sure, but he dreaded a row with himself the centre of it.

At last the elder Whiteoak spoke. "I'll tell you what I'll do, Finch. I'll ask Vaughan if you may practise on his piano. I'm sure he wouldn't mind. The housekeeper's deaf, so her nerves won't be upset. I'll have the piano tuned. It used to be a good one. Then you'll be quite independent."

Soon young Finch might be seen ploughing through the ravine on the dark December afternoons to the shabby, unused drawing-room at Vaughanlands. He brought new life to the old piano, and it, like land that had lain fallow for many years, responded joyfully to his labour, and sent up a stormy harvest of sound that shook the prismed chandelier. Often he was late for the evening meal, and would take what he could get in the kitchen from Mrs Wragge. Several times Maurice Vaughan asked him to have his supper with him, and Finch felt very much a man, sitting opposite Maurice with a glass of beer beside him, and no question about his smoking.

Maurice always managed to bring the conversation around to Meggie. It was difficult for Finch to find anything pleasant to tell about her in these days, but he discovered that Maurice was even more interested to hear of her cantankerousness than her sweetness. It seemed to give him a certain glum satisfaction to know that things were at sixes and sevens with her.

Finch had not been so happy since he was a very little fellow. He had perhaps never been so happy. He discovered in himself a yearning for perfection in the interpretation of his simple musical exercises, which he had never had in his Latin translations or his maths. He discovered that he had a voice. All the way home through the black ravine he would sing, sometimes at the top of his lungs, sometimes in a tender, melancholy undertone.

But how his school work suffered! His report at the end of the term was appalling. As Eden said, he out-Finched himself. In the storm that followed, his one consolation was that a large share of the blame was hurled at Renny. However, that did him little good in the end, for Renny turned on him, cursing him for a young shirker and threatening to stop the lessons altogether. Aunt Augusta and Alayne stood by him, but with caution. Augusta did not want her visit to become too unpleasant, and Alayne had come to regard her position in the house as a voyageur making his difficult progress among treacherous rocks and raging rapids. She could endure it till the New Year—when Eden was to take a position in town which Mr Evans had got for him—and no longer.

At this moment, when Finch, a naked wretch at the cart's tail, with fingers of scorn pointing at him from all directions, alternately contemplated running away and suicide, he suddenly ceased to be an object of more than passing scorn, and little Wakefield took the centre of the stage. Piers had for some time been missing cartridges. Wake had for an equal length of time seemed to have an unlimited supply of marshmallows. And a sneaking stableboy had 'split', and it was discovered that Wake was emptying the cartridges, making neat little packets of the gunpowder, and selling it to the village boys for their own peculiar violences.

When cornered, Wake had denied all knowledge of gunpowder, whether in cartridges or bulk. But Meg and Piers, searching his little desk, had come upon the neat little packets, all ready to sell, with a box full of coppers, and even a carefully written account of sales and payments. It was serious.

Meg said he must be whipped. The young Whiteoaks had set no high standard of morality for a little brother to live up to, but still this was too bad.

"Flog him well," said Gran. "The Courts stole, but they never lied about it."

"The Whiteoaks," said Nicholas, "often lied, but they never stole."

Ernest murmured: "Wakefield seems to combine the vices of both sides."

"He's a little rotter," said Piers, "and it's got to be taken out of him."

Alayne was aghast at the thought of the airy and gentle Wake being subjected to the indignity of physical punishment. "Oh, couldn't he please get off this time?" she begged. "I'm sure he'll never do such a thing again."

Piers gave a short scornful laugh. "The trouble with that kid is he's been utterly ruined. If you'll let me attend to him, I'll wager he doesn't pinch anything more."

"I strongly disapprove of a delicate child like Wakefield being made to suffer," said Lady Buckley.

The culprit, listening in the hall, put his head between the curtains at this and showed his little white, tear-stained face.

"Go away, sir," said Nicholas. "We're discussing you."

"Please, please——"

Renny, who had been captured for the conclave and who stood gloomily, cap in hand, with snow-crusted leggings, turned to go. "Well, I'm off."

"Renny!" cried his sister, peremptorily. "Why are you going? You have got to whip Wake." The opposition of Alayne and Augusta had turned her sisterly anxiety to correct the child into relentless obstinacy.

Renny stood with bent head, looking sulkily into his cap. "The last time I licked him, he shivered and cried half the night. I'll not do it again." And he turned into the hall, pushing Wakefield aside and slamming the front door behind him.

"Well, of all the damned sloppiness!" broke out Piers.

"Don't worry," said Meg, rising. "Wakefield shall be punished." Her immobile sweet face was a shade paler than usual.

"This isn't a woman's job," declared Piers. "I'll do it."

"No. You'll be too hard on him."

"Let me flog the boy," cried Grandmother. "I've flogged boys before now. I've flogged Augusta. Haven't I, Augusta? Get me my stick!" Her face purpled with excitement.

"Mamma, Mamma," implored Ernest, "this is very bad for you."

"Fan her," said Nicholas. "She's a terrible colour."

Meg led Wakefield up the stairs. Piers, following her to the foot, entreated: "Now, for heaven's sake don't get chicken-hearted. If you're going to do it, do it thoroughly."

"Oh, don't you wish it were you?" exclaimed Pheasant, tugging at his arm.

"Which?" he laughed. "Giving or getting one?"

"Getting, of course. It would do you good."

Nicholas and Ernest also came into the hall, and after them shuffled Grandmother, so exhilarated that she walked alone, thumping her stick on the floor and muttering: "I've flogged boys before now."

Finch draped himself against the newel post and thought of thrashings of his own. Augusta and Alayne shut themselves in the living-room.

Eden came out of his room above to discover the cause of the disturbance, but Meg would not speak. With set face she pushed Wakefield before her into her room and closed the door. However, Piers, in vehement tones, sketched the recent criminal career of the youngest Whiteoak.

Eden perched on the handrail, gazing down at the faces of his brothers, uncles, and grandmother with delight. He said, dangling a leg:

"You're priceless. It's worth being interrupted in the very heart of a tropic poem to see your faces down there. You're like paintings by the great masters: Old Woman with Stick. The Cronies (that's Uncle Nick and Uncle Ernest). Young Man with Red Face (you, Piers). Village Idiot (you, Finch). As a matter of fact, I was at my wits' end for a rhyme. Perhaps brother Wake, in his anguish, will supply me with one."

"What's he saying?" asked Gran. "I won't have any of his back chat."

Ernest replied mildly: "He's just saying that we look as pretty as pictures, Mamma."

"She's beginning at last," announced Piers, grinning.

A sound of sharp blows cascaded from Meg's room, blows

that carried the tingling impact of bare skin. Staccato feminine blows, that ceased as suddenly as they had begun.

"He's not crying, poor little beggar," said Eden.

"That's because he's not hurt," stormed Piers. "What does the woman think she's doing? Giving love taps to a kitten? Good Lord! She'd hardly begun till she'd stopped. Hi, Meggie, what's the matter? Aren't you going to lick the kid?"

Meg appeared at the door of her room. "I have whipped him. What do you want me to do?"

"You don't mean to say that you call that a licking? Better not touch him at all. It's a joke."

"Yes," agreed Nicholas, "if you're going to tan a boy, do it thoroughly."

Grandmother said, her foot on the bottom step: "I'd do it thoroughly. Let me at him!"

"Steady on, Mamma," said Nicholas. "You can't climb up there."

"For God's sake, Meggie," exclaimed Piers, "go back and give him something he'll remember for more than five minutes!"

"Yes, yes, Meggie," said Ernest, "a little swishing like that is worse than nothing."

"Give him a real one! Give him a real one!" bawled Finch, suddenly stirred to ferocity. He had suffered, by God! Let that pampered little Wake suffer for a change.

Boney screamed: "Jab kutr! Nimak haram! Chore!"

Meg swept to the top of the stairs. "You are like a pack of wolves," she said at white heat, "howling for the blood of one poor little lamb. Wake is not going to get one more stroke, so you may as well go back to your lairs."

Eden threw his arms about her, and laid his head on her comfortable shoulder.

"How I love my family!" he exclaimed. "To think that after the New Year I shall be out of it all. Miss such lovely scenes as this."

Meg did not try to understand Eden. She knew that he was pleased with her because he hugged her, and that was enough.

"Do you blame me for telling just how heartless I thought they were?"

"You were perfectly right, old girl."

"Eden, I hope you won't mind what I'm going to say, but

I do wish Alayne would not interfere between me and the children. She has *such* ideas."

"Oh, she has the habit of wanting to set everything right. She's the same with me. Always telling me how unmethodical I am, and how untidy with my things. She means well enough. It's just her little professorial ways."

"Poor lamb!" said Meggie, stroking the shining casque of his hair.

Wake's voice came, broken by sobs: "Meggie!"

Meg disengaged herself from Eden's arms. "There, now, I must go to him, and tell him he's forgiven."

The party downstairs had retreated after Meggie's attack, leaving a trail of wrangling behind them. Piers reached for his cap, and, stopping at the door of his grandmother's room, said, loud enough for Alayne to hear: "They're spoiling the two kids among them, anyway. As for Eden, he's no better than another woman!"

"He's like his poor flibbertigibbet mother," said Gran.

The cloud under which Wakefield awoke next morning was no more than a light mist, soon dispelled by the sun of returning favour. Before the day was over he was his own dignified, airy, and graceless self again, a little subdued perhaps, a little more anxious to please, a shade more subtle in the game of his life.

The game of life went on at Jalna. A stubborn heavy game, requiring not so much agility of mind as staying power and a thick skin. The old red house, behind the shelter of spruce and balsam, drew into itself as the winter settled in. It became the centre of whirling snow flurries. Later on, its roof, its gables, and all its lesser projections became bearers of a weight of slumbrous, unspotted snow. It was guarded by snow trees. It was walled by a snow hedge. It was decked, festooned, titivated by snow wreaths, garlands, and downy flakes. The sky leaned down toward it. The frozen earth pressed under it. Its inhabitants were cut off from the rest of the world. Except for occasional tracks in the snow, there was little sign of their existence. Only at night dim lights showed through the windows, not illuminating the rooms, but indicating by their mysterious glow that human beings were living, loving, suffering, desiring, beneath that roof.

Christmas came.

Books for Alayne from New York, with a chastely engraved card enclosed from Mr Cory. More books, and a little framed etching from the aunts up the Hudson. An over-blouse, in which she would have frozen at Jalna, from Rosamond Trent. Alayne carried them about, showing them, and then laid them away. They seemed unreal.

There were no holly wreaths at Jalna. No great red satin bows. But the banister was twined with evergreens, and a sprig of mistletoe was suspended from the hanging lamp in the hall. In the drawing-room a great Christmas tree towered toward the ceiling, bristling with the strange fruit of presents for the family, from Grandmother down to little Wake.

A rich hilarity drew them all together that day. They loved the sound of each other's voices: they laughed on the least provocation; by evening, the young men showed a tendency toward horseplay. There was a late dinner, dominated by the largest turkey Alayne had ever seen. There was a black and succulent plum pudding with brandy sauce. There were native sherry and port. The Fennels were there; the two daughters of the retired admiral; and lonely little Miss Pink, the organist. Mr Fennel proposed Grandmother's health, in a toast so glowing with metaphor and prickling with wit that she suggested that if he were three sheets in the wind on Sunday he would preach a sermon worth hearing. The admiral's daughters and Miss Pink were flushed and steadily smiling in the tranced gaiety induced by wine. Meg was soft and dimpled as a young girl.

A great platter of raisins smothered in flaming brandy was carried in by Rags, wearing the exalted air of an acolyte.

Seeing Rags' hard face in that strange light carried Renny as in a dream to another very different scene. He saw Rags bent over a saucepan in a dugout in France, wearing a filthy uniform, and, oddly enough, that same expression. But why, he could not remember. He had picked Rags up in France. Renny looked up into his eyes with a smile, and a queer worshipping grin spread over Rags' grim hardbitten face.

The raisins were placed on the table in the midst of the company. Tortured blue flames leaped above them, quivering, writhing, and at last dying into quick-running ripples. Hands, burnished like brass, stretched out to snatch the raisins. Wake's, with its round, child's wrist; Finch's, bony and predatory; Piers', thick, muscular; Grandmother's, dark, its hooklike fingers glittering with jewels—all the grasping, eager hands and the watchful faces behind them illuminated by the flare; Gran's eyes like coals beneath her beetling red brows.

Pheasant's hands fluttered like little brown birds. She was afraid of getting burned. Again and again the blue flames licked them and they darted back.

"You are a little silly," said Renny. "Make a dash for them, or they'll be gone."

She set her teeth and plunged her hand into the flames. "Oh—oh, I'm going to be burned!"

"You've only captured two," laughed Eden, on her other side, and laid a glossy cluster on her plate.

Renny saw Eden's hand slide under the table and cover hers in her lap. His eyes sought Eden's and held them a moment. They gazed with narrowed lids, each seeing something in the other that startled him. Scarcely was this unrecognized something seen when it was gone, as a film of vapour that changes for a moment the clarity of the well-known landscape and shows a scene obscure, even sinister—— The shadow passed, and they smiled, and Eden withdrew his hand.

Under the mistletoe Mr Fennel, Grandmother having been carefully steered that way by two grandsons, caught and kissed her, his beard rough, her cap askew.

Uncle Ernest, a merry gentleman that night, caught and kissed Miss Pink, who most violently became Miss Scarlet.

Tom Fennel caught and kissed Pheasant. "Here now, Tom, you fathead, cut that out!" from Piers.

Finch, seeing everything double after two glasses of wine, caught and kissed two white-shouldered Alaynes. It was the first time she had worn an evening-dress since her marriage.

Nicholas growled to Ernest: "Did you ever see a hungry wolf? Look at Renny glowering in that corner. Isn't Alayne lovely tonight?"

"Everything's lovely," said Ernest, rocking on his toes. "Such a nice Christmas!"

They played charades and dumb crambo.

To see Grandmother (inadvertently shouting out the name of the syllable she was acting) as Queen Victoria, and Mr Fennel as Gladstone!

To see Meg as Mary Queen of Scots, with Renny as

executioner, all but cutting off her head with the knife with which he had carved the turkey!

To see Alayne as the Statue of Liberty, holding a bedroom lamp on high ("Look out, Alayne, don't tilt it so; you'll have the house on fire!"), and Finch as a hungry immigrant!

You saw the family of Jalna at their happiest in exuberant play.

Even when the guests were gone and the Whiteoaks getting ready for bed, they could not settle down. Ernest, in shirt and trousers, prowled through the dim hallway, a pillow from his bed in one hand. He stopped at Renny's door. It was ajar. He could see Renny winding his watch, Wake sitting up in bed, chattering excitedly. Ernest hurled the pillow at Renny's head. He staggered, bewildered by the unexpected blow, and dropped his watch.

"By Judas," he said, "if I get you!" With his pillow he started in pursuit.

"A pillow fight! A pillow fight!" cried Wake, and scrambled out of bed.

Ernest had got as far as his brother's room. "Nick," he shouted, in great fear, "save me!"

Nicholas, his grey mane on end, was up and into it. Piers, like a bullet, sped down the hall. Finch, dragged from slumber, had barely reached the scene of conflict when a back-handed blow from Eden's pillow laid him prostrate.

Nicholas' room was a wreck. Up and down the passage the combatants surged. The young men forgot their loves, their fears, their jealousies, the two elderly men their years, in the ecstasy of physical, half naked conflict.

"Boys, boys!" cried Meg, drawing aside her chenille curtain.

"Steady on, old lady!" and a flying pillow drove her into retreat.

Pheasant appeared at her door, her short hair all on end. "May I play, too?" she cried, hopping up and down.

"Back to your hole, little hedgehog!" said Renny, giving her a feathery thump as he passed.

He was after Nicholas, who had suddenly become cognizant of his gout and could scarcely hobble. Piers and Finch were after him. They cornered him, and Nicholas, from being the wellnigh exhausted quarry, became the aggressor, and helped to belabour him.

Eden stood at the top of the stairs, laughingly holding off little Wake, who was manfully wielding a long old-fashioned bolster. Ernest, with one last hilarious fling in him, stole forth from his room, and hurled a solid sofa cushion at the pair. It struck Eden on the chest. He backed. He missed his footing. He fell. Down the stairs he went, crashing with a noise that aroused Grandmother, who began to rap the floor with her stick.

"What's up? What have you done?" asked Renny.

"My God! I've knocked the lad downstairs. What if I've killed him!"

The brothers streamed helter-skelter down the stairs.

"Oh, those stairs," groaned Eden. "I've twisted my leg. I can't get up."

"Don't move, old fellow." They began to feel him all over. The women emerged from their rooms.

"I have been expecting an accident," said Augusta, looking more offended than usual.

"Oh, whatever is the matter?" cried Alayne.

Ernest answered, wringing his hands: "Can you ever forgive me, Alayne? Piers says I've broken Eden's leg."

21

EDEN AND PHEASANT

SIX WEEKS had passed and Eden was still unable to leave his room. As well as a broken leg, he had got a badly wrenched back. However, after the first suffering was over, he had not had such a bad time. It was almost with regret that he heard the hearty red-faced doctor say that morning that he would soon be as fit as ever. It had been rather jolly lying there, being taken care of, listening to the complaints of others about the severity of the weather, the depth of the snowdrifts, and the impossibility of getting anywhere with the car. The inactivity of body had seemed to generate a corresponding activity of mind. Never had he composed with less effort. Poetry flowed through him in an exuberant crystal stream. Alayne had sat by his couch and written the first poems out for him in her beautiful legible hand, but now he was able to

sit up with a pad on his knee and scrawl them in his own way
—decorating the margins with fanciful sketches in illustration.

Alayne had been a dear through it all. She had nursed him
herself, fetching and carrying from the basement kitchen to
their room without complaint, though he knew he had been
hard to wait on in those first weeks. She looked abominably
tired. Those brick basement stairs were no joke. Her face
seemed to have grown broader, flatter, with a kind of Teutonic
patience in it that made him remember her mother had been
of Dutch extraction, several generations ago; it was there—
the look of solidity and patience. A benevolent, tolerant face
it might become in later life, but plainer, certainly.

She must have been disappointed, too, at his inability to
take the position got for him by Mr Evans at the New Year.
Though she had not said much about it, he knew that she was
eager to leave Jalna and have a house of their own. He had
refused to let her put her money into the buying of one, but he
had agreed that, he paying the rent from his salary, she might
buy the furniture. She had talked a good deal about just how
she would furnish it. When his leg was paining and he could
not sleep, it was one of her favourite ways of soothing him, to
stroke his head and furnish each of the rooms in turn. She had
chosen the furniture for his workroom with great care, and
also that for his bedroom and hers. He had been slightly
aggrieved that she spoke of separate rooms, though upon
reflection he had decided that it would be rather pleasant to
be able to scatter his belongings all over his room without the
feeling that he was seriously disturbing her. She was too
serious: that was a fact. She had a way of making him feel like a
naughty boy. That had been charming at first, but often now it
irritated him.

There was something strange about her of late. Remote,
inward-gazing. He hoped and prayed she wasn't going to be
mopy. A mopy wife would be disastrous to him, weigh on his
spirits most dreadfully. She had slept on the couch in their
room during the first weeks after the accident, when he had
needed a good deal of waiting on at night. Later, she had taken
all her things and moved to a big low-ceiled room in the attic.
She spent hours of her time there now. Of course, all he had
to do was to ring the little silver bell at his side, and she came
flying down the stairs to him, but he could not help wondering

what she did up there all alone. Not that he wanted her with him continually, but he could not forgive her for seeking solitude. He was really very happy. He was well except for a not unpleasant feeling of lassitude. He had also a feeling of exquisite irresponsibility and irrelevance. This interval in his life he accepted as a gift from the gods. It was a time of inner development, of freedom of spirit, of ease from the shackles of life.

He had scarcely felt the chafing of those shackles yet, and he did not want to feel them. He should have been a lone unicorn, stamping in inconsequent gaiety over sultry Southern plains, leaving bonds to tamer spirits.

He was just thinking this, and smiling at the thought when Pheasant came into the room. She was carrying a plate of little red apples, and she wore the vivid smock bought for her by Alayne.

"Meggie sent you those," she said, setting the plate beside him. "As a matter of fact, I think you eat too much. You're not as slim as you were."

"Well, it's a wonder I'm not thin," he returned with some heat. "God knows I've suffered!" He bit into an apple, and continued: "You've never had any real sympathy for me, Pheasant."

She looked at him, astonished.

"Why, I thought I'd been lovely to you! I've sat with you, and listened to your old poetry, and told you what a wonder you are. What more do you want?"

He reclined, drumming his fingers on the afghan that lay over him, a faint smile shadowing, rather than lighting, his face.

She examined his features and then said darkly: "You're too clever, that's what's the matter with you."

"My dear little Pheasant, don't call me by such a horrid word. I'm not clever. I'm only natural. You're natural. That is why we get on so famously."

"We don't get on," she returned, indignantly. "Uncle Ernest was saying only the other day what a pity it is you and I quarrel so much."

"He's an old ninny."

"You ought to be ashamed to say that. He has done everything in his power to make up to you for hurting you. He has read to you by the hour. I don't think he'll ever get over the shock of seeing you hurtle downstairs with his pillow on top of you."

"I agree with you. It was the most exhilarating thing that has happened to him for years. He looks ten years younger. To have knocked an athletic young fellow downstairs and broken his leg! Just when he began to feel the feebleness of old age creeping on! Why, he's like a young cockerel that's saluted the dawn with its first crow."

"I think you're sardonic."

"And I think you're delicious. I especially admire your wisdom, and that little tuft of hair that stands up on your crown. But I do wish you'd put it down. It excites me."

She passed her hand over it.

"Do you know," he said, "that you pass your hand over your head exactly as I do. We have several identical gestures. I believe our gesture toward life is the same."

"I think your greatest gift," she said, stiffly, "is flattery. You know just how to make a woman pleased with herself."

She was such a ridiculous little child, playing at being grown up, that he could scarcely keep from laughing at her. Neither could he keep the tormenting image of her from his mind when she was away from him. He lay back on the pillow and closed his eyes.

Outside, the snow-covered lawns and fields, unmarked by the track of a human being, stretched in burnished, rosy whiteness toward the sunset. The pines and hemlocks, clothed in the sombre grandeur of their winter foliage, threw shadows of an intense, translucent blueness. And in the hard bright intensity of that northern ether, every smallest twig was bitten against its background as though with acid. An atmosphere hateful to those who see it in alien loneliness, but of the essence and goodness of life to the native born.

When Eden opened his eyes and turned toward her, she was looking out on this scene. He thought there was a frightened look in her eyes. A faint sound of music came from Uncle Nick's room. He was playing his piano as he often did at this hour.

"Pheasant."

"Yes?"

"You look odd. Rather frightened."

"I'm not a bit frightened."

"Not of me, of course. But of yourself?"

"Yes, I am rather frightened of myself, and I don't even know why. I believe it's that wild-looking sky. In a minute it will be dark and so cold. You'll need a fire here."

"I am on fire, Pheasant."

He found her hand and held it. He asked: "Do you think Alayne loves me any more?"

"No, I don't think she does. And you don't deserve it—her love, I mean."

"I don't believe I ever had it. It was my poetry she loved, not me. Do you think she loves—Renny?"

She stared at him, startled. "I'd never thought of that. Perhaps she does."

"A nice mix-up."

"Well, I should not blame Alayne. Here she is pitchforked into this weird family, with a husband who is absolutely devoted to himself, and a most remarkable-looking and affectionate brother-in-law."

"'Remarkable-looking and affectionate'! Heavens, what a description!"

"I think it's a very good description."

"Well, I suppose Renny is remarkable—but 'affectionate'! That scarcely describes making love to another man's wife. I don't believe Alayne would fall for him unless he did make love to her. But 'affectionate'—I can't get over that."

"How would you describe your holding my hand? That's affectionate, isn't it?"

He took her other hand and laid both hands on his breast. "I shan't mind about anything," he said, "if you will only care for me." He drew her closer, his face stained by the afterglow that transformed the matter-of-fact room into a strange and passionate retreat.

Pheasant began to cry.

"Don't," she implored. "Don't do that! It's what I've been afraid of."

"You care for me," he whispered. "Oh, my darling little Pheasant! Say that you do—just once. Kiss me, then—you know you want to. It's what you've been dreading, but—desiring, too, my dearest. There's nothing to be afraid of in life; nothing to be ashamed of. Just be your precious self."

She flung herself against him, sobbing.

She did not know whether or not she loved him, but she knew that that room had a sultry fascination for her, that the couch where Eden lay was the centre of all her waking thoughts, that his eyes, blazing in the afterglow, compelled her to do as he willed. She hated Piers for being absorbed in his cattle, seeing nothing of her temptation, not saving her from herself, as he should have done. He knew that she was not like other young girls of his class. She had bad, loose blood. He should have watched her, been hard with her, as Maurice had been. His idea was to make a 'pal' of his wife. But she was not that sort of wife. He should have known, oh, he should have known, saved her from herself—from Eden!

As she wept against Eden's shoulder, her tears became no longer the warm tears of surrender, but the tears of black anger against Piers, who had not saved her.

22

WAKEFIELD'S BIRTHDAY

WAKEFIELD AWOKE each morning now with a feeling of gay excitement. The reason for this was that Finch had given him his Boy Scout bugle. Finch had got over being a Boy Scout very quickly. The only thing about it that had suited him was the fact of his being a bugler. However, he soon tired of that, and, coming to the conclusion that he was not the stuff of which good Boy Scouts are made, he gave it up entirely. To perform his little duties with bright alertness, to be ready, to be helpful, to do a kind act every day, seemed beyond him. So he had skulked out of the organization, and locked his bugle in the under part of the secretary in his room, where Wake might not meddle with it.

Now he had given it to Wake for his birthday. Having once decided to do this, he did not hold it till the day itself. The little boy had been in possession of it for a fortnight. And every morning he wakened with his nerves tingling with delicious excitement, for there, at the head of the bed, was the bugle, and he must not get up until he had sounded the reveille. It was thrilling to sit up in bed and send forth from swelling chest and distended cheeks those glorious brazen notes. Feeble, croaking they might sound to the listener, but to Wake they were round with a noble roundness and stirring to the soul.

Luckily, he was usually the last of the family to awake. But this morning was his birthday and he had been the very first. All, all had been roused by that sleep-shattering reveille. Renny, stretched on his back, his arms flung above his head, had been dreaming of galloping on a great wild horse along a steep precipice. Suddenly, with a neigh that shook the universe, the horse had leaped over the precipice, and plunged with him into the sunlit sea.

With a convulsive twitch of the body, Renny awoke into the sunlight of the early morning, his face so comic in its astonishment that Wakefield laughed aloud, lost his wind, and sputtered helplessly into the instrument. Then Renny laughed too, for the sight of his young brother sitting up in bed, so alert, so important, with hair on end and one dark eye cocked roguishly at him above one bulging cheek, was so ridiculous. He was ridiculous, and he was pathetic too. 'Poor little beggar,' thought Renny, 'a human being like myself, who will have a man's feelings, a man's queer thoughts one day.'

"It's my birthday," quoth Wakefield, wiping his chin.

"Many happy returns," said Renny, trying not to look as though he had a delightful present for him.

"I shall probably not live to be as old as Gran. But I may reach ninety if I have good care."

"Oh, you'll get good care, all right. Cuddle down here a bit. It's early yet."

Wake laid the bugle on the table at the head of the bed and flung himself down into the bedclothes. He burrowed against Renny, putting his arms about his neck.

"Oh! I'm so happy," he breathed. "A picnic today if you please. The first of the season. It's June. The first of June! My birthday!" His eyes were two narrow slits. "Renny, have you a—you know what?"

Renny yawned prodigiously, showing two rows of strong teeth. "Well, I guess I'll get up."

"Renny, Renny!" He bumped and struggled against his elder's chest. "Oh, Renny, I could kill you!"

"Why?"

"''Cos you won't tell me."

"Tell you what?" Renny held him as in a vice.

"You know what."

"How can I know if you won't tell me?"

"Oh, you beast, Renny! It's you who won't tell me!"

"Tell you what?"

"Whether you have a—you know what—for me."

Renny closed his eyes. "You sound half witted this morning," he said, coldly. "It seems a pity, when you've reached such an age."

Wakefield examined his brother's hard, weather-bitten visage with its relentless-looking nose. Certainly it was a forbidding face. A face that belonged to a man who was his adored brother and who had no birthday present for him.

He, too, closed his eyes, murmuring to himself: "Oh, this is terrible!" A tear trickled down his cheek and fell on Renny's wrist.

The elder Whiteoak gave the younger a little shake. "Cut that out," he said. They looked into each other's eyes.

"It nearly broke me."

"What did, Renny?"

"Why, the present."

"The *present*?"

"Rather. The birthday present."

"Oh, Renny, for God's sake——"

"Stop your swearing."

"But *what* is it?"

"It's," he plunged the word into Wake's ear, "a pony—a beautiful Welsh pony."

After the first ecstatic questions, Wake lay silent, floating in a golden haze of happiness. He did not want to miss the savour of one lovely moment of this day of days. First a pony, then a picnic, and in between, an orgy of other presents. A birthday cake with ten tall candles. At last he whispered. "Is it a he or a she?"

"A little mare."

A mare! He could hardly believe it. There would be colts—tiny, shaggy colts. His very own. It was almost too much. He wriggled against Renny. Adoring him.

"When will she—oh, I say, Renny, what's her name?"

"She has no name. You may name her."

No name. A nameless gift from the gods. Oh, responsibility overpowering, to name her!

"When will she come?"

"She is here, in the stable."

With a squeal of joy Wake leaped up in the bed; then, espying the bugle, he had an inspiration.

"Renny, wouldn't it be splendid, if I'd sound the reveille and then we'd both instantly get up? I'd like terribly to sound the reveille for you, Renny."

"Fire away, then."

Solemnly the boy placed the bugle against his lips and took a prodigious breath. Renny lay looking at him, amused and compassionate. Poor little devil—a man some day, like himself.

Loudly, triumphantly, the notes of the reveille were sounded. Simultaneously they sprang out on to the floor. June sunshine blazed into the room.

Downstairs, Wakefield said to Finch: "What do you suppose? Renny has given me a pony. We've just been out to the stable to see her. A little pony mare, mind you, Finch. There'll be colts one day. And thanks again for the bugle. Renny and I both got up by it this morning. And there's to be a picnic on the shore, and an absolutely 'normous birthday cake."

"Humph," grunted Finch. "I never remember such a fuss on any of my birthdays."

"You have always had a cake, dear," said Meggie, reproachfully. "And don't forget that nice little engine thing, and your bicycle, and your wristwatch."

"You don't expect the family to rejoice because you were born, do you?" asked Piers, grinning.

"No, I don't expect anything," bawled Finch, "but to be badgered."

"Poor little boy, he's jealous." Piers passed a sunburned hand over Finch's head, stroking downward over his long nose, and ending with a playful jolt under the chin.

Finch's nerves were raw that morning. He was in the midst of the end-of-the-term examinations, and his increasing preoccupation with music seemed to render him less than ever able to cope with mathematics. He knew with dreadful certainty that he was not going to pass into the next form. The fact that his music teacher was not only pleased with him but deeply interested in him, would not make up for that. Combined with a skulking sense of helpless inferiority, he felt the exalted arrogance of one whose spirit moves on occasion in the free and boundless spaces of art.

With a kind of bellow, he turned on Piers and struck him in the chest. Piers caught his wrists and held them, smiling lazily into his wild, distorted face.

"See here, Eden," he called. "This little lamb is baaing because we celebrate Wake's birthday with more pep than we do his. Isn't it a crime?"

Eden lounged over, his lips drawn in a faint smile from his teeth, which held a cigarette, and joined in the baiting.

All morning Finch's heart raged within him. At dinner Meggie and her grandmother both chose to correct him, to nag at him. He slouched, they said. He stuck his elbows out. He bolted his food so that he might be ready for the last helping of cherry tart before poor dear Gran. Furious, he muttered something to himself to the effect that she might have it for all he cared, and that if it choked her——

She heard.

"Renny! Renny!" she shouted, turning purple. "He says he hopes it chokes me—chokes me—at my age! Flog him, Renny; I won't stand it. I'll choke. I know I will."

She glared wildly at the head of the house, her eyes blazing under her shaggy red brows.

"Mamma, Mamma," said Ernest.

"It's true," growled Nicholas. "I heard him say it."

Renny had been talking to Alayne, trying not to notice the disturbance. Now, in sudden anger, he got up and in a stride stood over Finch.

"Apologize to Gran," he ordered.

"Sorry," muttered Finch, turning white.

"No mumbling! Properly."

"I'm very sorry, Grandmother."

The sight of his hunched shoulders and unprepossessing, sheepish face suddenly threw his elder into one of his quick passions. He gave him a sound and ringing cuff. Perhaps it was because Finch was not properly balanced that day. In any case it always seemed easy to send him sprawling. The next second he was in a sobbing heap on the floor, and his heavy chair had fallen with a crash.

Alayne smothered a cry, and stared at her plate. Her heart

was thudding, but she thought: "I must hang on to myself. I must. He didn't mean to do it. He will be sorry. They drove him to it."

Renny sat down. He avoided looking at her. He was humiliated at having been drawn into violence before her. However, if she thought him a brute, so much the better.

Finch gathered up himself and his chair, and resumed his place at the table with a look of utter dejection.

"Now will you give back chat?" asked Grandmother, and she added after another mouthful of tart: "Somebody kiss me."

She kept asking what time the picnic was to be, for she was even more excited about it than Wake. She had her bonnet and cape on long before the hour when the phaeton was to convey her to the shore. She had the picnic hampers ranged beside her chair, and passed the period of waiting by a prolonged and bitter discussion with Boney as to whether or not he should forage among the edibles.

The picnic party was separated into the same parts as the church party, with the difference that Finch rode his bicycle instead of walking, and Piers arrived late on horseback, for it was a busy season with him.

As he tethered his mare to an iron stake which had been driven into that field before any of them could remember, he glanced toward the picnickers to see where Pheasant was. He had not had so much of her company of late as he would have liked. To the regular spring work of his men and himself had been added the setting out of a new cherry orchard and the clearing of a piece of woodland for cultivation. Piers was as strong and wholesome as a vigorous young tree. He was ambitious and he was not afraid of work, but it did seem rather hard that he had so little time to spare in these lovely days of early summer for happy and indolent hours with Pheasant. She seldom came out into the fields or orchards with him now, as she used to do. She looked pale too, and was often petulant, even depressed. He wondered if she were possibly going to have a child. He must take good care of her, give her a little change of some kind. Perhaps he could arrange a motor trip over the weekend. The poor girl was probably envious of Alayne, who had Eden always at her side.

He saw Pheasant standing on a bluff, her slender figure

outlined against the sky. Her short green dress was fluttering about her knees. She looked like a flower poised there above the breezy blueness of the lake.

The phaeton has been drawn down the narrow stony road that led to the water's edge between two bluffs. Hodge had loosed the horses, and had led them out into the lake to drink. A fire had been lighted on the beach, and around it the family, with the exception of Pheasant and old Mrs Whiteoak, were enjoying themselves in their own fashions. Wake, with up-turned knickers, was paddling along the water's rim. Renny was throwing sticks for his spaniels. Nicholas and Ernest were skipping stones. Meg, in a disreputable old sweater, was bent over the fire, cherishing the tea kettle. Alayne was carrying driftwood. Lady Buckley, very upright on a rug spread on the beach, was knitting at something of a bright red colour.

Before Piers joined the others on the beach, he went to speak to his grandmother, who sat regarding the scene from the safety of her seat in the phaeton.

"Well, Gran, are you having a good time?"

"Put your head in so I can kiss you. Ah, there's the boy! Yes, I'm having a very good time. I used to bring the children to picnics here more than sixty years ago. I remember sitting on this very spot and watching your grandfather teach the boys to swim. Nick was a little water-dog, but Ernest was always screaming that he was going down. Oh, we had the times! This was a grand country then."

"I suppose so, Gran."

"Yes, the wood pigeons were so thick they'd fly in clouds that would throw a great shadow. The farm boys would trap them. Pretty, pretty things, with eyes like jewels. They'd put the pretty eyes out of one, the brutes! And they'd throw it in a field; and when the flock saw it fluttering they thought it was feeding and they'd alight in a cloud, and the boys and men would shoot them by hundreds."

"No such shooting now, Gran."

"Go and see when tea will be ready. I want my tea. And, Philip—I mean Piers—keep your eye on Pheasant; she's young, aye, she's young, and her mother was bad, and her father a rip. She's worth watching."

"Look here, Gran, I don't like your saying such things about Pheasant. She's all right."

"I dare say she is—but she's worth watching. All women are, if they've any looks. I want my tea."

Piers was smiling at the old lady's advice as he strode along the beach. He was tolerantly amused by her, and yet he thought, 'There's a grain of truth in what she says. Girls are worth watching. Still, there's no one about but Tom Fennel that she could—Eden, there's Eden; he has nothing to do—might amuse himself—poets—immoral fellows. I'll spend more time with her. I might take her to the Falls for the weekend. There's that new inn there. She'd like that, poor little young 'un.'

The lake was the colour of lapis-lazuli. Some gulls, disturbed by the barking of the dogs, wheeled, petulantly crying, above its brightness. Beyond them a coaling schooner, with blackened sails, moved imperceptibly, and a steamer bound for Niagara trailed its faint streamer of smoke. Little sailing-boats were languishing in some yacht-club race.

Piers went up to Renny, whose eyes were fixed on Flossie swimming after a stick, while Merlin, having retrieved his, barked himself off his feet in agonized demand for another opportunity to exhibit his powers. As Piers approached, the spaniel shook himself vigorously, sending a drenching shower over the brothers' legs.

"She has got it," said Renny, his eyes still on Floss, and he called out to her, "Good girl!"

"Damn Merlin!" said Piers. "He's soaked my trouser legs."

"All in white, eh?" observed Renny, looking him over.

"You didn't expect me to come in overalls, did you? Have we time for a swim before tea?"

Renny bent and put his hand in the water. "It's not very cold. Suppose we do. Tea can wait."

"Where is Eden?" asked Piers, casting his eyes over the party.

"He was up on the bluff with Pheasant a bit ago." Looking up, they saw his fair head rising just above the grass where he lay stretched at Pheasant's feet.

"I won't have him hanging about her," burst out Piers.

"Tell him so, then," said Renny, curtly.

"By the Lord, I will! I'll tell him so he'll not forget." His mind suddenly was a seething sea of suspicions. "Why, even

Gran thinks there's something wrong. She was warning me just now."

"No need to get in a stew," said Renny, throwing the stick for Merlin, who leaped to the water with a bark of joy, while his place was immediately taken by a dripping, importunate Flossie. "Eden and Alayne will be leaving before the first of July. Evans has a job for him then."

"What a loafer he is!"

"You didn't expect him to work with a broken leg, did you? Don't grouse about anything now: this is Wake's birthday party. Come on and have our swim." He shouted to Wakefield: "Wake, should you like to go in for a swim?"

Wakefield came galloping through the wavelets.

"Should I? Oh, splendid! What if I had the pony here? She'd swim out with me, I'll bet."

"Eden!" called Renny. "We're going in swimming. Better come."

They stared up at him as he scrambled to his feet and began to descend the steep path down the side of the bluff. He still limped from the effects of his fall.

"Won't it be pretty cold?" he asked.

"We might have Meggie boil a kettle of water to warm a spot for you," said Piers.

"Where's Finch?" asked Renny. "Finch will want to come."

Wakefield answered: "He's in the little cove already, lying on the sand."

The four made toward the cove.

"Don't let Uncle Ernest come," said Eden. "He's sure to hurt me."

"Uncle Ernest!" shouted Renny. "Eden says you're not to come. You're too rough."

"Eden, Eden," cried Ernest, but with a certain pride, "I wish you would let me forget that."

Grandmother's voice came from the phaeton, sharp with the anguish of hunger: "When are we going to have tea? I told Piers to fetch me tea!"

"I am bringing you a molasses scone to stay you, Mamma," said Augusta. She was carefully making her way across the shingle, the buttered scone in her hand.

When the four brothers reached the little willow-fringed

cove, they found Finch lying face downward, his head propped on his arms. "Still sulking?" asked Piers. "Did you know, Renny, that the poor youth is obsessed by the idea that we make more of Wake's birthday than his? Isn't it heartrending, Wake?"

Wakefield, smiling and self-conscious, stared down at Finch's prostrate form.

"If I get this leg chilled," observed Eden, "I might have rheumatism."

"You won't get chilled if I am with you," said Piers, pulling off his coat.

When the others had plunged into the lake, and Wake was already screaming with delight and terror at Piers' hands, Renny returned to Finch and said with a fatherly air: "Better come in, Finch; it'll do you good. You've been studying too much."

"No. I d'want to," mumbled the boy against his arm.

"Don't be a duffer," said Renny, poking him with his bare foot. "The more Piers sees he can rattle you the more he'll do it."

"'Tisn't only that."

"Well, look here. It was too bad I gave you that cuff before the others. But you were too damned cheeky. Come along and forget it."

Finch rolled over, disclosing a distorted red face.

"Is there no place I can be let alone?" he bawled. "Have I got to go to the end of the world to be let alone? All I ask is to be let alone, in peace here, and you all come prodding me up!"

"Stay alone, then, you little idiot!" Renny tossed away the cigarette he was smoking and strode to the water's edge.

All very well, Finch thought, for a lordly being like Renny, safe, always sure of himself, unmenaced by dreadful thoughts and bewitchment, of whom even Piers stood in some awe. With his head propped on his hand, he watched his brothers swimming, splashing, diving, the sunshine glistening on their white shoulders. As a creature apart, he watched them, with the idea in his mind that there was a conspiracy against him, that each member of the family played a different part against him, talking him over among themselves, sneering and laughing at him; but, in spite of himself, a slow smile of pleasure in their glistening grace, their agility, crept over his features. Their robust shouts were not unmusical. And the shine of their sleek heads, blond and russet and black, pleased his eyes. He saw that Piers was rough with Eden, and he was glad. He wished they would fight, half kill each other, while he reclined on the sand looking on.

Eden came limping out of the water.

"Are there any towels?" he asked. "Run and ask Meg for towels, like a good fellow, Finch."

Oh, yes! He was a good fellow when there was an errand to be run. But he hurried across the shingle to his sister.

"Towels? Yes, here they are. This big red-and-white one for Renny, mind! And the two smaller ones for Eden and Piers. And send Wake to me. I must give him a good rubbing so he shan't take a chill."

A sudden mood of savage playfulness came over Finch. Snatching the towels, he went, with a wild fling of his body, back toward the cove. There he hurled the twisted bundle at his brothers.

"There are your old towels!" he yelled; and as he crashed among the brushwood beyond the willows, he called back, "You're to go to Meggie, young Wake, and get walloped!"

Alayne had joined Pheasant on the bluff, and presently Renny too mounted the path, his damp russet head appearing first above the brink, like the ruffled crest of some bird of prey. He threw himself on the short thick clover that carpeted the bluff, and lighted his pipe.

"It seems rather hard," said Pheasant in her childish voice, "that Alayne and I could not have bathed. By the noise you made we could imagine the fun you were having."

"It was too cold for girls."

"It is a scientific fact," she said, sententiously, "that our sex can endure more cold than yours."

"We had no bathing-suits."

"We should have all brought bathing-suits and made a proper party of it. You have no idea how stupid it is to sit twiddling one's thumbs while you males are enjoying yourselves. 'Men must work, and women must weep'—that is the Whiteoak motto. Only you translate it into: 'Men must play, and women——' Do help me out with something really biting, Alayne."

Alayne answered only with a shrug. Renny continued to

stare out across the moving brilliance of the water, puffing at his pipe. With a sort of taciturn tyranny he overrode the younger girl's desire for chatter and chaff. She too fell silent, plucking at the grass, and then, after a sidelong glance at the other two, she rose and began slowly to descend the path.

"Why are you going, Pheasant?" called Alayne sharply.

"I think someone should help Meggie to lay the cloth."

"Very well. If I can be of use, please call me."

Now a shudder of excitement ran through her. It was the first time in weeks that she had been alone with Renny. She almost wished that she had followed Pheasant.

For some time he had avoided her. Their rides, which had been interrupted by the heavy snowfalls of January and the illness of Eden, had not been resumed. Although they lived in the house together, they were separated by a wall, a relentless wall of ice, through which each was visible to the other, though distorted by its glacial diffusions. Now on the cliff, in the sunshine, the wall seemed likely to melt, and with it the barrier of her intellectual self-control. If she could only know what he was feeling! His very silence was to her a tentative embrace.

Like incense, the sweetness of the wood smoke rose from the beach. Wake's little naked figure was darting here and there like a sandpiper.

She studied Renny's profile, the carved nose, the lips gripping the pipe, the damp hair plastered against the temples. It was so immobile that a heavy depression began to drown her mood of passionate excitement. Looking at him, remembering Eden, she began to feel that she had had enough of Whiteoaks. She had bruised her soul against their wanton egotism. This Renny whom she loved was as remote, as self-sufficient, as that rock out yonder. His look of passionate immobility might be the mask of nothing more than a brooding desire to acquire some mettlesome piece of horseflesh for his stalls. Yet how could that be, and she have that feeling that his very silence was an embrace! Two shadowy arms seemed to spring from his shoulders toward her, crushing her to him, kissing her with the passion of his kisses in the orchard with, added to them, all the hunger of these months of self-restraint.

His fleshly arms had not moved. One lay across his thigh,

the other slanted toward his pipe, the bowl of which lay in his palm.

He took his pipe from his lips, and spoke in a low, husky voice. His words overwhelmed her. She was like a mariner who, fearing certain shoals, watching with both dread and desire for the light that warned of their nearness, is suddenly blinded by that light full in the eyes. Excitement, resentment, depression, all left her. She was conscious only of his love.

"I love you," he said, "and I am in hell because I love you. And there is no way out."

The magical experience of sitting on the cliff with Renny, hearing these words from his mouth, in his restrained voice, filled Alayne with a sense of reckless surrender rather than tragic renunciation. Like a crop from virgin soil, this first profound love gushed upward from her being to embrace the hot sun of his passion.

With Renny it was very different. A man who had loved women both casually and licentiously, who could not speak their language, who had thought to have and craved to have no other sort of feelings toward them, he felt himself betrayed by this new and subtle passion that went deeper than mere possession, that could not be gratified and forgotten. In his eyes was something of the bewilderment of the animal that finds itself wounded, unable to exercise the faculties which had been its chief delight. Love, which had hitherto been to him as a drink of fresh water, now tasted of the bitter salt of renunciation.

He muttered again: "There is no way out."

She said, almost in a whisper: "No, I suppose there is nothing to be done."

It was as though a traveller, pointing to the rising moon, had said to another: "There is no moon."

He caught that strange denial of her words in her tone. Looking into her face, he perceived the warmth and pathos there. He exclaimed, with a groan: "I would cut everything —take you away, if only—he were not my brother!"

In an odd, choking voice that seemed to come from a long way off, she reminded him: "Your half brother."

"I never think of that," he said, coldly. His attachment to his brothers was so tenacious that it always had annoyed him to hear them spoken of as half brothers.

After a moment of silence that seemed made manifest by a veil of wood smoke that rose and hung over them for a space, she said, with a tremor in her voice: "I will do whatever you tell me to."

"I believe you would," he answered. With sudden realization, he knew that her life was to her as important as his to himself, and yet she was putting it into his hands with heroic selflessness.

They became aware that those on the beach were calling to them and, looking down, they saw that they were beckoning. The cloth was laid; already Nicholas, with the help of Piers, was letting himself down heavily into the unaccustomed posture of sitting on the ground.

"Tea is ready. Come down! Come!" echoed the voices.

The two rose mechanically, like two untroubled puppets, under the blue immensity of heaven, and turned toward the path.

"Your heels are too high for such a rough place," he said. "Let me take your hand."

She placed her hand in his, and he held it in his thin, muscular grasp till they reached the shingle.

23

JUNE NIGHT AT JALNA

TWO MEMBERS of the picnic party did not return with the others to Jalna. Piers went through the ravine to Vaughanlands, and with Maurice Vaughan drove to Stead to a meeting of fruit growers. Finch too went to Vaughanlands, but he cycled along the country road and entered by the front road into the house. He knew Maurice was going out with Piers, and since the housekeeper was almost totally deaf, he might make music with all the wild fervour that he chose, with no one but himself to hear.

All day Finch had been straining toward the hour. Yet he knew that he should at this moment be in his room at home 'swatting' for the physics exam tomorrow. He should not have gone to the picnic at all, though he had compromised by taking a textbook with him to study at odd moments. In reality, he had not read one word of it. The book had been nothing more than a mask, behind which he had hidden for a while his angry, sullen face. When he had fastened it in its strap to the handlebar of his bicycle, he had muttered something about going to study with George Fennel. He had lied, and he did not care. This evening he must be free. His soul must stretch its wings in the spaces of the night. Music would set him free.

This new freedom, which music had the power to cast over him like a bright armour, was most of all freedom from his own menacing thoughts and, better still, freedom from God. God no longer frightened him, no longer pursued him in his loneliness, following him even to his bed with face that changed from thunderous darkness to fiery whiteness, from old to young. On evenings when music had made him brave and free he marched home through the ravine, singing as he marched, and no more afraid of God than of the whippoorwills that called to their loves among the trees, or of the quivering stars.

Sometimes the thought of being loved by God rather than pursued by Him, filled him with ecstasy, blinded him with tears. Often, and more often as the months flew on, he did not believe in God at all. God was nothing but a dragon of childhood, Fear personified, of which a Scottish nurse in tiny boyhood had sown the seed. Yet he did not want to lose this fear of God entirely, for it had in it the power of submerging the more terrible fear of himself. Once, in a strange flash of inwardness, he had thought that perhaps God and he were both afraid, each afraid of his own reflection as seen in the other's eyes. Perhaps, even, God and he were one——

In the forsaken house he sat very upright on the piano stool, only his hands moving firmly and with spirit over the keys. The piece he played was no more pretentious than that which any boy of talent might execute after an equal number of lessons. Nevertheless, there was something special in Finch's playing, in the way his sheepish air gave place to confidence when he sat before the piano, in the firm dexterity of his beautiful hands—such a contrast to his unprepossessing face— which kept him in his teacher's mind long after the lesson was over. More than once the teacher had said to a colleague: "I have one pupil, a boy named Whiteoak, who isn't like any of the others. He has genius of some kind, I am sure, but whether music is its natural expression, or whether it is just a temporary outlet for something else, I can't yet make out. He's a queer, shy boy."

Finch sat playing now, neither shy nor queer. The room was dark except for the moonlight that serenely fell across his hands on the keys. Through the open window the rich sweet scents of this June night poured in a changeful stream, now the odour of the cool fresh earth, now the heavy scent of certain yellow lilies that grew beneath the window, now the mixed aroma of wild flowers, last year's leaves, and rich mould, that poured up from the ravine. The breeze blew in, now warm and gentle as love's first kiss, now with a chill borne from some sequestered place not yet warmed by the summer sun.

All these scents and warmths and coolnesses Finch wove into his music. He had a strange sensation that night that many years had fled by with averted faces since the hour of the picnic. That all those he knew, indeed all the people of the world, were dead. That he alone lived, and was creating by his will, his music, the June night of a new world.

He felt the wondrous elation of creating, and at the same time a great sadness, for he knew that the world he was creating could not last; that it was no more than the shadow of a shadow; that the dancing streams, the flying petals, the swift winds that were born beneath his fingers would dry and wither and fall as the music sank to silence.

A clock on the chimneypiece struck ten in a thin far-away tone. Finch remembered tomorrow's examination. He must go home and study for a couple of hours, try to get something into that brain of his besides music. But, at any rate, his brain felt clearer for the music. He felt wonderfully clear-headed to-night. All sights and sounds seemed to him magnified, intensified. With luck he might in the next few hours absorb the very problems upon which the questions of the examination would be based. The worse was that, as he had told Meggie he was going to study with George Fennel, he must go a long piece out of his way in order that he might arrive from the direction of the rectory. The night was so mild that some of the family were almost certain to be about, and if he appeared out of the ravine, it would at once be suspected that he had been at Vaughanlands.

Just one piece more! He could not tear himself away yet.

He played on, losing himself in the delight of that growing sympathy between his hands and the keyboard. Then he gently closed the piano and went out on to the veranda, shutting the door behind him.

A puff of warm air met him, as though it had been deliberately blown on him to entice him into the woods, to keep him there till he forgot all the things he had so painfully learned at school, and knew only the mathematics of the seasons, and the language of the trees. He mounted his wheel and rode across the lawn.

The basin where the house stood was flooded by moonlight, like a shallow bowl with golden wine. The air was full of whisperings and stirrings. The very grass across which he glided seemed a magic carpet.

He flew along the road, faster and faster, through the little hamlet, past the rectory (there was a light up in George's attic room, and poor George swatting away!). What if he went in and spent the night with George? He could telephone to Jalna.

No, he wanted to be by himself, George was too solid, too prosaic for him tonight. He could see his slow smile, hear his "Whatever puts such fool ideas into your head, Finch?"

Down the lane into the old woods of Jalna. The black pine trees blacker than the blackest night. How did they manage it? No darkness could obliterate them. How lovely the little birch wood must look in the moonlight! All the silver birches in their own fair communion in the midst of the black pines! If he left his wheel here, he might go to the birch wood and see it in this first silvery night of June; take a picture of it back to his room in his mind's eye.

His 'mind's eye'. What a singular phrase! He thought of his mind's eye—round, glowing, rapturous and frightened by turns.

> The mind has a thousand eyes,
>   And the heart but one;
> Yet the light of a whole life dies
>   When love is done.

It must have been the eye of his heart which he had been imagining—that flaming, rapturous, terrified eye. 'When love is done——' Love had not begun for him. He thought it never would. Not that kind of love. He was not at all sure that he wanted it.

He was running lightly along the woodland path that wound among the pines. There were before him five slender young birches, sprung from the trunk of a fallen and decayed pine, like five fabled virgins from the torso of a slain giant. Beyond them the birch wood lay in the mystery of moonlight, the delicate, drooping boughs seemed to float above the immaculate boles.

This was the spot where one morning he had seen Renny standing with a strange woman in his arms. The place had ever since been haunted by that vision. He was therefore scarcely surprised when he heard low voices as he reached the outer fringe of trees. Was Renny up to his love games again? He halted among the young ferns and listened. He peered through the strange misty radiance that seemed to be distilled from the trunks and foliage of the birches themselves rather than to fall from above, and tried to see who were the two who had sought this hidden spot. Every nerve in his body was quivering, taut as the strings of a musical instrument.

At first he could make out nothing but the dew-wet mistiness of light and shade, the strange lustre that hung above a patch of greensward. All about him the air was full of mysterious rustlings and sighings, as though every leaf and blade and fern frond were sentient. Then the murmur of voices, the sound of long, passionate kisses drew his gaze toward a particular spot, sheltered by some hazel bushes. Scarcely breathing, he crept closer. He heard a low laugh, and then the voice that laughed said, "Pheasant, Pheasant, Pheasant," over and over again.

It was Eden's voice.

Then rushing breathless words from Pheasant, and then a deep sigh, and again the sound of kisses.

Oh, they were wicked! He could have rushed in on them in his rage, and slain them. It would have been right and just. They had betrayed Piers, his beloved brother, his hero! In imagination he crashed in on them through the hazel bushes, trampling the ferns, and struck them again and again till they screamed for pity; but he had no pity; he beat them down as they clung about his knees till their blood soaked the greensward and the glade reverberated with their cries——

He was dazed. He drew his hand across his eyes. Then he moved closer toward them through the hazels, not seeing where he was going, dizzy. Her voice gasped: "What was that?"

He stopped.

There was silence, except that the beating of his heart filled the universe.

"What was that?"

"Nothing but a rabbit or a squirrel."

Finch dropped to his knees. With great caution he turned and began to creep away from them. He crept till he reached the path into the pine wood then he got to his feet and began to run. He sped along the needle-strewn path with great strides like a hunted deer. His mouth was open, his breath coming in sobbing gasps.

When he reached the place where he had left his wheel, he did not stop. Nothing mechanical could move with the speed of his swift, avenging feet. He ran down the lane, waving his arms; he flew across the pasture, past a group of sleeping cattle; missing the bridge, he waded across the stream through the thick, clinging watercress; slipped, and sprawled on the bank into a great golden splash of kingcups; and pressed on toward the stables.

Piers had just driven into the yard when he arrived. Finch ran up in front of the car, his wild white face and dishevelled hair startling in the glare of the lamps. His hand was on his side, where a pain like a knife was stabbing him.

"What's the matter?" cried Piers, springing out of the car.

Finch pointed in the direction whence he had come.

"They're there," he said, thickly. "Back there—in the woods!"

"What the devil is the matter with you?" asked Piers, coming around to him. "Have you had a fright?"

Finch caught his brother by the arm and repeated: "In the wood—making love—both of them—kissing—making love——"

"Who? Tell me whom you mean. I don't know what you're talking about." Piers was impatient, yet, in spite of himself, he was excited by the boy's wild words.

"Eden, the traitor!" cried Finch, his voice breaking into a scream. "He's got Pheasant in the wood there—Pheasant. They're wicked, I tell you—false as hell!"

Piers' hand was as a vice on his arm.

"What did you see?"

"Nothing—nothing—but behind the hazel bushes I heard them whispering—kissing—oh, I know. I wasn't born yesterday. Why did they go so far away? She wouldn't have let him kiss her like that unless——"

Piers gave him a shake. "Shut up. No more of that. Now listen to me. You are to go straight to your room, Finch. You are to say nothing of this to anyone. I am going to find them." His full, healthy face was ghastly, his eyes blazed. "I'll kill them both—if what you say is so, Finch. Now go to the house."

He asked then, in a tone almost matter-of-fact, just where Finch had seen them, why he had gone there himself. Finch incoherently repeated everything. Something of their excitement must have been transmitted to the animals, for the dogs began to bark and a loud whinny came from the stables. The moon was sinking, and a deathlike pallor lay across the scene. Piers turned away, cursing as he stumbled over the tongue of a cart. A mist was rising above the paddock, and he ran into this obscurity, disappearing from Finch's eyes, as though swallowed up by some sinister force of nature.

Finch stared after him till he was lost to view, then stumbled toward the house. He felt suddenly tired and weak, and yet he could not go to the house as he had been bid. He saw a light in Alayne's room. Poor Alayne! He shuddered as he thought of what Piers would do to Eden, and yet he had done right to tell of this terrible thing. He could not have hidden such evil-doing in his heart, connived at their further sin. Still it was possible that his own evil imagination had magnified their act into heinousness. Perhaps even they were no worse than others. He had heard something about the loose morals of the younger generation. Well, Pheasant was only eighteen, Eden twenty-four; they were young, and perhaps no worse than others. What about Alayne herself? Was she good? Those long rides with Renny, her moving into a room by herself, away from Eden—Finch had heard a whispered reference to that between Meg and Aunt Augusta. Would he ever know right from wrong? Would he ever know peace? All he knew was that he was alone—very lonely, afraid—afraid now for Eden and Pheasant, while a few minutes ago he had thought only of crushing them in the midst of their wickedness.

He crossed the lawn and followed the path into the ravine. The stream, narrower here than where he had waded through it crossing the meadows, ran swiftly, still brimming from heavy spring rains. Luxuriant bushes, covered by starry white flowers, filled the night with their fragrance.

Renny was sitting on the strong wooden handrail of the little bridge, smoking and staring dreamily down into the water. Finch would have turned away, but Renny had heard his step on the bridge.

"That you, Piers?" he asked.

"No, it's me—Finch."

"Have you just come back from the rectory?"

"No, Renny, I've been—practising."

He expected a rebuke, but none came. Renny scarcely seemed to hear him, seemed hardly aware of his presence. Finch moved closer, with a dim idea of absorbing some of his strength by mere proximity. In the shadow of that unique magnificence he did not feel quite so frightened. He wished that he might touch Renny, hold on to his fingers, even his tweed sleeve, as he had when he was a little fellow.

Renny pointed down into the water. "Look there," he said.

Looking, Finch saw a glossy wet back gliding across the silver shimmer of the stream. It was a large water-rat out on some nocturnal business of his own. They watched it till it reached the opposite bank, where, instead of climbing out as they had expected, it nosed among the sedges for a moment and then moved into the stream again, slowly passing under the bridge. Renny went to the other side and peered after it.

"Here he comes," he murmured.

"Wonder what he's after," said Finch, but he did not move. Down there in the dark brightness of the water he saw a picture—Eden lying dead, with Alayne wringing her hands above his body; and as the wavelets obliterated it, another took its place—Piers, purple-faced, struggling, kicking on a gallows. Icy sweat poured down Finch's face. He put out a hand gropingly, and staggered from the bridge and up the path. On the ridge above the ravine he hesitated. Should he go back and pour out the whole terrible tale to Renny? Perhaps it was not too late, if they ran all the way, to prevent a disaster.

He stood, gnawing at his knuckle distractedly, the clinging wetness of his trouser legs making him shiver from head to foot. He seemed incapable of movement or even of thought now; but suddenly he was stirred to both by the sound of Eden's laugh, near at hand, on the lawn. Then Pheasant's voice came, speaking in a natural, unhurried tone. Piers had somehow missed them, and while he was crashing through the woods in pursuit, they were strolling about the lawn, as though they had been there all the while.

Finch moved out from the darkness and stood before them. Eden had just struck a match and was holding it to a cigarette. The flame danced in his eyes, which looked very large and bright, and gave an ironical twist to the faint smile that so often hovered about his lips.

Pheasant uttered an exclamation that was almost a cry.

"Don't go in the house," said Finch, heavily. "I mean—go away. I've told Piers about you. I heard you in the birch wood, and I ran back, and told Piers——"

Eden held the still flaring match near Finch's face, as though it were some supernatural ray by which he could look into his very soul.

"Yes?" he said, steadily. "Go on."

"He's after you. He—he looked terrible. You'd better go away."

Pheasant made a little moaning sound like a rabbit caught in a trap. Eden dropped the match.

"What a worm you are, brother Finch!" he said. "I don't know where we Whiteoaks ever got you." He turned to Pheasant. "Don't be frightened, darling. I will take care of you."

"Oh, oh!" she cried. "What shall we do?"

"Hush."

Finch said: "He'll be back any minute," and turned away.

He could not go into that house with its peacefully shining lights, where the others were still talking perhaps of the picnic, all unwitting of the thunderbolt that hung over them. He skulked around the house, through the kitchen garden, through the orchard, and out on the road that led to the churchyard.

The church steeple, rising from among the tapering cedars, pointed more sharply than they toward the sky. The church had gathered to itself the darkest shadows of tree and tomb, and drawn them like a cloak about its walls. The dead, lying beneath the dewy young grass, seemed to Finch to be watching him, as he climbed the steep steps from the road, out of hollow eye sockets in which no longer was boldness, or terror, or lust, but only resigned decay. They no longer were afraid of God. All was over. They had nothing to do but lie there till their bones were light as the pollen of a flower.

Ah, but he was afraid of God! Fear was his flesh, his marrow, his very essence. Why had the moon sunk and left him in this blackness alone? What had he done? He had ruined the lives of Piers and Eden and Pheasant and Alayne. Were Eden and Pheasant sinful? 'Sin'? What a mad word! Could there be sin? All the mouldering bones under this grass—their sins were no more than the odours of spring growth, warm earth, sticky leaf-bud, blessed rain—sweetness. But there was that saying: 'To the third and fourth generation'. Perhaps he was suffering tonight for the heavy sin of some far-off White-oak. Perhaps that baby sister, over whose grave he stood, had given up her little ghost because of some shadowy bygone sin. He pictured her lying there, not horrible, not decayed, but fair and tender as the bud of an April flower, with little hands held out to him.

Hands held out to him—— Oh, beautiful thought! That was what his lonely spirit yearned for—the comfort of outstretched hands. A sob of self-pity shook him; tears rushed to his eyes and poured down his cheeks. He cast himself on the ground among the graves, and lay there, his face against the grass. All the accumulated experience of the dead beneath him, passing into his body, became one with him. He lay there inert, exhausted, drinking in at every pore the bitter sweetness of the past. Hands stretched out to him, the hands of soldiers, gardeners, young mothers, infants, and One far different from the others. Hands from which emanated a strange white glow, not open-palmed, but holding something toward him—'the living Bread'—Christ's hands.

He knelt among the mounds and held up his own hands, curved like petals, to receive. His thin boy's body was torn by sobs as a sapling in a hailstorm. He put his hands to his mouth —he had received the Bread—he felt the sacred fire of it burn through his veins—scorch his soul—Christ in him.

Overcome, he sank beside his mother's grave and threw his arm about it. Little white daisies shone out of the dark grass like tender, beaming eyes. He pressed closer, closer, drawing up his knees, curling his body like a little child's, thrusting his breast against the grave, and cried: "Mother, oh mother—speak to me! I am Finch, your boy."

24

THE FLIGHT OF PHEASANT

MAURICE VAUGHAN was sitting alone in his dining-room. When he and Piers had returned from Stead, he had brought the young fellow into the house for a drink and some cold viands which he had got himself from the pantry. If he had had his way, Piers would still be there, smoking, drinking, and talking with ever less clarity about fertilizers and spraying and the breeding of horses. But Piers had refused to stay for long. He had to rise early, and for some reason he could not get Pheasant out of his head. His thoughts kept flying back to her, to her little white face, her brown cropped hair. Her thin eager hands seemed to tug at his sleeve, drawing him home. He had been abstracted all the evening.

However, Maurice had scarcely noticed this. All he craved was company, the warmth of a human presence to pierce the chill loneliness of the house. When Piers was gone, he sat on and on, slowly, heavily drinking without enjoyment, slowly, heavily thinking in the same numbing circle which his mind, like the glassy-eyed steed of a roundabout, had traversed for twenty years.

He thought of Meg, tender and sedate, a noble young girl, as she was when they had become engaged. He thought of his old parents, their fond joy in him, their ambition, with which he was in accord, that he should become one of the most brilliant and influential men in the country. He pictured his marriage with Meggie, their life together, their family of lovely girls and boys. There were six of these children of his fancy. He had named them all—the boys with family names, the girls with romantic names from the poets he had once admired. From the eldest to the youngest, he knew every line of the six young faces and had a right to know them, for he had shaped them out of the shadows to satisfy the hunger of his heart. For them he had a love he had never given to Pheasant.

He thought of that affair with her mother, of their meetings in the twilight, of her clutching his knees and begging him to marry her when she found she was with child, of his tearing himself away. Then the basket with the baby, the note—here a feeling approaching nausea made him shift in his chair—the family consternation, the family conclaves, Meg's throwing him over, his parents' death, financial distresses, the end of ambition. And so on through the whole gloomy business of his life, in which the brightest spot was the War, where he had been able for a time to forget the past and ignore the future.

As he completed the circle, the room reeled a little with him; his chin sank on his breast, and the electric light brought out the increasing whiteness of the patches on his temples. He did not sleep, but consciousness was suspended. The sound of someone softly entering the room did not rouse him. With his heavy underlip dropped, his eyes staring into space, he sat motionless as a sullen rock buried in the heaviness of the sea.

Pheasant felt a pang of pity as she saw him sitting alone in the cold, unshaded, electric light. 'He looks frightfully blue,' she thought, 'and he's getting round-shouldered.' Then her mind flew back to her own tragic situation, and she went to him and touched him on the arm.

"Maurice."

He started, and then, seeing who it was, he said in a surly tone: "Well, what do you want?"

"Oh, Maurice," she breathed, "be kind to me! Don't let Piers into the house. I'm afraid he'll kill me."

He stared stupidly at her, and then growled: "Well, it's what you deserve, isn't it?"

"Yes, yes, I deserve it! But how did you know? Have you seen anyone?"

He considered a moment, staring at the decanter on the table.

"Yes, Piers was here."

"Piers here? Oh, he was searching for me!" She wrung her hands frantically. "Oh, Maurice, please, please don't let him in again! I've been wandering about in the dark for hours, and at last I thought I'd come to you, for after all I am your child. You've a right to protect me, no matter what I've done."

He roused himself to say, "What have you done?"

"Didn't Piers tell you anything?"

"No."

"But he was searching for me?"

"No, he wasn't."

"Then how did you know something was wrong?"

"I didn't."

"But you said I deserved to be killed."

"Well, don't you?" he demanded, with drunken raillery.

"Maurice, you're drunk. Oh, whatever shall I do?" She threw herself on his knees, clasping his neck. "Try to understand! Say that you'll not let Piers kill me." She broke into pitiful wails. "Oh, Maurice, I've had to run away from Piers, and I love him so!"

"He was here a bit ago," said Vaughan, staring around as though he expected to find him in a corner. Then, noticing her head against his shoulder, he laid his hand on it in a rough caress, as a man might stroke a dog.

"Don't cry, youngster. I'll take care of you. Glad to have you back. Damned lonely."

She caught his hand and pressed a dozen wild kisses on it.

"Oh, Maurice, how good you are! How good to me! And how good Piers was to me—and I didn't deserve it. Hanging is too good for me!" And she added, melodramatically: "'Twere better I had never been born!'"

She rose then and wiped her eyes. She was a pitiful little figure. Her clothes were torn from running distractedly through a blackberry plantation. Her hands and even her pale face were bleeding from scratches. She had lost a shoe, and the stockinged foot was wet with mud.

"Yes, 'twere," he repeated, agreeably.

With a certain pathetic dignity, she turned toward the door. "Will it be all the same to you, Maurice, if I go to my room?"

"Same to me—wherever you go—absolutely."

How different this hall, she thought, as she dragged herself up the bare stairs, from the luxurious hall at Jalna, with its thickly carpeted stairs, its dark red rugs, its stained-glass window. The great moose head which had been her especial terror in childhood now glared down its long hard nose at her, with nostrils distended, as though it longed to toss her on its cruel horns.

She felt dazed. She scarcely suffered, except for the aching

248

in her legs, as she threw herself across her old bed. With half shut eyes she lay staring at the two pictures on the wall opposite, 'Wide Awake' and 'Fast Asleep', which had once hung in Maurice's nursery. Darling little baby pictures; how she had always loved them—— She wished she had the strength of mind to kill herself. Tear the sheets into strips and wind them tighter and tighter around her throat, or, better still, hang herself from one of the rafters in that back room in the attic. She saw herself dangling there, purple-faced—saw horrified Maurice discovering her—saw herself buried at the crossroad with a stake in her inside. She did not know whether that was still done, but it was possible that the custom would be revived for her——

She fell into a kind of nightmare doze, in which the bed rocked beneath her like a cradle. It rocked faster and faster, rolling her from side to side. She was not a real, a wholesome infant, but a grotesque changeling, leering up at the distraught mother who now peered in at her, shrieking, tearing her hair. Again the scream rent the silence, and Pheasant, with sweat starting on her face, sprang up in bed.

She was alone. The electric light shone brightly. Again came the loud peal—not a scream, but the ringing of the doorbell.

She leaped to the floor. The lock of the door had been broken many years. She began to drag at the washstand to barricade it.

Downstairs the sound had also penetrated Vaughan's stupor. He lurched to the door, which Pheasant had locked behind her, and threw it open. Renny and Piers Whiteoak stood there, their faces like two pale discs against the blackness. Renny at once stepped inside, but Piers remained in the porch.

"Is Pheasant here?" asked Renny.

"Yes." He eyed them with solemnity.

Renny turned to his brother. "Come in, Piers."

Vaughan led the way toward the dining-room, but Piers stopped at the foot of the stairs.

"Is she upstairs?" he asked in a thick voice, placing one hand on the newel post as though to steady himself.

Vaughan, somewhat sobered by the strangeness of the brothers' aspect, remembered something.

"Yes, but you're not going up to her. You'll let her alone."

"He won't hurt her," said Renny.

"He's not to go up. I promised her."

He took the youth's arm, but Piers wrenched himself away.

"I order you!" shouted Vaughan. "Whose house is this? Whose daughter is she? She's left you. Very well—let her stay. I want her."

"She is my wife. I'm going to her."

"What the hell's the matter, anyway? I don't know what it's all about. She comes here—done up—frightened out of her wits—I remember now. Then you come like a pair of murderers."

"I must see her."

"You shall not see her." Again he clutched Piers' arm. The two struggled beneath the sinister head of the great moose, under the massive antlers of which their manhood seemed weak and futile.

In a moment Piers had freed himself and was springing up the stairs.

"Come into the dining-room, Maurice," said Renny, "and I'll tell you what is wrong. Did she tell you nothing?"

Maurice followed him, growling: "A strange way to act in a man's house at this hour."

"Did she tell you nothing?" asked Renny, when they were in the dining-room.

"I don't remember what she said." He picked up the decanter. "Have a drink."

"No, nor you either." He took the decanter from his friend and put it in the sideboard, decisively locking the door.

Vaughan regarded the action with dismal whimsicality.

"What a to-do," he said, "because the kids have had a row!"

Renny turned on him savagely. "Good God, Maurice, you don't call this a row, do you!"

"Well, what's the trouble, anyway?"

"The trouble is this: that brat of yours has wrecked poor young Piers' life."

"The hell she has! Who is the man?"

"His own brother—Eden."

Vaughan groaned. "Where is he?"

"He made off in the car."

"Why didn't she go with him? Why did she come to me?"

"How can I tell? He probably didn't ask her. Oh, the whole rotten business harks back to me! It's my fault. I'd no right

250

to let Eden loaf about all winter, writing poetry. It's made a scoundrel of him!"

A wry smile flitted across Vaughan's face at the unconscious humour of the remark.

"I shouldn't blame myself too much if I were you. If writing poetry has made Eden into a scoundrel, he was probably well on the way beforehand. Possibly that's why he turned to it."

There was a deep understanding between these two. They had confided in each other as they had in no one else. Renny, stirred by the disclosures of the night, burst out: "Maurice, in thought I am no better than Eden! I love his wife. She's never out of my mind."

Vaughan looked into the tormented eyes of his friend with commiseration.

"Do you, Renny? I had never thought of such a thing. She doesn't seem to me your sort of girl at all."

"That is the trouble. She isn't. If she were, it would be easier to put the thought of her aside. She's intellectual, she's——"

"I should say she is cold."

"You're wrong. It is I, all my life, who have had a sort of cold sensuality—no tenderness went with my love for a woman. I don't think I had any compassion. No, I'm sure I hadn't." He knit his brows as though recalling past affairs. "But I'm full of compassion for Alayne."

"Does she love you?"

"Yes."

"What about Eden?"

"She had a romantic devotion to him, but it's over."

"Does she know about this?" Maurice lifted his head in the direction of the room above.

"Yes. I only had a glimpse of her in the hall—the house was in an uproar. She had a strange, exalted look as though nothing mattered now."

"I see. What is Piers going to do?"

"Piers is a splendid fellow—tough as an oak. He said to me, 'She's mine; nothing can change that. I'm going to fetch her home.' But I should pity Eden if he got his hands on him."

"They are coming down. Heavens, they were quiet enough! Must I speak to them?"

"No, let the poor young beggars alone."

The two came slowly down the stairs. Like people leaving

the scene of a catastrophe, they carried in their eyes the terror of what they had beheld. Their faces were rigid. Piers' mouth was drawn to one side in an expression of disgust. It was like a mask of tragedy. They stood in the wide doorway of the dining-room as in a picture framed. Maurice and Renny smiled at them awkwardly, trying to put a decent face on the affair.

"Going, eh?" Maurice said. "Have something first, Piers." He made a movement toward the sideboard.

"Thanks," returned Piers in a lifeless voice. He entered the dining-room.

"Where's that key, Renny?"

Renny produced the key; a tantalus was brought forth, and a drink poured for Piers. Maurice, with Renny's eye on him, did not take one himself.

Piers gulped down the spirits, the glass rattling grotesquely against his teeth. Under the ashen tan of his face, colour crept back. No one spoke, but the three men stared with gloomy intensity at Pheasant, still framed in the doorway. The magnetic currents between the members of the group seemed palpably to vibrate across the atmosphere of the room. Then Pheasant, putting up her hands, as though to push their peering faces back from her, exclaimed: "Don't stand staring at me like that! One would think you'd never seen me before."

"You look awfully done," said Maurice. "I think you ought to have a mouthful of something to brace you. A little Scotch and water, eh?"

"I might if I were asked," she returned, with a pathetic attempt at bravado. She took the glass in a steady little hand, and drank.

"I shall come along later," said Renny to Piers. "I'm going to stop a while with Maurice." But he continued to stare at Pheasant.

"I know I'm a scarlet woman, but I think you're very cruel. Your eyes are like a brand, Renny Whiteoak."

"Pheasant, I was not even thinking of you. My—my mind was quite somewhere else."

Piers turned on Maurice in a sudden rage. "It's all your fault!" he broke out, vehemently. "You never gave the poor child a chance. She was as ignorant as any little immigrant when I married her."

"She doesn't seem to have learned any good from you," retorted Vaughan.

"She has learned all of decency that she knows. Was she ever sent to school?"

"She had two governesses."

"Yes. They both left inside of six months, because they couldn't live in the house with you."

"Oh, I suppose it is my fault that she inherits her mother's instinct," returned Maurice, bitterly. "And Renny has just been telling me that it is his fault that Eden is a scoundrel. We've taken on a lot of responsibility."

"You are talking like fools," said Renny.

"Please do not quarrel about me," put in Pheasant. "I think I'm going to faint or something."

"Better take her out in the air," said Renny. "The liquor was too strong for her.

"Come along," said Piers, and took her arm.

The touch of his hand had an instant effect on Pheasant. A deep blush suffused her face and neck; she swayed toward him, raising her eyes to his with a look of tragic humility.

Outside, the coolness of the dawn refreshed her. He released her arm, and preceded her through the grove and down into the ravine. They walked in silence, she seeming no more than his shadow, following him through every divergence of the path, hesitating when he hesitated. Centuries before, two such figures might have been seen traversing this same ravine, a young Indian and his squaw, moving as his silent shadow in the first light of morning, primitive figures so much akin to the forest life about them that the awakening birds did not cease twittering as they passed. On the bridge above the stream he stopped. Below lay the pool where they had first seen their love reflected as an opening flower. They looked down into it now, no longer able to share the feelings its mirrored loveliness excited in them. A primrose light suffused the sky and in a deeper tone lay cupped in the pool, around the brink of which things tender and green strove with gentle urgency to catch the sun's first rays.

An English pheasant, one of some imported by Renny, moved sedately among the young rushes, its plumage shining like a coat of mail. Careless, irresponsible bird, Piers thought, and for one wild instant he wished that she were one with the bird—that no man might recognize a woman in her but himself; that he might keep her hidden and love her secretly, untortured by the fear and loathing he now felt.

Pheasant saw, drowned in that pool, all the careless irresponsibility of the past, the weakness, the indolence, that had made her a victim of Eden's dalliance. If Piers loathed her, how much more she loathed the image of Eden's face which faintly smiled at her from the changeful mirror of the pool! Just to live, to make up to Piers by her devotion for what he had suffered—to win from his eyes love again instead of that look of fear which he had turned on her when he entered the bedroom! She had expected rage—fury. And he had looked at her in an agony of fear. But he had taken her back! They were going home to Jalna. She longed for the thick walls of the house as a broken-winged bird for its nest.

"Come," he said, as though awakening from a dream, and moved on up the path that led from the ravine to the lawn.

The turkeys were crossing the lawn, led by the cock, whose blazing wattles swung arrogantly in the first sunrays. His wives, with burnished breasts and beaming eyes, followed close behind, craning their necks, alternately lifting and dragging their slender feet, echoing his bold gobble with plaintive pipings. The hens paused to look with curiosity at the boy and girl who emerged from the ravine, but the cock, absorbed by his own ego, circled before them, swelling himself rigidly, dropping his wings, urging into his wattles a still more burning red.

Down the wet roof Finch's pigeons were strutting, sliding, rooketty-cooing, peering over the eaves at the two who slowly mounted the steps.

Inside, the house lay in silence except for the heavy snoring of Grandmother in her bedroom off the lower hall. It was as if some strange beast had a lair beneath the stairs, and was growling a challenge to the sun.

They passed the closed doors of the hall above and went into their own room. Pheasant dropped into a chair by the window, but Piers, with a businesslike air, began collecting various articles—his brushes, his shaving things, the clothes which he wore about the farm. She watched his movements with the unquestioning submissiveness of a child. One thought sustained her: 'How glad I am that I am here with Piers, and not flying with Eden as he wanted me to!'

When he had got together what he wanted, he took the key from the door and inserted it on the outside. He said, without looking at her:

"Here you stay, till I can stand the sight of your face again."

He went out, locking the door behind him. He climbed the long stairs to the attic, and, throwing his things on the bed in Finch's room, began to change his clothes for the day's work. In the passage he had met Alayne, looking like a ghost. They had passed without speaking.

25

FIDDLER'S HUT

THREE WEEKS later Mr Wragge was an object of great interest one morning to a group of Jersey calves as he crossed their pasture. They ceased gambolling, butting, and licking each other, to regard him with steadfast scrutiny out of liquid dark eyes. He was in his shirt sleeves, his coat being thrown over one arm, for the day was hot; his hat was tilted over his eyes, and he carried, balanced on one hand, a tray covered with a white cloth. He was smoking, as usual, and his expression was one of deep concern.

When he reached a stile at the far end of the paddock, he set the tray on the top, climbed over, then, balancing the tray at a still more dangerous angle, proceeded on his way. It now lay through an old uncared-for apple orchard, the great trees of which were green with moss, half smothered in wild grape-vines and Virginia creeper, and their boughs, like heavy wings, swept to the long coarse grass. Following a winding path, he passed a spring, where long ago a primitive well had been made by the simple process of sinking a wooden box. The lid of this was now gone, the wood decayed, and it was used by birds as a drinking fountain and bath. The liquid gurgle of the spring as it entered the well made a pleasant undertone to the song of birds with which the air was merry.

Embowered in vines, almost hidden by flowering dogwood, stood the hut where Fiddler Jock, by the consent of Captain Philip Whiteoak, had lived in solitude, the story of whose death young Finch had told Alayne on their first walk together.

Here Meg Whiteoak had been living for three weeks.

Before approaching the threshold, Mr Wragge again set down the tray, put on his coat, straightened his hat, threw away his cigarette, and intensified his expression of concern.

"Miss W'iteoak, it's me, ma'am," he said loudly, as though to reassure her, immediately after knocking.

The door opened and Meg Whiteoak appeared, with an expression as sweetly calm, but a face paler than formerly. "Thank you, Rags," she said, taking the tray. "Thank you very much."

"I'd be gratified, ma'am," he said anxiously, "if you was to lift the napkin and tike a look at wot I've brought you. I'd be better pleased if I knew you found it temptin'."

Miss Whiteoak accordingly peered under the napkin and discovered a plate of fresh scones, a bowl of ripe strawberries, and a jug of thick clotted cream such as she liked with them. A sweet smile curved her lips. She took the tray and set it on the table in the middle of the low, scantily furnished room.

"It looks very tempting, Rags. These are the first strawberries I've seen."

"They are the very first," he announced, eagerly. "I picked them myself, ma'am. There's going to be a wonderful crop, they s'y, but it don't seem to matter, the w'y things are goin' on with us these days."

"That's very true," she said, sighing. "How is my grandmother today, Rags?"

"Flourishing amazing, ma'am. My wife says she talked of nothink but 'er birthd'y the 'ole time she was doin' up 'er room. She 'ad a queer little spell on Thursday, but Mr Ernest, 'e thought it was just that she'd eat too much of the goose grivy. She looked remarkable well yesterd'y, and went to church the sime as usual."

"That is good." She bit her full underlip, and then asked, with an attempt at nonchalance: "Have you heard anything about Mrs Eden's leaving?"

"I believe she's to go as soon as the birthd'y celebrations are over. The old lidy wouldn't 'ear of it before. Ow, Miss W'iteoak, she's only a shadder of 'er former self, Mrs Eden is; and Mr Piers is not much better. Of all the people in the 'ouse those two show the wear and tear of wot we're goin' through the most. Of course, I've never seen Mrs Piers. She ain't never shown up in the family circle yet, but my wife saw 'er lookin' out of the winder, and she says she looks just the sime. Dear me, some people can stand anythink! As for me, I'm not the man I was at all. My nerves 'ave all gone back on me. It's almost like another attack of shell shock, you might s'y."

"I'm very sorry, Rags. You do look pale."

He took out a clean folded handkerchief and wiped his brow. "It isn't as though my own family relations was wot they were, ma'am. Mrs Wragge and me, we 'ad our little altercations, as you know, but, tike it as a 'ole, our life together was amiable; but now," he dolefully shook his head, "it's nothing more nor less than terrific. Me being on your side and she all for Mr Renny, there's never a moment's peace. W'y, yesterd'y—Sunday and all as it was—she up and shied the stove lifter at me 'ead. I escaped to the coal cellar, where she pursued me, and as for 'er language! Well, Mr Renny 'e 'eard the goings on and 'e came rattling down the basement stairs in a fine rage, and said if 'e 'eard any more of it we should go. The worse was, 'e seemed to blime me for the 'ole affair. I never thought I'd live to see the d'y 'e'd glare at me the w'y 'e did."

"That's because you are on my side, Rags," she said, sadly.

"I know, and that makes it all the worse. It's a 'ouse divided against itself. I've seen deadlocks in my time, but I've never seen a deadlock like this. Well, I'll be takin' aw'y wot little appitite you 'ave with my talk. I must be off. I've a thousand things to do, and of course Mrs Wragge puts all the 'ard work on to me as usual. And if you'll believe me, ma'am, she's so evilly disposed that I 'ad to steal those little scones I brought you."

He turned away, and when he had gone a few yards he put on his hat, removed his coat, and lighted a cigarette. Just as he reached the stile he met Renny Whiteoak crossing it.

Renny said sarcastically: "I see you have a path worn to the hut, Rags. Been carrying trays to Miss Whiteoak, I suppose."

Rags straightened himself with an air of self-righteous humility.

"And if I don't carry trays to 'er, wot do you suppose would 'appen, sir? W'y, she'd starve; that's wot she'd do. It would look rather bad, sir, for a lidy to die of starvation on 'er brother's estite, and 'im livin' in the lap of luxury."

This remark was thrown after the retreating figure of his

master, who had strode angrily away. Rags stared after him till he disappeared among the trees, muttering bitterly: "This is all the gratitood I get for the w'y I've slaved for you in war and in peace! Curses yesterd'y, and a sneer and a dirty look tod'y. You ill-tempted, domineerin' red-'eaded slavedriver! But you've met your match in Miss W'iteoak, let me tell you—and serves you right."

With this he climbed over the stile, and returned meditatively to the basement kitchen.

When Renny reached the hut, he found the door open, and inside he could see his sister sitting by the table, pouring herself a cup of tea. She looked up as she heard his step, and then, with an expression of remote calm, dropped her eyes to the stream of amber liquid issuing from the spout of the teapot. She sat with one rounded elbow on the table, her head supported on her hand. She looked so familiar and yet so strange, sitting in these poverty-stricken surroundings, that he scarcely knew what to say to her. However, he went in, and stood looking down at the tray.

"What particular meal is this?" he asked.

"I have no idea," she answered, buttering a scone. "I keep no count of meals now."

He looked about him, at the low, rain-stained ceiling, the rusty stove, the uneven, wormeaten floor, the inner room with its narrow cot bed.

"This is an awful hole you've chosen to sulk in," he commented.

She did not answer, but ate her scone with composure, and after it two strawberries smothered in cream.

"You'll make a charming old lady after you've spent ten years or so here," he gibed.

He saw a sparkle of temper in her eyes then.

"You will have the satisfaction of knowing that you drove me to it."

"That is utter nonsense. I did everything I could to prevent you."

"You did not send that girl away. You allowed Piers to bring her into the house with me, after her behaviour."

"Meggie, can't you see anyone's side of this question but your own? Can't you see that poor young Piers was doing a rather heroic thing in bringing her home?"

"I will not live under the same roof with that girl. I told you that three weeks ago, and you still try to force me."

"But I can't allow you to go on like this!" he cried. "We shall be the talk of the countryside."

She regarded him steadfastly. "Have you ever cared what the countryside thought of you?"

"No; but I can't have people saying that my sister is living in a tumbledown hut."

"You can turn me out, of course."

He ignored this, and continued: "People will simply say that you have become demented."

"It will not surprise me if I do."

He stared at her, positively frightened. "Meggie, how can you say such things? By God, I have enough to bear without your turning against me!"

She said, with calculated cruelty: "You have Alayne. Why should you need me?"

"I have not got Alayne," he retorted furiously. "She is going away the day after Gran's birthday."

"I do not think she will go away."

"What do you mean?" he asked, suspiciously.

"Oh, I think you have a pretty little game of progressive marriage going on at Jalna. No, Alayne will not go away."

His highly coloured face took on a deeper hue. Its lines became harsh.

"You'll drive me to do something desperate," he said, and flung to the door.

She pushed the tray from her and rose to her feet.

"Will you please go? You are mistaken if you think you can abuse me into putting up with loose women in my house. As to being the talk of the countryside, there must be strange stories about the married couples of our family already."

"Rot! It's all within the family."

"All within the family? Just think those words over. They've got a sinister sound, like the goings on in families in the Middle Ages. We should have been born two hundred years ago at the very least. No woman who respects herself could stay at Jalna."

He broke into a tirade against her, and all hard, narrow-minded women. She followed him to the door, laying her hand on the latch.

"You can never argue, Renny, without using such dreadful language. I can't stand any more of it."

He had stepped outside, and his spaniels, having traced him to the hut, ran to meet him with joyous barks, jumping up to paw him and lick his hands. For an instant Meg almost relented, seeing him there with his dogs, looking so entirely her beloved Renny. But the instant passed; she closed the door firmly and returned to her chair, where she sat plunged in thought, not bitterly reviewing the past as Maurice did, nor creating an imaginary and happy present, but with all her mind concentrated on those two hated alien women in her house.

Renny, returning to his stables, found Maurice there, waiting to talk over some proposed exchange. He was in the stall with Wakefield's pony, feeding her with sugar from his pocket. He turned as Renny entered.

"Well," he said, "how are things going now?"

"Like the devil," he returned, slapping the pony sharply, for she had bitten at him, not liking the interruption of her feast. "Piers still keeps Pheasant locked in her room, and goes about with an expression like the wrath of God. Uncle Nicholas and Aunt Augusta quarrel all day long. He's trying to worry her out of the house and back to England, and she won't go. He and Uncle Ernest aren't speaking at all. Alayne is looking ill, and Grandmother talks ceaselessly about her birthday. She's so afraid that something will happen to her before she achieves it that she refuses to leave the room."

"When is it?"

"A week from today. Alayne is staying here till it's over; then she goes back to New York, to her old position with a publisher's firm."

"Look here; why doesn't she divorce Eden? Then you and she could marry."

"The proceedings would be too beastly unsavoury. No, there's no hope there."

Something vicious in him prompted him to tease the pony. He cuffed her till she drew back her lips, showed all her teeth, bit at him, neighed, and finally reared and struck at him with her sharp hoofs. Maurice moved out of the way.

"Stop it, Renny," he said, half angry, and half laughing at the display of temper by the pair. "You'll make her an ugly little brute for Wake to handle."

"That's true." He desisted at once, red-faced from temper, rather ashamed of himself.

"It's a pity Alayne could not have seen that."

"Yes, isn't it?" He began to stroke the pony. "Here, give me a lump of sugar, Maurice."

"No, I'll give it to her myself. She and I are friends. We have no quarrel to patch up. Have we, pet?"

He offered her sugar, but, too upset to take it, she wrinkled her lips and cast baleful glances at them both. As they left the loose-box, Maurice asked: "How is Meg, Renny?"

"I've just been to see her. She's still stuck in that awful hut, sulking. Nothing will budge her. It looks as though she would spend the rest of her days there. I don't know what I'm to do. If you could only see her! It would be pathetic if it weren't ridiculous. She has a few sticks of furniture she took from the attic. The floor is bare. They say that all she eats is the little that Rags carries over to her. I met him with a tray. The fellow is nothing but a spy and a tale-bearer. He keeps her thoroughly posted as to all that goes on in the house. Aunt Augusta was for starving her out, forbidding Rags to take food to her; but I couldn't do that. She shut the door in my face just now."

"It's appalling."

They walked in silence for a space, along the passage between stalls, among the sounds and smells they both loved—deep, quiet drinking, peaceful crunching, soft whinnying, clean straw, harness oil, liniment.

Vaughan said: "I've been wondering—in fact, I lay awake half the night wondering—if there is a chance that Meg might take me now. Pheasant being gone, and Jalna in such an upset, and things having reached a sort of deadlock, it would be a way of solving the problem for her. Do you think I'd have a show?"

Renny looked at his friend with amazement.

"Maurice, do you really mean it? Are you still in love with her?"

"You know perfectly well I've never cared for any other woman," he answered, with some irritation. "It's not easy for you Whiteoaks to understand that."

"I quite understand, only—twenty years is a long time between proposals."

"If things had not turned out as they have, I should never have asked her again."

"I hope to God she'll have you!" And then, fearing that his tone had been too fervent, he added: "I hate to see you living such a lonely life, old man."

Meg had come out of the cottage, and was bending over a spray of sweetbriar that had thrust its thorny way up through a mass of dogwood. She loved its wild sweetness, and yet it made her sadder than before. Maurice noticed, as she raised a startled face to his, that her white cheeks were dappled by tears. One of them fell, and hung, like a bright dewdrop, on the briar.

"I'm sorry if I frightened you."

His voice, unheard for so many years, came to her with the sombre cadence of a bell sounding through the dark. She had forgotten what a deep voice he had. As a youth, it had seemed too deep for his slenderness, but now, from this heavy frame, she found it strangely, thrillingly moving.

"I had no right to intrude on you," he went on, and stopped, his eyes resting on the spray of briar; for he would not embarrass her by looking into her tear-stained face. Why did she not wipe her cheeks? He reflected, with a shade of annoyance, that it was just like Meggie to leave those glittering evidences of her anguish in full view. It gave her a strange advantage, set her on a plane of suffering above those around her.

Unable to speak, he rolled a cigarette deftly—in one hand, for the other had been crippled in the War. He could not have found a more poignant way of pleading his case. She had passed him often on the road and seen that he was going grey. She had heard that one of his hands was useless, but it was not until she saw the wrist in its leather bandage, above the helpless hand, that she realized how alone he was, how pathetic, how he needed to be taken care of. Renny was hard, careless, unhurt; he was arrogant, immovable. Eden was gone. Piers clung to his wretched young wife. Finch was unsatisfactory, moody. Wake was a self-sufficient little rogue. But here was Maurice, her unhappy lover, seeking her out with a strange, hungry expression in his eyes.

The droop of his mouth stirred something in her that she had forgotten, something buried for years and years. It did not stir weakly, feebly, like a half dead thing, but boundingly, richly, like the sap that thrilled the growing things in this June day. She swayed beneath the sudden rush of its coming and put out a hand to steady herself. Colour flooded her face and neck.

He dropped the cigarette and caught her hand.

"Meggie, Meggie," he burst out. "Have me—marry me! Meggie, oh, my darling girl!"

She did not answer in words, but put her arms about his neck and raised her lips to his. All the stubbornness was gone from their pretty curves, and only the sweetness was left.

26

GRANDMOTHER'S BIRTHDAY

THE DARKNESS had just fallen on Grandmother's birthday. It had descended slowly, seeming reluctant to draw the curtain on that day of days. But now the sky was a royal purple, and quite a hundred stars twinkled with all the mystic glamour of birthday candles.

Grandmother had not slept a wink since dawn. Not for worlds would she have missed the savour of one moment of this day, toward which she had been straining for many years. She could sleep all she wanted to after the celebration was over. There would be little else to do. Nothing to look forward to.

With her breakfast had come all the household to congratulate her, wish her joy, and other birthdays to follow. She had put her strong old arms about each body that, in succession, had leaned over her bed, and after a hearty kiss had mumbled: "Thank you. Thank you, my dear." Wakefield, on behalf of the tribe, had presented her with a huge bouquet of red, yellow, and white roses, an even hundred of them, tied with red streamers.

The day had been a succession of heart-touching surprises. Her old eyes had become red-rimmed from tears of joy. The farmers and villagers of the neighbourhood, to whom she had been a generous friend in her day, besieged her with calls and gifts of fruit and flowers. Mr Fennel had had the church bell ring one hundred merry peals for her, the clamour of which, sounding through the valley, had transported her to her childhood in Ireland; she did not know just why, but there it was; she was in County Meath again!

Mrs Wragge had baked a three-tiered birthday cake, which had been decorated in the city. On the top, surrounded by waves of icing, was a white-and-silver model of a sailing vessel such as she had crossed the ocean in, from India. On the side, in silver comfits, the date of her birth, 1825. This stood on a rosewood table in the middle of the drawing-room, beside a silver-framed photograph of Captain Philip Whiteoak. How Grandmother wished he could have seen the cake! She imagined herself, strong and springy of step, leading him up to the table to view it. She pictured his start of surprise, his blue eyes bulging with amazement, and his, 'Ha, Adeline, *there*'s a cake worth living a hundred years for!'

Oh, the feel of his firm, muscular arm in her hand! A dozen times that day she had kissed the photograph. At last Ernest had been moved to say: "Mamma, *must* you kiss it so often? You are moistening off all the gloss."

Now night had fallen and the guests were arriving for the evening party. The Fennels, the admiral's daughters, Miss Pink, and even old friends from a long distance. Her chair had been moved to the terrace, where she could see the bonfire all ready to be lighted. It had taken her an unconscionably long time to make the journey there, for she was weak from excitement and lack of sleep. In the summerhouse two violins and a flute discoursed the insouciant, trilling airs of sixty years ago, filling the air with memories and the darkness with plaintive ghosts. Grandmother's sons and eldest grandson had spared no trouble or expense to make the party a memorable one.

On her right hand sat Ernest and Nicholas, and on her left Augusta and Alayne. Augusta remarked to Alayne: "What a blessing that Meg is off on her honeymoon, and not sulking in Fiddler's Hut! It would have spoiled the party completely if she had been there, and even more so if she had come."

"She wasted no time when she finally made up her mind, did she?"

"No, indeed. I think she was simply shamed into it. She might have gone on living there for ever. Renny would never have given in." Lady Buckley regarded with complacency her nephew's tall figure, silhouetted against the flare of the musician's torches.

"I am afraid," said Alayne, "that Meg hated me very much after our quarrel about Pheasant. I know that she thought my attitude toward her positively indecent."

"My dear, Meg is a narrow-minded Victorian. So are my brothers, though Ernest's gentleness gives him the appearance of broad-mindedness. You and I are moderns—you by birth, and I by the progression of an open mind. I shall be very sorry to see you go tomorrow for I have grown very fond of you."

"Thank you; and I have of you—of most of you. There are so many things I shall miss."

"I know, I know, my dear. You must come back to visit us. I shall not leave Jalna while Mamma lives, though Nicholas would certainly like to see me depart. Yes, you must visit us."

"I'm afraid not. You must come to see me in New York. My aunts would be delighted to meet you."

Augusta whispered: "What do they know about Eden and you?"

"Only that we have separated, and that I am going back to my old work."

"Sensible—very. The less one's relatives know of one's life the better. I had no peace in my married life till the ocean rolled between me and my people. Dear me, Renny's lighting the bonfire. I hope it's quite safe. I wonder if you would mind, Alayne, going down and asking him to be very careful. A spark from it smouldering on the roof, and we might be burned in our beds tonight."

As Alayne moved slowly down the lawn, the first sparkle curled about the base of the pyramid of hardwood sticks that had as their foundation a great chunk of resinous pine. A column of smoke arose, steady and dense, and then was dispersed by the sudden and furious blossoming of flowers of flame. In an instant the entire scene was changed. The ravine lay, a cavernous gulf of blackness, while the branches of the nearby trees were flung out in fierce, metallic grandeur. The torches in the summerhouse became mere flickering sparks: the stars were blown out like birthday candles. The figures of the young men moving about the bonfire became heroic; their monstrous shadows strove together upon the rich tapestry of the evergreens. The air was full of music, of voices, of the crackling of flames.

Out of the shadow thrown by a chestnut tree in bloom,

Pheasant ran across the grass to Alayne's side. She seemed to have grown during those weeks of her imprisonment. Her dress looked too short for her. Her movements had the wistful energy of those of a growing child. Her hair, uncut for some time, curved in a quaint little tail at her nape.

"This freedom is wonderful," she breathed. "And all that pretty firelight, and the fiddles! Try as I will, Alayne, I can't help feeling happy tonight."

"Why should you try not to be happy? You must be as happy as a bird, Pheasant. I'm so glad we had that hour together this morning."

"You've been beautiful to me, Alayne. No one in the world has ever been so good to me. Those little notes you slipped under my door!"

Alayne took her hand. "Come, I am to go and tell Renny to be careful. Aunt Augusta is afraid we shall be burned in our beds."

The three youngest of the Whiteoaks were in a group together. As the girls approached, Finch turned his back on them and skulked into the shadow, but Wakefield ran to meet them and put an arm about the waist of each.

"Come, my girls," he said, airily, "join the merry circle. Let's take hands and dance around the bonfire. If only we could get Granny to dance, too! Please, let's dance!" He tugged at their hands. "Piers, take Pheasant's other hand. Renny, take Alayne's hand. We're going to dance."

Alayne felt her hand being taken into Renny's. Wakefield's exuberance was not transmittable, but he ran hither and thither, exhorting the guests to dance, till at last he did get a circle together on the lawn for Sir Roger de Coverley. But it was the elders who were moved to disport themselves, after a glass or two of punch from the silver bowl on the porch. The younger ones hung back in the shelter of the blazing pile, entangled in the web of emotions which they had woven about themselves.

Eden was not among them, but the vision of his fair face, with its smiling lips, mocked each in turn. To Renny it said: 'I have shown you a girl at last whom you can continue to love without possessing, with no hope of possessing, who will haunt you all your days.' To Alayne: 'I have made you experience, in a few months, love, passion, despair, shame, nough for a lifetime. Now go back to your sterile work and ee if you can forget.' To Piers: 'You sneered at me for a poet. Do you acknowledge that I am a better lover than you?' To Pheasant: 'I have poisoned your life.' To Finch, hiding in the darkness: 'I have flung you, head first, into the horrors of awakening.'

Renny and Alayne, their fingers still locked, stood looking upward at the flame-coloured smoke that rose toward the sky in billows endlessly pursuing each other, while, after the crashing of a log, a shower of sparks sprang upward like a swarm of fireflies. In the glare their faces were transfigured to a strange beauty, yet this beauty was lost, not registered on any consciousness, for they dared not look at each other.

"I have been watching two of those sparks," she said, "sparks that flew up, and then together, and then apart again, till out of sight—like us."

"I won't have it so. Not till out of sight, extinguished—if you mean that. No, I am not hopeless. There's something for us beside separation. You couldn't believe that we'll never meet again, could you?"

"Oh, we may meet again—that is, if you ever come to New York. By that time your feelings may have changed."

"Changed! Alayne, why should you want to spoil our last moments together by suggesting that?"

"I suppose, being a woman, I just wanted to hear you deny it. You've no idea what it is to be a woman. I used to think in my old life that we were equal: men and women. Since I've lived at Jalna, it seems to me that women are only slaves."

Someone had thrown an armful of brushwood on the fire. For a space it died down to a subdued but threatening crackle. In the dimness they turned to each other.

"Slaves?" he repeated. "Not to us."

"Well—to the life you create, to the passions you arouse in us. Oh, you don't know what it is to be a woman! I tell you it's nothing less than horrible. Look at Meg, and Pheasant, and me!"

She caught the glint of a smile. He said: "Look at Maurice, and Piers, and me!"

"It's not the same. It's not the same. You have your land, your horses, your interests that absorb almost all your waking hours."

"What about our dreams?"

"Dreams are nothing. It's reality that tortures women. Think of Meg, hiding in that awful cabin. Pheasant, locked in her room. Me, grinding away in an office."

"I can't," he answered, hesitatingly. "I can't put myself in your place. I suppose it's awful. But never think we don't know a hell more torturing."

"You do, you do! But when you are tired of being tortured you leave your hell—go out and shut the door behind you, while we only heap on more fuel."

"My darling!" His arms were about her. "Don't talk like that." He kissed her quickly, hotly. "There, I said I wouldn't kiss you again, but I have—just for goodbye."

She felt that she was sinking, fainting in his arms. A swirl of smoke, perfumed by pine boughs, enveloped them. A rushing, panting sound came from the heart of the fire. The violins sang together.

"Again," she breathed, clinging to him. "Again."

"No," he said, through his teeth. "Not again." He put her from him and went to the other side of the bonfire, which now blazed forth once more. He stood among his brothers, taller than they, his hair red in the firelight, his carved face set and pale. Recovering herself, she looked across at him, thinking that she would like to remember him so.

In a pool of serene radiance, Grandmother sat. A black velvet cloak, lined with crimson silk, had been thrown about her shoulders; her hands, glittering with rings, rested on the top of her gold-headed ebony stick. Boney, chained to his perch, had been brought out to the terrace at her command, that he might bask in the light of the birthday conflagration. But his head was under his wing. He slept, and paid no heed to lights or music.

She was very tired. The figures moving about the lawn looked like gyrating, gesticulating puppets. The jigging of the fiddles, the moaning of the flute, beat down upon her, dazed her. She was sinking lower and lower in her chair. Nobody looked at her. One hundred years old! She was frightened suddenly by the stupendousness of her achievement. The plumes of the bonfire were drooping. The sky loomed black above. Beneath her the solid earth, which had borne her up so long, swayed with her, as though it would like to throw her off into space. She blinked. She fumbled for something, she knew not what. She was frightened.

She made a gurgling sound. She heard Ernest's voice say: "Mamma, must you do that?"

She gathered her wits about her. "Somebody," she said, thickly, "somebody kiss me—quick!"

They looked at her kindly, hesitated to determine which should deliver the required caress; then from their midst Pheasant darted forth, flung herself before the old lady, and lifted up her child's face.

Grandmother peered, grinning, to see which of them it was, then, recognizing Pheasant, she clasped the girl to her breast. From that hug she gathered new vitality. Her arms grew strong. She pressed Pheasant's young body to her and planted warm kisses on her face. "Ha," she murmured, "that's good!" And again—"Ha!"

A SELECTION OF POPULAR READING IN PAN

CRIME

Agatha Christie
THEY DO IT WITH MIRRORS   25p

Victor Canning
QUEEN'S PAWN   30p
THE SCORPIO LETTERS   30p

Dick Francis
FLYING FINISH   25p
BLOOD SPORT   25p

James Eastwood
COME DIE WITH ME   25p

Ed McBain
SHOTGUN   25p

GENERAL FICTION

Mario Puzo
THE GODFATHER   45p

Rumer Godden
IN THIS HOUSE OF BREDE   35p

Kathryn Hulme
THE NUN'S STORY   30p

George MacDonald Fraser
ROYAL FLASH   30p

Rona Jaffe
THE FAME GAME   40p

Leslie Thomas
COME TO WAR   30p

C. S. Forester
THE MAN IN THE YELLOW RAFT   30p

Andrea Newman
A BOUQUET OF BARBED WIRE   35p

Arthur Hailey
HOTEL   35p
IN HIGH PLACES   35p

Nevil Shute
REQUIEM FOR A WREN   30p